Karin Baine lives in No... husband, two sons and he... collection. Her mother an... collection of books inspir... ...of reading and her dream of becoming a Mills & Boon author. Now she can tell people she has a *proper* job! You can follow Karin on X, @karinbaine1, or visit her website for the latest news—karinbaine.com.

Louisa Heaton lives on Hayling Island, Hampshire, with her husband, four children and a small zoo. She has worked in various roles in the health industry— most recently four years as a Community First Responder, answering 999 calls. When not writing Louisa enjoys other creative pursuits, including reading, quilting and patchwork—usually instead of the things she *ought* to be doing!

Discover more at millsandboon.co.uk.

NURSE'S NEW YEAR WITH THE BILLIONAIRE

KARIN BAINE

RESISTING THE SINGLE DAD SURGEON

LOUISA HEATON

MILLS & BOON

All rights reserved including the right of reproduction in whole or in part in any form. This edition is published by arrangement with Harlequin Enterprises ULC.

This is a work of fiction. Names, characters, places, locations and incidents are purely fictional and bear no relationship to any real life individuals, living or dead, or to any actual places, business establishments, locations, events or incidents. Any resemblance is entirely coincidental.

This book is sold subject to the condition that it shall not, by way of trade or otherwise, be lent, resold, hired out or otherwise circulated without the prior consent of the publisher in any form of binding or cover other than that in which it is published and without a similar condition including this condition being imposed on the subsequent purchaser.

® and TM are trademarks owned and used by the trademark owner and/or its licensee. Trademarks marked with ® are registered with the United Kingdom Patent Office and/or the Office for Harmonisation in the Internal Market and in other countries.

First published in Great Britain 2024
by Mills & Boon, an imprint of HarperCollins*Publishers* Ltd,
1 London Bridge Street, London, SE1 9GF

www.harpercollins.co.uk

HarperCollins*Publishers* Macken House, 39/40 Mayor Street Upper, Dublin 1, D01 C9W8, Ireland

Nurse's New Year with the Billionaire © 2024 Karin Baine

Resisting the Single Dad Surgeon © 2024 Louisa Heaton

ISBN: 978-0-263-32177-7

11/24

MIX
Paper | Supporting responsible forestry
FSC™ C007454

This book contains FSC™ certified paper
and other controlled sources to ensure responsible forest management.

For more information visit www.harpercollins.co.uk/green.

Printed and Bound in the UK using 100% Renewable Electricity
at CPI Group (UK) Ltd, Croydon, CR0 4YY

NURSE'S
NEW YEAR WITH
THE BILLIONAIRE

KARIN BAINE

MILLS & BOON

This one is for Keith and Matthew because
apparently they haven't had one yet...

CHAPTER ONE

JO KIRKHAM CLOSED her eyes, clenched her fists and prayed she wouldn't die.

'I never get used to this either.' Isabelle Stroud, the reason she was on this tiny seaplane imagining plummeting to her death, gently patted her on the knee and did her best to put Jo at ease.

It wasn't working. Being flown out on a private jet with all the privileges and luxuries of working for a wealthy family was entirely different to island hopping in a contraption where she was way too close to the cockpit. The one consolation was that Bensak, the private island owned by Isabelle's entrepreneur son, wasn't too far away.

She never would have dreamed she'd willingly spend Christmas Day travelling, arriving at her destination late on Boxing Day, completely missing the usual festive celebrations. But a free trip to the Fijian islands was the best thing that had happened to her in a long time.

Politeness forced her to open her eyes to address the elderly woman she was here to take care of for the duration of their stay. 'I've only ever flown commercial. This is all new to me.'

Isabelle was recovering from a stroke and Jo had been employed as her private nurse to continue her treatment; making sure she took her medication, keeping an eye on her blood pressure and blood sugar and helping her with her physiotherapy in between appointments. All to try and prevent another stroke from occurring. Her patient was recovering well, with only her mobility still providing a cause for concern, but she might not be so lucky the next time.

The plane hit a pocket of air and bumped them in their seats. Jo bit back a panicked scream and dug her nails deeper into her palms.

'Believe it or not I wasn't on an airplane until I was fifty-four years old,' Isabelle confided, her light blue eyes sparkling at the memory.

'Really?' With the billions the family were reputed to have, Jo imagined fleets of all manner of vehicles at their disposal. Able to transport them anywhere in the world at a moment's notice. A far cry from the daily commute, sardined onto the train with all the other minions whose livelihoods depended on working for rich overseers.

Not that the Stroud family were her sole employers. As a private nurse she took work with whoever needed her, and looking after Isabelle so far had been a joy rather than a chore. Of course, she still had to provide essential medical assistance, which put a great deal of responsibility on her shoulders, but this particular job had its perks. Like accompanying her charge out to the family's private island for New Year's Eve celebrations in a few days.

'We had to work hard for our money. My husband, John, built the business up from the ground and it was years before we were able to take a holiday abroad. It was my son who completely transformed the company and made it what it is today. I've been lucky enough to see the benefits of that. Unfortunately, John didn't live long enough to see Stroud Technologies become the phenomenon it is now. I only wish he were here with me to enjoy all of this. He'd be proud of Paul and everything he has achieved.' She gestured out the window to where the island was coming into view in the midst of the turquoise waters. Paradise.

'I'm sure he would be.' Jo reached across her seat and gave Isabelle's fragile hand a gentle squeeze.

Paul Stroud wasn't just a successful businessman; he was an inventor. Creating all sorts of innovative, and expensive, electrical products that made Stroud Technologies a household name. As well as making the family their fortune.

Isabelle offered her a watery smile. Although they came from completely different worlds, sometimes it felt as though they were more than nurse and patient. She might only have been working with her for a couple of months, but there was a genuine connection between them, and Isabelle had been as beneficial in assisting Jo in recovering from her troubles, as Jo had been in Isabelle's stroke aftercare.

These last couple of years had been tough. Once upon a time, Jo had run her own business with her partner, Steve, providing agency nurses and healthcare assistants to private clients. She'd worked as a nurse herself before starting the business and built it into a successful agency, which afforded her a beautiful big house, where she'd lived with Steve and looked forward to a happy future with him.

Now she was bankrupt, back living with her parents with whom she had a strained relationship to say the least, and was spending the holidays working so she could afford to rent a flat the size of a matchbox. All because Steve had emptied their joint account and fled the country, leaving her behind to face all the unpaid bills and deal with the fallout. He'd broken her spirit as well as her heart, and it had taken her a long time to crawl back out of the black pit of despair he'd tossed her into.

Still, she was taking one day at a time, and today's view was stunning.

'Brace yourselves,' the pilot told them just before they came down with a bump and a splash, and Jo gave a silent prayer of thanks for their safe arrival.

'It looks as though we have a welcome committee.' Isabelle waved out the window to the family members already assembled and awaiting their arrival. They'd flown out ahead, leaving Jo to accompany Isabelle.

She'd be lying if she said she wasn't a little apprehensive. Although she'd met some of the family members, spent a lot of time in Isabelle's home, being part of this gathering was out of her comfort zone. She hadn't been very sociable since her ex had ruined her life, and these were people who moved in some serious social circles. As she escorted Isabelle down onto the golden sand she had to pinch herself that she was here at all.

'Welcome to Bensak Island.' Paul greeted them with open arms, wearing an open-necked white cotton shirt and loose white cotton trousers, looking every inch like the head of a hippy commune. Barefoot, long haired and donning the requisite leather thong necklace, he was either going through some belated mid-life crisis, or he was beginning to believe his own hype. He was the leader of his kingdom on this island.

But Jo couldn't deny his generosity or hospitality.

'Thanks,' she said, dodging the kiss he tried to plant on her lips so he came into contact with her cheek instead.

'Mother.' He met Isabelle with double kisses, but she batted him away.

'It's getting late. Just take us to our rooms, Paul. I'm tired.'

He looked a tad crestfallen by her dismissal, but Jo had been with her patient long enough to know that her crotchetiness was often due to her arthritis. The long journey to get here, not to mention the cramped confines of their last mode of transport, would have taken their toll on the elderly lady's frail body.

'I should probably get your mother settled for the night. It's been a long day.' Jo tried to take some of the sting out of the moment, and Paul immediately perked up.

'Of course. I'll get someone to take you to your quarters.' With a snap of his fingers he summoned what looked like a glorified golf buggy to take them to their accommodation.

Whilst the journey there wasn't smooth, it was worth it to reach their destination. A sprawling, glass-fronted mansion, which appeared to stretch for ever appeared in the midst of the green landscape.

'My son doesn't do understated,' Isabelle mused upon seeing Jo's reaction.

She'd heard about this place, the celebrities and rumoured royals who'd stayed and partied here over the years, but it was something else seeing it materialise like a mirage before her. Knowing this was going to be her home for the next week.

'I'll show you to your rooms and have someone bring you dinner. You can catch up with everyone tomorrow after a good night's sleep.' Paul jumped out of the cart that drew up alongside them and helped his mother out.

'That's okay, Mr Stroud. I'm here in a work capacity

to take care of your mother,' Jo reminded him. Not sure she was ready to be presented to the wider circle of family and friends.

'Nonsense. You're part of the family now. Even Taylor's coming tomorrow to be part of the celebrations. Everyone is going to have a great time.' Paul seemed to be trying to convince himself of that.

Jo had heard that his relationship with his eldest was strained. She'd met his stepson, Harry, and stepdaughter, Allegra, but Taylor had been absent from the family home as long as she'd known them. From everything Isabelle had told her, he despised everything his family stood for, so she wondered why he would've agreed to a New Year's Eve party on the private island, and what made him so superior to the rest of the family.

Whether it was the humidity, or the guilt of leaving her parents behind in snowy England that was keeping her awake, Jo couldn't keep lying in bed staring at the ceiling. She had been afforded every luxury, but she was still restless. Tiptoeing past Isabelle's adjoining room so as not to disturb her, Jo decided to explore the villa a little further.

She'd only seen part of the sprawling property on the way in, but it was enough to intrigue her. Along with the requisite swimming pool and relaxation area, she was sure she'd also seen an open air gym. Not that she was keen to do anything too energetic in this heat, but she was curious as to what other surprises were in store. There was also the matter of her rumbling stomach and her parched throat to attend to. Paul had kept his word and had dinner served to Jo and Isabelle in their rooms, but as delightful as the seafood platter had been, it hadn't quite filled her. The mini fridge provided for them was also in Isabelle's room and she hadn't wanted to disturb her. Yes, this late-night visit was basically a search for the kitchen to find herself a midnight snack…

Padding barefoot along the cool tiled floors, she by-passed the other bedrooms and huge bathrooms, until she came to the large open plan kitchen.

'Wow.' It was about ten times the size of the box room she'd been living in at her parents' place for the past two years.

She trailed her fingers across the marble countertops and stainless steel appliances. Everything was spotless, and the floor-to-ceiling windows provided a stunning view out to sea. Although it was dark, the glow from the silver moon reflecting on the frothy waves outside was as much light as she needed.

Jo helped herself to a bottle of water from the American-style fridge and carried it over to the window, holding it against her fevered skin as she listened to the soothing sound of the waves. It was all surreal. Usually on Boxing Day she'd still be lying in something of a food hangover from Christmas Day, the remnants of unwrapped presents lying all around the Christmas tree, listening to her father complain about the lack of good programmes on TV. Here, there was no sign Christmas had even happened. It really was a different world. A fantasy land that made her believe she could really leave everything that had happened to her these past two years behind and start again. Maybe she could do so with the money she was being paid to work the holidays.

Not that that was the sole reason she'd agreed to come. Isabelle was a lovely lady and she wanted to be here for her so she could enjoy the celebrations with the rest of the family. Plus, it gave Jo some time away from her parents, and she reckoned they could all do with a break from one another. At least when she was around Isabelle she didn't feel as though she was treading on eggshells, afraid to say the wrong thing and upset her. Regardless of how much still needed to be said.

Things hadn't been right between herself and her parents since she discovered she was adopted upon opening a new bank account. Until then, she hadn't needed, much less seen, her birth certificate, and had ordered a copy of it unaware of the ensuing consequences. Finding out her parents had lied to her her whole life had affected eighteen-year-old Jo deeply, leaving her feeling betrayed and lost. Everything she'd ever known, apparently a lie. She hadn't been ready then to make contact with her biological parents, concentrating on her studies and her nursing career. A part of her not really wanting to accept the truth. After the break-up with Steve, feeling lost, she'd made an attempt to reach out to her birth family. Searching for some sort of stability. Only to find they'd died without her ever getting to know them. It had brought back all of those old feelings of resentment towards her parents, but she'd had to swallow down her pride to ask for their help. In return for lodgings and support she'd suppressed all the questions and anger she'd been holding on to for over a decade for the sake of harmony. The atmosphere at home had been strained ever since, because she blamed them for not letting her discover who she really was.

A few days out of that pressure cooker environment would do wonders for her stress levels.

'Who the hell are you?' The unexpected gruff voice behind her made her jump, and she wasn't proud of the yelp she gave in response either. Clearly she was still wound a little tight.

'J-Jo,' she stuttered as she turned around, responding to the sudden interrogation, regardless of the man's rude manner.

Looking at him attired in a navy tailored suit, she felt extremely underdressed in the moment, aware that she was clad only in her white cotton nightshirt, which wasn't meant to be seen by anyone else, bought only for comfort. She certainly hadn't accounted for it coming under the scrutiny of a handsome, dark-haired stranger who was looking at her as though he could see straight through it. Despite her unease, she resisted her initial urge to try and cover up, and fronted this awkward interaction out. After all, she didn't know who she was speaking to either, and she had as much right to be here as he did. Probably. Unless he was some kind of high-end burglar who'd travelled all this way to rob the Stroud family under the cover of darkness.

'Jo who?' he demanded, but with the few seconds she'd had to recover from the fright, Jo now resented the attitude this stranger was taking with her.

'Who is asking?' she countered, not feeling the need to justify her presence here when she'd been invited, *employed*, by the Strouds to be here.

'Taylor Stroud.' His answer was sufficient to form an O on her lips.

The prodigal son.

'I thought you were arriving tomorrow.'

'I got here early. Again, I'm asking who you are.'

She wondered if he was like this with everyone or if it was evident to him from this brief interaction that she didn't belong, wasn't one of the rich and famous acquaintances who were probably free to come and go as they chose without providing proof of ID.

'Joanna Kirkham. Jo. I've been employed to take care of your grandmother.'

It was hard to see in this limited light, but she was sure he rolled his eyes at her.

'Oh. You're *that* Jo.' The way he said it made it sound as though her reputation had preceded her, and not in a good way. She couldn't for the life of her figure out what she'd done to deserve his obvious disdain. Other than come from a working-class background.

'Yes. I'm her nurse.' For some reason she felt compelled to add her professional status, though that should have been pretty obvious by now. Her explanation only brought forth a snort of derision.

'Of course you are.'

What the hell was that supposed to mean?

Mr Stroud Jr began to walk towards her, and she backed up against the windowpane as his angular features were highlighted in the moonlight. The high cheekbones and strong jaw would've made him a handsome man if not for the stern look on his face.

'And tell me, Jo, do you often snoop around your clients' houses in the middle of the night?'

It was her turn to frown at the accusation she was doing something untoward. 'You tell me, *Taylor*, do you often hang around in formal attire waiting in the dark to attack strangers?'

'I walked in on you, remember? And you didn't answer my question.'

Jo folded her arms across her chest, her patience and politeness wearing thin. 'No, I don't snoop around anyone's house at night. However, when I'm staying in a very humid room and I don't want to disturb the lady sleeping next door, I will go to the kitchen to get a cold drink.

Your family told me to treat the house as my own. I wasn't aware I was under curfew.'

Taylor made a *humph* noise, which suggested he had no comeback to that one.

'Well, I'm a doctor, so I can take care of her from here.'

'Er, Isabelle wants me here, and the family are paying me to look after her. I'm sure you can find something else to do with your time.' She wasn't sure what kind of doctor he was. For all she knew, he'd simply bought the title. The family were certainly rich enough to do whatever they chose. His siblings seemed happy enough to ride the family coattails and didn't feel the need to get in the way of her doing her job. She didn't know what made Taylor so special, or why he appeared to have a problem with her being here.

'I assure you my grandmother's interests are all I have at heart. It's the only reason I came here. I'm not prepared to let anyone take advantage of her.' With that, he tilted his nose in the air, turned on the heel of his expensive leather shoes, and walked away.

'What's that supposed to mean?' she asked into the darkness. The ominous silence that followed his exit told her perhaps this trip away wasn't going to be as relaxing as she'd hoped.

Taylor stomped back to his room and wrenched his tie off before stripping completely and stepping into the shower. The cold water made him take a sharp breath at first, but he soon acclimatised. He needed it to cool off after his unexpected interaction with Jo.

Guilt still ate away at him that he'd been abroad when his beloved grandmother had taken ill and he was only able to see her now, two months on. By the time the news had come through to him she was already recovering at home. He'd video called, and if he'd thought her life was in imminent danger, he would've found a way to get back. However, she'd insisted that he needn't fuss and should concentrate on his work. He'd kept up to date with her recovery, but this was the first chance he'd had to take a break from work.

This mysterious nurse who'd apparently inveigled her way into his grandmother's life in such a short time had already made him wary, and meeting her hadn't done anything to assuage his fears. The family name was a magnet for people who thought they could take advantage and make themselves a few quid. He should know. He'd once thought he'd met the woman of his dreams, someone who was as philanthropic as he hoped to be. But the whole time, she'd been secretly stashing away his money into her own bank account. He wasn't that trusting any more.

Although he still preferred to make use of the family fortune in a more altruistic manner than his father, he was careful about the people he let into his life these days. On this occasion he thought his family should have adopted the same attitude when it came to choosing a companion for his grandmother. From what he could ascertain they knew nothing about this 'Jo', other than the fact that she was capable of doing her job. It wasn't enough for him to entrust his beloved grandmother's welfare to a complete stranger. Con men, and women, were very adept at gaining people's trust. Going under the radar until it was too late and the damage had been done. At least he was able to come out here and provide an objective opinion on this woman and her motives. He could also use the opportunity to provide some medical aid to the locals on neighbouring islands, so this trip hadn't simply been a jolly jaunt added to his carbon footprint.

Taylor needed to know he was doing his best to help others, to remind him he wasn't anything like his father who preferred to sit and count his money than spread the wealth.

As a doctor, he hadn't been able to save everyone who came to him for help, but he could rest easy knowing he'd always done his best. He couldn't say the same about his father.

At thirteen, Taylor had been old enough to remember his father sending him and his mother packing with a hefty cheque, and moving his mistress and her young children into the family home in the same day. It wasn't something easily forgiven. Although he'd still had contact with his father, he'd always felt as though he was something of a nuisance in his father's new life. He'd spent the next couple of years pinballing between two homes, until he found stability at university. He'd no longer felt part of a family. None of what had happened was Harry's, or Allegra's fault, but they weren't close. They had little in common and were very different people. Taylor liked to think he had more of his mother's traits. She was someone who hadn't been too proud to go back to work for a living and was quite happy in her part-time job and living out in the country. His stepfamily seemed to take easily to the good life, and were content to wallow in luxury without a thought for others. It was difficult not to be resentful of the fact that his mother had been treated so appallingly, whilst they'd had everything they'd ever wanted.

Of course, Taylor had enjoyed something of the same pampered lifestyle, but he'd made a vow never to be as callous as his father had been. As soon as he was able to make a difference in other people's lives, he did everything he could to not be just another selfish billionaire only looking out for himself.

He rarely saw any of his family when he was so busy with his work abroad, but he did have a soft spot for his paternal grandmother, Isabelle, who had always been very loving towards him. She'd made time for him when his father always seemed too busy with work or his new family to bother with him. Her illness had been a shock, and her current circumstances were the reason he was here. His grandmother was still vulnerable, and he knew a thing or two about opportunists taking advantage of kind-natured people.

One thing was for sure, he wasn't going to let this Jo have sole access to his grandmother. He was going to shadow her every move whether she liked it or not.

CHAPTER TWO

'CAN I GET you anything else to eat, Isabelle?' Jo lined up her client's medication on the table for her to take along with a glass of water, eyeing up the buffet-style spread laid out for the guests to help themselves.

'I'm fine. Sit down and eat your breakfast, Jo.'

Jo did as she was told and helped herself to some fresh fruit and yogurt before taking a seat across from Isabelle. Since her late-night encounter with Taylor Stroud, Jo had been unsettled, analysing his every remark. He'd insinuated she was looking after his grandmother for some sinister motive other than simply doing her job. Now she was paranoid the rest of the family would find her lacking in her duties in some way.

'Did you sleep well last night?' She knew sometimes Isabelle's arthritis kept her awake and could provide pain relief if needed.

'Yes, thanks. The fresh air must agree with me. How about you? Did you have a good night's sleep?'

Jo was tempted to tell her about the exchange with her dear grandson, then realised it wouldn't be very professional, and she didn't want to give him any ammunition to use against her.

'The heat made it difficult for me to sleep so I went

to the kitchen to get myself some water. I hope that was okay?'

'Of course, dear. Paul told you to make yourself at home.'

She almost asked for that in writing so she could wave it in Taylor's face.

'I might just take some water to bed with me tonight so I don't disturb anyone.'

'Morning.' Taylor arrived as stealthily as he had last night and went to kiss his grandmother on the cheek.

'Taylor! This is a nice surprise. I thought you were supposed to be arriving later today?' Isabelle's eyes lit up at the sight of her grandson and Jo couldn't help but wonder why.

She had to admit he looked good in his light blue linen shirt and cargo shorts. More casual and relaxed than the last time she'd seen him, but no less intimidating as he slid her a dark look.

'I got in last night. I wanted to get a real feel for the place.'

Jo bit her lip.

'I'm so glad you made it.' It was obvious how pleased Isabelle was at him gracing their presence, regardless of the fact that he'd apparently been absent when she'd needed him most.

'I'm so sorry I wasn't there when you were ill. I promise I'll make it up to you.'

'It's fine. I told you to stay where you were, didn't I? You were more use working out there than you could have been to me. Besides, I have Jo now.'

'And me. I brought my medical kit with me. I thought I'd give you a quick examination.' Taylor produced a small bag and proceeded to take out his medical equipment.

It was taking all of Jo's restraint to keep the bubbling anger inside her from manifesting at the end of her fist. 'There's no need, Mr Stroud.'

'Doctor Stroud,' he corrected her with an insincere smile as he placed a blood pressure cuff around Isabelle's arm.

She tried to count to ten in her head so she wouldn't say something in front of her patient that she might come to regret. Unfortunately, she only made it to five. 'As I was saying, *Doctor* Stroud, there's no need for you to trouble yourself. I've already attended to your grandmother's medical needs this morning. Including checking her blood pressure. I'm quite capable of doing my job, thank you.'

'I'm sure you are, but why not make use of a doctor when you have one here?' He put his stethoscope on, presumably so he couldn't hear the rest of her protest, then started pumping up the cuff.

Jo was forced to wait patiently until he'd taken the reading, even though she wanted to scream at him. She didn't know what she'd done to deserve his suspicion, or interference, but she was being severely tested. It took a lot of patience to look after the people she was employed to help. They needed someone to work with them as they recovered from serious illness that left them debilitated. Even Isabelle had needed some time to recover her speech and movement after the stroke. That's why families employed Jo, because she had the skills and patience it took. There was just something about this man that shredded her very last nerve.

Jo folded her arms, foot tapping, waiting until he'd finished his exam. 'Well?'

'Everything seems fine.'

'I told you,' she hissed through gritted teeth.

'It never hurts to get a second opinion now, does it, Jo?' She didn't appreciate the smug look on his face.

'Good. Now that it's settled that I'm not going to pop my clogs, perhaps I can get on with my day.' It was Isabelle who eventually put an end to the verbal sparring between them. 'Though I need you to do me a favour, Taylor. Could you put those muscles of yours to use and move the mini fridge in my room into Jo's for me? It will be more convenient for her than having to walk all the way to the kitchen.' Isabelle's request apparently took them both by surprise as the look on Taylor's face was probably the same as Jo's. She certainly hadn't asked for it.

'There's no need—'

'Of course. I'll do it later.' Taylor cut off her protest with a promise to carry out his grandmother's wishes at a later time. Hopefully when Jo was nowhere in sight.

'Perhaps we could see about getting her a fan too. I'm not sure the air conditioning is enough,' Isabelle campaigned unnecessarily on her behalf.

'Honestly, there's no need to trouble anyone—'

'I'll speak to Dad and see what we can do. We wouldn't want Ms Kirkham to be uncomfortable.' Although he was playing the role of accommodating host very well, Jo could hear the sneer in his voice.

'Speaking of which, Jo, you must be roasted in that outfit. You don't have to wear it out here. Didn't you bring something more suitable to wear?' Isabelle peered at the blue button-down uniform she had donned to spite Taylor, though she was regretting the non-breathable fabric.

'I thought it would serve as a reminder to everyone that I'm staff. I'm here for you and no other reason.' She directed that at Taylor in case he thought she was here simply for a free holiday.

Isabelle tutted. 'There's no need for that. Yes, you're my nurse, but you're also a friend and a guest. If anyone has a problem with that, they can take it up with me.'

Jo shot Taylor a satisfied smirk and revelled as he cleared his throat, clearly uncomfortable. Good. Now he knew how it felt.

'I thought you might like to go for a walk after breakfast, Grandmother. I could get your chair and take you to the waterfalls if you'd like?' Taylor ignored her and carried on a conversation with his grandmother as though Jo wasn't even in the room.

'That's what I'm here for,' she reminded him.

'As am I. I don't get to spend nearly enough time with my grandmother and I thought this week would be the perfect opportunity.' Taylor gave her a sickly-sweet smile.

'We can all go. It sounds wonderful and how lovely for me to have two medical professionals on hand to tend to my every need.' Isabelle clapped her hands as though she'd come up with the perfect solution. Jo couldn't think of anything worse.

'I'd rather not—'

'I don't think—'

Taylor and Jo stumbled over one another's words in their hurry to get out of the arrangement.

Isabelle set her napkin down on her plate and slowly rose to her feet. 'Jo, you go and get changed into something more suitable for the climate. Taylor, go and have a word with the chef and see if he can prepare us a light picnic to take with us. I'm looking forward to this little outing.'

She was so aglow with excitement at the prospect of

getting out and about, neither of her attentive subjects were apparently able to dissuade her from the plan. Jo didn't see that she had any choice but to nod and agree to her client's wishes.

Taylor supposed this little jaunt would give him an opportunity to keep an eye on his grandmother's new best friend, even if he wasn't relishing the thought of spending the day in her company. Certainly they hadn't got off to the best of starts when it appeared Ms Kirkham was the apple of everyone's eye around here. When he'd asked his father what he knew of her this morning he'd described her as 'part of the family'. Something he'd take as an insult if he were her. In his eyes, the Stroud family hadn't done anything to be proud of. At least not with the fortune and possibilities at their disposal.

He did his best to share the wealth and provide aid to the less fortunate. Not that it meant much to his father, or his step-siblings who thought that his job was a pet project like their whims into starting their own clothes labels or interior design. Various fields in which they had no experience or qualifications, merely an interest at the time. He wasn't sure they understood how much training he'd had to be where he was, or if they cared. At least his mother was proud of him, even if he didn't see her as often as he should. Work kept them both busy, but they kept in touch.

The only time he'd felt accepted by his father was when he'd been with Imogen. She seemed to blend in seamlessly with his stepfamily. Now he knew why. She'd apparently been as motivated by money as they were. Once they'd split up he was back to being the pariah of the family. Almost as if they blamed him for taking her away from them. As though it was his fault she'd had to resort to lying and stealing money from him. He'd been left feeling, again, that he hadn't been good enough to be loved. Just as he'd felt when his father took on a new family. He'd since given up trying to gain their approval and was happier on his travels, alone.

When it came to his father's new family, he couldn't get over the feeling that they could do so much more if they weren't so concerned with themselves and that constant desire to add to their bank balance. Goodness knew why when they already had enough money to last them a lifetime.

'Do you have a parasol to keep the sun off you?' he asked his grandmother as he met her on the veranda.

She scowled at him. 'I'm not some fragile Edwardian noblewoman who'll faint at the first glimpse of the sun. Jo made sure I have sun cream on, and I have a hat.'

She plonked a large-brimmed straw hat on her head as she got into her wheelchair, not looking her chipper self. He wished he'd been a fly on the wall when Jo had displayed similar concerns, sure she wouldn't have received any better reception than he just had. It gave him some satisfaction to think of his grandmother putting up something of a fight against Jo as she'd attempted to administer some protection against the sun. Perhaps his grandmother wasn't as vulnerable as he'd imagined, though he only had her best interests at heart.

'We just don't want you getting burnt, or suffering from heat stroke. We're both trying to take care of you, Isabelle.' Jo appeared then and he was chastened by her words. It was true, they were both simply making sure she was safe and he shouldn't have taken any pleasure in the idea of his grandmother resisting attempts to help her. Although he still had his suspicions about Jo, perhaps for one afternoon, he could set them aside so they could enjoy a walk.

'I'm not a child,' his grandmother huffed, letting them know her fighting spirit was still going strong. Something he was grateful for when her health hadn't been the best.

Taylor had worried about her since the stroke, but he was more afraid now that in his absence he'd let a snake into the nest. The one thing he could do was let it be known that he wasn't going to stand for any kind of manipulation of a vulnerable person.

'We know you're not, Isabelle, but as you said, you have two medical professionals by your side. We would be lacking in our duties if we let anything happen to you.' Jo soothed their patient with some common sense and soft-soaping.

Sufficient that Taylor's grandmother stopped grumbling. About appropriate attire for the weather at least.

'Well let's get on with it, or it'll be dark by the time we get moving.'

'Yes, Grandmother,' he said with a sigh, happening to catch Jo's eye. She gave him a half-smile and for a moment they appeared to bond, before she looked away again.

They both reached for the handles of the wheelchair at the same time.

'I've got it.'

'She's my grandmother.'

'Now, now, there's no need to fight over me. Taylor, dear, you push me, and Jo can walk alongside me. She's a much prettier view.'

Taylor had to agree with his grandmother as he took control. Jo walked ahead, following the path he assumed his father had made down to the waterfall. It was a wonder he hadn't had the whole thing tarmacked, or built a bridge to the mainland to make life easier for himself. He wasn't sentimental about destroying natural beauty.

Speaking of which, *Jo looks lovely today.*

'Pardon?' She turned around and he realised with horror that he'd voiced that out loud.

'I was just remarking on how much better you look out of your uniform. I mean, in your casual clothes.' He stumbled over his excuses, somewhat taken aback by his response to the sight of her today.

His journey to the island had been fraught with delays and hot, cramped conditions, and as a result his mood had been…irascible. He hadn't been able to see her clearly in the dark, and his mind had been elsewhere. Now, however, with the sunlight shining through her white shirt dress, which showed off her curvy figure and toned legs, he could see she was as beautiful as the local scenery. Even her clear green eyes seemed to be sparkling like the tropical waters surrounding the island. She looked at home here.

'Well, I didn't want you to think I was forgetting my place here.' She narrowed those beautiful eyes at him and he felt himself flush with shame at his behaviour last night. He didn't like to be judged himself, either by his own family or outsiders, and it hadn't been fair of him to make assumptions about her. It didn't mean he wasn't wary about her motives for getting close to his grandmother and the rest of the family, but he wouldn't find anything out by being hostile.

'Sorry about last night. It had been a bit of an arduous journey for me to get here. I shouldn't have taken it out on you.' Taylor heaved the backpack containing their refreshments further up onto his back.

'It's fine.' Jo sighed. 'Let's just enjoy the day. Can I

carry that for you? I want to do something useful. I'm still on the clock after all.'

Her tongue-and-cheek comment along with her offer to help went some way to thawing relations between them as Taylor handed over the bag.

Isabelle glanced between them both. 'Is there something going on between you that I don't know about?'

Taylor didn't want to upset her by admitting his suspicions, or embarrass himself by getting a telling off from his grandmother who wouldn't hear a bad thing said about her nurse. So he decided not to mention his late night altercation with Jo, and hoped she would do the same.

'Not at all. We're just getting to know one another. Aren't we, Taylor?' Jo fixed the backpack around her shoulders and batted her eyelashes at him, apparently on board with this truce. For now.

'One big happy family.' He grinned, navigating the wheelchair down the lane towards the vast green landscape ahead.

'What about your family, Jo? Do they mind that you're not home for Christmas?' Isabelle said.

Taylor didn't miss Jo's brief scowl at his grandmother's questions. He wondered what the background story was, and if they had more in common than he'd first thought. Perhaps she didn't get along with her family either.

'It's just Mum and Dad at home. I'm sure they're glad I'm out from under their feet for a while.'

'Oh? You still live at home?' Taylor's curiosity piqued at this new information. He would have had Jo pegged for an independent woman who valued her personal space. Certainly he hadn't been able to move out of home quick enough to stay in student digs as soon as he'd been old enough. A life of luxury wasn't everything if you had a social conscience too. He'd wanted to go out on his own and make a difference in the world. As well as getting some space from those who didn't understand him, and vice versa. It was ironic that he'd ended up adding more money to the family pot with his innovative medical invention—a portable device able to test bloods on site for all manner of ailments and send the information to the nearest hospital via satellite phone. A lifesaver in some of the remote areas he worked in. Money-making had never been his objective, only a need to improve a service for his patients.

Jo plucked a long blade of grass from along the side of the laneway and folded it between her fingers. 'At the moment. I'm hoping to get another place of my own this year.'

It was a carefully worded comment that prompted so many more questions. Why did she have to move back in with her parents if she'd previously lived in her own place? Did she live with someone else? Had there been a break-up? He hadn't seen a wedding ring on her finger, but he knew from bitter experience that any failed relationship was painful to deal with. Of course, her private life wasn't any of his business. Unless it had any bearing on her role here. He was sure his father had done some background checks before employing her as a carer for his mother, and he was sure she was capable of doing her job, but he was concerned that she might be using it to get close enough to take advantage of his grandmother.

'I'm sure they're missing you. What do you usually do at Christmas?' Taylor's grandmother appeared oblivious to Jo's caginess, probing deeper into her personal circumstances. He listened on with fascination. His questions could wait for another date. Presumably when he'd done a little bit more research and had information he might be able to confront her with. Perhaps she had nothing to hide and he was simply projecting his past painful experience onto someone who wanted nothing more than to help an elderly lady, but that instinct he'd developed since his break-up for smelling trouble was on high alert.

'We just have a quiet one. I didn't miss anything, I'm sure.'

'New Year's out here is going to be entirely different. My son doesn't do understated, or quiet. He has quite the party planned.'

'So I hear. I'm looking forward to the celebrations.' Jo swung around again, her blond ponytail swishing as she abruptly ended the conversation and began marching ahead.

Yup. She was definitely hiding something, and Taylor was determined to find out what.

The view was stunning. As they made their way into the clearing, Jo could only stand and stare in awe. The sound of the thundering waterfall was deafening, but welcome. Hopefully drowning out any more questions about her home life. Although Isabelle had been sympathetic to her plight, she didn't want to have to confess about the break-up of her relationship and subsequent financial difficulties to Taylor. It was embarrassing enough that she'd been left destitute without having to recount the details leading up to it to someone who probably didn't have any concept of what it meant.

Taylor had been born into money, and by all accounts, made more of it every time he breathed. She wasn't jealous, she just wished her own circumstances were different. Enough that she could live a quiet life without the constant worry about how she was going to survive, or what the future held. Issues she was certain someone like Taylor would never have to deal with. Good for him.

'There's a little shady spot here. Why don't we stop for a moment?' Taylor was still able to make his voice heard above the roar of water spilling down the rock face, and Jo was keen to have a little break too. With the weight of the bag on her back, and the heat of the sun shining down, she was beginning to flag.

'Good idea.' She dropped the bag where she stood and unpacked the blanket Taylor had put in for them to sit on. He spread it on the ground and held out a hand to his grandmother to help her out of the chair.

'I think I'll just stay where I am, thanks, in case I can't get up again. You and Jo sit down. You've been doing all the heavy work.' Isabelle, either oblivious to the friction between her companions, or choosing to ignore it, was forcing them to sit down together in enforced harmony.

Jo perched on the farthest piece of the tartan blanket that she could, but it made no difference when Taylor joined her, his body and long legs dominating the space. So much so that his thighs were touching hers, and she could feel his body heat through the thin fabric of her dress. Despite being out of the direct sun, her skin became feverish. It was the closest she'd been to a man since the break-up. That was the only reason she was responding the way she was. It had absolutely nothing to do with the muscular thigh pressed intimately against her outer leg.

'Jo?'

'Hmm?'

'I was just asking if you'd like a drink?' Taylor was looking at her with amusement and she realised she'd been so caught up in her body's physical reaction to him, and what it meant, that she hadn't heard the question.

'Sorry. I was miles away. Yes, I'd love a drink of lemonade. Thank you.' At this point it didn't matter. She just needed something to cool down the heat of her embarrassment. The last thing she needed was to find herself attracted to an arrogant billionaire who clearly despised her. Actually, worse than that was the thought that he might be able to tell.

Taylor poured them all a drink and she busied herself laying out the spread the kitchen had provided for their little outing. Lots of fresh fruit and dainty sandwiches for them to snack on. She plated up some food for Isabelle before tucking in herself.

'It's lovely down here, isn't it? The young ones like to swim in the pool there.'

'It looks refreshing,' Jo agreed, following Isabelle's wistful gaze down to the clear pool at the foot of the waterfalls.

'I might go in for a dip.' Taylor got to his feet, kicking off his footwear and unbuttoning his shirt.

Jo swallowed, trying not to stare, even though curiosity as to what was beneath that shirt was getting the better of her.

'You go too,' Isabelle urged her.

'I couldn't possibly…' Jo spluttered, uncomfortable with the idea of stripping off down to her bikini to frolic in the water with Taylor. She had only put it on under her dress in case she got the opportunity to do a little sun worshipping, in private. Who wouldn't come out here and hope to go back to wintry England without a tan?

'Ah, come on. We can keep an eye on Gran from down there.' Taylor whipped off his shirt, baring his smooth, delineated torso.

Jo took a sip of lemonade to quench her sudden thirst.

'I'm just going to close my eyes for a few minutes so you may as well go and enjoy yourself.' Isabelle handed Jo her empty plate and settled back into her wheelchair for a nap.

Jo didn't know what defence she had left, save for saying she didn't want to cavort half naked with Taylor in the water for the sake of her peace of mind. She didn't want to lust over someone who'd made her a candidate for anger management classes within five minutes of meeting him.

'I'll maybe just go and dip my toes in. That way I'll be able to race back if you need me.'

Eyes closed, Isabelle simply mumbled her agreement as her grandson tore on down towards the water. He was like a different person today. Carefree. Fun. Accommodating. Even at breakfast there had still been an atmosphere between them, almost resentment about her presence here. Now, however, he was acting as though they were besties. Perhaps that's exactly what it was, an 'act' for his grandmother's benefit. A truce they'd silently agreed to so as not to upset her, but which was now causing Jo anxiety. Because she didn't want to like him. Her life was messy enough without the added complication of a crush on her employer's son.

Even if she ever got over the pain of her ex's betrayal, Taylor was probably the worst person to set her sights on. All those close to her seemed to let her down and she'd learned the hard way that the only person she could trust was herself. She was even having doubts about that now...

Jo carefully picked her way through the foliage in her now bare feet, casting a glance back every now and then to make sure Isabelle was all right. The spray drifting on the breeze from the waterfall was cooling on her skin, and the tall trees and giant palm leaves were providing shade. It was paradise.

Whilst Taylor had headed up to a greater height, she walked down towards the water's edge in the shallows to paddle her feet.

With a Tarzan-like call, Taylor leapt off the ledge and landed with a splash in the pool, causing a shower to soak Jo in the process. The sudden cold made her gasp as she fought for breath.

'Sorry,' Taylor called to her as he emerged from the clear water, washing his hands over his face and hair. Though the grin on his face showed no sign of apology at all.

Jo looked down at her dress, which was practically see-through anyway now. She looked at Taylor who walloped both hands down on the surface of the water and caused another soaking. His smile growing wider by the second.

'Oh, you're asking for it—' A need for revenge over-riding common sense and self-preservation, Jo whipped off her dress and waded into the water in her bright yellow bikini.

Taylor didn't move. Challenging her to do her worst. With a determined stride, she made her way towards him until he was within reaching distance. Two hands in front of her, she pushed a wall of water at him, then swam away laughing as he shook his head from side to side like a wet dog after the resulting tsunami. Revenge was so very sweet. And wet.

Before he could retaliate, she ducked in behind the waterfall into a secret rocky grotto. Taylor quickly followed, breaching the curtain of water to join her. Okay, so her hiding place wasn't so secret after all.

'Believe it or not this is the first time I've been here,' he told her, coming to stand near her, water dripping down his muscular chest.

'The waterfall?' It was hard to concentrate when they were so close, seemingly locked away from the rest of the world, and she was increasingly aware of her own state of undress. Especially when his gaze flicked appreciatively over her body. Jo crossed her arms over her chest, feeling her nipples harden in the cool air.

Taylor sank back down into the water and broke the intimacy of the moment that seemed to be happening between them. 'Er, no. I mean the island.'

'But your family own it.' She couldn't believe that he wouldn't take advantage of exclusive access to this place any time he wanted. Given the chance, she was sure she could happily spend the rest of her days here. Especially if she had a full staff of people on hand taking care of her every need.

He shrugged. 'My father owns it. He owns a lot of things. It doesn't mean I want to be part of the whole show.'

Jo raised an eyebrow. 'But you are. Aren't you part of the empire? Why wouldn't you enjoy the benefits that come with that?'

He was such a complex character. Someone who appeared to have the world at his feet, but resented it at the same time. His stepbrother and stepsister didn't seem to have a problem with it, embracing the life of luxury and privilege the family name afforded them. Jo didn't recall ever hearing about their careers outside of Stroud Technologies. It was obvious that there was a story behind Taylor's reluctance to be part of the family, and a reason why he was choosing now to make an effort with them.

The frown was back, transforming his otherwise handsome face into that surly man she'd met last night in the dark. Then he sighed and relaxed again. 'Trust me, it's conflicting for me too. I think the money my family has is obscene, yet it enables me to help out disadvantaged communities I probably wouldn't be able to reach otherwise.'

'But you're a doctor. I'm sure that would've happened anyway.' Whilst she admired the fact that he'd carved out his own career, she didn't see what the conflict was with his family's status. He could choose to walk away from it altogether if he felt so strongly, be financially independent. Something she hoped to be again someday.

'Not to the same extent. I run free clinics abroad when I can.'

'Is that why you decided to come out here?'

'Partly,' he said ominously. 'Anyway, enough about me. We should probably get back.'

Taylor made a move first and she followed. Except she slipped on a rock underfoot and went under the water, spluttering as the water went up her nose and down her throat, making it difficult to breathe. Then, as she was beginning to panic, two large hands were at her waist, lifting her up out of the water.

'Are you okay?'

After she was done coughing and wiping the water from her eyes, she could see Taylor staring at her, concern etched on his face. He was standing close, holding her by the arms.

'I'm fine, thank you. I just lost my footing and swallowed some water.'

'Just take some deep breaths,' he said, holding her whilst she did so.

She would have been embarrassed if it wasn't for the other emotions and sensations currently flooding her body. The awareness of his touch upon her, his genuine concern and kindness towards her—all things that had been missing from her life for so long—awakened something else inside her. Desire.

'You're shaking. It must be the shock.'

Before Jo had a chance to protest, Taylor had swept her up into his arms and was treading water, carrying her back to dry land. She had no choice but to wrap her arms around his neck for support, creating further skin to skin contact. The steady beat of his heart as she pressed against his chest was as reassuring as his body heat.

'You can put me down now,' she tried to insist once they were out of the water, but Taylor was undeterred, carrying her back to the picnic spot.

'What on earth has happened?' Isabelle was visibly distressed at the sight, and Jo could've kicked herself as well as Taylor for worrying her unnecessarily.

'Nothing. I had a little fall. Taylor is overreacting.' She narrowed her eyes at him, trying to get him to set her down when she was extremely aware there wasn't very much keeping their naked bodies apart.

'As a medical professional too, I'm sure you would do the same.' The mood had changed between them again as he teased her. She supposed it should be easier than the sexual tension she didn't know how to deal with, but she didn't like him to think he had the upper hand. Life had taught her never to give control away, and at present, she was very much at his mercy.

'Hmm, not sure I have the upper body strength. I would've had to drag you up here by the ankles instead.' She pried herself away from his bare chest and made an attempt to stand on her own.

'Thank goodness we didn't have to do that then.'

He dumped her unceremoniously onto the blanket and wrapped it around her until she was swaddled like a newborn, and virtually unable to move.

'This really isn't necessary,' she spat. He was enjoying her discomfort way too much.

'I'll go and get our clothes. You stay here and dry off.'

She didn't have much choice, but she was grateful that he'd at least covered her up. Once they had their clothes back on perhaps she wouldn't feel so vulnerable and out of her comfort zone.

Taylor let out a shaky breath as he jogged away, needing some space. And a cold shower. The pool at the waterfall would have to do. Carrying a wet, half-naked Jo in his arms had seemed like a good idea at the time, but he'd been left feeling decidedly…uncomfortable. It was natural to be attracted to the blonde beauty, but that didn't mean he had to act on it. If only his body would take that on board.

He'd tried to downplay the moment he'd chosen the worst possible time to respond to her as a hot-blooded man, rather than a suspicious bystander, by teasing her. At least it had put her off the scent that he was attracted to her, even if it was liable to make things between them frosty again. That was probably preferable in the circumstances.

He dived back into the cool water, momentarily cleansing himself of his sin. It wouldn't do to have inappropriate thoughts about the woman he'd come here to investigate. Perhaps if it hadn't been for his past experiences, he would never have thought to be suspicious of his grandmother's nurse. However, his ex had got close to the family too, only to siphon away a great deal of his money whilst he'd been deceived by her charms. It wasn't the money that bothered him, it was the betrayal, the lies and deceit, which had been more difficult to move past. He didn't wish for his grandmother to be hurt the way he'd been if Jo had similar intentions.

In his case, it had been a beautiful woman who'd convinced him she was as dedicated to helping others as he was, who'd used his generosity for her own benefit. Soliciting handouts for alleged charitable acts she'd claimed to be carrying out. Something he'd never thought to check on. He'd believed he was helping to establish a new venture abroad providing medical care for disadvantaged people, because she'd told him all of her great plans in detail, and he'd never thought to question her legitimacy. A mistake that had cost him dearly, and not just in a financial sense. That broken trust was something he didn't think could ever be repaired, and the reason he couldn't take Jo at face value.

Appearances could be deceptive, and he wasn't sure his grandmother would recover if she experienced such a brutal betrayal. He certainly hadn't.

It was inconvenient to say the least to find his body had apparently forgotten to be as wary as the rest of him when it came to beautiful women.

Once Taylor had recovered his composure, and was sure he wouldn't embarrass either of them, he did one last lap and climbed out of the pool. His sodden shorts wouldn't leave anything to the imagination if he couldn't control his impulses, so he hoped they'd dry quickly once he was out in the sun again.

Taylor stopped to grab Jo's dress from the nearby rocks, still damp from his horsing around earlier. It was a reminder that he'd started the nonsense, and any resulting moments of intimacy had been entirely his own fault. He'd let his guard down so much with her he'd almost shared some very personal information and private thoughts about his relationship with his family. Along with the reasons he was out here. That hadn't been part of the plan, but it was easy to see why the rest of the family had been so beguiled by her. He would have to stay alert around her for the duration of his stay on the island.

By the time he reached the others, Jo had already packed their things away, and was standing waiting in that sunny two-piece bikini. He tossed her dress over but didn't miss the way her eyes lingered on his body as he put his shirt back on.

'Could we walk on down to the beach? I'd like to feel the sea air on my face for a while.' His grandmother's request was surprising on top of the outing they'd just undertaken, considering she'd appeared to doze off whilst they'd been at the pool.

'Wouldn't you like to go back and rest for a while, Isabelle?'

'Jo's right. We wouldn't want you to overdo it.' He'd been hoping they'd all be going their separate ways, giving him some space from Jo to remember exactly why he was here.

'I've been sitting here whilst you two were playing in the water. Now it's my turn.' Taylor's grandmother folded her hands in her lap and tilted her chin up into the air, letting them both know there would be no further argument.

He and Jo took up their positions and made the trip to the shore, even though it meant doubling back on themselves. Of course, despite his best intentions, he couldn't fail to notice that Jo's dress was clinging intimately to her curves, and he prayed for the torture to end.

CHAPTER THREE

ISABELLE SEEMED DETERMINED to get her own way today, regardless of whatever cost to Jo's peace of mind. She was used to her client's strong will, and was usually a fan. After all, that's what had helped her recovery so far. That stubborn determination had driven her to recover most of the use in her left-hand side again, which had been partially paralysed after the stroke. Isabelle, despite her frailty, had worked with a physiotherapist to regain her strength and thankfully, much of her mobility. However, in the circumstances, Jo longed for some compliance so she could retreat to her own quarters.

Which didn't include a view of Taylor's wet shorts cupping his backside. It was her own fault for falling so behind, but she'd been attempting to avoid small talk with him. Or worse, the easy repartee they seemed to have fallen into. When they got too comfortable with one another she apparently forgot about the man who'd 'greeted' her in the dark last night. And that was the version of Taylor Stroud she needed to cling to if she was to go home from this trip unscathed.

'Isn't that glorious?' Isabelle's words didn't do the sight justice when Jo finally saw it for herself.

Of course she'd seen the stunning vista on her arrival to the island, but actually being on the beach looking out at the Pacific Ocean was something else. Whilst Taylor pushed his grandmother down the wooden walkway, Jo pulled off her sandals and walked on the fine golden sand, revelling in the feel of it beneath her feet. If she ignored the development the Strouds had made nearby to make it their home, she could almost imagine she'd been cast away on a desert island. With the palm trees providing shade and already having found fresh water, she wondered if she could've survived here without the chef and kitchen staff back at the house. The soothing sound of the waves breaking on the shore made all of her problems seem so far away she wished she could stay here for ever.

'Yet everyone else is sitting up by the pool.' Taylor sighed, and Jo understood his frustration, yet was selfishly glad they were the only ones here.

It would've been spoiled by pampered guests stretched out with cocktails in their hands, video calling their friends and live blogging instead of living in the moment.

'They'll come down later for drinks. There are daybeds and a beach bar further on up,' Isabelle said.

'Of course there are,' Taylor darkly responded to his grandmother's new information.

'Well, I like it here.' Jo dumped the bag on the sand and stretched.

'I'd like to take a walk down to the sea.' Isabelle bent down to take off her shoes, clearly feeling the need to experience the sand between her toes too.

Jo and Taylor both rushed to assist her, each taking an arm to help her up out of the wheelchair.

'None of your shenanigans this time. I've just about dried out,' Jo warned Taylor as they made their way down to the water, arm in arm with the elderly woman.

He simply grinned in response, as if to say he wasn't

making any promises. Though Jo didn't imagine he would do anything to upset his grandmother. They clearly doted on one another, even though they hadn't seen much of each other in the time she'd been working for the family. It made her wonder why he kept his distance, and why he was back on the scene now. He'd made his distaste over his family's wealth clear, so it didn't make any sense why he'd choose to come to the island that was the ultimate display of grandstanding.

'I can't remember the last time I did this.' Isabelle lit up like a child seeing the ocean for the first time. Jo was glad they could do something nice for her after the trouble she'd had with her health lately. It was the reason she'd been employed by the Strouds, to care for her through her recovery, but seeing a patient back on their feet wasn't always part of Jo's experience. Often when she was involved with an elderly patient it was towards the end of their lives and they weren't as mobile as Isabelle was.

'I can manage on my own now,' she insisted, paddling out into the sea.

Jo and Taylor let go of her and watched on like two anxious parents.

'Don't go out too far,' she called, but Isabelle simply waved her away.

'She's a stubborn so-and-so,' Taylor laughed.

'It must run in the family.'

'Don't knock it. It's what makes us survivors.' A strange expression crossed Taylor's face, then disappeared as quickly as it appeared.

The Stroud family didn't strike Jo as 'survivors', rather entrepreneurs who'd been fortunate compared to most people. Though she agreed with the sentiment. It was sheer pigheadedness that had got her through her troubles.

A determination that she wouldn't let her ex ruin her life. Something she was still working through. Taylor was giving all the signs of someone who'd gone through a similar rough time, even if it wasn't a severe lack of money that could possibly have caused him problems.

'I hear you,' she muttered, drawing an inquisitive glance from Taylor.

Suddenly, Isabelle let out a yelp and toppled back into the water. Jo didn't think twice about running to her, with Taylor alongside.

'Isabelle?' She was lying flat on her back, her face contorted in pain.

'I... I think something...stung me.' Her breathing was shallow, her words slurring.

'We need to get her out of the water.' Taylor grabbed hold of his grandmother under one arm, and Jo got the other so they could pull her out onto the sand. Her heart was racing, but her nursing instincts took over from the fear and anxiety surrounding the situation.

'There's something moving in the water...' Jo pointed at a strange, spiky looking fish nearby as Taylor checked the wound site.

'I thought it was just a rock...' Isabelle's voice was starting to sound distant, as though she was drifting into unconsciousness. Whatever happened, Jo knew she had a better chance of survival if they kept her awake.

'Stay with us, Isabelle. Can you tell me how you're feeling?'

'Hot... I feel sick...'

'It could be a stonefish. I did a bit of reading up about the local wildlife before I came out.' Jo knew that particular species could be deadly and had to be acted upon immediately.

'There's a puncture site on her foot—barbs of some sort still in it,' Taylor surmised.

Jo felt Isabelle's forehead. 'She's burning up.'

'Her blood pressure's dropping, heartbeat irregular, and the entire leg is beginning to swell already. That's the venom in her blood stream. We need to get those barbs out.' The pain on Taylor's face as he lifted her bleeding, discoloured foot suggested he blamed himself for somehow failing his grandmother. Jo recognised it because she felt the same way.

Then she realised Isabelle had stopped breathing and her nursing instincts well and truly kicked in. 'Taylor, she's not breathing. I'm starting CPR.'

Jo couldn't stop to see how he took the news. Instead, she tilted Isabelle's head back and made sure her airways were clear before starting to deliver chest compressions.

Cardiac arrest meant the heart was no longer pumping blood around the body, preventing oxygen to the brain. If Jo didn't make any attempt to keep the blood and oxygen circulating herself, Isabelle would die in minutes.

Kneeling in the sand, the water lapping around her, Jo began CPR. With the heel of one hand in the centre of Isabelle's chest, she placed her other hand on top and interlocked her fingers. Arms straight, she pushed down hard in a desperate hope to revive Isabelle. 'One, two, three—'

Carefully, Taylor pulled out the small barbs from Isabelle's foot and set them aside, sweat forming on his forehead with the sustained effort he was putting in to try and save his grandmother's life.

'How the hell are we going to get an ambulance out here?' Despite all of their efforts, Jo knew it could be in vain if they didn't get Isabelle to hospital for proper treatment. She was beginning to tire, and goodness knew she couldn't keep this up until someone happened to stumble across them.

'Let me take over, Jo,' Taylor pleaded, apparently sensing her struggle.

'I can manage.' She didn't want him to think she wasn't capable when this was the very reason she'd been employed to look after his grandmother.

'Please. I need to do something useful.' It was a plea she couldn't ignore when he looked so anguished. Jo could relate to that feeling of helplessness. That's exactly how she'd felt for two years after what her ex had done, trying to wrestle control of circumstances that had been taken out of her hands. At least here she could relieve one person of that feeling, if only for a moment.

'Okay.' She relinquished control, for both his and Isabelle's sakes as her arms were beginning to feel the strain.

Taylor came to her side and they quickly switched positions.

'My phone's in the bag. Phone my dad and tell him what's happened. We need a helicopter, plane, anything to get her to the nearest hospital. We can't wait for help to come to us.' Taylor carried on, arms outstretched, fingers linked, pushing down on his frail grandmother's chest. It seemed Taylor's doctor side had come to the fore too, even though this was his loved one lying unresponsive.

Jo emptied the contents of the bag onto the sand until she spotted his phone. He shouted out his password so she could access his contacts and phone his father. She tried not to panic him as she relayed what had happened, told him their whereabouts and left the rest up to him. All the while she was watching Taylor work, and praying for a miracle. This wasn't what any of them had imagined when they'd flown out here for New Year's celebrations.

'Look in that bag and see if there's any hot water to soak the wound. It's the best temperature to treat this kind of injury.'

Jo followed Taylor's instruction and located the flask of hot water Isabelle had no doubt requested for her afternoon tea. Not wanting to cause any further injury, she tried a little of the steaming liquid onto her hand to make sure it was bearable before pouring it onto the wound.

Jo marvelled at his extensive knowledge and wondered how often he treated this kind of injury. It was certainly something she'd never had to deal with before and wasn't ashamed to admit she was a little out of her depth.

'Listen! I think I heard her take a breath.' Taylor stopped chest compressions and bent down to listen to Isabelle's chest, and checked her wrist for a pulse.

Jo held her breath until he confirmed it.

'She's breathing.'

'Isabelle? Can you hear me? It's Jo. We need you to try and stay awake for us, okay?' Jo did her best to reassure her as she came to on the sand with her and Taylor leaning over her.

Isabelle was shaking and mumbling incoherently now, and they moved quickly to get her into the recovery position. Now that the immediate danger appeared to have passed, the shock and disbelief at what had happened seemed to set in. She found herself suddenly teary, but the only thing more surprising than that was Taylor reaching out to give her hand a squeeze. Perhaps a silent signal to let her know he was feeling equally emotional, but also a reminder that he was here with her. A touching gesture she would never have expected from someone who'd made no attempt to hide the fact he resented her very presence so far.

It was possible there was a thaw setting in, hopefully due to the fact he was finally realising they were both here for Isabelle's benefit.

The moment was soon interrupted by a cacophony of noise and chaos as the family came running down onto the beach crying and yelling, followed by the arrival of a helicopter further up. Taylor covered his grandmother with his body, protecting her from the sand and debris whipped up.

They weren't ideal conditions for a patient transport with no paramedics or stretchers, but between them they managed to get Isabelle on board. Jo made a move to get in alongside her, but that idea was shot down by Taylor.

'I'll go with her in case anything happens. I'll phone ahead to the hospital and let them know we're coming.'

'Okay. You're the doctor,' Jo conceded and backed off. It was his grandmother and he was the senior medical professional here. It was his call.

Nobody should be relying on her judgement these days. She was someone who apparently hadn't known who she'd got into bed and business with despite spending every minute of every day with Steve. As a result, she questioned everything she did lately. Letting her patient walk into unknown waters and almost die as a result was simply another example of her bad decision-making. It was no wonder Taylor had trouble trusting her. He clearly had better judgement than she could ever hope for.

'Thanks, Jo. For everything.' Out of the blue, Taylor offered her his gratitude, along with a half-smile. She supposed it was his way of apologising for the way he'd treated her up until now, as well as recognition that she'd been partly responsible for saving his grandmother's life.

Hopefully he'd remember that the next time their paths crossed.

As the helicopter rose up into the sky she knew Isabelle was in the best hands, and hoped for a positive outcome. However, she couldn't shake off the notion that she'd let Isabelle and her family down. She'd been distracted today, her thoughts straying to Isabelle's grandson instead of the real reason she was out here, and if she couldn't do her job then she was no use to anyone.

Taylor let himself into the villa, doing his best not to alert anyone to his presence. He wanted some downtime before he faced the family. Even though he'd already spoken to his father and reassured everyone that his grandmother was going to be fine, he knew he'd be bombarded with a hundred and one questions. After a long day he wasn't ready for that just yet.

He was just thankful that he and Jo had been there. Though he had experience of working in exotic climes, it was Jo who'd spotted the stonefish and saved precious time, which might otherwise have been wasted trying to find out what had happened. As scary as the whole situation had been, at least they'd been able to move swiftly to help his grandmother and he was grateful for Jo's calming influence as well as her medical expertise.

As he'd waited at the hospital for news, he'd had time to reflect on everything that had happened on the island since his arrival. It was possible, he supposed, that he'd got Jo all wrong. Certainly, she'd been as concerned as he for his grandmother's welfare and had done everything in her power to save her. She'd even been a little emotional by the end of it all. He should probably give her a break, stop giving her a hard time and let her get on with the job she'd come here to do. At least once his grandmother had recovered and was back on the island with them, or they both went back to England.

The hospital had treated his grandmother with antivenom, given oxygen and fluids upon arrival. If she'd been stung elsewhere, or he and Jo hadn't acted so quickly, she might not have survived. Something he didn't want to share with his family. If there weren't any complications, she should be back with them in a day or two, so he didn't see the point in upsetting anyone unnecessarily.

He went to his room to change out of the clothes he'd been wearing all day into some more comfortable jogging bottoms and T-shirt. Fooling around with Jo at the pool seemed like a lifetime ago now after spending most of the afternoon and evening in the tiny hospital on one of the bigger neighbouring islands. It was clear they were struggling with the ratio of staff to patients, and he'd even had to volunteer his services to help out so he could get his grandmother the treatment she needed. At least it gave him validation about this whole trip being more than sussing out Jo's motivations. It was obvious they needed extra funding out here, and in the meantime he'd set up an emergency clinic of his own nearby. For now, he needed something to eat and drink, and a moment to collect his thoughts.

He made his way to the kitchen and flicked the light on. Only to find Jo sitting at the breakfast bar, jacket on and suitcase at her feet.

'What are you doing?'

'I, er, I'm…what's happening to Isabelle? Your father said she's recovering well.' She deftly changed the subject, but Taylor wasn't going to walk away without an explanation.

'She is. All her test results were fine, but they're going to keep her in for a couple of days just to make sure there are no complications or aftereffects. Now, what are you doing?' This had all the hallmarks of their first meeting. Although this time around he was more irritated by the thought of her leaving than her presence. A development he'd never expected and wasn't sure how to deal with.

'I'm glad she's going to be okay. I let her down.'

'How did you work that one out? We were both there at her command, got her medical treatment and saved her life.'

'I think you did most of that, but that's not the point. If I'd done my job properly, we wouldn't have even been there. She'd done too much, been in the sun too long—'

'And none of that had anything to do with what happened. You don't need to play the martyr, Jo. It was an accident no one could have foreseen.'

'Which might never have happened if I'd been vigilant.' Jo seemed determined to beat herself up over what had happened, and whilst it was always unnerving when a loved one was involved in a medical emergency, this hadn't been anyone's fault. Taylor didn't understand why she was doubting herself when she'd done everything that could possibly have been expected of her and more.

'So, what, you're going to fly back home?'

'I hadn't figured that bit out yet. It's not as easy as booking a flight online. I was sitting here thinking about what I was going to say to your father so he'd help me out.'

'Do you always run away when things don't go your way? That's not very reassuring for your patients, is it?' He knew he was being facetious, but he wanted her to see how ridiculous she was being. Even if that meant riling her up in the process.

'I'm not running away. I've never run away from anything in my life. But I was paid to do a job here and since your grandmother is in hospital there's no need for me to stay, is there?'

Taylor didn't doubt for one second that Jo was the sort of person who would always face a challenge head on, which made her apparent decision to flee all the more mind-boggling.

'As far as I know you were paid for the duration of this trip, so if you leave now, you'd be in breach of contract. It's an agreement you had with my father, not my grandmother.'

She gave him the side-eye. 'Really? You're going to sue me if I leave?'

'Probably not, but I'm under strict instructions from my grandmother to make sure you enjoy your free time on the island until she comes back. I don't know about you, but I don't want to tick her off.' Strictly speaking, that wasn't one hundred percent true, but he was sure that's what she meant when she told him to make sure Jo was all right. And he felt bad for judging her so harshly when she was actually an excellent nurse who had proved her worth today.

It was sufficient for the defiant tilt of Jo's chin to falter a little. 'She's not mad at me?'

'No one is mad at you. So stay, enjoy your vacation.' He moved to help her take her jacket off as proof she wasn't going anywhere.

'I'm not sure I'd feel right lounging around when I'm supposed to be working, with your grandmother in hospital.'

'Well, you can always help me out. I'm running a free

clinic on a neighbouring island. An extra pair of hands is always welcome.'

'I suppose…if it means I'm doing something constructive and not self-indulgent…'

'It's a deal then. Get some sleep. We'll be leaving early.' Taylor walked away before she had the chance to change her mind.

It was refreshing to find she had the same work ethic and conscience as he had, even if it didn't fit with the notion he had of a manipulator ingratiating herself with the family. Unless that was what she wanted him to believe… He didn't want to fall for that shtick twice. Spending time running a busy clinic would certainly help him learn more about the sort of person she was, and whether or not he had completely misjudged her after all.

CHAPTER FOUR

ISLAND-HOPPING IN THE sun wasn't something Jo had ever pictured herself being a part of, especially given her financial status, but that's exactly what she was doing. Even though she was going to work, it all seemed very glamorous. However, she'd insisted on wearing her uniform today, so she, and everyone else, would know why she was here. Taylor had chosen a light white cotton shirt teamed with some board shorts for a more casual, and comfortable, look.

'Are you okay?' he asked, helping her out of the boat they'd taken across to Loloma, one of the small neighbouring islands.

'Yes. A bit apprehensive about what lies ahead, I suppose. I've never done anything like this before.'

'You'll be great. Honestly, you'll get as much out of doing this as the community will get from you helping.'

'So you do this a lot?' Jo lifted some of the medical supplies Taylor had unloaded from the boat and followed him across the beach. There was a lot more foliage on this island compared to the one the Stroud family currently resided on, the tree line starting at the far end of the sand and continuing as far as the eye could see. It made her wonder about the people who lived here. How many there

were, where they lived, and how they'd feel about her and
Taylor landing here.

'When I can. It takes some organising. You know,
transport, liaising with the local hospitals, and the community etcetera.'

'At least funding isn't a problem.'

'No. It does have its perks I guess.' He didn't look
happy about it and Jo knew he was conflicted over the
matter. But she appreciated the effort he went to for the
money to make a difference in other people's lives. Not
everyone would give their time and energy for something
that didn't result in payment or accolades. As he said, the
reward for him must've come in helping others. An ad-
mirable quality that wasn't in plentiful supply. Certainly
not with her ex.

'And the locals don't get upset by outside interference?'
She was trying to choose her words carefully, but she
wanted to be sure he wasn't seen as some arrogant rich
saviour riding in on his horse for the sake of his own ego,
even if she knew it wasn't true.

'Trust me, I can be very diplomatic when I need to be.
I only go where I'm sure my services are wanted. So far
that hasn't been a problem as people are desperate in some
cases for accessible medical care.'

His words satisfied her that she wasn't about to walk
into a protest about their arrival on the island and some
of the tension left her body.

'And where exactly are we setting up this clinic?' She
had yet to see any sign of life, save for the man who'd
dropped them off in the boat and was now halfway across
the sea in the opposite direction.

Taylor waited until they'd hiked up the trail between

the trees to the main 'road', which was essentially a dirt track, to respond. 'At the community centre. Over there.'

A very grand name for the hut that looked as though it had been thrown together using bits of old corrugated iron and planks of wood.

'It looks like it would topple down with one gust of wind.' She doubted the palm leaf roof would keep much rainwater out either.

'We could set up on the beach, but there wouldn't be much protection from the sun, and it could be a long day.'

'It's fine. Just not what I'm used to.' She didn't want to seem churlish, but it was a contrast to the conditions they'd been living in on the neighbouring island. Goodness knew how he got used to this after living his life in privilege, but Jo supposed that was what had pricked his conscience in the first place.

'I don't think someone like you will have a problem fitting in.'

'What's that supposed to mean?' The thought that he saw her as the poor relation immediately put her back up, regardless that it was true.

Taylor's smile neutralised her urge to scowl. 'I mean you're kind and compassionate, and everyone likes you. I don't think it matters where you are, or who you're with, you'll always be welcomed.'

It was a nice thing to say and the compliment put a spring in her step as they made their way over to the hut. 'Well, thank you, kind sir.'

'I mean it. I know we got off to a rocky start but I, er, I've learned not to take people at face value any more. Not everyone is what they seem, but I can see you're genuine, Jo.' It was a heartfelt attempt to build bridges with her, but it also made her wonder about what had happened in the past. Clearly, someone had given him cause to be so defensive, even if she wasn't the one who deserved his wrath.

'It's taken you long enough,' she joked, and managed to make him smile.

'I know. I guess it takes a near death experience with a loved one for me to trust anyone these days.'

'I'm sorry.' She knew exactly how that felt, and despite their differences, she was sorry he'd suffered some sort of betrayal.

'It's not your fault. We, er, just had some trouble a while back with someone getting close to the family and stealing some money. I shouldn't have assumed you were the same.'

'It's okay. When someone lets you down like that, it's difficult to get over, I know.' Although Taylor was referencing the family, his earlier comments, and the fact that he was the only one who'd been suspicious of Jo, led her to believe this was a personal matter for him. Perhaps they had more in common than they'd initially thought, even if he hadn't been left bankrupt by whoever had taken him for a ride.

He gave her a quizzical look, as though wondering what her story was, then appeared to decide to let the matter drop. Likely because he didn't want to go into detail about what had happened to him, and Jo wasn't going to push it, since she wasn't in a hurry to share her experience either.

'Anyway, it's all in the past, and I'm just glad you're here to give a helping hand.' They carried on over to the hut in silence, though it seemed to Jo as though they had made some sort of connection. Even if neither of them were ready to open up just yet.

There was a party of locals inside the community centre waiting to greet them, along with a table full of fresh fruit and snacks.

'Welcome.' A mountain of a man with a beaming smile came and shook their hands enthusiastically.

'You must be Isaac.' Taylor returned the handshake with gusto.

'I'm Jo. I hope you don't mind me tagging along today.'

'Not at all. Are you a doctor too?'

'A nurse. I can give first aid to any minor injuries that might come in.'

'We're very pleased to have you here. Everyone is looking forward to meeting you.' Isaac, whom she assumed was some kind of community leader, appeared to be in charge, or at least had been working with Taylor to make this happen.

He led them over to meet the rest of the group, all dressed in colourful casual wear, which made her feel way overdressed.

'What do you need?' Isaac asked once everyone had been introduced and they'd been furnished with drinks.

'A table and some chairs will do for starters. We might need a private area for examining patients too.' Taylor glanced around the small room, which looked as though it was used for everything from church services to school lessons.

Whilst Isaac and the others rearranged the furniture for their makeshift clinic, Taylor pulled over an old-fashioned free-standing chalkboard. 'We could use this as a screen.'

As he pulled a chair in behind it, Jo began unpacking medical supplies onto one of the empty tables that wasn't currently laden with food.

'Okay, I think we're ready for business.' Taylor took a seat at the table and clapped his hands together.

'Good, because there's a queue forming outside already.' Isaac peered out the door before waving the first patients inside.

Before they knew it the room was crammed with people chatting and helping themselves to refreshments. Jo got the impression this was the way they welcomed everyone to the island and whilst it was a lovely atmosphere, they'd come here to do a job.

Clearly Taylor felt the same way as he got to his feet and banged for attention on the table. 'Hi, everyone. I want to thank you all for coming to our clinic today. Obviously, we want to see as many of you as we can today, so if we could ask you to form some sort of queue it would make this go smoother.'

Everyone stopped and stared, listening to his words, but no one made a move.

Jo sidled up to Taylor. 'Why don't I take names and details and triage here first, then I'll send them back to you.'

'Good idea. Thanks, Jo.' A relieved Taylor touched her lightly on the arm, but it was enough to leave her skin tingling. Reminding her of the moment they'd shared at the waterfall.

She shut down the thoughts capable of making her hot and bothered because she had work to do, and was grateful for it. Otherwise, she would have nothing but Taylor and the memories of him wet and half-naked to occupy her thoughts until Isabelle was back.

'You can button your shirt again, Mary. It's nothing to worry about, but your heart is racing a bit. That's what could be causing the dizzy spells. I'm going to refer you to a specialist on the mainland and they can organise some scans for you.' Taylor couldn't administer any medication here; she would have to have an ECG to see what was going on first, but he could make the referral.

'Thank you, Doctor.' The elderly woman began to rummage in her handbag.

'There's no payment necessary. This is a free clinic.' He'd had to repeat that a lot over the course of the morning. Although they didn't have much, these were proud people who seemed to want to pay for their time today. So far, he'd accumulated quite a collection of food and handmade gifts in kind for treating people today and he didn't want to refuse in case he offended anyone.

'It is just a token of my appreciation,' she said, pulling out a beautiful hand-painted fan.

'Thank you so much.' Taylor accepted it graciously before showing Mary out again. He took a moment to check in with Jo too. She'd done an excellent job of sorting the clinic into something more organised and efficient than he'd ever managed in these sorts of conditions. Since she was able to treat some of the more superficial injuries and ailments, she was sharing the workload too. Though she was beginning to look a little flushed, and no wonder with the lack of air conditioning in the basic facilities they were working in.

'How's it going?' he asked, handing her the fan Mary had just gifted to him.

She took it and immediately began to fan herself. 'Good. A few cuts and sprains to deal with. That's all I can really do with just a first aid kit.'

'I know. It's frustrating, but short of building my own hospital in every one of these areas, that's all we can do in terms of being hands-on. I can diagnose the obvious and make referrals, but in terms of further investigation and ongoing treatment, they have to go to the mainland.'

He wished he could do more, but supplies were limited. The most he could do was make donations towards the hospitals themselves, which he did, to pay for more staff and specialised equipment.

'Obviously these people still need your help or else we wouldn't have such a big turnout. I'm sure it's not as easy to go island hopping without your own private helicopter.' She was teasing him, but he appreciated her validation of what he was trying to do in places like this. It gave him the motivation to continue his work, even if it sometimes felt like a drop in the ocean of what was needed.

'I see everyone's been showing their appreciation to you too.' He nodded towards the flower leis and shell necklaces around her neck and decorating the table.

'They're so lovely here. I think we could probably move here permanently and be treated like royalty for the rest of our days.'

'I think I've had my fair share of pampering, but you certainly deserve to be treated like the queen you are.' The idea of just the two of them being out here away from the rest of civilisation was tempting, if not a complete fantasy. At least the simple life wouldn't have him constantly on alert, suspicious that everyone who came into his life was there for nefarious reasons.

Although, it was getting more and more difficult to imagine Jo was anything like his ex. Especially when she looked content with so little. He didn't think all the jewels in the world would put as big a smile on her face as the seashell necklace that she was playing with around her neck.

'Maybe after I've finished here,' she said, getting back to her paperwork.

'So, who have we got next?'

'Michael Reyus, a diabetic. Looks like gout.' She handed him the patient's details with a smile and she looked so at home here, so content, he wished this could have been a permanent arrangement. Sometimes she looked as though she had the weight of the world on her shoulders.

'You need to keep this nice and dry to give it a chance to heal, okay?' Jo finished dressing the nasty cut on her patient's hand.

'Does that mean I can't fish?' The panic in the man's eyes was understandable when it was how he made his living. It was also how he'd injured himself, a slip of the knife when he'd been gutting his catch.

'You could use a plastic bag to keep the water from getting into it. Just be careful you don't get it infected. If there's any sign of swelling, or you have a temperature, make sure to get some medical advice.' She was sorry they wouldn't be here to do a follow-up on the patients they'd met today. In the brief time they'd spent with the locals, she'd got to know and like every one of them. They deserved to have the same medical treatment most people took for granted.

'Thank you.' The relief on his face was surpassed by his gratitude as he shook her hand and left her with a whittled wooden fish. A hobby she hoped he would set aside for a while given his recent history.

'We're going to need a bigger boat to transport all of this back with us. We could open our own souvenir shop,' Taylor commented as he turned the fish over in his hands.

'Well, I'm taking every single gift home. I'll have some lovely memories every time I look at them.'

'I told you it was worth the trip.'

'Indeed, it is, but how do you do it? How do you walk away after? In our line of work, we're used to seeing patients through their treatment. This must feel like setting something in motion and never seeing it through to the conclusion.' Taylor gave her the impression of someone who liked to be in control. She didn't imagine it was easy for him to walk away and absolve himself of any responsibility when he seemed to take on more than any ordinary person could handle on their own.

'It's not ideal, but it's more than these people are currently getting in the way of medical treatment. At least with mobile clinics I can see more patients.' Taylor gathered up more paperwork, obviously trying to help as many people as he could while they were here.

Jo couldn't help but wonder what motivated him, what drove him. Okay, so he wanted the family money to be put to good use, but there was more to it. With no apparent partner of his own, his work seemed to be his life. As though he was running from something else. She should know, when she'd been doing the same for the past two years.

'I'm sure they're all very grateful. I know I am for you letting me take part.' It showed a lot of trust on his part. Especially after their initial meet. For someone who liked to keep a tight rein, he was opening up his world and putting his faith in her medical abilities along with his own.

'Help! I need some help!' A man burst in through the door, rushing towards them carrying a screaming child in his arms, blood everywhere.

'Get him over here.' Taylor cleared one of the tables so they could lay the young boy down, whilst Jo rushed to chivvy everyone else out of the hall.

'This is an emergency. If you could all just give the

boy some privacy and wait outside until we treat him, it would be greatly appreciated.' Although the waiting patients were all peering over her shoulder, trying to get a better view of what was happening, Jo managed to herd them all outside.

She closed the door and rushed back to see what she could do to help.

'What happened?' Taylor asked the father as he stripped off the child's bloodied shirt.

Jo grabbed Taylor's medical bag along with a first aid kit and carried the supplies over.

'He was wrestling with his brother. We've told them time and time again that someone's going to get hurt, but they don't listen...'

'There are lacerations all over his face and body.' Taylor peered closer. 'I think there's glass in some of the wounds.'

'He fell through the glass table. It shattered. I didn't know whether to pull the glass shards out or leave them where they are.' The father was understandably distraught over his son's injuries. Although the cuts could be superficial, there was always that chance that a shard could penetrate vital organs or arteries, causing the patient to bleed out. They would have to do a careful examination of every wound.

'Did he lose consciousness at any time? Any vomiting?'

'No.'

Hopefully that meant he hadn't suffered a concussion during the fall.

'What's his name?' Jo asked, setting out antiseptic and gauze to dress the cuts.

'Jack. I'm his father, Dessie.'

'Okay, Dessie. We're going to have to clean and dress his injuries. You can take a seat or wait outside.' She knew they would work better if he wasn't standing over their shoulder.

'I—I think I'll wait outside. Get some fresh air.'

'We'll give him some pain relief to help him. Does he have any allergies we should be aware of?'

'No.'

'Don't go, Dad.' Jack reached for his father, but Jo stood between them.

'We're going to take good care of you, Jack.' Then, turning to Dessie, she added, 'We'll come and get you if we need you.'

'I'll be right outside, son. The doctor's going to make sure you're all right.' Dessie dropped a quick kiss on his son's head and left one last lingering look before he walked out, hands on his head, torn about whether or not he was doing the right thing.

'Jack, we're going to have to clean all your cuts and make sure we get any glass out. It's going to sting a bit. We'll give you something to help with the pain, but I need you to be brave, okay?' Taylor spoke softly to the terrified child before he did anything. It was always a sign of a good doctor when they took time to explain to the patient what they were doing, no matter what age they were dealing with.

He gave the boy some pain relief, asked him about his favourite wrestlers, and generally won over his trust before attempting to treat him. Jo admired his compassion, and the understanding of how terrified the child was in the circumstances. Honesty and kindness were always the best policy with children. Trauma wasn't easily forgotten, as she could testify all these years later.

If her parents had only explained to her at an early age, believed in her that she could process and deal with it, then news of her adoption wouldn't have felt like such a betrayal. Finding out for herself when she was practically an adult had made her question not only who she was, but who she'd been living with for her entire life. Trust, once lost, wasn't easily given again.

Taylor handed her a pair of tweezers, showing he had faith enough in her to let her do the important work with him. Carefully, and methodically, they set to work cleaning the numerous cuts, and extracting the bits of glass embedded within.

'There are a few here that are going to need stitches.' Taylor rummaged in his medical bag to find the necessary supplies and set to work closing the larger wound sites.

Jack winced.

'You're being so brave,' she assured him, brushing his dark hair from his forehead. It made her think of all the times she'd fallen and been patched up by her mother. Her soothing words a comfort. Their bond so strong, once upon a time. Now, even though they were living in the same house, they felt like strangers forced together.

'We need to turn you over, Jack. We'll be as gentle as we can.' Taylor's instructions brought her back into the room, and the needs of their patient.

He'd suffered the most injuries to his arms and face, but there was always the chance he could have landed on some glass during the fall. They gently rolled him onto his side at first and Jo slid a towel onto the table to try and cushion him a little bit as they moved him onto his front. Jack's little cry of discomfort struck deep at her heart, wishing she could make everything better for him.

She wasn't a parent, but that natural instinct to protect a vulnerable child came to the fore. Not for the first time she thought about the parents who'd given her away. Had they done so for her own benefit, or had it been a selfish act? She'd never know because she'd since learned of their passing. The denial of her true identity for so long preventing her from ever finding out or getting to know her birth family. More reasons she didn't think she could ever forgive those who'd lied to her throughout her childhood.

'I think there's a big piece of glass stuck in here. I could do with some better light to see what I'm doing...' Taylor was crouched down, studying a deep gash near Jack's spine.

Jo knew if there was something left in there it could cause severe damage to nerves, or organs, and being so close to the spine could even result in paralysis.

She rushed around the room making sure all the curtains were wide open, then grabbed a small table lamp from the back of the room. Plugging it in to an extension cord, she carried it over and held it close to the wound so Taylor could see better.

'Thanks.' He took a moment to flash her a grateful smile and in that moment she felt a bond between them. They were working as a team. Something they fell into as easily as they had when Isabelle had been injured. She wasn't used to that, having been on her own for so long, concentrating on her own survival. It was nice to have company again, someone working towards the same goals. She could easily get used to it. Though that was where the danger lay. Any time she relied on anyone, they let her down, betrayed her trust and left her broken.

'It's deep in there. Ideally we'd get him to hospital...' Taylor didn't finish his sentence, but she understood what he meant.

In a hospital environment they'd be able to numb the area before attempting to extract the glass, but they didn't have that luxury here. Even if they had the means to transfer him immediately, one wrong move, a bump in the road, and there was a chance of doing further serious injury. Perhaps paralysis, or even death, depending on how deep the glass was, and how close it was to vital body parts. This one in particular was too close to the spine to take a chance. Even removing it ran the risk of doing more damage, though she was sure Taylor would do his utmost to avoid that.

'I'll open the wound a little more so you can get inside there.' She set the lamp down on the table so it was still lighting up the important area for them to see where they were working.

'Jack, this is going to hurt a little, but there's some glass in there that we need to get out quickly. I need you to be a big boy and be as still as you can. It'll all be over soon, then we can bring your dad back in.' Jo gave him some warning before they began the procedure, knowing it wasn't going to be pleasant.

She pulled the skin slightly apart so Taylor could get inside the wound with the tweezers, earning a cry from Jack.

'I'm so sorry. We'll be as quick as we can.' She watched Taylor dig in with a grimace, but when he got hold of the shard and gently eased it out, she was able to breathe again.

'All done,' Taylor announced, the relief evident in his voice as the tension seemed to leave his shoulders.

'You're so brave.' Jo leaned in and whispered in Jack's ear, suddenly tearful for everything he'd endured.

Taylor moved quickly then to close the site and dress it to prevent any infection and Jo was able to go and get Dessie to reunite him with his son. 'You can come in and see him now. Just be very careful, he's going to be tender.'

Jack sobbed as his dad came in.

'Is he going to be okay?' he asked Taylor, who was cleaning the boy up and wiping away as much blood as he could.

'I'll send some painkillers home with him but he's going to have to rest up and give those cuts a chance to heal over. I'll see if Isaac can arrange transport home for you both. We don't want to move him any more than is necessary.'

'I can go home?'

'Yes, Jack, but no more wrestling for a while. Okay?' Jo was sure she wasn't the only one in the room who would've given him a great big hug if he wasn't so delicate right now.

'You're going to have to keep an eye on him tonight, Dessie. The first sign of a temperature, or any nausea, get him to the hospital. Actually...' Taylor pulled out his phone. 'Call me. I can come here, or get you to the hospital myself. I'm only a phone call away.'

'Thank you.' Dessie looked relieved and thankful as he took down Taylor's contact information.

Jo knew Taylor would keep his word and get help here the second it was needed, even if it meant calling in a few favours from his father. At least he wasn't someone who would prioritise his principles over someone's health. It was good to see he was a man of action, as well as words. The more time she spent with him, the less he seemed like the rest of his family, and the more there was to appreciate about him. He wasn't just a philanthropic rich kid who looked good in a pair of wet shorts. Taylor Stroud was a true humanitarian, a man she was glad she'd got to know, and someone she was going to miss when she went home.

Uh-oh!

* * *

Between them all, they managed to lift Jack into the back of Isaac's truck, with strict instructions from Taylor to go slowly. It wasn't the first emergency he'd had to deal with in such a remote area, or even the first time he'd run a clinic jointly with anyone. However, it was the first time he'd done it all with Jo, and he had to say, he kind of liked it.

Of course, he wished young Jack hadn't gone through such a harrowing time, but Jo had been good at keeping him calm. They'd also got through more patients than he'd expected because they'd been able to share the work. She might be used to working one-on-one these days, but she'd been more than capable of organising and triaging the patients to make his working day go as smooth as possible in the circumstances. Although he ultimately preferred to be the one in control whenever he did one of these trips, he could see the benefits of having a partner. At work at least. In terms of his personal life, it would be a long time before he'd trust anyone enough to let them into his private world and run the risk of being hurt again.

Taylor didn't think he'd ever be able to have a proper relationship again even if he met someone he wanted to have in his life. He'd be waiting, looking for signs that something wasn't quite right, expecting that final devastating blow to his heart. His ex had made him that way— distrusting, wary and unable to completely give himself to another person.

He'd believed he'd found someone with common interests and passions, a woman he would possibly spend the rest of his life with, and she'd been lying and scheming the whole time. The happiness he'd felt had been fake. It gave him some insight into the way his mother had felt when her marriage to his father had ended so cruelly and abruptly.

Perhaps he'd ignored any signs that something was wrong in his own relationship because he'd been so desperate to find the security and stability he hadn't had from his family. To be with someone who accepted him for who he was. Imogen had pretended to understand him, to share common passions and interests, and he'd foolishly accepted it as fact when all along it had been a lie. All so she could get her hands on his money. It was so cliché, and he should have seen it a mile away, but he'd been so blinded by love. Now it would take a miracle for him to ever feel that way about someone again.

Taylor wondered if that was the family curse. That because of their wealth, it wouldn't be possible to ever find someone who could see past it. The only thing he could rely on, the only good thing in his life now, was his work. It was a pleasant change to have Jo here helping him with it when it was usually something of a lone experience.

They managed to see a couple of the more urgent patients before they started to lose the light and began to wrap things up. By the time Isaac came back, they were ready to leave.

'Did Jack and Dessie get home safely?' he asked, before Isaac even had time to shut off the engine.

'Yes. They're fine, and very grateful that you were here today to help. I wish we had you permanently.' Isaac clapped him on the back. A hearty thump given with genuine affection and appreciation.

'And I wish we could do more, I really do, but we have to get back to Bensak.'

Jo nodded as she joined them outside the hall carrying

some of their medical supplies. 'Do we just meet the boat back on the shore?'

'Oh, the boat won't be coming back tonight,' Isaac informed them with a grin.

'Pardon?'

'Why not?' Jo sounded as anxious as he was suddenly feeling at the news.

He was exhausted, hungry and had been looking forward to heading back to unwind. Now he was as tense as the first night he'd arrived on the family retreat.

'It's too dark now, and the wind is getting up. The weather changes quickly here. There will be no boat until the morning.'

Taylor's mouth dropped open, no words seeming to come, whilst Jo looked visibly pained at the thought of remaining here with him for the night. 'But where are we going to stay?'

'I have a bed in my house you are welcome to use.' Isaac's offer did little to lessen the abject horror on Jo's face.

'We can't share a bed. Taylor, can't you do something? You could get us a helicopter out of here.' There was a rising sense of panic in Jo's voice, and though he could understand her anxiety about being stuck here with him for the night, he couldn't justify making an SOS call like that.

'If it's going to be dark and stormy, I don't really want to put someone's life in jeopardy simply because we might be a bit uncomfortable for one night. I'm sure we can manage.'

He could see Jo churning everything over in her mind and gradually coming to accept this was happening. 'Where are we going to sleep?'

'If you don't want to camp out on the beach, we could just pull up a few chairs here. Would that be okay, Isaac?'

'Of course. I can bring you some blankets, if you're happy to stay here.' Isaac look relieved they'd no longer be his responsibility, and they weren't going to insist on trying to get off the island.

'I wouldn't say happy…' Jo mumbled and dropped the bags she was carrying, making it clear she was reluctant, if resigned, to the change of plans.

'We'll have shelter, there's plenty of food and drink left, and on the plus side, we'll be able to check Jack over in the morning again.' He was trying to look at the positives. It was more than a lot of people had, and it wouldn't be the first time he'd had to rough it. It was ironic that it wasn't him that was struggling with the idea of leaving luxury behind for one night. Unless it was more about who she was stranded here with.

They'd clashed at first, but they'd also had some bonding moments over his grandmother, and the patients they'd treated. He didn't think she was still holding a grudge over his rude attitude that first night, but there was obviously something more than the lack of Egyptian cotton sheets concerning her. For him, the increasing concern was the amount of time they were spending together. He was becoming increasingly close to Jo, and if he was honest, spending the night here with her didn't seem as much of a disaster to him as it clearly did to her. Which was a red flag in itself…

They had a lot in common, including their medical backgrounds, and, he suspected, their need to keep their personal lives private. He knew nothing of her, or her life, beyond caring for his grandmother, but he found himself wanting to find out more. All signs that he needed to be careful. He'd been there before, and the last time a woman had piqued his interest, he'd been left devastated by betrayal. Taylor had to make sure his professional admiration for Jo didn't stray into something more dangerous.

CHAPTER FIVE

JO WASN'T USUALLY one to panic. She was used to being calm in a crisis, a prerequisite in her line of work. This felt different. Out of her comfort zone.

It wasn't a life-threatening situation, and perhaps she was overreacting, but the thought of being alone with Taylor all night was giving her heart palpitations. After spending all day in his company she needed to retreat back into her own space and put some distance between them so she could gather her thoughts, remember all the reasons she was here and why liking him was a bad idea.

She couldn't trust her judgement any more. Certainly not when it came to men. Steve had destroyed everything. Not just her business, and her sense of security, but he'd taken away the very essence of who she was. Jo Kirkham was no longer a successful businesswoman content in both her professional and home life. Now she was an employee, a lodger and completely at the mercy of others. It wasn't an ideal situation for someone who thought they could no longer trust another soul.

Besides, if she'd been duped by people she thought were her parents her whole life, as well as a man she'd given herself completely to, she had to be careful about getting close to new people. Her heart was a liar and not to be trusted. She was managing to survive now, but she didn't think she could withstand another betrayal. There was too much risk involved in letting a stranger further into her life.

Without other people or distractions, being stuck here together in this small hall was only going to force them to get to know each other better. Since the more he revealed about himself, the more reasons there were to like him, she was worried to say the least.

'Thank you.' Jo took the bundle of blankets Isaac's wife, Elizabeth, had very kindly brought them. He and his children followed behind bringing cushions and trailing a mattress with them.

'It might be more comfortable than those hard chairs, for one of you at least. It can get cold at night. We've brought you some water and food too. There should be enough to see you through the night at least.' Isaac threw the mattress down in the middle of the floor and once the children had finished hitting each other with the cushions, they arranged them on the mattress.

Jo felt ashamed about her reaction to having to stay the night when they were all being so hospitable.

'You really shouldn't have gone to all this trouble, but thank you.' Taylor shook Isaac's hand, showing their appreciation. They could easily have been left to fend for themselves, but as Taylor had reminded her, they had food and shelter and should be grateful.

'It's the least we can do for you after you looked after our little community so well today. I'll let you know the minute we can get someone to take you back home in the morning. We'll let you get settled for the night.' Isaac rounded up his children and ushered them back out as noisily as they'd entered the hall.

'Thanks again.' Jo gave Elizabeth an awkward hug,

squashing the bale of bedding between their bodies as she did so, but she was reluctant to let them all go. As soon as they walked out it was just her and Taylor left here alone until morning.

'They're lovely people, aren't they?' Taylor was smiling to himself as he closed the door and sealed them in the hall for the night.

'Yes. I hope I didn't come across as a petulant, spoiled tourist. It was just a shock to find we weren't going to be able to leave the island.'

'I'm sure they understand. Although I get the impression they'd be more than happy for us both to stay here and become part of the community permanently.' Taylor's words, though in jest, made her shiver.

There was something about the thought of them living and working together here for ever that was more than tempting. She had to cling to the recent traumatic memories of doing just that with Steve to prevent her from getting carried away with the fairy tale again.

'I think one night will be more than enough.' Jo set about making the bed up with the blankets Isaac and his family had provided, whilst Taylor concerned himself with the contents of the foil-covered dishes they'd brought.

'Mmm, chicken,' he said, munching down on a drumstick. The barbecue aroma began to waft across the room, making Jo's stomach rumble and reminding her she hadn't eaten for a while.

Jo opened another of the food containers to reveal a vegetable rice dish. She grabbed a fork and dug in.

'You want some?' She offered the spicy accompaniment to her dining companion and they did a swap so she could help herself to some of the delicious-smelling chicken.

They stood, eating directly out of the dishes, grinning at each other, until they'd had their fill.

'You'd think we'd never seen food,' Taylor remarked as they stacked the empty dishes on the table.

'We must've been hungry.'

'It's all the excitement that does it. That adrenaline rush when an emergency comes in always makes me hungry afterwards.'

'Does it happen often? I'm not sure I'd like to be stuck in the middle of nowhere with a life-or-death emergency with everyone relying on me.' Today had been different. Although Jack had suffered a serious injury, the pressure hadn't been solely on her to save his life. With her usual clientele, as soon as they developed any health complications the hospital was the first point of contact. In places like this that luxury wasn't available.

'Now and then. It's part of the job, isn't it?'

'I guess so. Don't you ever just want something more secure? To settle down?' Despite everything she'd gone through, Jo mourned that version of her, so full of optimism and certainty that she'd found happiness with Steve. Like most people, she'd thought that her future was all set because she had a partner to share her life with. Now all she wanted was a permanent position and a house to call her own again. Peace.

'I could have that if I wanted. I did, once upon a time. It's not all it's cracked up to be.'

'Oh?'

Taylor hesitated before he continued, as though pondering whether or not to share any more with her. He pulled up one of the plastic chairs and sat down.

'I, er, did the whole eight to five in a GP practice, had my own place, and a steady relationship. Imogen was a director of a local charity, and I thought we had the same world view. We talked about setting up our own charity project providing medical services to disadvantaged people abroad. She even left her job to help set it up. We'd agreed I'd keep working in the meantime, and I was funding all of it.'

Jo didn't like the sound of where this was heading, or the dark shadow that was beginning to creep over Taylor's handsome features as he spoke about it.

'I'm guessing it didn't work out the way you expected it to?'

'That's an understatement. The whole thing was fake. There was no charity. Unless you count the Imogen Potter designer handbag fund. She'd been pocketing all the money, and when I found out she just laughed, said I could afford it.'

'That's terrible. Did you report her?'

'What was the point? She was right—I could afford it, and dragging her through the courts wasn't going to change anything. It was my heart, my trust, that had taken a bigger hammering than my wallet.' He gave Jo a half-hearted smile that did nothing to hide the hurt he was clearly still feeling over the incident. It was understandable when she was struggling two years on to forgive her ex for everything he'd done, and she wasn't sure she ever would. Even when she had paid off her debt and moved on, she knew that betrayal would live on inside her. That broken trust left an indelible mark and changed a person.

'I know how that feels...'

'Oh? Do tell. I don't want to be the only sad sack running away from my problems out here.' Taylor leaned forward, resting his head on his hand, batting his eyelashes at her.

He did make her laugh.

Jo took a deep breath. It wasn't something she'd shared with anyone unless they'd needed to know. Like bank officials and employees, and all the other people she'd had to face when her ex skipped out of town.

She pulled up a chair and sat down too. 'I used to have my own business, with my partner, Steve. We had a lovely house, and I pictured us raising a family together.'

'And he didn't?'

'Obviously not. He did a runner, and hasn't been seen since.'

'And the business?'

'It's gone. That's why I'm back working as a private nurse. So I think I win the sob story contest.' She tried to make light of it because she didn't want him to see how much she was still hurting over the whole ordeal. It wasn't going to define who she was, but it was still impacting on her, and would until she was able to get back her independence.

'I'm sorry,' he said eventually.

'It hasn't been easy for either of us, but hey, we're not the bad people in either scenario. We're the good guys.' Something she had realised over the course of these past two days was that Taylor most definitely was one of the good guys. Even if he didn't always let people see it at first.

She could have sworn he muttered something like, "I hope so."

Taylor watched as Jo settled into the hard plastic chairs, rearranging the cushions below her head into a makeshift pillow.

'What are you doing?'

'I'm going to sleep. It's been a long day. You can take the mattress.'

'Absolutely not. You can't think much of me if you think I'm the sort of man who'd expect you to sleep in a chair while I'm lounging in a bed.'

'I think a lot of you. That's why you're having the bed. You organised this clinic. I'm here on your dime. You're about a foot taller than I am, and I can sleep anywhere. Just get into bed, Taylor.' With that, she rolled onto her side, her back to him. Preventing him from extending the argument.

Since it didn't make any sense for both of them to spend an uncomfortable night trying to sleep on two chairs pulled together, he resigned himself to taking the comfier option. Even though he was embarrassed about doing so.

He pulled off his shirt with a sigh, kicked off his shoes and climbed under the covers. Dealing with small, remote communities, working in difficult conditions, was easier for him than managing personal relationships. Regardless that Jo wasn't a girlfriend, he'd involved himself in her relationship with his grandmother. That meant she was part of his life now too. At least for the duration of this New Year's trip.

He lay staring into darkness, his mind working overtime thinking about everything that had happened since he arrived on the island. Sometimes his thoughts drifting back to Imogen and how foolish he'd been in trusting her so completely. Then he wondered about Jo and what she'd told him about her relationship. If she had suffered the way he had.

He drifted in and out of consciousness, the wind howling outside keeping him from falling into a deep sleep. The rattle of the loose windows became louder and louder until he was fully awake. He sat up and pummelled his pillow into submission in the hope of getting a more comfortable sleep, only to catch sight of Jo curled up in the corner. She had the blanket pulled up to her chin but her teeth were chattering from the cold.

'Jo? Are you all right?'

'I'm fine,' she said, shivering.

'Get into this bed before you end up with hypothermia,' he insisted, glad when she rushed over and climbed in beside him.

Her whole body was shaking as she curled up into a foetal position next to him.

'You're freezing. Why didn't you tell me?'

'And admit I needed your help?' she chattered through her grin.

'Come here, you silly sod.' Taylor forgot all of his concerns in light of her plight. He put an arm around her and pulled her close into him.

'Next you'll be telling me to strip off to generate more body heat.'

Her jest in the midst of her obvious discomfort made him chuckle. 'Feel free. Or we could just pull the covers up around us.'

Despite the joking around, her comment had sparked images and feelings that were definitely not appropriate for someone trying to rescue a damsel in distress. Then she mischievously pressed her cold nose and frozen feet against his body to jolt him back into the moment.

'I think I can feel my toes again,' she said once she stopped shaking.

'Good.'

She was curled around his body now, her head in the crook of his shoulder, and her arm splayed across his chest. It should've felt uncomfortable both physically, and emotionally, but it wasn't. When Jo's breathing became steady, her chest rising and falling against him, for some reason, Taylor felt at peace. As though he'd found a missing piece of himself.

Instead of freaking out about the implications of that, or concerns about how vulnerable he was making himself, he began to drift into a peaceful slumber.

Jo became increasingly aware of the hard body she was pressed against as she came to. She should've scrambled out of bed to safety, away from Taylor and the threat he posed to her equilibrium. But she didn't.

It was such a pleasant sensation waking up next to him, feeling safe and secure in his arms, that she was reluctant to leave his embrace. He'd been her source of warmth and comfort in the night, and now he was the romantic fantasy she'd been missing in her life. She'd rebelled against the idea of getting involved with anyone else since her ex had done the dirty on her, but Taylor was reminding her of the good things to be found in a relationship. Even if he wasn't aware of it.

Even if he could never be the one for her.

There were so many things Jo didn't know about him, and she could never dare risk her fragile heart on someone so emotionally closed off. She should remember the first night they'd met, when he'd been so cold, instead of thinking about how she'd shared his warmth last night. He wasn't any more settled in life than she was, and could never bring her the peace of mind she longed for.

Maybe someday she might learn to trust again, and let someone into her life. For now she simply wanted to enjoy the feel of Taylor beneath her, and pretend that this was real.

Perhaps sensing her awake, he began to stir, but Jo continued to feign sleep for as long as she could.

He stretched and yawned, finally forcing her to relinquish her hold on him.

'Morning,' he said sleepily, his eyes still dazed with sleep.

She turned her face up to greet him and before she knew what was happening, he had bent to give her a brief kiss on the mouth. They both froze, staring at each other now wide-eyed at the realisation of what had just happened. However, rather than freaking out and reclaiming her personal space, Jo found herself leaning in for more. Taylor accepted the invitation and before they knew it, they were in a passionate embrace.

So much for not getting too close...

Lips crushed against lips, arms wrapped around one another, they lost themselves in the passion that had suddenly awakened between them. As though it had been there all this time bubbling beneath the surface and the intimacy of sharing a bed together had given them permission to release it. To embrace this desire neither knew the other had been harbouring.

Jo groaned against him, her brain too befuddled by the taste of him, the feel of him against her, to think clearly. Taylor merely responded by grabbing her backside and pulling her into his ever-hardening body. It was gratifying to feel his arousal pressed against her, confirming this wasn't just a case of mistaken identity. That he hadn't simply woken up in a daze and kissed her believing her to be someone else. Taylor wanted her, and heaven help her, she wanted him too.

All of those issues that had been holding her back from getting involved with another man seemed to evaporate in the face of her need for him. The only thing that mattered right now was how he was making her feel. Wanted. Wanting.

The practicalities of giving into temptation, or how it would affect the rest of their time on the island didn't enter her head. As though she was purposely blocking them out to indulge this erotic fantasy. Until there was a knock on the door and Isaac called in from outside.

'Are you awake in there?'

The second the real world broke through the erotic haze, Jo practically bounced out of bed. Putting some much-needed distance between her and Taylor, though wrenching herself away hadn't erased the memory of him. He was still imprinted on her lips.

'Yes,' Taylor shouted back, his voice gruff.

Jo couldn't even bear to look at him, her skin flushed with embarrassment as well as arousal. She hadn't just lowered her defences, she'd blasted right through them in her desperation to have him. Clearly her body was still craving that intimacy with a partner, even if her head was telling her it was a bad idea. Next time that voice needed to shout a little louder to make sure it was heard. Goodness knew what Taylor would think of her when she'd been about to give herself so willingly to him. He didn't know her well enough to understand this type of behaviour wasn't the norm for her. Which also made it so unnerving. What was it about him that had made her act so out of character? Her head wasn't usually so easily turned by a handsome face. Perhaps it was the knowledge that he had a good heart, making him as attractive on the inside as he was on the outside, that had captured her attention.

Whatever it was, she couldn't let it happen again. There was no happy ending to be had here, and if she did ever dare to venture into a relationship, it was going to be with someone she could trust to deliver that.

Not only was Taylor part of the family that employed her, but by his own admission, he didn't want to settle down. He was scarred by his own past relationships, always on the move. Those were not the qualities needed in her ideal man.

'Good morning. I hope you slept okay?' Isaac peered in around the door, checking the coast was clear for him to come in.

Thankfully his good manners had prevented him from walking in on something that would have mortified all of them. As it was, Jo felt the need to keep herself busy folding up the blanket she'd been using last night so she didn't have to face him.

'Like babies,' Taylor lied on her behalf.

She was glad of it. A man like Isaac would have blamed himself if they'd said they'd been cold and uncomfortable, regardless that he'd offered hospitality at his own home. Now Jo realised why she'd been so afraid of sharing a bed with Taylor in the first place. Deep down that attraction towards him had obviously been building and she must've known it subconsciously. Although the discovery that she had feelings for Taylor was unexpected, she could take steps now to avoid being alone with him. The other problem was that he was aware of it now too.

'If you're ready to leave, the boat is here. Of course, you're welcome to stay and have breakfast first—'

'No. We can leave now.' Taylor cut off Isaac's invitation, and though Jo would be glad to escape their almost indiscretion, his eagerness to go was a tad jarring.

She might regret acting on her impulses, but it didn't do her self-esteem much good to find out the feeling was reciprocated. It was possible he'd simply reacted like any other hot-blooded man waking up to a woman in his bed. Any woman. It didn't mean he was attracted to her the same way she was to him. Despite her decision to pretend nothing had happened, the thought that their early morning smooch hadn't been as special as she imagined was a bitter pill to swallow.

Taylor was grateful for the noisy boat engine making conversation impossible. Even if he and Jo were sitting as far apart as could be in the tiny space available.

He'd messed up.

Disoriented, disarmed and half asleep, he'd reacted to the sight of Jo next to him in bed before he'd engaged his brain. If he'd taken time to think about what he was doing he'd have remembered he was supposed to be objective about her presence. Not an active participant.

It hadn't helped that she'd kissed him back with abandon, lighting a fire inside him that had taken some time to extinguish. Even now he was worried that if she as much as smiled at him it would spark straight back to life. Not that she'd glanced in his direction since Isaac had walked in. No doubt regretting the incident as much as he had. He'd ducked out to check in with Jack before they headed for the boat, giving them both some time out from the pressure cooker they'd found themselves in.

The problem was he regretted complicating things between them, but not the kiss itself. It was good to know there was still a passion inside him for more than his work. After Imogen, he'd thought that part of him had died, with no interest in the opposite sex. Yet that had been disproved by how close he'd come to Jo in just a matter of days, despite all of his reservations. Although now he knew how she felt in his arms, how responsive she was to his touch, it was going to be difficult to forget.

'Thank you.' He handed the skipper a handsome tip for his trouble as the boat came to rest in the shallows, then helped Jo out.

Even that simple contact now had the ability to spark his body to life and he wondered if it was going to be like that every time, and how he was going to stand it. They still had days left on the island. Time to fill, and no place to hide. A ticking time bomb he was afraid would explode with devastating consequences, leaving multiple casualties, and no way back.

He wasn't used to feeling this helpless to his desires. Since the split with Imogen, the opposite sex hadn't held much fascination for him. Betrayal by one woman had erected barriers around his heart to repel everyone else who might be capable of causing him the same pain. He'd channelled all of his energy and passion into his work, with no interest beyond a passing glance at the opposite sex. Until now.

This chemistry he had with Jo had managed to break through those defences. It seemed all-consuming, penetrating his thoughts at inconvenient times, and distracting him from his usual focus. All for what? It couldn't go anywhere. She was his grandmother's nurse, recovering from her own emotional wounds, and only in his life through circumstance. They were such different people, from contrasting backgrounds, and they could never work as a couple. That's why it was such a bad idea to even think about getting involved. It could only end badly, and they'd both had enough painful endings for one lifetime.

He hoped now they were back on the island they would both remember that.

With their equipment on their backs, they schlepped through the water, and made their way back up the sand bank towards the villa. Jo suddenly stopped and turned to face him, her lips pursed into a straight line.

'Look, before we get to the house, I think we should talk about this morning.' It was clear by the look on her face it wasn't a subject she was comfortable discussing, though they both knew it was necessary if they were going to move past it.

'I'm sorry. I shouldn't have kissed you like that.'

'I think we're both to blame, but that's not the point.' He swore her cheeks went pink at the mere mention of it and he wondered briefly if she had been as unaffected as she was trying to project. 'I want to make it clear I'm not looking for anything…romantic.'

'Nor am I.'

'Good. The last thing I want is to jump into a relationship with another man I know nothing about. Or with anyone, actually. Maybe I'll become a nun…'

'Now, that would be a shame. You definitely don't kiss like a nun.'

She was blushing now, and regardless of his intention to try and put the moment of madness behind them, Taylor couldn't help but push her buttons some more. Perhaps because he was sure the immediate danger was over. Jo was no more interested in a relationship than he was. And there was just a satisfaction to be had in knowing that perhaps she'd enjoyed the kissing as much as he had. No matter how unexpected, or inconvenient it was to both of them. And he wanted to test his theory.

'We both got a little carried away,' Jo admitted.

'Oh? So you were into it? That puts things in a very different light.'

'I don't see how. We kissed. We shouldn't have. End of story.'

He took a step closer, saw her nostrils flare and her jaw clench. 'Why not? We're both adults, single and clearly have chemistry. What harm is there in a little kiss?'

Taylor was treading on dangerous ground. One wrong step and he knew he'd be in trouble too, but he couldn't seem to help himself. Some invisible force was driving him on, desperate to touch her again, to feel that same sense of abandon he'd experienced upon waking. They were attracted to one another and if neither of them was interested in anything beyond the physical, maybe it was worth exploring. Just because they weren't going to live happily ever after together, it didn't mean they had to ignore this new feeling of desire creeping in on them.

He reached out and caught a strand of her hair dancing in the wind. Her eyes fluttered shut as though she was anticipating the kiss, and called his bluff. Now it was he who was on the back foot, his teasing having backfired, because he was becoming flushed and bothered.

'There you are!'

They'd been so caught up in each other they'd been unaware of his father approaching. Taylor dropped his hand and stepped away from Jo.

'Yes, we're just heading back to the house to get washed and changed, Dad.' At least then they could retreat to opposite ends of the villa and he could get a cold shower. Something that would hopefully wash away this desperation he'd suddenly developed to keep touching and kissing Jo.

'I'm sure you've both had a tough night. We're just

glad you're back in one piece. That's why we've organised lunch later this afternoon for you down at the beach.'

'That's really not necessary, Mr Stroud.' Jo had already started walking again, understandably keen to get away from him.

He felt ashamed for the teasing, for making her uncomfortable and for causing even more trouble.

'It's all sorted. Everyone wants to hear what you've been up to.'

Taylor exchanged a loaded look with Jo. A silent agreement that *no one* would hear exactly what that entailed.

'Dad, it's been a long couple of days. We're exhausted.'

'Oh, don't be a spoil-sport, Taylor. We need some excitement, something to talk about other than your grandmother's health to lighten the mood. I want to hear all about your adventures. So we'll see you both down at the beach bar in an hour.' Clearly, his father wasn't going to take no for an answer. He jogged away without even offering to carry any of their bags.

'Sorry.' He apologised to Jo again, although this one wasn't his fault. 'It looks as though we're both required to attend. He's very persuasive.'

'It must run in the family.' Jo walked away before he could figure out if she meant that as a good thing or a bad thing.

CHAPTER SIX

JO LET THE multiple shower heads in the luxury shower blast her in the vain hope they would wash away those inappropriate feelings she was beginning to have towards Taylor. A few words, the slightest touch, and her body was begging for more from him. She'd sworn off men after Steve, a relationship the last thing on her mind when she'd been fighting just to stay afloat. Now her libido was reminding her that she had other needs.

'Get yourself together, Jo.'

So far the self-motivation talks hadn't been doing much good, when all the reasons she shouldn't want him went out the window the second she looked into those gorgeous brown eyes. But there was no future for them as a couple. Come the New Year they'd be going their own ways, probably in completely different directions.

But he's so hot...

That coquettish little voice in her head swooned, making a mockery of the strong, independent woman she'd been up until recently. Now she was expected to spend the rest of the day with Taylor and his family, instead of being allowed to avoid him so she could make an attempt to get those defences back in place.

When her skin was in danger of either turning wrinkly, or being flayed from her body, she shut off the shower and grabbed a towel. A perusal of her meagre wardrobe left her a little deflated. She hadn't packed to impress, never expecting to be socialising with the family outside of her duties to Isabelle. These were people to whom money was no object. The idea of getting their clothes second hand unthinkable, but she'd had to be frugal these last couple of years. Charity shops and preloved sites online had become her lifeline. Hopefully her dress code wouldn't draw any negative attention, or *any* attention in fact. She'd be content to simply blend into the background. That's why her uniform was more of a security blanket. It rendered her invisible a lot of the time, but today that wasn't going to be an option.

She supposed it hadn't proved to be the barrier she'd hoped for yesterday anyway.

In the end she decided she wanted to be comfortable in the sun rather than attempting any sort of formality. She chose a light cotton sundress with tie strings at the shoulders. It was a cheery lemon colour with little sprigs of lavender embroidered all over. A bargain find in one of her local charity shop haunts, which looked as though it had never been worn. It mightn't be high fashion, or cost the price of a month's wages, but it should keep her cool. Ironic when she'd been shivering only hours ago. That's what had caused all the trouble. If she hadn't climbed in beside Taylor, they might not have succumbed to temptation in the first place.

She slipped on a pair of strappy white sandals and brushed out her hair. It would dry in the sun. There was no need to spend hours styling it because this wasn't a date. This was lunch with her employer and his family. She didn't have to impress anyone, merely get through it.

That's what she told herself as she made her way down

to the beach, not daring to wait around for company. With any luck she could plonk herself in a corner somewhere, well away from temptation.

A hope that was quickly extinguished when she heard footsteps running up behind her and turned around to find Taylor beaming at her. 'Are you ready for this?'

'No.'

'Don't worry. We're just there to provide some entertainment.'

'That's really not helping, Taylor.' She rolled her eyes at him, trying not to be swayed by the sight of him in his leaf print, short-sleeved shirt and linen trousers. He looked so relaxed and smelled fresh and clean. Jo was doing her best not to imagine him in the shower, even though his hair was still wet and his shirt was clinging to his damp skin. It briefly occurred to her that they would've been showering at the same time, but she had to push that thought far from her mind before any X-rated images had time to form. She was supposed to be regaining control over her urges, not developing more.

'They just want some tales of life in the real world so they can gasp with horror and thank their bank balance it's not them.' He always sounded so cynical when he talked about his family, and though she understood why she wished he could reconcile his way of life with theirs. For his own sake.

He would only twist himself in knots trying to make them into people they weren't. She should know. Growing up she thought she had the perfect family, the idyllic upbringing. Finding out that she'd been adopted had changed everything. Her parents became strangers to her, who'd lied about who she was her entire life. She wished she could go back in time and have the relationship with them she'd once had, at least then she wouldn't feel as alone as she did now.

Though she'd understood when they explained they'd kept her real parentage a secret because they didn't want to cause her any pain, their relationship had been altered for ever.

And then Steve had upended her life. At a time when she needed to feel some security, she'd begun the search to trace her birth family. Already fragile and feeling betrayed, that devastating news of their deaths had brought all of that resentment back to the fore. Everyone close to her had let her down. First Steve, taking everything, then her parents, denying her that closure with her birth family. She'd felt completely adrift ever since, not knowing who she really was, or who she was supposed to have been. It seemed every time she figured that out, her identity was ripped away from her. If she wasn't Steve's future wife, or Jo Kirkham, then who was she?

After the break-up she should've been able to lean on her parents, cry on her mum's shoulder and revert to a child in need of comfort. Except that new layer of betrayal, that feeling that her parents were responsible for keeping her from making that important connection with her birth family, seemed to destroy what was left of their relationship. She'd only gone back home to stay with them out of necessity, and everyone knew it. Now they tiptoed around each other, leading their own lives. It was sad really and she wished they could find some sort of resolution, but she didn't know how. They probably needed a good talk to clear the air and for her to air her grievances, but she didn't want to rock the boat when they were providing her with a roof over her head.

She didn't even have any friends to turn to any more.

Most of them disappeared with her ex. Either embarrassed by her change in circumstances or not wanting to get drawn into any drama. So she'd effectively been on her own since, fighting her way back. Probably for the best when she found it so difficult to let anyone get close these days. It seemed the only way to keep herself protected. Opening up her world to anyone now just seemed like inviting trouble, giving them carte blanche to mess with her heart.

Although Taylor didn't have her money worries, his life seemed pretty solitary too. Only around his family when he had to be. She hoped some day they could all find a way to live in harmony when it wasn't an ideal situation for anyone.

'How do you deal with that?' Unlike her, Taylor didn't strike her as someone who would bite his tongue or put on a show to keep anyone happy.

He shrugged. 'They know how I feel. I tell them often enough. I just hope someday I can get through to them and that they'll make an effort too. We're just very different people. I've come to realise that now, after spending half my life wondering why my mother and I weren't good enough for my dad. Why he needed to replace us.'

'I'm sure it's not like that at all. You know, my parents kept the information that I was adopted from me, until I discovered the truth at eighteen. It changed our relationship for ever when I found out my birth parents had died without me ever meeting them. Please don't let anything stop you from being with your family. One day it'll be too late to change anything.'

'I know that was upsetting for you, Jo, but couldn't you forgive your parents too? Perhaps they were simply trying to protect you. That's how much they love you.' Taylor's outside view of her situation was simplistic at best, but Jo realised it was also true.

She'd been so caught up in anger and grief these past two years she'd neglected the reasons why her parents had been so afraid of telling her the truth. It had been easy to put the blame on them being selfish. Ironically, it had taken her telling Taylor to hold on to his family at any cost, for her to realise she didn't want to lose the one she had. That they had been acting out of fear, and love for her. They still needed to have that big talk, but perhaps she could cut them some slack and try to salvage her relationship with them. After all, it was the only one she had in her life now. Another reason Taylor should keep trying with his family when he was as closed off to other people as she was, and might need his loved ones around him some day too.

'I'll talk to them when I get home. I promise. What about your family? What would it take for you to feel closer to them?'

His heavy sigh told of his frustration at the situation more than his words ever would. As though he didn't expect it to ever happen, and he knew he was fighting a losing battle. 'Anything. Just have some awareness of the world beyond their cosy bubble. Dad's always about the next big product, the "must have" that becomes another source of income to fund his next project. I'm sure he makes charity donations, probably for tax purposes, but I'd like him to give something back that came from the heart.'

'Like setting up a mobile clinic.' She couldn't help but smile knowing that was the kind of person Taylor was. A man with a heart, and a conscience as big as his bank balance.

'Yeah.' He gave her a lopsided smile that made her tummy flutter with nervy butterflies. 'Or a whole hospital. He can afford it.'

By now they'd reached the beach bar, which went way beyond the title and the picture she'd had in her mind of a grass hut serving drinks. The bar itself, although it did have some sort of thatch and bamboo roof, was as big as she'd ever seen. She imagined with more than the one member of staff currently mixing drinks behind the counter they could serve hundreds if the Strouds ever decided to throw a festival of some sort.

There were huge daybeds arranged into a sort of cul-de-sac. They were so close together she wondered if this arrangement was specially for this afternoon. She imagined on a normal day they'd be spread out to afford people more privacy and a better view of the ocean. This set-up seemed more in keeping with the 'story time' vibe Taylor had suggested they'd planned.

The rest of the family and his siblings' partners were already spread out on the luxury seating awaiting their arrival. Unfortunately, that meant Jo and Taylor had been left to share one of the bed areas.

'Glad to see you made it back in one piece, bro.' Taylor's stepbrother, whom she recognised from back home, reached up from his prone position to high-five him.

'You too, Jo. I'm sure it can't have been easy being stranded there last night. I would've been terrified.' The youngest of the Stroud offspring, Allegra, fanned herself in horror at the thought.

Jo had to do her best not to laugh. Taylor's predictions of his family's reactions had been pretty spot on.

'It wasn't too bad. The local community really made us feel welcome, made sure we had plenty to eat and were comfortable for the night.' Even the mention of their night together made her think about their passionate embrace and sent her temperature rising.

'Sit down, sit down. Tell us everything.' Taylor's father headed back from the bar carrying a cocktail, followed by several staff who distributed similar colourful concoctions to the rest of the party.

Jo accepted the sunset-coloured drink garnished with gaudy paper decorations and streamers, then tried to manoeuvre herself onto the thin mattress-like cushion without spilling it. Something told her the cream-coloured upholstery wouldn't survive it. She shuffled back and tried to keep herself propped upright on the many oversized cushions that were lying around. When Taylor came to join her, the bed dipped in the middle, causing them to roll closer to each other, but she couldn't scrabble away without making it obvious she was affected by him and had to remain where she was. For somewhere designed to be the ultimate luxury chill-out area she wasn't comfortable in the slightest.

With everyone sitting listening in anticipation she knew the onus was on them to make conversation.

'Well, we set up a clinic in the local community centre. A man called Isaac made the arrangements and before long we had a queue of people waiting to see us. All bringing us gifts.' She showed off the seashell necklace she was wearing.

'You have to understand these people have to get a boat or a plane over to the mainland just to get seen to,' Taylor interjected. 'That's if they can afford to do so, and if there's transport available. A pop-up clinic like the one we provided won't make any difference long-term, but we advised and treated as many people as we could. Having

Jo there meant I could see twice as many people since she was able to see to a lot of the minor injuries and queries for me.' Taylor joined in her account to point out the necessity of the work he did, not, she suspected for praise, but in an attempt to garner them into action themselves.

'That's very commendable of you, Jo.' Though Mr Stroud's comment was probably well meant, it made her wince at his lack of tact. Not only had he missed the point, but he'd neglected to acknowledge his son's incredible contribution. He was the architect of the whole thing after all.

She was beginning to see where Taylor's frustration with his family came from.

'What happens in emergencies?' his stepsister asked, pulling her feet up on her bed until she was almost in the foetal position.

'Well, they have to try to get them to the mainland where the hospital is, but failing that, they have to deal with the problem themselves. You can see the issue…in these remote areas the mortality rate is a lot higher than the cities that have accessible medical help.' Again, Taylor tried to reiterate why investment of time and money was so important in the work that he did.

'We actually had an emergency when we were there yesterday. A young boy had an accident, and his body was peppered with shards of glass. As we were removing them, Taylor found one embedded very close to his spine. I dread to think what would have happened if he hadn't been able to successfully remove it.' Jo thought it was equally important for Taylor's family to recognise the difference he personally was making in this quest.

'Really?' It was Taylor's stepmother, Victoria, who voiced her surprise at this snippet of information. As though she wasn't aware of her stepson's abilities, and they'd been under the impression his medical qualifications had been little more than a hobby. That they'd been indulging his ventures abroad in the same fashion as his siblings' interests in racing cars or running a fashion line.

Jo turned to look at Taylor, silently questioning why he hadn't told them in detail about the work he did. He avoided eye contact with her, instead getting up to help himself to some of the snacks that had been laid out on the glass-topped rattan table set up in the middle of their little commune.

'Yes. Taylor's so much more than a doctor. He's an emergency service in his own right.' She didn't miss the smirk on Taylor's face even if he didn't rise to the bait.

'I don't know how you do it.' His stepsister fanned herself again, and Jo marvelled in the difference between the siblings. She admired Taylor even more for going out on his own when he could easily have led this pampered lifestyle safe from the horrors of the real world.

'I think you deserve something to eat after all of that.' Mr Stroud senior got to his feet and helped his wife up with him. She was wearing a cloud of chiffon and seemed to glide towards the bar area that had been laid out with silver platters full of barbecued delights.

With no signs, nor smell, of the food cooking, Jo had to assume it had been barbecued elsewhere so the smoke wouldn't offend the hosts. A contrast to the dinner she'd shared with Taylor last night, which they'd eaten out of tinfoil parcels with their hands. Perhaps he'd been adopted too…

Whilst everyone headed up to the bar, Jo headed straight for Taylor. 'Why don't you tell them what you do? You're amazing and they should know it.'

He gave her a sad sort of smile. An acceptance of the situation even though it was obviously unfair. 'It's not about me, is it?'

Jo acted on impulse then, throwing her arms around his neck to hug him, and offer a little comfort. Forgetting the no touching rule she was supposed to have in place. He rested his head momentarily on her shoulder, his arms slipping around her waist, as he gave a small sigh. Then he let go and joined the others at the buffet laid out—the reason they were here.

She took a moment to compose herself before following him over to the bar area. The moment surprising her in all sorts of ways. Not only had her reaction been unexpected, but so had his. Taylor had leaned into that hug like he really needed it. She knew how it felt to be among family and still feel alone. For the duration of that brief embrace they'd been kindred spirits, and her heart ached for both of them.

'Have you heard anything about your mother's progress?' she asked Mr Stroud, making small talk as they mingled with their plates of food.

'Yes, I checked in with the hospital this morning. They're hoping she can be discharged in a day or two. Hopefully she'll be back for the New Year's Eve party.'

Jo stopped herself from suggesting that it might be more advantageous for the lady's health to go back home and rest, knowing it wasn't her place to do so. If the hospital had said she could still participate in the festivities Jo doubted Isabelle would be put off either. It certainly seemed important to her son that everyone should be here for the party.

'I'm so glad. I was worried about her.' Selfishly, having her charge back meant Jo would be busy again, and less likely to stray back into temptation in the form of her gorgeous grandson.

So he's gorgeous now, huh? that smug little devil on her shoulder who wouldn't be silenced whispered into her ear. Reminding her that the attraction wasn't simply going to disappear because Isabelle was coming back.

'The doctors at the hospital have been wonderful,' he gushed, seemingly oblivious to his own son's achievements.

'You know Taylor provides an extremely valuable service to these communities. He was amazing out there yesterday. You know you should think about going with him some time to see for yourself.' Jo hoped she'd given him some food for thought, but at the same time hoped she still had a job when they got back home.

Once she'd made some excruciating small talk with everyone, she managed to slink back to the daybeds unnoticed. As soon as an acceptable amount of time had passed, she'd excuse herself and go back to the villa. She kicked off her sandals and climbed onto the Taylor-free mattress, which was surprisingly comfy when she wasn't sweating over being in such esteemed company.

With her head on the cushions, she didn't think it would hurt to close her eyes for a while. After all she hadn't had much sleep last night. Jo drifted off with the sound of the sea and the white noise of the other guests chatting playing her a lullaby.

'Jo.'

Even though Jo knew Taylor running hand in hand with her along the shore was a dream, it seemed so real. She couldn't wipe the grin off her face, and she swore she could even hear his voice.

'Jo.'

It was getting louder now, and for some reason he was shaking her by the arm.

'Everyone's gone back to the house. I don't want to leave you out here all night.' Taylor's voice sounded as though it was right in her ear now.

Another shake, and the romantic beach stroll began to fade away. Consciousness loomed until she was blinking back into reality and staring into Taylor's velvety brown eyes. He was kneeling next to the daybed, his hand on her arm, apparently trying to get her to wake up.

'Hello, sleepy-head.'

'Hello.' She gave him a lazy smile. He really was a pretty picture to wake up to.

'We didn't want to wake you up when you were sleeping so soundly, but everyone's gone back to the villa and I told the staff they could finish for the day. I didn't want to leave you here on your own.'

Fully awake now, embarrassment flooding every cell in her body, Jo sat up. 'I'm so sorry. That must've seemed so rude after all the trouble they'd gone to.'

'It's fine. They knew we were both exhausted, and let's face it, it was the staff who did all this.' Taylor definitely had a lovely bedside manner, capable of putting her immediately at ease with his humour.

The fairy lights that she hadn't noticed strung up around the canopies suddenly came on as the natural light began to fade. It was magical.

'This is so beautiful.' She lay back down again to appreciate the view.

To her surprise, Taylor climbed up onto the bed and lay down beside her. 'I guess it is. Stuff like this I take for granted.'

'Well, I think you've proved you don't need it. Still,

it's a nice change from a freezing cold community hall.' Though they were effectively tucked up in bed together again.

'I don't know, it had its charms…' He turned to look at her, and Jo's heart gave a happy sigh.

'It's been a weird couple of days, hasn't it?' She tried to change the subject, afraid of what would happen if they lingered on last night's events. Despite the open air and the sea breeze around them, the air seemed thick with tension. Anticipation of what tonight would bring.

'You're telling me.' Taylor released her from his hypnotic gaze, flopping onto his back to stare up at the night sky and the stars beginning to wink at them from above. 'Dad told me he was proud of me. Then he literally patted me on the back.'

He seemed genuinely taken aback by the praise. Whilst Jo was pleased for him, it also shouldn't be such a big deal for his father to acknowledge he was doing something worthwhile. Of course, Taylor didn't need anyone to validate him. He knew what he was doing was incredibly important. But like everyone, deep down, she suspected he craved his family's approval. It would ruin the moment if she told him it was likely her who'd prompted his father's unexpected display. He didn't need to know that, and it would likely embarrass him to find out she'd been canvassing on his behalf. Besides, they'd see his brilliance for themselves eventually. It had only taken her a matter of hours to realise what an amazing person he was.

'It's about time. Next thing you know he'll be funding a new hospital wing in your name.'

Taylor narrowed his eyes at her. 'Let's not get too carried away. I'll settle for him realising I'm not just playing doctor.'

'Well, you're definitely not doing that any more than I'm playing nurse.' It wasn't meant as anything more than a throwaway comment. Yet the way he was looking at her suggested it had been so much more. As though she'd suggested playing doctors and nurses together.

The atmosphere seemed to change between them then. The darkness prettified by the fairy lights, and the gentle swish of the waves on the shore only increasing the romance of the moment as they lay together.

'You do wonders for my self-esteem, you know that?'

'I wouldn't have thought you needed any help in that department. You always seem so sure of yourself.'

'It's all an act. More like self-preservation than anything else. If I exude confidence, then no one else can take advantage of me. Or something like that...'

An overwhelming surge of something seemed to wash over Jo as he opened up to her. That vulnerability making all her defences melt away too. Because she recognised it. That need to put on an act, to hide the hurt and just keep on going. She didn't have to imagine what his ex had put him through, because she'd felt it too. The betrayal, the thought of never trusting anyone again, and the loss not only of the relationship, but also the person you'd once been. It was devastating. His heart was as broken as hers.

'I can understand that... I haven't been able to forgive my parents for keeping my adoption secret, and it will take a lot for me to trust anyone again. When Steve came along, I let him into my life—'

'And he betrayed you all over again. I'm so sorry, Jo, but you're not the one to blame here. If anything, you're the victim. You shouldn't be punishing yourself for something he did when you still have a life to live. Don't shut yourself off from the world.'

'Says you. Isn't that exactly what you're doing too, Taylor? Flitting from one place to another, never staying long enough to get close to anyone so they don't hurt you the way Imogen did. You were the victim there too. You deserve happiness as much as I do.'

'And what? That means leaving myself open to someone else who wants to steal and lie their way into my heart?'

'I'm just saying that it might be nice to share the life you have with someone. You don't have to be alone.'

He sighed. 'I've made my peace with the life I have, but you seem stuck somewhere that's making you unhappy. You deserve so much more, Jo.' Taylor put an arm around her and pulled her close.

'We both do.' She leaned into him, and the moment seemed reminiscent of last night. Only this time she wasn't in search of warmth. At least not in the purely physical meaning. Right now, she felt as though she'd found someone with whom she shared a connection, but didn't have to fear. They both knew how it felt to be betrayed, and neither of them was ready to open up fully to the idea of another relationship. That didn't mean they couldn't explore the intimacy that usually came as part of the deal. For two years she'd been avoiding the idea of being with another man because she didn't want her feelings hurt. Perhaps with Taylor she could finally relax and enjoy the physical closeness he offered without having to keep herself protected at all times. Because Taylor would be out of her life again as quickly as he'd entered it.

When the kiss came, it felt like the most natural thing in the world. There were no alarm bells ringing, or red lights flashing, because she wanted it. She needed the comfort, the romance and the passion she'd already tasted on his lips.

This time they started slow, letting that fire burn steadily between them. She hadn't realised how much she'd missed the intimacy of a simple kiss until Taylor had first pressed his lips against hers. That feeling of letting go, of giving herself completely, physically and emotionally in that moment came as a relief. She could feel his hands on her waist through the thin fabric of her dress, branding her, claiming her as his. The thought of which made her tremble; arousal and anticipation coursing through her body.

His mouth was crushing hers now, his tongue flicking tantalisingly against hers, that fire spreading, raging out of control. She was burning everywhere he touched her, and places where she wanted him to touch her. Aching, craving, needing Taylor. Only Taylor.

'What if someone sees us?' Her voice was breathy, heavy with desire and excitement. She wanted this, but she was an employee of his father's, and certainly not an exhibitionist.

'I'm on it.' Taylor jumped up and unfurled the canopies on all sides, so they fell down creating a curtain all around them. Ensconcing them in their own private room on the beach.

'Very nifty,' she said watching him work.

'I have my uses.' His eyes twinkled with the promise of more, making her tingle all over at the thought of him working more of his magic on her.

This was her moment to change her mind if she wanted to. When she was able to think clearly without Taylor touching her, kissing her, and rendering her a slave to her libido. She didn't need the lifeline because she wasn't going anywhere. Especially not now that Taylor was pulling off his shirt, exposing that hard body she couldn't resist reaching out to stroke. His shaky intake of breath when she touched him was reassuring. This wasn't the norm for him either.

They'd both been wounded by their exes. Afraid to trust or get close to anyone again. She wondered, if like her, he'd been too hurt to share a bed with anyone since. Not only did it give them a deeper connection, but it also made her feel more relaxed that she wasn't the only one out of her comfort zone. Based on a kiss alone she didn't think they'd have a problem with compatibility, but there was always the worry that she would be found lacking in some way. Especially when it had been so long since she'd been intimate with anyone.

Then Taylor was kissing her again and all of her anxiety melted away.

He slipped the straps of her dress over her shoulders, sliding his hands over her skin and raising goose bumps in his wake. With greedy palms, he pushed her strapless bra down and cupped her breasts. Jo gasped at the strong grip, sighed as he brushed his thumbs over her nipples, turned to liquid when he pinched them between his fingers. It didn't matter that they were in the lap of luxury on a private island, she knew he could make her feel this way wherever they were.

Taylor's trousers were already riding low on his hips, and they didn't take much coaxing from an eager Jo to slide on down past his backside along with his boxers. He kicked them off so he was gloriously naked, prompting her to strip off the rest of her clothes too. She lay beneath him, her breath coming in short, shallow gasps. This was her at her most vulnerable. She was trusting Taylor with her heart, her body and her peace of mind. When he paused to look at her, she held her breath, hoping that he wasn't going to find her wanting in any way. If he rejected her now she didn't think she'd ever be able to trust again.

'You're beautiful,' he finally said, letting her breathe again.

His ever-darkening eyes and hardening body led her to believe he was being genuine. It did wonders for her confidence, giving her the bravado to reach for him. To stroke the epitome of his masculinity. He closed his eyes and his intake of breath soon exhaled on a sigh as she moved her hand along his rock-hard shaft. The sense of power she felt, at a time when circumstances had been out of her control for so long, was an aphrodisiac all of its own. Not that she needed one when this gorgeous man was naked and...*oh*... Now he was flicking his tongue over her nipples, sucking almost until that point of pain. The balance of power had definitely tipped in his favour again.

They seemed determined to drive one another to the brink of madness, touching, teasing, tasting one another's bodies. Mouths clashing, hands exploring, she was molten at her core; ready for him.

'What about contraception?' she asked, barely clinging to the last atom of common sense in her body.

Taylor swore, as though in the heat of their passion he'd forgotten too. It was easily done when they were so engrossed in one another; so close to that relief and release they were searching for.

He only left her for a moment to retrieve his wallet from his trousers, rummaging with shaking fingers for that little foil packet. Jo waited impatiently as he sheathed himself, kissing his neck and nibbling on his earlobe until he was groaning with frustration. She liked that she could drive him wild. That she could make him feel the way she did.

He pushed her back down onto the bed, kissed her all over until she was writhing and wanton beneath him, desperate to make that last connection.

When Taylor joined his body with hers, she clutched him tight, trying to stay grounded when she was already soaring.

'You feel so good.' Jo could hear the restraint in his voice as he kissed her, made sure she was comfortable, relaxed, before taking things to the next level.

It was tempting to race ahead, to get to that finish line as soon as possible, but she suspected they both needed much more than that final release. They needed the intimacy, the comfort to be had in sharing their bodies with one another. The ultimate test of trust.

CHAPTER SEVEN

TAYLOR TOOK HIS TIME, moving slowly at first. Giving them both the opportunity to adjust to one another, to revel in the sensation. She felt like heaven. So soft and warm around him he knew he'd never want to leave.

Neither of them had planned this, but from the moment he'd kissed her it had seemed inevitable. That level of passion wasn't something found every day, and clearly couldn't be contained. There was a chemistry between them they hadn't been able to ignore, and now would be impossible to forget. Especially now he knew she didn't want anything serious.

She'd thrown his own words back at him. Made him think about how he'd been a victim too, had been punishing himself. Denying any chance he'd had to find happiness in anything other than his work. Although he still wasn't ready to jump into a relationship, and might never be, seeing his situation in a different light gave him permission to enjoy this moment with Jo. To totally let himself go just for a little while.

Jo squeezed her inner muscles around him and short-circuited his brain so he couldn't think straight, only feel. And he wanted more. She was raking his skin with her nails, wrapping her legs around him to draw him in deeper, urging him not to hold back. Driven by lust he picked up the pace, every thrust of his hips bringing him closer to the edge. He didn't want to get there before Jo.

With one hand, he cupped her breast, her pert nipple too tantalising to resist. He sucked hard, causing her to buck against him with a gasp. Whilst teasing the pink tip with his teeth and tongue, he reached down between their bodies and pressed his thumb into her soft mound. Her gasp spurred him on, thrusting, teasing, sucking, until they were both slick with her arousal.

When her orgasm hit, she muffled her cry in the crook of his neck, rocking with him until her body was limp. Taylor's restraint broke, and a primal roar ripped from him as he gave into that final bliss. He climaxed so hard and fast he felt as though he was giving her a piece of his soul.

In a way, he was. Jo was the only person he'd let down his defences with since Imogen. Not only had he shared his passion project with her, and details of his personal life, but now he'd shared his body too; he'd given her everything he could. And it still wasn't enough. Because deep down he was still wary, of everyone capable of hurting him. That meant holding back.

As wonderful as Jo was, he wasn't able to take that final leap into a relationship. Not that she wanted that either. She'd made it clear she wasn't ready for a serious commitment. Perhaps that was why he'd given into temptation, because he knew she wasn't expecting more than he was willing to give. He didn't know if he could ever trust anyone, including himself, not to break his heart, or his trust again.

He lay down beside her, his heart thumping, and his chest heaving as he recovered from his exertions.

'That was amazing.' Jo practically purred as she curled her body around him and pulled the decorative throw up over their bodies. He suspected the move was more about covering her nudity, making her feel less exposed, than the need for warmth. Despite the cool night air, their bodies were slick with sweat.

'I didn't even use all my best moves.'

'Oh? Are you saving them for next time?' she asked, batting her eyelashes, attempting a casualness that didn't quite work because of the hitch in her voice.

Jo was asking if this was a one-time deal and he didn't know how to answer that without spoiling the mood. He didn't want to upset her, but he also had to be realistic. It wouldn't be fair to lead her on when he still wasn't in the right head space for a relationship. Not to mention their different lifestyles, which wouldn't be conducive to anything long-term even if he was to consider it.

'Listen, Jo…'

'Such a serious face.' She mocked him with a scowl and pursed lips to make him smile and feel even worse.

Taylor sighed. 'This was great, but I, uh, I don't know where I'm going to be from one month to the next. I can't commit to anything.'

'I didn't ask you to.'

'You know what I mean… I'd like to do this again. Preferably somewhere more private. Where I have all night to show you my moves.' There would have to be something seriously wrong with him not to want to do this again, but he wouldn't risk anyone getting hurt in the process.

'I'm curious to find out what else you have in your locker, Taylor, when you've already surpassed yourself. That doesn't mean I'm looking for anything beyond that. We can keep things casual. Believe me, I've enough going on in my life without the hassle of another relationship. I'm still recovering from the last one. As, I suspect, are you.'

'You want to do this again? Just sex?' It was a tempting idea, and would mean he could have Jo in his life for a little while longer. Without the worry that she was going to break his heart.

'Why not? No promises, no commitment. Just company, and great sex. Sounds ideal to me. I think it'll help both of us move on from the past.' When she put it that way, Taylor didn't see any problem, other than having to get used to an empty bed again once it was all over.

There was just something about the arrangement that seemed a little…off. Clinical even. It was obvious they were both holding back from committing to anything because of their past relationship issues, but things got messy when emotions got involved. Painful. Perhaps this was the ideal solution. At least for now.

'I suppose we could keep seeing one another for the duration of this trip. Then, once the New Year comes, we'll go our separate ways with some very nice memories to take with us.' It meant he wasn't even committing to anything beyond these few days together. By setting a time limit, there was no risk of things getting complicated. New Year's was their deadline, and it would be nice to start afresh once he left the island.

'What about your father?'

'I'm not into threesomes. Especially not with close family members.'

Jo rolled her eyes at him. 'I think one Stroud man is more than enough for me to handle, thank you. I meant that I'm technically an employee. I'm here to look after his mother. Not for a romantic getaway.'

Taylor traced a fingertip over her décolletage and was rewarded when she bit her lip. It was clear once wasn't going to be enough for either of them.

'I don't see why you can't do both. No one else has to know. We have a day or two before my grandmother comes back anyway.'

'You mean sneak around?'

'We can be stealthy, yes. Sex ninjas.' In one quick motion he pulled the cover up over their heads, making Jo squeal with surprise.

'I like the sound of that,' she said as they were cocooned in their own little blanket bubble, her eyes twinkling in the semi darkness. He wished they were on their own, on a mini break together, free to explore the island without fear of incurring his father's wrath.

They both knew he wouldn't approve. Not least because of the nature of their agreement to keep things purely about sex. It was definitely no one else's business. He didn't want what they had together to be reduced to something shameful. Then he could leave what had happened between them here and move on without regret or recriminations. He didn't want Jo to lose her job either. She had a life to go back to, and she obviously needed the money to help her get back on her feet.

He wished so many things were different.

The only way he knew how to make reality disappear was to lose himself in Jo. He kissed her again, and with their naked bodies pressed tightly together it wasn't long before his attentions were focused elsewhere.

'Why don't we take this back to the house?' At least then they'd have some privacy and there was the chance of spending the night together. He couldn't remember the last time he'd woken up next to someone in bed. The closest he'd come was kipping down with other medical professionals who'd volunteered their time on similar outreach programmes with him. It wasn't quite the same. On those occasions he'd usually spent the night trying not to touch whoever happened to be sharing a hostel or a tent with him. He wasn't always guaranteed a bed, never mind the luxury of his father's villa.

'Like this?' Jo gestured to her naked form, giving him an excuse to drink in the sight of her again. 'I'm not sure I want to be caught streaking across the beach, thanks.'

'Now, there's an idea.' He could just picture her running across the sand under the moonlight carefree into his arms.

'What?' She eyed him cautiously.

'Skinny dipping. When was the last time you did that?'

'Uh, never.'

'You don't know what you're missing. We used to do it all the time as medical students when we went on trips to the beach. There's something very liberating about stripping off outside in the night air. As though you're casting off all of your problems, even for a few minutes.'

'Sounds like heaven.' She sighed, as though she had the weight of the world on her shoulders. Taylor wanted her to forget everything bringing her down for as long as possible. There would be time enough for reality to crowd them and bring them back down to earth from their post-sex high.

'So you're in?' He was seizing on the slight waiver in her first refusal to even entertain the idea.

'I'd be mortified if anyone saw me.' It wasn't a flat-out no.

'No one will come down this way now when they have everything they need back at the villa. I'll take a look and make sure there's no one around. We'll see if anyone's coming down and can make a run for the sea if needs be.'

She didn't look convinced, but Taylor decided to take

the initiative anyway and ducked outside. He walked around the bar and a little bit along the shore, looking out for any signs of life. It was as invigorating being naked in the open air as he'd remembered. Hopefully, he'd be able to convince Jo to join him. As well as thinking it would be good for her to let loose for a while, he knew it was another memory he'd have to cherish for the rest of his days. Much preferable to the times he'd larked around with uni mates dunking each other under the water and generally messing about. Back in the days when he'd been oblivious to anyone else's needs but his own.

'The coast is clear,' he said, sticking his head around the curtain of the bed.

'I'm not sure about this…' She was hesitant, but she did get up, their blanket wrapped around her body for now.

'Come on…live a little.' He held out his hand to take hers and led her out into the open.

She looked furtively around and seemed to relax when she was convinced there was no one else lurking nearby. Taylor waggled his eyebrows suggestively at her and watched with a grin as she dropped the blanket and revealed herself to him.

'Aah!' She let out a shriek, grabbed his hand and ran down towards the sea.

'The water's freezing!' Her eyes were sparkling in the darkness, wide and full of the thrill of the moment.

He felt it too.

'But it feels great. Right?' They waded out until the water was up to their shoulders, their nakedness hidden from sight should anyone venture out on a late-night walk along the shore.

'I'll tell you when I get my breath back.'

'I'm proud of you for doing this.' He meant it. Even

though the water was cold, and he couldn't feel anything from the neck down, he was glad they were doing this and being silly together. It made a change from the serious life-or-death work he did every day, and he'd forgotten what it was just to have fun for the sake of it. He suspected it was the same for Jo after everything she'd been dealing with recently.

'So am I. I never thought I'd do anything like this. It is kind of freeing. Maybe I'll become a naturist.' Jo seemed to be in her element. She jumped up out of the water giving him a flash of her beautiful round breasts before splashing the water around him soaking them both.

'Maybe we should find our own deserted island and just live off the land, like a regular pair of castaways.' He moved towards her, suddenly feeling the urge to have her in his arms again.

'I wish.' She slicked her wet hair back with both hands, looking like some sort of water nymph, bewitching him and liable to drag him to a watery death, but he didn't care. He'd die a happy death with a naked Jo coiled around his body.

'You're beautiful.' The words slipped out of his mouth unbidden, but true.

He kissed her. Not caring about the cold noses or other frozen body parts. He cupped her backside and held her flush against him, wishing he'd taken his own advice and gone back to the warmth and comfort of the villa in the first place.

'Let's go before we end up with hypothermia,' Jo said eventually, reading his mind and taking him by the hand.

They walked back to the daybeds, his arm around her, as though strolling around naked was commonplace for both of them, and there was no one else in this world. It didn't take them long to pull their clothes on again, both eager to get back to the house as soon as possible.

Jo didn't know what had come over her. She was like a different woman since she'd met Taylor. These past two years she'd been nothing but cautious. Hurt and feeling guilty about the other people who'd been affected by her ex's betrayal, her life had become a struggle for survival and trying to clear up the damage he'd left in his wake. Not to mention the devastation caused by the news that her birth parents had died without her ever getting to know them, finding out that part of her was now lost for ever.

Taylor had reminded her who she was. Not only was she someone who could make a difference in other people's lives, but she was also a woman with a lot of life to live. She'd enjoyed working with him, getting to know the man he was, but she'd also loved the person she was with him. A young woman having fun. She'd only been able to do that because she trusted him. It was a risky strategy, but so far it seemed to be working.

Now as they made their way back to the villa, bodies still wet and smelling of the ocean, it was as thrilling as running on the shore naked. Equally as exhilarating because she knew what was waiting for her beyond the bedroom door already.

Taylor was keen for them to have some privacy so he could show her his 'best moves'. Judging by the time they'd already spent together she knew she was in for something special. She only hoped they wouldn't wake the rest of the house with their antics or else they'd have some serious explaining to do.

When Mr Stroud senior had asked her to come on this trip for his mother's sake, so she could enjoy the New Year celebrations with the rest of the family, Jo would never have believed this was where she'd end up. Nor that she would have agreed to a casual sex arrangement with his son. It seemed an ideal set-up for two people who were afraid to commit in case they got hurt. She just prayed it stayed that way. Sharing her life with someone in any capacity again was a risk, and if it backfired on her she doubted she'd trust anyone ever again. As long as she kept their New Year's end date in mind, hopefully there wouldn't be any emotional fallout.

'Are you okay, gorgeous?' Taylor must have mistaken her introspection for apprehension, but there was absolutely no need. She'd never been as sure about anything as she was about spending the night with him. Sleeping with him had been the only bit of happiness she'd had in over two years, and getting the chance to do it again was a no-brainer. Who wouldn't want to be ravished by a handsome doctor, worshipped and brought to the point of orgasm again and again?

'I'm fine. I just don't want to get caught sneaking into your room.' That was the one thing she was wary of, apart from having her heart and her trust broken all over again. She didn't want to lose her job, as well. She couldn't afford to.

'We'll be as quiet as church mice. At least until we get to my room.' He gave her a wink that suggested reasons for them to be making a lot of noise. All of which made her tremble more with the anticipation of his promises.

When they reached the front door, he put his finger on his lips. They were giggling like naughty teenagers about to be busted sneaking in from a party they'd been told they weren't allowed to attend. Hand in hand they tiptoed down the quiet hallways to his room. Once they were inside, the door closed, locking them away in their own world again, they let passion flare to life again. Kissing and tearing each other's clothes off like they'd been denied each other a lifetime, rather than a few minutes.

She hoped it would be like this every time they got together. It would give her something to look forward to, as well as something to cling to when she was back to her lonely life. For two years she'd been consumed by work and trying to earn a living. There hadn't been any real joy in her life since everything had fallen apart. Neither her work life, nor her home life, were making her particularly happy. Perhaps this was the start of things beginning to turn around.

Once she had enough money saved for a deposit, she'd move into her own place. A picture flashed into her mind of what that would be like as it so often did. Maybe she might eventually be able to travel. This trip had given her a taste for that. Except when she thought about travelling somewhere hot and sultry, Taylor inevitably became part of the scene, lying in bed next to her. She shook off the romantic fantasy, a little perturbed by those thoughts creeping in uninvited. It was a dream that went too far and she needed to rid herself of the notion that this was anything other than a short fling. It was enough for now. A step forward without rushing in too fast into a new relationship.

They tumbled into bed, keen to pick up where they'd left off. Rolling around atop the mattress in a tangle of limbs and naked bodies, clinging to one another as though their lives depended on it. In that moment, he felt like Jo's whole world. Nothing else mattered except his kisses, his touch and the things he was doing to her. Taylor made her feel alive for the first time in years. Before then she'd been nothing more than an automaton simply going through the motions. Wake, work, sleep, repeat.

Now she was a real girl. A woman who had feelings, wants and needs, that were apparently all wrapped up in Taylor. He already knew how to make her happy, to satisfy her and to make her moan in ecstasy.

This must be one of his moves he'd boasted about...

Lying back, with Taylor appreciating every inch of her body with his mouth and his tongue, Jo had never felt so wanted. Even when she'd been with Steve, she didn't remember being so relaxed and turned on at the same time. Probably because there had always been a difference in the balance of power between them, with him always in control.

In hindsight, she'd worshipped him too much, never seeing any wrong in him. Oblivious to his faults until it was too late.

Perhaps in her desperate search for stability she'd clung to the idea of him, and who they could be together. Hopefully a family someday. He'd used that belief in him to his advantage, swindling her out of her business as well as that dream. She'd handed him too much of her power, deferred to him when it came to the business as a way of showing him how much she loved him. It was different with Taylor. When they worked together it had felt like sharing the load equally. A mutual respect and understanding of each other's roles. That hadn't been the case with her ex who'd always treated her as his inferior despite the fact it had been her business. He'd joined her later as a partner after they'd started going out together. When she'd signed over half of her business, she hadn't realised her life as she knew it would never be the same. And not in a good way.

Only now was she beginning to be optimistic about the future, and Taylor had been a part of that by making her feel so good. She hadn't thought another man, or great sex, would be part of her life, but she could see now what she'd been missing out on. With any luck her life now on would be full on every level and the euphoria wouldn't begin and end on this island.

Taylor was teasing her intimately with his tongue, dipping in and out, bringing her to the edge over and over. Until she was begging him to help her reach that final release. Only then did he retrieve a condom from his nightstand and give her what she was craving.

He filled her, drove deep inside her until she felt as though she was flying high above her own body. Then he withdrew from her, bringing her crashing down to earth. Taylor flipped her onto her side, and thrust inside her again from behind, the change of angle causing new sensations, equally arousing. His hands were on her breasts, squeezing, tugging at her nipples, and flooding all of her erogenous zones at once. Hot breath in her ear, lips on the sensitive skin at her neck—this man knew what he was doing. He seemed to anticipate what she needed, and more. Even the sound of his breath getting shallower as he came closer to climax was a turn-on. She rocked back against him, meeting the thrust of his hips with her own, both gasping as they climbed higher and higher. Then he reached between her legs, dipped a finger inside her and stroked until she was completely undone.

She tried to muffle her cry into the pillow so she wouldn't wake the house even though she wanted to scream her release from the hilltops. Taylor followed soon after, his groan sending aftershocks rippling through her body. As if they'd both ridden out an earthquake and lived to tell the tale. She supposed in a way they had. The earth had definitely moved, and she was sure something else had shifted between them too as they drifted off to sleep still lying in one another's arms.

CHAPTER EIGHT

'I SUPPOSE WE should make an appearance or it's going to look suspicious if we're both MIA.' Taylor snuggled up behind Jo, showing no sign of getting out of bed.

She knew he was right, but she preferred where she was. It was nice waking up in the morning to a hard male body wrapped around hers making her feel safe and protected. Convincing her that she didn't have to be on her own any more.

It was tempting to pull the covers over their heads again and forget the real reason she was on this island.

The sound of the villa coming alive, footsteps outside as the staff began their working day taking care of the Stroud family, finally roused her. She was supposed to be one of them. Here to work, not lounge around in bed pretending this was her world.

'I'll run the gauntlet back to my room and try and avoid bumping into anyone.' The thought of potentially embarrassing them both and causing upset to the rest of the family brought her back down to earth with a bump.

In an ideal world they wouldn't have to sneak around. And she wouldn't have to think of herself as a second-class citizen. More than that, there wouldn't be a clock ticking down on their time together and they'd see each other whenever they pleased, because they'd both recovered from the scars of their last relationships.

However, the reality was that none of that was possible and she had to be thankful for the snatched time they could have together.

She threw back the covers and retrieved yesterday's clothes from the bedroom floor.

'I'll grab a shower then see you in the kitchen for breakfast. You're welcome to join me for both.' With Taylor striding naked towards the bathroom, it was very tempting, but she didn't want to leave any later before attempting to get back to her own room unseen.

'Maybe next time.' She planted a kiss on his lips on her way out of the door, clearly leaving them both wanting more.

Although her heart was pounding, adrenaline pumping through her veins as she made her way stealthily back to her own room, it wasn't the same as last night. That had been about letting herself go, enjoying the moment with Taylor, and the thrill of it all. This was fear of being discovered and being made to feel ashamed. She didn't want that to ruin what they had.

Once back in her own room she was able to relax. She flicked on the shower, stripped off and stepped into the cubicle. The warm water on her skin reminded her of Taylor's caress, and everywhere he'd touched her. Despite wanting to stay and recall those vivid memories, she was kind of hungry. Jo hadn't eaten much last night and between the late-night swim, and everything else she'd been up to, she'd worked up an appetite.

If she was being truthful, she couldn't wait to see Taylor again. With the circumstances making it difficult for them to be together in the open, she wanted to take any opportunity she had without raising suspicion. Everyone else was going to be at breakfast at some point, so, as long as they could keep their hands off one another, she and Taylor could at least be around each other in company. Anything else would probably have to wait until they were under cover of darkness again.

After rinsing the ocean out of her hair, Jo donned the bikini she'd bought in the hope she would get to see something of the sun. Without Isabelle to look after, or planned work trips with Taylor, perhaps she'd get to lie by the pool for a while after all. That's what everyone else around here seemed to do to fill their days. And, if it meant she got to lust over Taylor in a pair of swim shorts too, it would make their anticipated alone time even hotter than last night.

She pulled on a blue and green cover-up, so she wasn't parading about the villa half naked, and followed the smell of coffee and bacon.

'Good morning.' She breezed into the dining room and tried to hide her disappointment that Taylor wasn't there with his parents.

'Morning, Jo. I hope you didn't sleep outside all night. Taylor promised he'd wake you.' His stepmother poured herself an orange juice, and didn't look the least bit concerned, despite the words coming out of her mouth.

'He did. Thank you.' It was impossible not to think of what else he did for her, which made an awkward atmosphere when she was alone with his parents.

Jo helped herself to some cereal and milk before joining them at the dining table, praying Taylor would make an appearance soon.

'I spoke to the hospital this morning. We're making arrangements to get mother back as soon as possible. She should be back here late afternoon if all goes well.'

'That's great news, Mr Stroud. I'm sure you'll be glad to have her back, as will I.' Regardless that resuming her duties would curtail Jo's time with Taylor, she was looking forward to seeing Isabelle again, and seeing for herself that she was all right.

'You should make the most of your free time before you have to get back to work,' Mrs Stroud said with a sniff, clearly not impressed that she'd been slacking in her duties despite the circumstances. A reminder that she was merely the hired help. Also, that finding out she was sleeping with Taylor would most certainly warrant instant dismissal.

A sobering thought when she needed every penny she was getting for this trip if she ever hoped to move out from her parents' place.

Then Taylor appeared and she thought it a risk worth taking. He was beautiful. The white T-shirt clinging to his chest emphasised the muscular body she'd explored thoroughly last night, and his wet hair made her think of the offer she'd turned down to join him in the shower. She must have been mad.

'Yes, Jo, you should spend the morning round the pool. I'm sure mother will keep you busy for the rest of this trip.' Taylor's father graciously gave her the go ahead to laze around until her services were required.

'What's this?' Their conversation had clearly caught Taylor's attention as he looked between Jo and his parents.

When his gaze lingered on Jo, she felt her temperature rise. It was going to be difficult not to give away what they'd been up to together when she lit up like a Christmas tree every time he looked at her.

She fought the urge to melt into her chair and attempted a casual response.

'I…er…your father…um…' The more she stuttered, the

wider Taylor's grin grew. He tilted his head to one side and waited for her to spit it out.

'We were just telling Jo she's free to use the pool until your grandmother gets back.' Mr Stroud put her out of her misery and answered on her behalf.

'I might do the same. I'm exhausted today for some reason.' The sultry look he shot her was even more devastating to her equilibrium than the grin.

'I think you both deserve some down time. I'm sure you're worn out after your exploits.'

It was all Jo could do not to spit out the mouthful of cereal she'd taken, thanks to his father's well-meaning comment. All she could think about was her 'exploits' with Taylor last night on the beach, and in his bed.

'Definitely. It's really taken a lot out of me.' Taylor wasn't helping, acting as though they were in some bawdy seventies comedy where every other word had a double meaning.

'If you don't mind, I think I'll head out now whilst it's quiet.' Jo grabbed a piece of toast as she excused herself from the table, hoping to get some time by the pool before the others joined her. It was a bit intimidating being surrounded by the rich and beautiful whose swimwear was more about what they could show off on social media than any practical purpose. She was sure if she tried swimming in one of those cutaway bathing suits she'd end up exposing parts of her body she hadn't meant to.

'That's fine, Jo. As long as you're here for Isabelle when she returns.' Taylor's stepmother dismissed her with another casual reminder of her position.

She didn't let it bother her. It might be different if she was in a proper relationship with Taylor, knowing she would never be good enough for the family, but neither of them wanted that.

Still, as she walked away eating her toast, she bit into it with slightly more aggression than usual.

'Sorry about that.' Taylor jogged after her.

'It's fine. I'm here to look after Isabelle. Your stepmother just likes to remind me of that.'

Taylor winced. 'She forgets she used to actually work for a living too. Sometimes she treats staff as though they're not actually people. That's what's wrong with living in this bubble. There's no concept of the real world, or any self-awareness.'

'It wasn't that long ago you were saying the same sort of thing to me, Taylor.'

This time he looked as though she'd actually punched him in the stomach. 'I guess so. Sorry.'

Taylor appeared so contrite, and with those puppy dog eyes begging her for forgiveness, Jo had no choice but to let it go. After all he'd shown her how much he thought of her since.

'I suppose we're all guilty of making assumptions about one another. That first night I thought you were a rude, entitled, spoilt brat.'

Taylor shrugged. 'Sometimes I am.'

'No, you're not. Now I've got to know you, it's clear you're compassionate, kind and generous.' She didn't need to mention that he was also amazing in bed, when they were both well aware of that fact.

'If you say so…'

'I do.'

'Well, maybe my parents just need to get to know you better too.'

'To know me is to love me, eh?' She was joking, but the

worried glance he shot her made her realise what she was saying. Of course he didn't love her. They hardly knew each other for goodness' sake. But now she'd made things awkward between them when this wasn't supposed to be anything more than a casual arrangement.

Not least because the thought had its merits. She was beginning to wonder what it would be like to have him in her life, loving her, wanting to be with her on a long-term basis. And why that would be such a bad thing. She'd already done the hard part in letting him into her life. The thought of being part of a couple again wasn't a frightening prospect as it once had been, if it included Taylor.

He'd shown her that not all men were like Steve, capable of deceit and causing pain. There were some still out there who were honourable, and kind and might even have been hurt just as much as she had.

Perhaps, more importantly, he had helped her remember that she wasn't the one who'd done anything wrong. That she shouldn't be embarrassed by how she'd been wronged, and there was no need to punish herself by hiding away from the world. She deserved a life too. Even if it was never going to be the one she was starting to wish she had with Taylor.

Although the horror emanating from him simply by teasing him about loving her soon put a stop to that wistful daydream.

'Why don't we grab some loungers before the others hog them all.' Taylor swiftly changed the subject and directed her towards a sunbed, whilst he took another, putting a little distance between them. The playful banter, and any chance of further flirting, now put behind them.

Jo resigned herself to a quiet day at the pool after all. Perhaps it wouldn't be a bad thing for her to get back to doing her job looking after Isabelle. Then she wouldn't be fixating on Taylor and fanciful ideas that they could have anything more than they'd agreed on.

Taylor didn't know why Jo's jokey comment had thrown him so much. Only that he needed some space. Seeing her settling down on her lounger on the other side of the pool apparently wasn't far enough. Not when the sun was shining through her light top exposing the bikini she was wearing beneath and the body he'd got to know so well.

He was glad he was wearing sunglasses but was regretting the flimsy swim shorts.

Taylor lay down on his sun bed and tried to block out thoughts of Jo, but it wasn't easy. Never mind all the vivid memories of what they'd done together, but now the guilt of how his parents treated her was weighing heavy on his mind. As was her throwaway comment.

'To know me, is to love me.'

Although he'd only known her for a matter of days, he had come to care for her, and he was worried the more time they spent together the stronger his feelings might become. That wasn't what he wanted in his life. It hadn't escaped his notice that the whole reason he'd come here had faded into the background since he'd acted on his attraction towards Jo. He needed to take a step back if he intended not to repeat past mistakes.

With Imogen he'd fallen too hard, too fast, going all in and paying the ultimate price for his recklessness. He was afraid of the same thing happening again. Not because he thought every woman out there was going to fake a charitable cause and steal his money, but there was a likelihood that he'd end up with more war wounds. People had let him down time and time again. His father, and Imogen, specifically. He'd learned it was much safer for him to be on his own, keeping his heart to himself. The fact that he'd even agreed to this fling with Jo was a step out of his comfort zone, so the suggestion of more was merely asking for trouble. Especially when he was already growing closer to her.

'Hey, bro. It's not like you to put your feet up and take it easy with us mere mortals.' His stepbrother's shadow loomed over him blocking out the sun.

'Well, we're all here for a break, aren't we? I thought it was about time I had a day off.' It wasn't usually his style, but he figured he'd earned it. Last night on the beach hadn't been just about Jo cutting loose; he'd realised he did it too little, as well. His work was spurred on by guilt and sharing some of the wealth he'd taken for granted growing up. But now he was wondering if it was also driven by the need to keep his mind occupied with something other than his personal issues.

If he'd been running away from his problems and the pain of his breakup. Being with Jo had taken away some of that need to stay moving. He'd found there was some joy to be found in staying in one place when she was around. Of course she wasn't always going to be there, but since they only had a few days of this trip left perhaps it would do him some good to simply kick back for a while. Figure out his next move.

'Fair play, Tay.' Harry fist bumped him, happy with the explanation. Though Taylor knew no one needed an excuse around here to be idle. It was the order of the day as long as the money was still rolling in.

In terms of work, it was his father who did the majority of it to benefit the rest of the family. He was the one who came up with the ideas, and produced the prototypes for the tech market. Everyone else just seemed to be along for the ride. Of course Taylor felt some resentment when his mother had been left to fend for herself and his father's new family took it all for granted.

That was just one of the reasons he liked Jo. Her work ethic. She knew how to graft, and her recent experiences probably made her appreciate the good life they had out here better than most.

'And Jo's joining us too this morning, I see. That's just a coincidence I suppose?' Allegra sniffed as she walked past, catching the end of their conversation.

'There's not much else to do here, dear sister.'

'I guess…if you're not off saving the world.' Allegra flounced off, trying as always to denigrate the work he did. She was very much like his stepmother in that regard, and probably didn't think any more highly of Jo either. It shouldn't matter to him, but it did. He wanted them to see what a good person she was, that she was deserving of respect. As was he.

He'd never quite fit in to his father's new family. Probably because neither his father, nor his new wife, had made any effort to include Taylor. Both more concerned with the advantages money brought than taking time to parent him. Dumping his mother for a younger model also hadn't made the best impression on a young Taylor and he'd vowed to never be like his father. Instead, he wanted to do some good with the money and opportunities afforded to him. To atone for his family's selfishness. Especially on behalf of his mother.

Undisturbed by his siblings' arrival at the other side of the pool, Jo stood up and stripped down to her bikini before stepping into the pool. From behind his shades he watched her cute backside in the small triangle of fabric as she climbed down the ladder. Couldn't take his eyes off her as she swam lengths of the pool. And had to turn over onto his stomach when she eventually emerged from the water, smoothing down her hair, her swimwear clinging to her wet body.

As he willed away his body's natural reaction, and his lustful thoughts about his grandmother's nurse, he closed his eyes and enjoyed the feel of the sun on his skin. It wasn't often he got to appreciate the good weather in the countries he travelled to. More often than not it was an inconvenience, making his job harder than it should've been when there was no air con where he was working. Lying here, chilling out, was a novelty, and kind of nice. Despite the general hubbub of noise around him as the others made themselves comfortable around the pool, he felt himself drifting off.

Suddenly he was awakened by a scream, some shouting and a lot of splashing. He sat up and tried to focus on what was happening.

Everyone was standing around the pool with horror written all over their faces. Jo was back in the pool swimming with Allegra's partner, Bobby, seemingly unconscious in her arms. The water was turning a frightening shade of red, and he noticed a trail of blood at the side of the pool.

'Taylor! Can you give me a hand?' Jo's anguished cry was enough to spur him into action, immediately alert now.

'What happened?' Moving the others out of the way, he knelt down, and with Harry's assistance, helped haul the dead weight of his sister's unconscious boyfriend from the pool.

Allegra was wailing and crying and doing nothing of any practical nature as the rest of them worked together.

'He was messing about dive bombing into the pool. I think he slipped and hit his head on the side, knocked himself out.' It was Jo who passed on the relevant information, breathless from her effort to help get him out of the water.

'How long was he under the water?' Taylor asked, checking his pulse. He wasn't breathing and was unresponsive.

'Not long. I jumped in straight away.' She clearly hadn't even stopped to take off her cover as it clung to her like a wet second skin.

'He's not breathing. I'm going to start CPR.' Taylor's assessment was met by more wailing.

'Do you want me to give him rescue breaths?' Jo asked kneeling down beside him as he tilted the man's head back to open the airways.

'If you're happy to do that?' He knew not everyone was comfortable with that these days and he could just carry on with the chest compressions he'd started.

'Of course.' Jo waited until he'd finished pumping the man's chest, then she pinched the nose, made a tight seal over his mouth with her own, and delivered a couple of breaths.

They checked his pulse and breathing again and when there was no response, they repeated the process. At this point Taylor couldn't be sure what damage had been done, or where, when there was blood everywhere. All he knew was that they had to get him breathing again and they were lucky Jo had been able to get to him as quickly as she had.

Suddenly, their patient started coughing, water spurting out of his mouth that must have been pushed out from his lungs during the CPR. Relief-fuelled adrenaline shot through Taylor.

'Help me get him into the recovery position,' he instructed Jo, who seemed to be the only other competent person around.

'Oh, thank goodness.' Allegra stopped screaming long enough to sob over him.

'Give him some room to breathe, sis. Bobby, we just need you to lie where you are for a while. You've had an accident and I need to check you over.'

'We need towels or blankets. Something to keep him warm.' Jo directed the others into action, and credit to them, they seemed glad to have something to do.

'Can someone get my medical bag from my room? He has a head injury and I need to stop the bleeding.' Although Bobby was conscious and breathing, he still wasn't out of the woods. Taylor needed to see what else was going on.

He used one of the towels to clean away the blood on Bobby's head, while Jo tried to make Bobby comfortable with some blankets handed to her.

'Here you go.' His brother handed him his bag and he set to work trying to find the head wound.

'There's a deep laceration to the back of his skull.' Jo parted Bobby's hair matted with blood to expose the injury.

'It's going to need stitches and you should probably get checked over at the hospital to make sure you haven't anything more serious going on, Bobby.'

'I'm not going to the hospital,' he mumbled, trying to show off how big and brave he was even now.

'Yes, you are.' Allegra spoke up. The one person Bobby wouldn't dare go against.

'I can patch you up, but you might need an X-ray. At the very least they'll need to check you over. I'll see if I can get us on the plane that'll be bringing grandmother back.' Taylor set to work stitching up the deep wound once Jo had cleaned the area. Then she dressed it with some cotton and gauze to protect from any infection.

'We should probably get you inside. Do you think you can stand, Bobby?' Aware that they needed to get him warmed up, Jo encouraged him to stand again. Taylor caught him under the arm, whilst she took the other and they manoeuvred him into the villa.

After they got him settled on the sofa, Allegra fussed around plumping cushions and tucking a blanket around him.

'He's going to need a change of clothes. Something to keep him warm.'

'What's going on?' Taylor's stepmother appeared just as he was issuing more orders.

'Bobby nearly drowned…he wasn't breathing. Taylor and Jo saved his life.' Allegra spilled the details through her tears.

'Taylor?' His mother looked at him with questioning eyes, as though she didn't believe what she was hearing. Even though Bobby was sitting shivering on the sofa in a state of shock with everyone else gathered around him.

'It's true. These guys are heroes.' Harry slapped him on the back and, clearly overwhelmed by the situation, Allegra grabbed Jo into a hug. Much to her surprise.

'We do have our uses,' Taylor mumbled, gaining a smile from a bemused Jo.

'Well, in that case we're glad we had you both here with us for the New Year's Eve party.' The praise from his stepmother was unusually heartfelt and Taylor was equally as glad for Jo as himself to receive it. It was important to him that she got the respect she deserved. He didn't want to think about why. Afraid that he held some deep secret desire for her to be accepted into the family in case their relationship should ever change to something more than casual.

It was also a reminder that his time with Jo was limited and he didn't want to waste any opportunity they might have to be together.

'I'm going to take Bobby over to the mainland when the plane gets here. In the meantime, we should probably go and get cleaned up.' He nodded towards Jo who was still wet from the pool and covered in as much blood as he was.

His stepmother wrinkled up her nose. 'Yes, I think that's wise before your grandmother gets here.'

At least it gave them an excuse to leave.

'I think Bobby's going to be okay,' Jo said as they walked down the hall.

Taylor didn't know what came over him, but he was suddenly overwhelmed by the urge to kiss her. So he did. He grabbed her and kissed her hard, her little moan against his lips his reward. Perhaps it was the adrenaline from everything that had happened, the admiration he'd felt watching her at work or that feeling of being part of something rather than alone, but he wanted to be with her. At that moment, the only important thing was Jo and making the most of having her in his life for the short amount of time they had together. The look in her eyes said she wanted the same.

This was dangerous territory he knew, but he'd been feeling all sorts of new sensations since meeting her, and for once he intended to lean into them. This trip would be over all too soon and the likelihood was that he'd never get to be with her again.

'Is that offer of a shower still going?' Her voice was thick with desire, and no matter what alarm bells had been going off previously, they were drowned out by the sound of his blood rushing in his ears.

With the knowledge that everyone else was occupied elsewhere, they stumbled into his room, kissing and tearing each other's wet clothes off. Once in the shower they slowed things down, lathering each other up, washing off and making out in between. Even towelling their bodies dry seemed like part of the foreplay before they climbed into bed together. It didn't matter what part of the day it was, sleeping together seemed inevitable. What they both wanted and needed.

They made love slowly, clinging to one another as they reached that peak together. Staring into one another's eyes as they fought to recover. Today had seen a shift between his family and Jo, and Taylor couldn't help thinking that it was the same for them. The mood had changed between him and Jo too. He couldn't be sure in what way or why, but he did know it was frightening and exhilarating all at the same time. Something he was curious about exploring further if circumstances allowed.

Jo was on pins and needles waiting for Taylor to come back. He'd gone over to the mainland with Bobby to get him checked out at the hospital. He might take these flights back and forth with a pinch of salt, but she didn't. Those small planes were always on the news having crashed leaving no survivors. She was beginning to realise how much he'd come to mean to her in such a short space of time, and not just because of the amazing sex.

For two years she hadn't let another man into her life. He was special to have even got that far. Beyond that, he was someone who made her feel part of something. A team, a relationship, the world in general. She'd been closed off since her ex's betrayal, shutting out everyone and everything to focus on working to pay off the debt she'd been left with. It was possible she'd even fallen out of love with her job because it was so tied up with money and never having enough to stay afloat. Taylor had renewed a passion inside her not just for him, but for the work they did too. They made a difference to people. He made a difference to her.

'A penny for them?' Isabelle's concern broke through Jo's reverie.

'They're not worth it. Sorry. Is there anything I can get you?' She'd met her elderly charge off the small plane as Taylor and Bobby had left, but in typical style she'd refused to take to her bed. Instead, they'd been sitting out on the veranda taking in the air. Away from the pool for obvious reasons, even though Mr Stroud had already employed people to thoroughly clean the area and drain the pool.

'I want to take a trip down to the beach,' Isabelle insisted, pulling her lilac shawl around her frail shoulders.

'I'm not sure that's a good idea after the last time. Your family wouldn't be happy for me to take you back down. We've had enough drama for one day.' She doubted when the family had organised this get-together they'd envisioned as many trips to the hospital, and she didn't want to have to add any more to the itinerary.

'It's not their decision, it's mine. I've been cooped up in a tiny room for days. I need some sea air and a view. Now, if you don't mind, you're paid to take care of me, and that means keeping me happy.' Isabelle folded her hands in her lap, and lifted her feet onto the footplates on her wheelchair ready to go. Leaving Jo no option but to follow her wishes.

'Okay, on your head be it.' She didn't mean it. Of course if anything happened she would take full responsibility, but for Isabelle to be so snippy with her she must really need a walk in the fresh air.

'I trust you to keep me alive as long as is humanly possible. I heard that you and my grandson have been saving lives in abundance lately.'

As Jo pushed the wheelchair down the path to the beach, Isabelle confirmed she'd already been informed of events during her absence. Not all events, Jo hoped. Although they were on good terms, she wasn't sure how the matriarch of the family would take to her being involved with her grandson. If deep down her attitude was the same as that of her daughter-in-law, Jo didn't think she'd be too impressed by the match.

'You weren't long in catching up on the gossip.' She'd only been here for about an hour and apparently already had the rundown over the cup of tea she'd shared with her son and daughter-in-law on arrival.

'Well, it sounds as though you've certainly been busy. I heard you and Taylor were off together working on a nearby island too.' Was it Jo's imagination or did it sound as though she was fishing for information about their relationship?

'Yes. He does amazing work. I was lucky to be a part of it, even for a day.'

'He's a good boy. He'll make someone an excellent husband someday, don't you think?' There was mischief in her voice, as if she held out some hope that Jo was going to be the wife for him. Although it was a romantic fantasy so far, Jo liked the fact that Isabelle thought it feasible she could become part of the family someday.

'I'm sure he would, but I don't think it's in his plans to settle down any time soon.'

'Ah, he just needs to meet the right woman who can convince him.'

Jo's skin began to heat up at the thought that might be her, but she soon cooled down again when she realised it couldn't possibly be. After all, they hadn't agreed on anything other than a casual arrangement. Chances were that he might meet someone else on his travels who would make him want to stay in one place and never come back. The thought of how upset that would make her wasn't in keeping with the idea of a no strings situation. That was entirely her own fault. She'd thought she could keep her feelings separate from a physical relationship, but it was dawning on her that wasn't the case. She cared for him, wanted something more, but she was afraid to take that chance on him and risk having her heart broken again. Worse, he might reject the idea altogether and she'd never see him again.

'Do you really think that's true, Isabelle? That there is someone out there for all of us who can make us believe in love again? Enough to risk everything?' It seemed like too big a dream to consider after everything she'd been through.

Isabelle waited until they were down at the edge of the sea before she answered. First taking in the smell of the sea, eyes closed, face tilted up to the sun. 'Did you know I was engaged to another man before I met my husband?'

'No. I didn't.' Jo wasn't sure where this was going, since she was effectively saying there'd been more than one man for her.

Isabelle nodded sagely. 'I'd known Edgar since I was little. He came from a wealthy family, and it was always expected that we'd marry. I certainly hadn't had thoughts of meeting anyone else. I was going to settle down and have a family with him and that was that. Then John Stroud came along and blew my world apart.'

She looked at Jo with such undisguised love it almost hurt.

'What happened?'

'Not to be indiscreet, or crass, but we had such passion together I forgot that I was meant to marry Edgar. John didn't have any money then, but I couldn't let him go out of my life. So, against my family's wishes, and all common sense, I called off my engagement and married John a couple of months later. I never looked back.'

Clearly. She had a family and a fortune, everything she'd ever want at her disposal. Still, Jo couldn't help but feel for the jilted fiancé in this happy little tale. Feeling very much as though she was the Edgar in this scenario, who'd been betrayed and left behind whilst his partner had sought a better life elsewhere.

'Surely that negates the idea of there being "the one", though?'

Isabelle shook her head and took hold of Jo's hand. 'Don't you see? Until you've felt that same passion, that same overwhelming desire to be with that person, you haven't met him yet. Edgar met and married someone else too. As much as it may have hurt him at the time, we obviously weren't meant to be together. I can tell you've had your heart broken, Jo, but don't lose hope. I know being with a man isn't the be all and end all, but keep your heart open and you never know what might happen.'

Unexpected and unwelcomed tears rushed to Jo's eyes

as those frail fingers gripped hers tightly before finally letting go. It was as if Isabelle knew exactly what had been going on in her absence and could tell what was in Jo's heart even though she'd been afraid to admit it to herself.

She was falling for Taylor, and if he didn't feel the same way she was inevitably going to get hurt. Either they both took the risk of being in a relationship or they had to end things now before she was in deep. It was all or nothing, with no guarantee of a happy ending. Even if Taylor was "the one", he might not want to be. So where did that leave her?

'Thanks for everything, Taylor. I don't know how I'll ever repay you.' Bobby clapped him on the back as they made their way back into the villa.

'Make a donation to charity in my name,' Taylor suggested in all seriousness, regardless that it was probably a futile ask.

'I will get right on that, buddy. Thanks again. I think I'll go and get myself a beer. Do you want one?'

'I'm good, thanks. I think I'll get an early night. I'm glad you're okay.' He left Bobby who went in search of Allegra and alcohol, not necessarily in that order.

After what seemed like an eternity of waiting in hospital corridors listening to Bobby's inane prattle about how much his trust fund was worth and his latest supercar, Taylor just wanted some down time. He also wanted to see Jo. Not for any particular reason other than today had reminded him of how much he actually enjoyed her company. It made the day so much more pleasant having someone to talk to, to work with and hopefully go to bed with at the end of the night. The only thing that had got him through the day spent with Bobby was the thought of getting back to her. It was amazing how quickly he'd accepted her as part of his every day. It should be worrying, but he was enjoying it too much to listen to those warning sirens going off somewhere in the distance. He'd had enough of being on his own, wounded and hiding from the world. Perhaps it was time to open up and let someone else into his life. He was beginning to think that by shying away from another relationship he'd been hurting, rather than protecting, himself. Failing to get close to someone as special as Jo.

With no sign of her anywhere, Taylor retreated to his room, the excitement of his return beginning to dissipate. He wondered if he was going to feel like this every time he returned to an empty bed now.

When he opened his bedroom door and found Jo lying asleep on his bed, it was like all of his Christmases come at once.

Loathed to wake her, he kicked off his shoes and eased himself onto the bed next to her. She stirred, a dreamy smile on her lips when she opened her eyes to see him. His immediate reaction was to kiss her fully awake.

'Sorry. I didn't mean to fall asleep. I just called in to see if you were back and I guess I got too comfy.'

'No problem. Although I would have come to find you the moment I came back, you know.' He was touched that she'd come to look for him at all. It proved she'd been thinking about him too. Whilst he wasn't sure what that meant for the long-term future, he was content being here with her now.

'Is Bobby okay? I have to say, your family seem to be in awe of your medical skills now. Perhaps now they've seen the evidence of it for themselves they'll appreciate you a bit more.'

'I won't hold my breath. As for Bobby, all his tests came back fine. He's going to have a nasty bump on his head, and I'll have to keep an eye on him to make sure the stitches don't get infected, but he should be fine.'

'That's good. I just wanted to be sure you both got back safely.' Jo went to sit up, but Taylor wasn't ready to lose her so soon when he'd been looking forward to spending some time with her.

'Where do you think you're going?'

She frowned. 'Back to my room. I'm sure you want to get some sleep.'

'Yeah, but that doesn't mean you have to go.' He patted the empty pillow beside him.

'Are you sure?' She eyed him with caution as though this was some sort of trick.

'Yes. I couldn't wait to get back and spend some time with you tonight. Even if it's just listening to you snore.'

'I do not snore.' She hit him on the shoulder but there was a great big smile on her face.

Taylor urged her back down onto the bed and gave a sigh of contentment when she snuggled into his side. 'I suppose it's more heavy breathing. Like a dormouse snore.'

'I do not snore.' There was less fire behind her denial as she cosied in next to him.

Even though they were fully clothed, Taylor pulled the covers over them, not wanting to disturb the comfortable moment. It was such a refreshing change to lie next to a woman in bed without any expectations. Of course, he'd enjoyed the sex too, but there was something special about simply being in one another's company.

He was aware of the dangers in believing they were a couple, but he was beginning to see the benefits of being with someone. Someone who had been hurt too, and who he didn't believe would purposely deceive him the way his ex had. Not only was he beginning to relax those unwritten rules he'd had in place for so long that meant he couldn't even consider getting involved with anyone again, but he was questioning whether he still wanted to keep moving.

Although he still wanted to help others, it would be nice to have someone to come home to at night like this. To have Jo curled up in his arms in bed; to wake up to in the morning, and lazily make love with her. All of those things he hadn't realised he'd missed, because it had all been tainted by his ex's deception. It didn't seem fair to deny himself that kind of happiness, which he was sure both of their partners had found elsewhere since.

He closed his eyes, weary and content. Dreaming about what it would be like to settle down with Jo somewhere and be happy not only at work, but also in his personal life. Was it too much to hope to have it all?

Jo watched Taylor sleep soundly next to her. She didn't have that luxury when her head was so full of worry, and her heart so full of something she was afraid to recognise. They only had a matter of days left together before the big party signalled the end of their time together. Whilst the fireworks and celebrations were supposed to signify a new start, it was coming to mean something different to her. It would herald the start of a new heartbreak.

She'd fallen for Taylor and it was going to be devastating to have to smile and cheer with everyone else when she'd be miserable inside, knowing she'd be leaving him behind. How could she have a happy New Year knowing Taylor wasn't going to be a part of it?

She didn't want to start another chapter of her life unhappy. Perhaps it would be better to cool things now, and give her a little time to get used to the idea of being on her own again. After all, going home as part of a couple had never been on the agenda anyway.

Lying here beside Taylor wishing for more than a casual arrangement wasn't going to help her process the fact that she was going to have to let him go sooner rather than later.

Jo tried to ease herself out of bed without disturbing him, but the moment her feet hit the ground he grabbed hold of her arm.

'Where do you think you're going?' he mumbled, eyes still closed.

'I should get back to my own room so I'll be there when your grandmother wakes.'

Taylor let go of her and rubbed at his eyes. 'Wouldn't you prefer to stay here with me and make the most of the morning?'

'Of course I would, but I have a duty to your grandmother. I have to administer her medication and check her blood pressure don't forget.'

'Well, I wouldn't want to get in the way of you doing that, but I will look forward to you coming to me tonight.' The promise of another night in Taylor's arms, coupled with the sultry look in his eyes, made Jo's stomach flip with anticipation.

Despite her decision to put some distance between them so she could get a grip on her emotions, there was always the possibility that it would only make her long for him more.

Once he was up and dressed, Taylor found himself going in search of Jo again. He had no desire to interfere in her work, but that need to be around her was all consuming. Most likely because in just a matter of days he'd be back to being on his own again. The staff, busy in the background making preparations for the big party, were a constant reminder of their time together ticking away. With each piece of bunting strung up outside, every food delivery, it was a dagger to his heart knowing the final countdown was on.

By the time he got to the dining room for breakfast it soon became obvious everyone else had already eaten and gone outside. After helping himself to some orange juice and toast, he wandered outside to take his breakfast on the veranda. Jo and his grandmother were sitting with a cup of tea, enjoying the morning air.

'Good morning,' he announced before inviting himself to sit at the table with them.

Jo glanced up, but quickly looked away again. 'We should probably get moving, Isabelle. It's not going to help your recovery by sitting in one place all day.'

She scraped her chair back and got up from her seat, leaving her tea half-drunk in her apparent hurry to get away from him. It wasn't the welcome he'd hoped for from her, and certainly didn't fit in with the way she'd been with him in the early hours of the morning. Taylor decided not to take it personally, as she was likely trying to keep up a professional façade in the presence of his grandmother.

'Jo's right. As long as you're feeling up to it, Grandmother, it will do you good to get out and about for a while.'

'Yes, Jo is going to show me some gentle yoga moves, but I fancy a change of scenery after lying in a hospital bed for days. We're going to take some exercise mats and head outdoors. I think we'll probably avoid the beach though this time.' His grandmother had the twinkle back in her eyes as she joshed about her ordeal. Something she was able to do now that she seemed to be recovering well.

'If you can hang on for a few minutes until I finish my breakfast, maybe I could come with you.' It would be nice to spend the morning with his two favourite people in the world and re-create the day they took the picnic to the waterfall, when he'd begun to see Jo in a different light. Although, he could do without another life-or-death scenario on this trip. There had already been more than enough medical drama.

'No. Sorry. We have a schedule to keep. Isabelle needs to be back for her medication before lunch.' Jo had already taken control of his grandmother's wheelchair, and was grabbing their belongings as she began to move away.

'No problem. I can grab something later.' He took a last gulp of juice and rushed to catch up with them.

Only for a scowling Jo to turn back. 'No, Taylor. You stay here. I'm busy.'

He was stunned into silence. Frozen to the spot by her dismissal, and more than a little hurt as they left him standing on the veranda. At least his grandmother gave him a little wave, but Jo didn't even turn to look back. He hadn't meant to interfere in her work, and never intended to get in her way—just wanted to be near her. Clearly she didn't feel the same need.

Somewhat dejected, Taylor flopped back down into his seat, wondering what had just happened. He hoped it was simply a matter of Jo reminding him that she was here to do a job. However, her furrowed brow and sharp tone suggested something more was going on. As though she was purposely putting some distance between them. He couldn't help but wonder if he'd done something wrong when things had been great between them last night. Amazing in fact. He made a note to apologise when he saw her again in case interrupting her morning with his grandmother had upset her more than he'd realised.

It wasn't a pleasant feeling thinking he'd done something wrong to cause her sudden withdrawal from him. The uncertainty, and questioning himself and his behaviour, reminded him of the last days of his relationship with Imogen. Believing he hadn't measured up as a partner, just as he hadn't measured up as a son. He'd felt her distance herself from the relationship just before he'd discovered her deceit. In fact, that's what had prompted him to look into the charity further. Trying to show more interest in what she was doing in a futile attempt to bring them closer together. Instead, he'd discovered her web of lies, and the secret bank account she'd been funnelling his money into. Though he didn't imagine Jo was doing the same, he'd rather she was upfront about what had changed between them so he could stop beating himself up over it. Especially when he was beginning to hope there might be a chance to see one another after this. If that was nothing more than a pipe dream, he'd rather know now.

'Oh, I didn't realise anyone was out here.' His father hovered nearby carrying his laptop under one arm, holding a cup of coffee in his other hand.

'I can leave if you want?' Taylor was beginning to think he wasn't welcome anywhere. He supposed that's what happened when you distanced yourself emotionally and physically from people. Once upon a time it wouldn't have bothered him, but these past few days with the family, and Jo, made him realise how nice it could be to have people in his life. Flaws and all. He and his family were never going to see eye to eye, but he was probably as guilty of judging them as much as he'd accused them of judging him. Perhaps they simply needed to get reacquainted with one another and for him to get to know why they acted the way they did. He could only do that if he made time in his busy schedule to come back and see them, spend time together. There was a thought niggling away at the back of his mind that it might be nice to do that with Jo too, if she'd be interested in seeing him again. After their most recent interaction he wasn't so sure.

'No. Stay. I'm just checking some emails. I want to be sure all the food and drink will be delivered on time for the party and I'm waiting for the fireworks expert to arrive.' His father set his stuff down on the table and pulled up a chair.

Taylor thought that this was probably the ideal moment to start having some quality time with his father at least. He couldn't remember the last time they'd actually sat down together and talked. Plus, it would take his mind off Jo for a while.

'We missed you at breakfast this morning. We all wondered if you'd gone out already on one of your missions.'

Taylor smiled, unsure how much of the fact he'd slept so soundly had to do with having Jo next to him for most of the night. 'No, just overslept. I guess all the excitement finally caught up with me.'

'Yes, it's highlighted the fact that we aren't equipped for medical emergencies out here. I mean, you're not going to be here the next time your grandmother or Bobby need life-saving treatment.'

'Well, as much as I'm glad to have been here in their hour of need, I'm not planning on taking up residence permanently.' Although it would be the ideal job for someone who wanted to live in paradise, on their own for most of the year except when his father's friends and family decided to visit. That wasn't Taylor.

'So, I've decided to invest in the hospital and emergency transport from the neighbouring islands. It's going to take a lot of time and money to organise it, but I think it will benefit everyone in the long run. I'm going to make some calls this morning to get the ball rolling.' It certainly explained why his father was up so early. When he was on vacation he tended to spend half the day in bed.

'That's great, Dad. I know everyone we've met at the hospital and on the other islands will be over the moon to hear that. They're crying out for investment in the health care system here.' Regardless that the move was primarily for selfish reasons, Taylor was impressed by his father's initiative. As far as he could see everyone was a winner in this scenario. Not only could visitors here be sure of adequate medical attention in the event of an emergency, but so could the people who lived in the area permanently. It would also undoubtedly provide more jobs locally, as well as boost the economy.

Perhaps his father was beginning to come around to his way of thinking after all, if he was willing to part with some of his money for the general good. It was a start at least.

Taylor bit into his toast, feeling optimistic about the future, and other projects he might be able to get his father interested in.

'I can tell, and I appreciate and admire everything you do. You did well yesterday, son.'

'So did Jo.'

'Yes, she's a real asset. I guess your grandmother thinks so too.'

'Why's that?'

'She had me set up a zoom meeting with her solicitor back home. Something about making provisions for Jo in her will. I know, I know, I tried to talk her out of it, but she's determined. And, as she reminded me, it's her money to do with as she wishes.'

Taylor nearly choked on the orange juice he'd washed down his toast with. The toast that his stomach was now considering rejecting.

'Grandmother has put Jo in her will?' It was hard to prevent his train of thought from venturing down a very dark path.

If Jo had heard this news first it would explain why she'd been off with him this morning. He'd put it down to something he'd done, but it was possible she was feeling embarrassed, or guilty, about the fact his grandmother had made such a grand gesture.

Taylor wanted to think it was simply something she'd felt moved to do by Jo's actions on the beach in helping save her life. Treating her just like any other member of the family because they'd become so close. Anything other than that would give him real cause for concern.

'As I understand it's for a considerable amount. Of course, she didn't tell me the details, and I didn't ask, but she said she wanted Jo to be able to start her life over again.'

'What does that mean?' It sounded as though there was some information about Jo that he hadn't been privy to.

'You know, after the bankruptcy...' His father dismissed it as though a trifle, when in reality, Taylor felt as though the ground was disappearing from under him.

'No, I don't know. What are you talking about?'

'I don't know all the details. Something to do with her ex stealing from her business... Anyway, it's down to your grandmother what she does with her money. I have more important matters to deal with before we head back to England.' Apparently, his father was ready to drop the subject. Taylor, however, was not. Bankruptcy suggested she was in real financial dire straits, perhaps desperate enough to do something uncharacteristic. Like take advantage of a rich, elderly woman who'd come to think of her as family.

'Aren't you worried that's the reason Jo has become so close to Grandmother? Perhaps this whole situation has been orchestrated to achieve this very outcome. Don't forget what happened with Imogen.' Taylor's mood had darkened from the bright, happy disposition he'd started the day with. It was obvious Jo had shared her sob story with his grandmother, and everyone else it would seem, apart from him. Garnering enough sympathy, and emotionally manipulating her kind client into helping her out. It was possible she'd only opened up as much as she had to put an end to his suspicions, and it had worked. He hadn't believed that someone who seemed so vulnerable in that moment would be capable of such cruelty.

Jo had every opportunity to tell him about her financial situation when they'd shared such personal information with one another. He'd told her things he hadn't told those closest to him, he'd felt such a connection with Jo. The fact that she'd held back the information suggested she'd been trying to keep it secret from him. Because she knew he was suspicious of her motives from the very start. He'd let his heart rule over his head. Again.

'Listen, Taylor, I know Imogen hurt you, but not everyone is out for what they can get. You know Jo. She's good at her job and we all trust her very much. Don't let your past experience cloud your judgement. She's a good person.'

'I wish I could believe that…'

This was everything he was afraid was going to happen. It was the reason he'd come out here. To prevent another con artist from getting close to the family and trying to take advantage of a vulnerable old woman. Manipulating her into doing something drastic like writing a complete stranger into her will. Except he'd let her creep into his affections and make him forget everything, save his need to be with her.

He felt naive for falling for another scam. Worse than that, he'd been starting to believe they might have had a future together. Instead, history was repeating itself. He'd opened his heart, only for someone else to take it and stomp on it. Using his weakness against not only him, but his family too. This time, however, he was going to take action before the damage was done. At least to his grandmother and her legacy. He feared it was already too late for his fragile heart.

'Taylor?'

Leaving his uneaten toast and half a glass of orange juice on the table, he got up to go in search of Jo and his grandmother to confront what had been going on behind his back.

'I think I'll go and check in with Grandmother. I want to make sure there are no long-lasting effects from her incident on the beach the other day.' Like being confused, coerced or agreeing to something she wouldn't ordinarily do.

'Thanks, son. I know I haven't been the father you've always needed, but I'm glad you're here. Not only to save everyone's lives—' he smiled at his own lame joke

'—but as part of the celebrations. Part of the family. You've made me very proud, and I promise I'm going to try and do the same for you.'

The only thing more unexpected than his father's new outlook was when he reached out to shake Taylor's hand.

'Thanks, Dad.' He didn't know what else to say, then his father pulled him into a bear hug, and he expressed his gratitude in the mutual embrace.

This trip had been a real rollercoaster of emotions, good and bad. At this moment in time, it felt as though he was at the top of the ride staring at the perilous drop ahead. Holding his breath in anticipation of the hardest part of the journey, waiting for it to be over so he could get back onto solid ground. Because he knew what he had to do.

He couldn't possibly ignore whatever arrangement Jo and his grandmother had come to in private. Not only did that mean he'd have to confront her about her motives for being here, for getting close to him and his family, but he'd be effectively ending things between them. That felt more of a punishment for him after everything they'd shared, and the hopes he'd had that it might continue into the new year.

If he couldn't trust Jo, he couldn't trust anyone.

CHAPTER NINE

As MUCH AS Jo loved her job, and Isabelle, she'd found herself wishing away the day. Once Jo got Isabelle settled for the night, she'd be free to go to Taylor. It hadn't been as easy as she'd imagined to stay away from him. Harder still when she'd seen the pained look on his face when she'd rejected his offer of company. In truth, there was nothing more she would've liked than to spend the day with him, but she was trying to get used to the idea of not having him around when she'd have to go home soon, without him. She only hoped he'd forgive her for her actions and welcome her back into his bed. After all, they only had a few nights left together. It could be a long time before she'd feel comfortable enough with anyone else to share this level of intimacy again, and she wanted to make the most of the physical connection she had with Taylor whilst she could. As long as he could forgive her for putting some emotional distance between them.

It had been a wrench for her to leave him to go back to an empty bed of her own this morning. Goodness knew what it was going to be like when they went their separate ways for good. Unless he'd had a change of heart about keeping their casual arrangement she had to stop fantasising about a life together that was never going to happen. Working and travelling to far-flung places together and making love on the sand as the waves crashed around them...

'Is there anything else I can get you, Isabelle?' She forced herself back down to earth and tucked Taylor's grandmother into bed, making sure she had everything she needed at hand.

'I'm fine, thank you. Just glad to be out of the hospital. It's made me more grateful than ever for the life I've been given, and appreciate the family I have around me. Taylor especially. Without you and him I mightn't even be here tonight.' She gave Jo a watery smile that made her heart catch.

Jo had become very fond of the elderly woman, and she was sure the feeling was mutual. 'We both care for you, and we're glad to have you back. Now, you've got some water by the bed in case you need it. Get some sleep.'

'I think I will.' Her eyes were already beginning to close, exhaustion beginning to set in after their afternoon taking in the sea air and, afterwards, a battle of wits over cards. Certainly a more relaxing day than they'd both had of late.

'Do you want me to leave the light on?' Jo backed away to let her get some rest, her pulse already racing at the thought of what the rest of the night might have in store for her with Taylor.

Isabelle shook her head. 'I imagine I'll be out for the count soon. I need to talk to you about something important though, Jo.'

'It can wait until tomorrow. Get some rest.'

'Tomorrow,' she mumbled, before nodding off to sleep.

Jo smiled and eased the door shut. Isabelle usually didn't have a problem sleeping through the night, but she had a mobile phone on her nightstand in case of an emergency. It meant Jo was free to go and seek out Taylor without worrying she might be needed back here.

With a quick change into something more suitable for meeting her lover, Jo went to find him. Doing her best to quell the rising sense of panic over the fact he'd been visibly absent today. He hadn't appeared at any mealtimes when she and Isabelle had dined with the others, though his father had explained it away by saying they were working on 'big plans' for the future. It hadn't helped to assuage her fears when she was sure whatever those big plans were, they didn't include her. After all, neither she nor Taylor had wanted a further crossover between his family and their 'arrangement'. It was none of her business what they were working on of course, but she was curious, and wary. Particularly because none of this had come from Taylor himself. Instead, she was the one seeking him.

'Taylor?' She knocked on his door, opening it when there was no reply.

The room was empty, the curtains still open, the bed unruffled. It appeared he hadn't been here in some time. She checked the kitchen and dining areas, took a stroll out on the veranda and by the pool, but there was no sign of him. Only lounging family members who hadn't seen him either. In the end she walked down by the waterfalls where they'd played in the water, using the torch on her phone to light the way.

For a split second she wondered if he'd already left the island. Jumped on a plane rather than have to admit he didn't want to be with her any more. Then she remembered all his stuff was still in his room. Though he could afford to replace it all with new if he chose to…

She was the one who'd thought to put some distance

between them, but now she was concerned he was no-where in sight. If, when she'd shut herself off from him this morning, she'd caused him half the anxiety and upset she was experiencing now, she was sorry for it. Perhaps it was time to stop pretending, and admit that she had feel-ings for him. Feelings which weren't going to disappear at the stroke of midnight on New Year's Eve. She was running out of time, and opportunities. If her hopes of something beyond this trip were to come to fruition, she had to put her heart on the line and tell him how she was feeling, and pray he felt the same. Of course, there was no guarantee he did, or would want more than this casual fling but she had to try.

Too often in the past she'd been afraid to confront the truth. Perhaps if she'd been brave enough she could've saved herself from the embarrassment of bankruptcy. If she was honest with herself there had been signs in her relationship with Steve that not all was well. She'd no-ticed him being more secretive when it came to his laptop or phone, hiding the screen from view. In hindsight he'd likely been moving money around between accounts, but at the time she'd convinced herself it was nothing to worry about. Just as she ignored that he'd been coming later to bed, if at all. She hadn't wanted to cause any upset and disrupt the happy life she'd built for herself. Unaware it was all a sham. Much like her childhood. Jo wondered if that was why she'd clung on to her relationship, afraid to push Steve away, because she needed stability, no matter what it cost her.

Now she wanted only to deal in truths, having had enough of secrets and lies to last a lifetime. She wasn't going to ignore her problems and hope for the best, she was going to take control. And, if Taylor decided he didn't want to be with her beyond the new year she would deal with it. Eventually.

She searched everywhere she could think of for him and, unless he was actually hiding behind the waterfall, Taylor wasn't taking a late-night dip either. There was only one last place to check, so she made her way to the beach. The lights draped around the daybeds were on, guiding her to where Taylor was sitting with a beer in his hands staring out at the ocean.

'Taylor?'

He looked up at her and frowned. 'Hey.'

Not the passionate reunion she'd been looking forward to all day.

'Rough day?' she asked, sitting down beside him, and swiping his beer for a drink.

'Help yourself,' he grumbled.

She didn't even like beer; she'd just wanted a way of breaking the ice. Something she hadn't needed to do before. Up until now they'd always fallen easily into conversation, even if it hadn't always been congenial.

'I haven't seen you all day.'

'Yeah. I've been busy helping Dad with something.' He seemed distant, couldn't quite meet her eye, and there was a distinct bristling when her hand touched his giving the beer back. And not in a good way. When they'd been trying to resist the attraction between them every accidental brush against one another had been electric, as if it could suddenly spark that passion to life. Now it felt as though he didn't want to be anywhere near her, and she didn't know what had changed. Other than spending last night cuddling, with no expectation of more. Or so she'd thought. Perhaps that had been enough to frighten him off. Too much tenderness for a man who purported to only want a physical relationship. It was a shame when it was the closest she'd been to anyone in a long time. Even her ex.

Their lives had been a whirlwind of business meetings, appointments with patients and families, always seeking work, hardly ever taking a break. In hindsight they hadn't made time for one another. It wasn't an excuse for his behaviour, nothing would ever justify the mess he'd left her in, or his betrayal. However, if they'd been closer, he might never have dreamed of doing it, of hurting her so much.

'He said you were working on a project together.'

'He wants to invest in the hospital and provide better transport links for the other islanders. It's mostly in case anything happens to any of the family again, I'm sure, but I can't turn down the offer when it would benefit so many people out here. So I've been making a few inquiries on his behalf to get the ball rolling.'

'That's fantastic. It's what you want, isn't it? For your father to do his best?' She couldn't understand why he wasn't psyched about the idea. Okay, so his father perhaps had his own best interests at heart, but it sounded as though this was going to be a public venture, not just for family use.

'Yes. Of course. It'll mean the world to people like Isaac and the other islanders.' Taylor set his beer down onto the table, his head dropped as he heaved out a sigh.

There was clearly something else bothering him. Her pulse sped up, along with her anxiety level, at the thought that it might be her. They had another couple of days on this island and if he was about to end things, it was going to make it very awkward for her to be here. Mostly because of having to face him, knowing what they'd shared, what they could have together, and knowing she wasn't enough for him either. The only consolation was that he wouldn't take her money when he ran. She didn't have any, even if he was as spiteful as her ex.

'I'm sorry about the way I acted this morning. I just wanted to be professional for your grandmother's sake.'

He suddenly turned to her. 'I know about the will.'

She could only stare at him blankly because she had no idea what he was talking about with the sudden change of subject. 'What will?'

'My grandmother's will. Don't pretend you don't know about it, Jo. Don't take me for an even bigger fool than you already have.' The vitriol with which he spat the words at her was physically wounding. He may as well have slapped her across the face.

'Isabelle? I have no idea about her will.'

Taylor tutted, and he was so tense she could feel his muscles clench beside her. 'Don't give me that. The first thing she did when she got back and spoke to you was phone her solicitor and have you added to her will.'

'I didn't know anything about that. I swear.' Under other circumstances she might have been touched by the unexpected gesture, but everything in Taylor's tone and body language suggested she was being accused of something. She wanted to be sick.

'If I know about it, I'm pretty sure you do too.'

'Honestly, Taylor, I had no idea. I never asked her to do that.' She was imploring him to believe her, knowing how that probably looked to him, but it certainly wasn't something she'd instigated. Apart from being unethical, she would never have taken a penny from any of her vulnerable clients. It was always their families she dealt with so she wouldn't be accused of anything underhand, taking advantage of those who put their trust in her. To hear Taylor basically accusing her of doing that very thing was

even more devastating than if he had told her he was ending their fling.

She wasn't like Steve, or Imogen, who had contrived
to steal and betray, and if Taylor thought that she was capable of that, he didn't have a high opinion of her at all.
It caused a sharp pain in her heart the like of which she
hadn't felt even when Steve had treated her so appallingly.

It meant he didn't know her at all, even after everything
they'd been through together. For him, perhaps their relationship had been purely physical after all. When, for
her, it had come to mean so much more. It was entirely
her own fault for getting carried away when they'd both
agreed this was never meant to be anything other than a
casual fling.

'Oh, I'm sure you didn't do anything as crass as ask her
outright to do that. You people are much sneakier about
getting what you want. It doesn't matter the cost to the
people who love and trust you the most.'

Jo was so gobsmacked she almost couldn't mount a defence. The wind literally knocked out of her lungs that he
could think so little of her. It was betrayal of a different
kind. A character assassination from someone she thought
she'd bonded with. Someone she'd imagined sharing her
life with. She'd got it all wrong again. It was becoming
apparent that she couldn't trust anyone, including herself.
Any fantasy that she could ever have a happy, successful relationship, was just that. Fantasy. A foolishness she
should stop giving head, and heart, space to.

Eventually, almost shaking with rage, she managed to
speak up. 'Taylor, are you seriously suggesting that I'm
some sort of con woman? That I get close to vulnerable
people to financially take advantage of them?'

'Maybe you don't even realise you're doing it. I don't

know.' He shrugged. 'Have you told her about what your ex did, and what your current situation is?'

Jo didn't think she had any other option but to be honest, even though it wasn't going to help her case. 'Isabelle asked me about my past. She could tell I'd been hurt, and I told her what my ex did. It wasn't a ploy to get money from her. You have to believe me, Taylor.'

'I don't know what to believe any more.'

'Your father thinks I had something to do with this too?'

'I don't think so, but then you've charmed everyone in the family, haven't you? Just like Imogen.' Still the accusations came that she'd somehow manipulated everyone into liking her for her own gain. It was something, she supposed, that Taylor was the only one who thought so, but still, it hurt. Not least because he kept comparing her to his ex who had gone out of her way to hurt him, when all Jo was guilty of was falling for him.

'I haven't done anything, and I'll ask Isabelle to take me out of her will tomorrow. I never asked for, or expected, anything. Other than respect, which I guess I've failed at if you think I'm capable of such a despicable thing.' She got to her feet, her shock and upset threatening to bring tears. If she started crying, he'd probably think she was only trying to get his sympathy.

'Even if that's true, and you didn't coerce her into writing you into the will, you omitted to tell me the truth about your financial situation. Probably because you knew I'd already sussed you out. I should have listened to my instincts from the start.' Taylor slammed his beer bottle down, displaying his anger at the situation, even though he'd got it all terribly wrong.

'I didn't tell you because I was embarrassed. You already seemed to have such a low opinion of me, I didn't want to give you any more ammunition. I haven't done anything wrong, except being a truly awful judge of character apparently. You clearly don't trust me, and after everything you've accused me of… I don't think I'll ever get over it.' How could she when she'd taken such a huge risk in letting him get close and he was able to hurt her so badly without a shred of proof? All he had were suspicions, and residual issues from his last relationship, which he was projecting onto her. Uncaring about the damage it would cause her. Both personally and professionally.

If he thought her so untrustworthy, that she'd been doing the same to him as his ex, then they had no future together in any capacity. He clearly couldn't move on from his past, and if it was so easy for him to distrust her, he'd always find some fault with her. Jo didn't need that kind of toxicity in her life. She needed, and deserved, love and respect. Not doubt and accusations.

'In case you're in any doubt, this is over between us, Taylor.'

'I'm sorry things had to end this way.' He didn't seem very sorry, more relieved. Perhaps this was his way of getting out of committing even to continuing their casual relationship.

'Well, they didn't, but since you don't hold a very high opinion of me, yeah, this is over.'

Taylor simply gave a curt nod of his head.

'Regardless of what you think, Taylor, I'm very fond of your grandmother. And the rest of the family. I would never do anything to hurt any of them.' That had included him up until a few minutes ago.

Who was she trying to kid? She'd come to the terrifying realisation that she'd fallen in love with him. That's what made this so excruciatingly painful.

He opened his mouth as if to say something, but stopped himself. Jo took it as her cue to walk away.

Somehow she managed to remain upright until she reached her bedroom before her legs collapsed from under her so she fell onto the bed. Feeling as though her world had crumbled around her all over again.

Taylor mightn't have stolen her money, but he'd left her in a mess all the same. He'd broken her trust just like everyone else in her life had done. She curled up, thinking about last night when she and Taylor had made love. It felt like a lifetime ago now. As though they'd been different people then. Before suspicion and distrust crept in and ruined everything.

Cocooning herself into a little hedgehog ball where no one else could get to her, hurt her, she let the tears fall.

She couldn't stay on the island seeing Taylor until the end of this trip, knowing what he thought of her. Not when she'd fallen for him, given him parts of herself she'd kept locked away for two years only to have it all thrown back in her face. Facing him for the next couple of days was a torture she couldn't put herself through when she was already hurting plenty. Never mind what the rest of the family would think of her once they heard about the will. She supposed Isabelle thought she was doing her a favour. An incredible gesture of kindness and generosity, which she was grateful for, even though she couldn't accept it. However well intentioned, far from helping to get her life back, she was now going to have to start afresh. This chapter was definitely over, and there hadn't been any happy ending.

* * *

'Morning.' Taylor greeted his father and grandmother who were taking tea on the veranda.

'It's afternoon,' his father corrected him.

He glanced at his watch for the first time and realised he'd slept through breakfast again. It was becoming a habit for someone used to surviving on just a few hours of sleep between clinics and flights. Although, last night it had been his guilty conscience keeping him awake until the birds' early morning chorus outside eventually sent him to sleep.

He didn't regret confronting Jo about the will; it would have been impossible to carry on while he harboured suspicions about her motives for being here. Especially when she appeared to have kept as many dark secrets as Imogen. All he could do was move on as usual and try and put her from his mind. If he could get through the next twenty four hours or so seeing her, and wondering how things could have been between them.

As he sat down, he could feel his father and grandmother glaring at him.

'What? I'm sorry I missed breakfast again. I had a couple of beers last night and I guess I'm just not used to it. I am on holiday.' He felt as though he had to justify his actions even though he was an adult. Probably because he was as disappointed in himself as they seemed to be with him. His grandmother was old-fashioned in her ways and preferred when they all dined together. Given a chance she would probably have them all sitting around the dining table using silver service and in formal dress. Though with his father's more laid-back approach to life he didn't think having a lie-in would have been the crime of the century.

'What did you say to Jo?' His grandmother's accusatory stare made him feel ten times worse than he already did.

He hadn't expected Jo to go running to his family and it only cemented the idea that she was up to something untoward by trying to cause friction between them.

'What has she told you?'

'Nothing. She's gone.' His father's very measured tone felt as though he was trying to hold back his anger. Taylor should have known he'd end up the villain of the piece when he'd simply been trying to protect everyone. It was clear they'd taken Jo's side in the matter even before he got to have his say. She'd left him to explain what she'd done and break their hearts.

'Your father said he told you about my will. Jo left me a note asking me to amend it, and remove her from being a beneficiary. It doesn't take a genius to work it out. I'm very disappointed in you, Taylor. I didn't think you of all people would begrudge someone less fortunate a little happiness.' It was obvious from the stricken look on his grandmother's face that she was heartbroken at losing Jo, but Taylor was sure it would be better for her in the long run that Jo was out of her life. Because he felt the same. He had to keep reminding himself that it was better to deal with the pain now than wait years down the line to find out she wasn't the person he'd thought she was. Just like his ex. It had been a pre-emptive move to deal with it now before he, or the rest of the family, got to rely on her too much.

'You don't understand…' He hated that she'd left him in this position, having to spell out to everyone how she'd been manipulating them all, and now that he'd caught her out she'd jumped ship.

'I understand that you upset her enough that she packed in the middle of the night and had me charter a plane back to the mainland first thing this morning.' At least his father answered how she'd managed to leave, avoiding him and any more awkward conversations between them.

'That wasn't what I wanted her to do.'

'Well, that's what she did, Taylor. So I'll ask you again, what did you say to her?'

'I told her I thought she was being underhanded, getting close to Grandmother in order to have access to the family fortune.' Why did it sound so silly now that he was explaining it to his father?

'I don't know how many times I have to reiterate this, but I'm not senile. I have all my faculties, and I'm entitled to add, or remove, anyone in my will however I see fit.'

'I know, Grandmother, but these people are clever manipulators. They get close to you, spin you a sob story, and the next thing you know you're signing over your life savings to them.' He should know how easy it was to be taken in by a pretty face and an apparent heart of gold.

'In case you haven't realised, Jo is not Imogen. Do you think I didn't do a background check before hiring her? I knew all about her financial difficulties, but she's a genuine person. I knew that from the first time I met her. You know it too.' His father hit him hard with the truth.

'This isn't about my will really, is it? Jo didn't know anything about it. As it happens, neither of you are very good at hiding your feelings. I'm just sorry I got caught in the crossfire, and now I've lost someone very dear to me because you're both afraid to admit the truth.'

'What do you mean?' Taylor was trying to process everything his father, and grandmother, were saying to him. Because he knew it was all true.

However, he couldn't get over the look of betrayal on Jo's face last night, or the nagging doubt that he might have got it all wrong. Whatever the reason, or whoever Jo really was, it was too late to go back and change what had happened. He'd been looking for an excuse to push Jo away, knowing he'd got too close. That continuing a casual fling wasn't going to be enough for him, and the idea of committing himself to more was terrifying.

So, at the first hint of trouble, he'd jumped ship. The thought that she might be after the family fortune reminded him so much of Imogen it had seemed the ideal excuse to shut down all thoughts of a relationship with Jo. Then he didn't have to deal with the very real feelings he was having towards her.

However, his cowardice had hurt all of those closest to him. Especially Jo. There was nothing in her behaviour, in the woman he'd come to know, that suggested a hint of malice. So he'd had to concoct a scenario giving him a reason to call things off, knowing he was getting in too deep. Transferring all the qualities he'd missed seeing in his ex onto Jo, in a failed attempt to protect himself. It hadn't worked, because he was hurting like hell without her.

'You light up around one another. It hasn't escaped anyone's notice that you're spending more time with the family lately too and I know that's because of Jo.'

Taylor opened his mouth to refute his grandmother's allegation but knew it was the truth.

'I've known her for months and I've seen a difference in her too over these past few days. She's happy. Or she was. When she first came to work with me, I could tell she was sad. It was me who asked about her past, she never volunteered the information. She didn't tell me until she trusted me.'

Taylor thought about how quickly she'd shared her past with him, and what that must have taken. After all, he'd felt close enough to open up to Jo about his ex too. It was something he'd taken for granted, but in hindsight it showed the trust she'd put in him. By using it against her he'd betrayed that trust, though he hadn't realised that at the time. It was no wonder she'd gone. And a miracle if she'd ever talk to him again.

If she had used his past against him, to inflict unnecessary pain in order to push him away, he wouldn't stick around either. Of course she'd been too embarrassed to tell him about the bankruptcy. He'd felt the same when he'd had to tell everyone about what Imogen had done. Now he was worried he'd never get to see Jo again, to tell he was sorry, or to ask for a second chance. That thought was sufficient to make him see how deep his feelings for her really went. He was in love with her. That's what had made the whole situation so terrifying, and why he'd been in a hurry to shut it down. Admitting he loved her meant opening himself up again, leaving himself vulnerable, and he'd been too cowardly to do so. Instead, it had been easier to push her away.

'I've been an fool, haven't I?'

The silence said everything.

'If you hurry, you might catch her before her flight back to England.' His father scribbled down the details on the crossword page of his paper before tearing it out and handing it over to Taylor.

'I—I need some time to think.' He stared at the piece of paper, not knowing what he wanted at that moment, but sure this was one of the most important decisions in his life he'd ever make.

'Just don't take too long or you mightn't get another chance,' his father said, and that was exactly the problem.

Taylor walked away clutching the scrap of paper as though it was the Holy Grail; there was no more running away. He had to face up to the truth of what he felt for Jo, and what he was going to do about it. Hopefully it wasn't too late.

Jo hadn't cared that she'd had hours to wait in the airport before the next available flight back to England; she'd had to get off that island and away from Taylor. She dabbed at her eyes under her sunglasses so she wouldn't show her red-rimmed eyes to the rest of the world. Hopefully no one would notice she was a heartbroken tourist going home in disgrace.

She still couldn't quite believe it herself.

The only thing worse than having to leave Isabelle, and a job she loved, was the knowledge that Taylor thought so little of her. That he thought everything she'd ever told him, everything she'd done, had been part of some elaborate plan to inveigle herself into his grandmother's will. It would've been laughable if it wasn't so painful.

The reason it hurt her heart more than her ego was because against all of her promises to herself, she'd fallen for Taylor. She'd risked her peace of mind, only to have it shattered by another man quick to betray her.

Now she had to go home with her tail between her legs. With no job, no money, no new start. And nursing a broken heart.

The announcement over the Tannoy that her flight was now boarding prompted Jo to take her place in the queue that had now formed at the gate. With her bag and passport in hand she waited patiently to be waved through onto the plane, away from Taylor and the memories she would associate for ever with this place. She was also sure this time of year was always going to become a sad occasion for her too. New Year's Eve, which should've been a celebration, marking a fresh start, but was instead tainted with the ugly memory of Taylor's accusations and her resulting heartbreak.

She moved forward to present her boarding pass and passport, one step closer to home. Suddenly, she felt a pressure on her arm and looked up to find Taylor there beside her, his hand wrapped tightly around her wrist. She blinked, wondering if she was imagining him there. Conjuring up one last reason to stay.

'I need to talk to you, Jo.' As her vision spoke, making him real, Jo's heart leapt at the thought that he'd come after her. That he wasn't ready for it to be over either.

Then she remembered how he'd spoken to her last night. The way he'd looked at her with such utter contempt, and knew she was still trying to fool herself.

'What are you doing here, Taylor?' She quickly quashed that initial surge of excitement at seeing him, wondering if he'd come to berate her some more. After all, she'd left without saying goodbye, or even standing up for herself.

'I just wanted to talk to you. I had to pay for a last-minute flight just for the privilege.' It occurred to her that he would've had to have a ticket to get through security. Not that the expense would mean anything to him.

'Madam? Are you boarding? The other passengers are waiting.' The airline employee at the desk politely, but firmly reminded her that there were other people here besides her and Taylor. She'd almost forgotten.

Not wishing to cause a scene, she moved to one side to allow the other passengers to board, with Taylor in pursuit.

'Have you come to search my bags and make sure I didn't steal the family silver on the way out?' She couldn't help but snap at him like a wounded animal, afraid he'd come to start round two of the fight.

He flinched. 'I deserve that. I was out of order last night.'

'Yes, you do, and yes, you were. I didn't do anything to warrant that treatment from you.' Jo was trying to keep her voice strong, so he didn't know how much his words had hurt her. That might just give the game away that she'd come to think of their relationship as more than a casual holiday fling.

'I know. I'm sorry. Can I convince you to come back? Grandmother is really missing you.'

'Oh, so you're here because Isabelle is unhappy that I've left?' Emotional blackmail wasn't going to be enough to convince her to return and go through the hell of being with Taylor for the duration of the Strouds' celebrations. All she wanted to do was lock herself in her room, climb into bed and sleep until her heart stopped aching.

It wasn't fair that he was here reminding her of what they'd had, and how awfully things had ended. She would've been better off never seeing him again and being left to work through her heartbreak in peace. He was probably only here to save his own skin when his relationship with his family was strained enough without him upsetting his grandmother. Whilst Jo was sorry she'd left Isabelle without a carer, she still had her family around her. They could always hire someone else when they got home to take care of her. It wasn't going to be so easy for Jo to move on.

'No, I'm here because I'm unhappy that you left. More so because I'm the one who caused you to leave.'

Jo gulped, feeling as though her heart had just leapt into her throat with hope. But she wasn't so easily fooled. People didn't always mean what they said. Sometimes words like 'I love you', or 'I want to be with you', had expiration dates. She was worried 'I'm unhappy that you left' might be in the same category, and that was no longer enough for her. For her to consider anything other than getting on a plane home, he needed to come up with something more. Something she could believe wholeheartedly. After the way he'd spoken to her last night, she thought it was going to be too big an ask.

'What is it you want from me, Taylor? Because it seems as though no matter how much I give of myself to you, it's never going to be enough for you to trust me.' As far as she could tell nothing had changed since last night, other than her deciding not to stick around for more blame and humiliation.

He hung his head. 'I'm sorry. I can't say it enough, I know. Since Imogen, I've found it difficult to trust. That's partly the reason I came out here in the first place. When I first learned about how close my grandmother and her nurse were, I was worried that you were here for nefarious reasons.'

'So you had it in for me from day one? That explains a lot.' Jo thought back to that first night and their altercation in the kitchen, which was very reminiscent of their argument last night. Both times she'd been bewildered by his hostile attitude towards her, though it had hurt more the second time around after how close they'd become.

'Have I said I'm sorry?' His lopsided smile and big

eyes were weakening her defences, but she wasn't giving in without a fight this time.

'Do you know what hurts most, Taylor? It's that we spent days working together, and sleeping together.' Despite her anger, she whispered the last bit. Not wanting everyone in the tiny airport to hear the private conversation and make assumptions about her character too.

'I know—'

'And you still thought I was only here to get written into a will that hopefully won't come into effect for years to come? You clearly don't think very highly of me, when I—I came to think a lot of you.' She barely held her cracking voice, and heart, together.

'That's the problem. I think too much about you. I can't stop thinking about you, Jo, and it scares the life out of me. I'm just waiting for something to rear its head and ruin everything. I guess when I heard about the will it was an easy out. I didn't mean to hurt you, I was trying to protect myself. I'm a selfish, thoughtless fool.'

Okay, so he seemed sincerely apologetic for his behaviour, but Jo needed to know what him being here actually meant. If he was simply trying to salve his conscience, or if he saw a future together in some capacity. Something which would bring its own problems.

'Yes, but you're my selfish, thoughtless fool.' Jo managed a smile.

'So…you'll come back with me?'

Jo thought about it, of spending New Year's celebrating with him and the family, but sooner or later they'd have to return to reality. If she didn't go now, it was going to be even harder second time around.

'I can't, Taylor. Our time together has made me realise I want more than a casual fling. If I'm going to share my life with someone, I want it to mean something. I don't think a long-distance, no strings relationship is going to work for me. If that's what you were thinking...'

'I will do whatever it takes to keep you in my life, Jo. If I learned one thing from pushing you away, it's that I don't want to be without you. I want to give us a chance too. If I have you, I don't need to keep running. Stay, and when we get back to England, I'll see about setting up there.' It was a big promise from Taylor, and she knew he wouldn't say it if he didn't mean it. Especially when he'd pushed her away last night.

Jo's head was in a spin. He was promising her the world, making a sacrifice she would never have expected, but he'd also hurt her deeply.

'Do you really mean that?'

'Yes. All I'm asking is that you come back to the island with me now. Please say yes.' Regardless that he was going all in, he wasn't even asking her for more than that now. Understanding that she'd been burned twice already, and would need time to think before committing to more.

'Madam? Are you boarding? The gate is closing.' The woman at the desk reminded her that she was supposed to be leaving, and as Jo glanced around, she could see that the room was empty of passengers now. Everyone else was on the plane and waiting for her.

Jo's head hurt as the pressure of the situation bore down on her. Having already made the difficult decision to leave, she was concerned that by staying she would open herself up to even more hurt.

'I'm sorry I pushed you away last night. The truth is, I was afraid of my feelings for you and jumped at the first excuse to put some distance between us.' Taylor pleaded his case, leaving her caught in this tug of war between her head and her heart.

'Madam?'

'I love you, Jo. It was only when I thought I was going to lose you for ever that I finally admitted that to myself. Please stay.' Taylor's public display of honesty, along with this surprising vulnerability, drew Jo closer to him than the door through which she'd been planning to make her escape.

If he was willing to make a commitment to their relationship and put everything on the line for her, moving on from his past, she had to forgive him. It was enough to persuade her to be brave too. 'I love you too, Taylor. Let's go back to the island together. Just as soon as we can figure out how to get back out of this airport...'

The beach, crowded with family and friends, the little fairy lights twinkling around the bar and daybeds, was almost as lovely as the night Jo and Taylor had spent there on their own. She'd had such a warm, welcoming response on her return; she was made to feel part of the family, and not just an employee.

Mr Stroud, and Isabelle, had insisted that she take the rest of the day off to settle back in and enjoy the New Year's Eve celebrations. She didn't know exactly what had transpired between them and Taylor in her absence, but no one had batted an eyelid when they'd come down to the beach party hand in hand.

He'd really made the effort to make her comfortable and included and as they stood on the beach with their glasses of champagne, she was looking forward to their future together.

'Ten, nine, eight...'

Mr Stroud paused the music to begin the countdown to the New Year and everyone joined in. 'Seven, six, five, four...'

Taylor turned to Jo and locked eyes on her as though they were the only people on the island. 'Three, two, one...'

A cheer went up at the same time as the very first firework. An expression of joy and excitement at the beginning of a new year. It all faded into the background as Taylor kissed her.

'Happy New Year, Jo. I hope this is just the start of our new life together, wherever it may be. I love you.'

Her heart fluttered, letting her know without doubt that he was the man she wanted to be with and maybe it was time for her to go all in too. 'I love you too, Taylor. That's why I want to travel and work with you.'

His eyes lit up as the sky filled with explosions of blues, reds and golds showering above their heads. 'Are you sure?'

Jo nodded. She'd given it a lot of thought over the past hours since coming back; she'd never felt so alive as she had working with him at the pop-up clinic. She didn't want safe any more, she wanted to follow her heart and see where it led.

'If this is the start of our new life together, I don't want either of us to compromise. It's time we stopped nursing old wounds and embrace our hopes and dreams instead. Here's to us. Happy New Year, Taylor.' She held her glass up to Taylor's. He clinked against it, then kissed her long and hard on the lips.

She knew then it didn't matter where they were, because he was her happy place.

EPILOGUE

'LET'S MAKE A run for it.' Taylor held his jacket up over his and Jo's heads and they ran out into the torrential rain.

Jo screamed as her light cotton dress was immediately soaked through, clinging to her skin. They ran the short distance from the community centre to their house. It was a dilapidated shack that Isaac and his team had renovated for them to stay in when they came back to Loloma Island. With the plans his father had implemented for the hospital and transport in the area, it was decided that Taylor would come to oversee proceedings. Of course Jo had wanted to come with him. They hadn't spent a minute apart in the six months since the New Year's party. Isaac and the others had welcomed them back with open arms when they'd suggested reopening the clinic in the meantime.

Despite the contrast between their basic amenities here, and the luxury villa on the neighbouring Bensak Island, this had become their home.

They let themselves into their little shack, only to find almost as much rain pouring in through the ceiling.

'I guess they aren't used to this much rain out here,' she said, glancing around at the puddles beginning to form on the floor.

'It won't last long. Don't worry.'

'I won't worry about anything as long as I'm with you,'

Jo said, meaning every word. Nothing else seemed to matter as long as they were together. She no longer had to stress over whether or not to trust him because he'd shown her how much he loved her every second since that day in the airport.

With Taylor's support she'd even been able to reconcile with her parents before they'd left England to come back out to Loloma again. They'd returned long enough for Jo to wrap up her work commitments, and speak to her parents. After a much-needed heart to heart, they'd all got to say their piece. A lot of tears and hugs later, Jo felt as though they really had another chance at becoming a family again. They understood how upset she'd been about the truth they'd kept hidden from her, and the impact it had on her. In turn, she'd come to realise that they'd thought they were acting in her best interests, trying to protect her. Something she'd come to relate to more lately…

Taylor slid his arms around her waist and held her to him, the rain still pouring in around them.

'Marry me,' he suddenly blurted out.

'Pardon me?' It wasn't something they'd discussed, or that she'd been prepared for. Though nothing about their relationship was conventional.

'Marry me. I want to make a commitment to you.'

'You don't have to.' As much as her heart was hammering in her chest with the romance of it all, she didn't want him to feel as though this was something he had to do to make her stay with him. She knew what a big deal it was for him when the idea of a relationship at all had freaked him out not so long ago.

'I want to.' He smiled, and dropped a kiss on her lips.

'Hold that thought… I have something to tell you that might make you want to jump on the first flight out of here.' She was hoping he wouldn't, that in making a commitment to them as a couple and having a future together, that her news would be welcome. If unexpected.

'No chance.'

Jo took a deep breath. 'I'm pregnant.'

She watched with bated breath as his frown transformed into a big beautiful grin.

'We're going to have a baby?'

Jo nodded. 'We're going to be a family.'

Taylor lifted her up and spun her around. 'All the more reason for you to say yes then. We'll be a proper family.'

'Of course it's a yes. I love you and I can't wait for us to be a little family.'

They sealed their future with a kiss, and Jo knew whether they settled here, England, or anywhere else in the world, she'd never want to be anywhere else but with Taylor.

* * * * *

If you enjoyed this story,
check out these other great reads from
Karin Baine

Festive Fling with the Surgeon
Midwife's One-Night Baby Surprise
An American Doctor in Ireland
Surgeon Prince's Fake Fiancée

All available now!

RESISTING THE SINGLE DAD SURGEON

LOUISA HEATON

MILLS & BOON

For Faisal, Hayley and Natalie. x

CHAPTER ONE

THE GARLAND CLINIC was situated midway down Harley Street. Pristine. As aesthetically perfect as any old town house could possibly be, its exterior was pure white, the glossy black door framed by two thick white columns, and the path that led to the door was black and white checked, lined by ball-shaped topiaries.

A brass plaque on the door let Isla and its clients know that this wasn't any ordinary house. It might look like an old domestic setting, but inside promised to be modern. Exacting and to a high standard.

She sucked in a deep breath, placed a smile upon her face and pushed open the door, revealing a warm and welcoming entryway. A long corridor lay straight ahead, but to her left was a reception desk with staff behind it. A receptionist in a crisp white blouse and black skirt and a guy in scrubs, holding a file in one hand and a phone in the other as he chatted to someone about a reservation he had the next evening.

The receptionist looked up at Isla and smiled. 'Can I help you?'

'Miss Isla French. I'm the new surgical nurse starting today.'

'Oh, yes! We've been expecting you. Why don't you take a seat and I'll see if Mr Garland is free?'

Isla took a seat. She'd met Mr Garland, the senior partner of the clinic. He had interviewed her, alongside Mr Sharma, one of the other surgeons. There should have been a third consultant there, a Mr Newton, she believed, the one she'd seen often in Mack Desveaux's gossip magazine when she'd been researching the clinic, but he'd been called away on an emergency, so they'd not met yet.

Both consultants had seemed very nice. Approachable. Friendly. Mr Garland specialised in breast reconstructions, Mr Sharma in liposuction and tummy tucks, whereas Mr Newton specialised in faces. Facelifts, rhinoplasties, that kind of thing.

It was exactly the kind of clinic she'd been looking for. Where she could continue to be a nurse, but where all the surgeries done were *elective*, cosmetic procedures. Nothing that was life or death. Nothing that provoked strong emotions. Nothing that could put her at risk.

Finding a clinic that she could get to on the bus had also been a bonus. Finding a place so close to the friend's flat she was staying in temporarily until she could find something more permanent had been like a sign that this job posting had been made just for her, and so she'd been thrilled to receive the phone call from Mr Garland that they'd like to offer her the position of surgical nurse.

'Would you like a beverage?' the receptionist asked. 'We have tea, coffee, water, juice?'

'I'm all right, thank you.'

'I'm Jane. Might as well get to know one another, seeing as we're going to be colleagues.'

'Isla.'

'Such a lovely name!'

Isla smiled. How were you supposed to respond to that? It wasn't as if she'd chosen it herself. But she didn't have too much time to worry. She heard footsteps coming down the stairs and then there was a very handsome man standing in front of her. Mr Newton. Plastic surgeon to the stars. Hair as black as a raven's wing, slightly rakish, slightly ruffled. Bed hair, she liked to think of it, but styled perfectly. He had icy blue eyes and dark stubble, cheekbones you could cut yourself with and a strong, square jaw. He turned his gaze over the waiting room, where he saw her and paused briefly before a wide smile broke across his face. 'Miss French? Mr Gabriel Newton. I don't believe I've had the pleasure yet.'

She was aware of how she must look. Gabriel Newton was clearly a man who assessed faces for a living. He scanned them, found their faults and automatically could think of how much better they might look once graced by his scalpel or bone hammer. And despite her having tried her best this morning, she knew she did not look as beautiful as the models and movie stars he was often seen out and about with.

Her hair was tied tight to the back of her head in a bun, as she liked to keep it out of the way when she was at work. She wore the bare minimum of make-up. A little eyeliner. A little lip gloss. Some concealer to hide the dark marks under her eyes, but that was it. And she'd never had cosmetic surgery. No plumpers. No fillers. Nothing. He probably looked at her and thought of all the ways she could be improved.

But she smiled back anyway. Because she was here to work. To be a professional, not to be a model, or a muse.

'Hello. Call me Isla.' She stood and held out her hand, trying not to be mesmerised by those blue eyes of his. She could see now, in person, why the paparazzi loved him so. He was a perfect sculpture of a man. Handsome. Beautiful. No doubt photogenic. He looked daring and racy and probably helped sell more magazines than he ought to, because of the company that he kept.

'Isla. Call me Gabe.'

He shook her hand and she felt something race up her arm. A tingle. A warmth. And then a flush of heat that suffused her face and neck.

Am I blotchy? I bet I'm blotchy.

The thought annoyed her. Irritated her. This was not what she'd wanted! She'd just wanted to return to work and get on with her day. Meet with everyone and then just be the best surgical nurse that she could be.

Not this.

Not this complication.

Putting it down to first-day nerves, she dismissed the idea that she might be even the slightest bit attracted to him and pushed the thought to one side. Because there was a danger of becoming enamoured with someone and just because they had a pretty face did not mean that they were a nice person. Danger could lurk behind even the nicest facades and she knew this to her detriment.

Gabe was gorgeous and rich, according to the gossip, but who was he really? Clever, no doubt, he was a surgeon, but beauty was superficial at best. So she could shove his good looks and her initial crush reaction into a box marked *Nothing Worth Worrying Over.* And *her* visage? Was nothing she wanted to do anything about. She'd never considered cosmetic surgery herself and so her face was her face and life was life. It had marred her with worry lines and crow's feet and dark shadows, but they told a story. They marked her as being someone who'd experienced things. Even if hardly any of them were pleasant.

So sue me if I'm not perfect.

She'd never wanted perfection. There was nothing interesting about perfection.

'Have you had the tour?' he asked.

'No.'

'Then let me show you around. It can be a bit of a maze, to begin with.' He had a dynamite smile. Lovely, straight teeth. Wide, full lips. And he smelt great. She could feel her senses going into overdrive and struggled to rein them in. As he showed her the consulting rooms, surgical rooms, recovery rooms, day ward, staffrooms, stock rooms, utilities, she kept getting wafts of his scent, flashes of his smile, and was acutely aware of his height and power.

He was a tall man. Over six feet, for sure. Broad shoulders, neat waist, his bespoke tailored suit clinging to him in ways that ought to be illegal. Gabriel Newton clearly worked out and looked after himself, but then she supposed he needed to, doing the job that he did. Gabe was a salesman. An advertising board. A look-at-what-you-could-be-too image. He had to look good. It made the clients, the patients, feel comfortable. Assured of their results. But as he showed her around, introducing her to various members of staff, she saw no obvious signs of surgery on his face. No scars. No nips. No tucks. Nothing pulled tight. He looked completely natural and she felt like looking up into the heavens and whispering, *Well done.*

'You can put your things here.' He indicated a free locker in one of the staff areas. They had a locker room, their own shower and toilet facilities. A small gym with workout equipment. A fully equipped kitchen and a lounge. It really was quite amazing!

Isla shrugged off her jacket and hung it up with her

bag. She closed her locker with the key and slipped it into her pocket.

'Scrubs are in here. Freshly laundered every day. Used ones go in that hamper over there—don't ever wear them home.'

'All right.'

'Can I make you a drink?' He checked his watch. 'You've got time before your first surgery.'

'Perfect. Tea, please.'

'Coming right up.' He gave her a dazzling smile that almost knocked her off her feet and she nervously sat down on one of the sofas, not sure what to do with herself.

'Do you know what my first procedure is?'

'You're in with me. Rhinoplasty.'

Nose job. 'Okay.'

'Phil says you've worked as a surgical nurse before. In plastics?'

Phil was Phillip Garland. The boss.

'A few times. I worked in a burns unit for a while, too. We did a lot of maxillofacial surgeries, but I've mostly worked in general surgery.'

'So you have a broad knowledge base?'

'I think so. I hear you specialise in facial procedures?'

He nodded as he poured boiling water into two cups that actually had saucers beneath. 'Yes. A lot of eyelifts, nasal augmentation, jaw reshaping—whatever the client wants, really.'

'Do you have a favourite type of surgery?'

He laughed and shook his head. 'The one where my client leaves feeling happy with their results.'

'A politician's answer.' Isla smiled knowingly, taking the cup and saucer from him when he brought it over and sat opposite her.

'A practised answer.' He agreed. 'But one that's true, I'm afraid. People come to me because they're unhappy with what they see on the outside. So if I can make them feel better on the *inside*, then that's what matters to me the most.'

'You have a counsellor on the premises, don't you?'

'We do. Every client that comes to us about needing a cosmetic procedure has to see our surgical counsellor and is given a cooling-down period before they're accepted to surgery. We like to know that they're ready. When you change how you look, when the mirror suddenly shows someone different, it can have an effect on well-being, even if they thought they wanted the change. Our counsellors are available to our clients for up to a year after their surgery, for no extra charge.'

'That's good.'

'We try to cater to our clients' every need. We adapt to suit them as much as we can.'

Isla smiled and sipped her tea.

'Do you live locally, or…?'

'Near Hammersmith. You?'

'Hampstead Heath.'

'Lovely. Do you have a view of the heath?'

'As a matter of a fact, we do.' He sipped his tea, then glanced at his watch. Some chunky, expensive number sat on his wrist. 'Oops. Better get going. I have a few things to do before surgery. You're happy you know where everything is?'

'If I get lost I can ask someone.'

He stood. Smiled. 'All right. I'll see you in surgery, Isla. I look forward to it.'

'Me too.' She stood as well and watched him go, feeling herself deflate slightly the second he left the room.

At that moment, in walked a male nurse. 'We all feel like that, don't worry.'

'Like what?'

'Like he takes all the air out of the room with him when he goes.'

She blushed. 'Oh, I didn't feel tha—'

'It's fine, honey, honestly. It doesn't help that the guy is single and probably the most eligible millionaire doctor in England right now. Pity he's straight, or I'd try my luck, to be fair. Mind you, wouldn't be the first time I'd turned a straight guy...' The nurse winked, then smiled at her, holding out his hand. 'I'm Justin.'

She laughed. 'Isla. Well, he's not my type, so...'

'Gorgeous, single, rich and clever isn't your type?' Justin took a moment to assess her, looking her up and down. 'Don't tell me...you prefer guys a bit rougher around the edges? Grungy-looking? A bit more blue collar?'

Isla shook her head. She didn't have a type. Not any more. Once upon a time it had been Karl. He'd been tall, dark and clever. A nurse in A & E. They'd bonded over who could tell the grimmest patient story and he'd won. Karl always won. He loved to control things. But he'd not been able to control events. He'd not been able to control that patient's family member that had ruined Isla's life and he'd certainly not been able to control how he felt about it, leading to the breakdown of their marriage. Men had been off her agenda ever since. Isla only ever viewed them as threats now. People to hold at a distance. The best men, in her opinion, were often anaesthetised.

'Let me guess...you're married?'

'Nope. Very much single.'

'Then what's wrong with you, honey?' Justin asked with a laugh as he left the staffroom, chuckling to himself.

Isla grimaced.

Some would say plenty.

Gabe was in the scrub room, getting ready for surgery and gazing through into the theatre at the staff inside.

His patient was already under, the anaesthetist having done their job, hooking the patient up to oxygen and monitoring their stats for any spikes or reactions. The two theatre nurses were busy setting up, Verity showing the new nurse, Isla, how Gabe liked his equipment to be laid out.

He'd met her only briefly, but she seemed to be competent. Phillip wouldn't have hired her if she weren't. She was friendly, he'd been able to talk to her with ease, but there'd been something about her that he couldn't quite put his finger on. It was niggling at him. Worrying away at him, at the base of his skull, as if he wanted to reach inside and scratch at it and make it go away.

What was it?

He liked that she was a natural beauty and did not try to over-emphasise her features. Her hair had been neatly tied back, as regulations expected, but there'd hardly been a lick of make-up on her face. Maybe that was it? He was so used to seeing women so perfectly made-up that when he saw one going au naturel, he noticed?

No, that's not it. It's something else. Why do I feel as if I know her? As if we've met before?

He knew her from somewhere. But if they had met before, then surely she would have mentioned it?

It would come to him. He knew that. Her name was not familiar to him, but it was really annoying to feel this way.

Gabe was a man who prided himself on his memory. He remembered names. Remembered faces. People. Places. So why couldn't he remember someone like her? She said she lived near Hammersmith—well, he'd never been there, but she had worked in a burns unit before and so had he, so maybe they'd worked together once. Maybe she'd been a scrub nurse for him before.

Her gaze met his through the glass and, startled, as if she'd caught him thinking about her, he looked down and away as he finished scrubbing. He needed to get his mind in the game. Needed to be thinking of the rhinoplasty. The patient.

Caron Latimer had come in to get her nose altered. Said that her nose had always bothered her, ever since she was a child. That her siblings had all inherited their mother's petite nose, but she'd inherited her father's Roman nose. She felt that the nasal bridge was too prominent, that her nose was too wide. She wanted something smaller. More like her mother's. She'd brought in pictures of what she wanted.

He'd listened to Caron, advised her. Taken pictures and created a digital model of her nose and then showed her on the computer what her new nose might look like on her face. He'd sent her home with these pictures. Told her to think about it. To talk to their counsellor, to make sure that this was what she wanted.

And she did. She'd lived with a nose that she hated for twenty-three years. It wore down her self-esteem. She felt self-conscious. Her mental health was being affected by it and she'd even taken days off work because some days she just couldn't face going in, because she worked in sales and she often caught customers' gazes focusing on her nose as they talked to her.

So he'd agreed to help her. To reduce the nasal bridge, to reshape her nose so that it was a little smaller and give her a little slope to her nose, rather than an arch.

Caron couldn't wait, she'd said. She'd been so excited when she'd come in this morning at seven a.m. to be prepped for the procedure.

And he couldn't wait to change her life.

That was the part of his job he loved the most. Making a difference. Giving someone a confidence they'd never had before. Making them feel that they could face the world with confidence again. And the work he did here, for the rich and the powerful and, yes, the celebrities, allowed him to fund his trips to India where he worked with acid-attack victims to try and improve their burns. Their scars. To make their lives a little easier.

As he entered Theatre, he looked to Verity, then Isla. 'Are we ready?'

Verity nodded.

The anaesthetist nodded.

Isla nodded.

She had the most beautiful eyes above that scrub mask. If he'd worked with her before, he would have remembered. Isla would have to remain a mystery for a little longer. 'Then let's begin.'

Gabe was a master of his craft and, unlike a lot of surgeons she'd worked with before, who very often ignored everyone around them whilst they were the star of the show, Gabe talked to everyone in the room, explaining what he was doing and why. As if he were in a teaching hospital.

'I'm going to perform a closed rhinoplasty,' he said.

A closed rhinoplasty involved the surgeon making incisions *inside* the nostrils, so that scars would not be shown on the face, rather than an open rhinoplasty in which the surgeon would cut across the skin *between* the nostrils.

'This patient has requested that I make her nose smaller. How do I do that, Verity?'

'By removing or shaving down cartilage and or bone,' she answered, as promptly as a robot.

'This patient also requires some reshaping of her nostrils. How am I going to do that? Isla?' he asked.

She felt a wave of heat wash over her, being put on the spot like this, but she'd seen rhinoplasties performed on accident victims so she felt confident with her answer. 'I assume you will break the nose bone and rearrange the cartilage.' Her cheeks felt hot and she met his gaze above his mask. Happily, she saw the corners of his eyes crease in a smile.

'Correct. And what are some of the risks to the procedure?'

'Breathing problems. Nosebleeds. Infection. Clots. Perhaps even an altered sense of smell.'

She heard Gabe let out a breath, before he nodded. 'Looks like Phillip hired the right person and I didn't need to be there, after all.'

It was a compliment. She had passed the first tests and she was proud of herself. If she could she would have turned to Verity to offer her a high-five, but that wasn't the sort of thing that a professional nurse did in Theatre. Instead Isla stood there knowing that everyone knew she deserved to be there. She might be new, but she was *not* inexperienced and she knew how to handle herself in a theatre.

It took just over two hours for Gabe to be happy he had done enough to reduce the nose to his patient's liking and, once he was done, he asked Isla and Verity to apply the splint and dressings whilst he scrubbed out.

'What did you think?' asked Verity when he'd gone.

'He's an amazing surgeon. Very good!' And she meant it. Watching Gabe work had been a privilege. The way his hands moved, his dexterity, his poise. It had been almost artful.

Verity laughed. 'I meant the surgery, but…okay. You wouldn't be the first nurse to have a crush on Gabriel.'

'I *don't*!' That was two people now who'd implied it was natural to have some secret feelings for Gabe Newton. It was her first day! She didn't need gossip like that carrying around her place of employment. That was not what she was here for! Isla wanted to do her job and nothing more and if that meant proving she was not smitten by Mr Newton's good looks, then she'd damn well show them. 'What surgery is next?' she asked, determined to change the subject.

'Mr Sharma. Buttock augmentation.'

'Right. I'll escort this patient to Recovery. I'll be back soon.'

'Okey doke. See you in a bit.'

'Phillip? What can I do for you?' Gabe had picked up the phone after an internal call had come through on the system.

'Gabe—just checking that you reminded our new theatre nurse about our ritual first-day dinner?'

Gabe closed his eyes in dismay as he realised he'd completely forgotten to mention it. The Garland Clinic had a habit of taking all new employees out for a meal after their first day at the clinic. It was like a welcome. A friendly hello-and-welcome-to-the-team thing. But they'd not had a new member of staff for such a long time, the whole thing had gone completely out of his head. 'Sorry, no. I forgot. Do you want me to go and check with her?'

'Would you, old boy? It's just I'm running a little late. My last patient went a little over time and now I've got a queue and I noticed that your clinic is over.'

'No problem. I'll track her down and ask and then email you.'

'Perfect. Thanks. I've booked a table at Jean Luc's. Seven p.m.'

Gabe brought up the staff rosters on his computer to try and work out where Isla would be. By all accounts she was in theatre with Mohammed, so he made his way there.

When he got there, Mo looked to be about halfway through his procedure. Gabe pressed the button on the intercom. 'Hi, I just wondered if I might have a quick word with our fabulous new nurse.'

Mo looked up over the patient to Isla and nodded.

Verity took her place as Isla walked over to the viewing window. She looked confused. A little worried.

'Something wrong?'

'No, nothing's wrong.' He smiled, to show he wasn't a threat, or a problem of any kind. 'Are you okay for dinner this evening?'

She blinked. 'Dinner? Oh, um…'

He watched as she went from shocked to desperate. Desperate to turn him down, and that was when he realised that maybe he'd phrased the question wrong. 'The new employee's dinner. With *everyone* there. Not just me,' he added quietly, almost feeling a blush come upon himself.

Isla stared at him as realisation hit. 'Oh! That! I remember Mr Garland mentioning it at interview, I'd forgotten. Um…well, yes. Yes! I can make the dinner. What time is it?'

'Reservation is at seven o'clock. Jean Luc's.'

'Right. Right. Dress code?'

'Smart.'

She continued to nod.

'So, that's a yes? I can tell Phil that you'll be there?'

'Yes!' She laughed. 'I thought for a minute there that you, that you were...' She laughed again, looked away. 'Seven is fine, though it might be a bit of a stretch for me to get home in time to change.'

'I'm sure we can let you go home a little early just this once.'

As she headed back to the surgery, Gabe came away from Theatre feeling slightly strange. Perturbed. What had just happened? She'd thought that *he* was asking *her* out personally!

He almost laughed, until he remembered that she'd been working out how she could possibly turn him down and that stopped him in his tracks. He wasn't used to women turning him down. Normally, they all said yes. Or asked him themselves.

But Isla had been going to say no. Politely. Nicely. Without hurting his feelings.

And that just made him like her all the more.

CHAPTER TWO

SHE'D BEEN ALLOWED to leave early, so that she could get home in time to change and get to the dinner. She'd looked up Jean Luc's on the Internet and stared open-mouthed at the prices for a while, before thanking her lucky stars that Mr Garland had told her when she'd accepted the posting that the clinic paid for the new employee's dinner.

I mean, thank God. If I had to pay, we'd be at the local pizza place.

Not that there was anything wrong with Mario's Pizza. She'd had many a happy night in front of the television, chowing down on a pepperoni taste sensation. There was no pizza on the menu at Jean Luc's. There wasn't much on the menu at Jean Luc's that she understood at all. Most of it was in French and she'd never remembered much of her French from school except for *je m'appelle* and she wasn't sure how far that would get her tonight.

Mr Garland and the other consultants, Mr Sharma and Mr Newton, were no doubt built for this sort of dining. A la carte. It wasn't really her thing and when she'd first heard about it, she'd actually tried to get out of it.

'Splendid! We're so glad you've accepted the job. Just a little heads up, the partners always take a new member of staff out for dinner after their first day. Special treat. A sort of welcome aboard the good ship Garland!'

She'd panicked. The idea of having to go to dinner with three men that she didn't know had terrified her.

'*Oh, I'm not sure that I—*'

'*Don't worry!*' he'd interrupted. '*You won't just have us there, the admin and other nursing staff will be there, too.*'

To be fair, that had made it a little easier. If the other staff were there, she'd feel a little more relaxed. Less like a mouse surrounded by three big cats.

The question was, what was she to wear? She'd only ever had a nurse's salary and, recently, she'd only been working part-time, so she'd not had much money to spare on cocktail dresses. She had two options to choose from. A little black dress that had saved her bacon on a number of occasions and a sleeveless, strapless white dress that clung to her figure and that she'd bought before her life had changed for evermore and she wasn't sure if she would ever wear it.

The white dress made a statement. The white dress ought to be worn by a woman who was comfortable in her own skin. The white dress was confidence.

She'd bought it years ago, when she had felt like a bad-ass. When she had felt indestructible and that nothing on this earth could hurt her.

But then it had.

Isla stared at them both. She could hide in the black dress. Pair it with a short black cardigan and kitten heels and if she added some jewellery, a necklace, some dangly earrings, maybe she'd get away with it looking more expensive than it actually was.

But her gaze kept getting pulled back to the white dress.

Jean Luc's demanded this dress. The Garland consultants demanded this dress. An all-expenses-paid à-la-carte dinner demanded this dress. This dress might make her feel…what? Better? More confident? Or would she feel as if she had a target on her back? Because *guys* would look at her in this dress.

She decided to put it on. Just to see what it would look like in the safety of her own home. Just to see if it would fit still.

I mean, it's been a few years. I've probably put on some pounds…

But it did fit.

It fitted like a glove. It made her shoulders and her arms look great. Yes, she'd been working out lately, figuring that physical strength was important if she was to start going back out into the world. The skirt ended just above her knees and had a small split on the left-hand side. Slipping her feet into a pair of nude heels made her legs look as if they went on for days. Even her calves were shapely!

She'd not noticed before. Normally when she studied herself in front of a mirror she was at the gym, in shorts and a tee shirt and sweating profusely and checking her form as she lifted weights. She'd never turned this way. Or that. Or pointed her toes in heels.

It's too much. I look way too much!

She almost took it off, so that she could retreat to the safety of the black dress, but a shawl in her wardrobe took that moment to slither off its hanger and make itself known and she knelt to pick it up and wrapped it around her shoulders, allowing herself to hide somewhat behind its silver fringing, and she just knew, in that moment, that she didn't ever want to go back to that little black dress.

The white dress stuck two fingers up at all that she had

gone through before and this was her new life. Her new start. So why not start it with confidence?

Isla picked up her mobile and dialled for a taxi before she lost her nerve.

Phillip had reserved for them the large oval table near the bay window and, as usual, was revelling in his role as host as Gabe joined them, Mohammed, Jane, Justin and Verity, greeting them all, dropping kisses onto the cheeks of the women and shaking hands and patting the backs of the men.

'Our guest of honour hasn't arrived yet,' said Phil as he saw him look around the table to the empty chair beside him.

'Oh. Maybe I should wait for her at the door?'

'No, no, the maître d' knows that we're waiting for her. He'll bring her straight to the table when she arrives. I take it her first day went well?'

Gabe nodded, settling into his seat. 'Very well, yes. I certainly had no problems—she was an excellent help in Theatre. Very knowledgeable. Professional.'

'Good! Good.' Phil sipped at his glass of water.

A waiter came to take their drinks order, but they asked him to wait until Isla arrived and as the waiter disappeared into the kitchen, Gabe's gaze fell upon movement by the entrance, where a woman had come in wearing a white dress.

He could view her only from behind, but she had beautiful honey-blonde hair that fell in a wave to just past her shoulders. She wore a wrap, or maybe it was a shawl, in silver that glittered and caught the light of all the candles in the room as she leant in to speak to the maître d'.

And then she turned to follow him in and Gabe realised, with shock, that it was Isla, their new theatre nurse.

'Wow.'

Heads turned at the table to see whom he was looking at and somehow he'd got to his feet without realising it. Phillip and Mohammed stood too and suddenly Isla was there, smiling, blushing, greeting the partners and all the staff and then she was in front of him, looking shy and tentative, and he leaned in to kiss her hello on the cheek and it was as if everything were in slow motion.

Her smile. Her eyes. Smoky and seductive.

Her scent. Light. Floral.

She looked…breathtaking! Completely unlike the woman he'd met today in the hall reception at the Garland Clinic. This Isla wore make-up and though she'd been beautiful without it, with the make-up, he was astounded. Drawn in to those soft blue eyes of hers, the way she looked at him from under those thick, dark lashes. Pulled to her soft pink lips, full and inviting, slicked with gloss. Magnetised by her womanly figure. A perfect hourglass.

Shocked, he looked away from her to see if she was having the same effect on everyone else, but instead he just found Justin looking at him with one eyebrow raised and an amused smile upon his mouth. That guy missed nothing.

And then they were seated and ordering drinks and the waiter disappeared again, this time to fulfil their order.

'You look wonderful,' he said, feeling the need to compliment her. 'Not that you didn't earlier on, but tonight is just…wonderful.' He laughed, embarrassed at his own inability to come up with another adjective.

'Thank you. You look *wonderful*, too.'

He'd thrown on his usual tuxedo. He'd had it made especially by Hugo Knight, a bespoke tailor in London who dressed a lot of male stars and celebrities.

'You, er…found this place, all right?'

She smiled. 'Not my job. I left that to the taxi driver, I'm afraid.'

'Of course.' *Idiot.*

'I'd like to propose a toast,' said Phillip, raising his glass, after the waiter had returned with their drinks. 'To Isla, our new theatre nurse! We are so very happy to have you join us and we hope that you will have many happy years with us at the Garland. We promise to try not to be too demanding. To Isla!'

'To Isla!' Gabe concurred, clinking his flute with everyone else's even though he'd read somewhere that clinking glasses was actually bad etiquette. You were only meant to raise your glass. But as Phillip and all the others were doing so, he knew he would feel bad if he didn't join them in the practice.

'Thank you, everyone. For making me feel so welcome.' Isla sipped her champagne as the waiter arrived with menus.

Gabe was looking at his for a moment when he realised that Isla looked a little confused.

'So it's true, then?' he asked, with a smile.

'What's that?'

'That even though your surname is French, it doesn't actually mean that you can read French?'

She blushed. 'I can read it. I just can't understand a word it says. Can you help me?' she whispered. 'I don't want to seem ignorant.'

He smiled back, amused. 'Of course. Let's see, there are three starters to choose from. There are mussels. Or there's a tomato and basil tarte tatin, or you can choose soupy cheese.'

Isla laughed. 'You make it sound so delicious!'

'I didn't say I was a perfect translator, but I understand the general gist.'

'Hmm, what are you going to have?'

'The soupy cheese. It's Gruyère and Camembert. I've had it from here before and it's fabulous.'

She nodded. 'Then I'll do the same. Mains?'

'Okay, let's see…five options: posh chicken casserole… posh steak and chips…posh fish quiche…posh fish on its own or a fig and ham salad.'

He could see that she was enjoying his tongue-in-cheek translation.

'Posh chicken casserole, I think.'

'Perfect choice. I'll join you.'

The waiter took everyone's order and disappeared back into the kitchen. Gabe couldn't help but smile as he was really beginning to enjoy himself, which was a surprise. He never usually enjoyed these employee dinners. He often found them to be very formal, very polite, the new employee not sure how to behave or what to talk about, and he often discovered that the dinner turned almost into a secondary interview with the new employee sharing their life story to date. He hoped that Isla wouldn't get interrogated that way, especially by Justin, who could be a bit persistent in his search for gossip.

'So…tell us *all* about yourself, Isla,' said Justin, right on cue. 'The bosses here know a little about you, but I'm totally in the dark. I've already asked around, but everyone's so light on the details!'

'What do you want to know?' asked Isla, smiling.

'Well, who you are. Where you came from. That kind of thing.'

'All right, well, um, I've always been a nurse. It was all I ever wanted to be from school. I don't know why. No one else in my family had worked in medicine. My first posting was in A & E, which I liked. Nice. Fast-paced. Huge variety of patients, which I liked. Occasionally, I got to work in Theatre and realised that I loved that the most, so I did some extra training and here I am.'

Justin nodded, lips pursed as if he was considering the information carefully. 'And you're here alone tonight. Should we infer from that that you're single?' He waggled his eyebrows.

'Yes and happily so.'

'Pretty thing like you? Won't take long, I'm sure.'

Gabe couldn't help but notice the impertinent wink Justin gave him when Isla took a sip of her drink. He knew the implication, but he would never choose to date a colleague and he was in no position to date anyone. Not with his situation. Not with Bea. It was all too complicated and that was why he *only* went on *first dates* with women. If they could even be called dates, that was. He gave women who wanted to be seen with him a good time. A great meal, fabulous conversation, maybe a bit of dancing, but then he waved them goodbye. The women he got spotted out and about around town with were not the kind of women who would be able to deal with Bea, his daughter. They came as a package and they were a complicated package. Dating, falling in love, were not on his agenda, thank you very much. The women he was seen with used him, as much as he used them. For mutual exposure.

'I'm not really looking for anyone right now,' Isla said.

Phew. Good. That let him off the hook.

'Why ever not?' Justin pushed. He really was on form tonight.

She shrugged and Gabe could tell she was feeling as if she had her back against the wall. Justin really could be a horrific snoop, so he decided to rescue her.

'I think it's a good thing. To be single. You can live your life your own way. By your own rules.'

Isla looked gratefully towards him and nodded. 'Absolutely.'

'Well, you would say that, Gabe. Don't think I haven't seen what you get up to most weeks. I see your face every month in that celebrity gossip rag. I think Mack Desveaux is obsessed with you.'

Mack Desveaux. The bane of his life. A kid he went to school with, who'd always been on the periphery of his life until he'd discovered that when he'd begun to date Ellis, she'd also been seeing someone else—Mack. When she'd realised her feelings for Gabe, she'd ended it with Mack, but Mack had never ended it with Gabe. Hounding him relentlessly as if he just couldn't get past his losing to him. 'I can't control the free press, Justin. *You* should know that,' he said, taking a sip of his own drink.

Justin blushed. He'd once been dragged into the press because he'd attended a charity ball that had also been attended by some minor pop-star celebrities and he'd offhandedly been rude to one, snatched her mobile phone from her hand and thrown it into a swimming pool because he'd thought the young woman had been flirting with the guy that he liked.

'Yes, well…'

Isla turned to Gabe, one eyebrow raised, intrigued, and he figured he'd just tell her later. But he wouldn't let

Justin bully her. The guy could be awful sometimes if he was bored.

At that moment, the food arrived and their Gruyère and Camembert fondue was placed before them. It smelt divine and came with two little side pots filled with croutons and perfectly cubed types of bread. Sourdough. Rye. Plain white. Wholemeal. One with sun-dried tomatoes in and what tasted like cranberries.

It was delicious!

'Nice?' he asked Isla.

'It's gorgeous! Thank you for the recommendation.'

'No problem.' He didn't know why he'd felt the need to take her under his wing and protect her from the vultures. Gabe just knew that it felt good. This wasn't the type of place Isla was used to. He could tell. She didn't seem comfortable at all and she'd come here alone, all quietly spoken and shy, yet still rocking that amazing white dress.

He couldn't help but notice how good she looked in it. He'd not noticed her figure at work, but, then again, she'd been in scrubs mostly, a hairnet, a face mask. Tonight, she wore the dress, the dress did not wear her, and she looked stunning. Clearly she took care of her body. Arms and legs didn't get that toned just from working in Theatre. You had to work at it. He knew, having spent hours in a gym himself. Though a lot of his gym use was because he felt angry, or that there'd been an injustice with his life, or whenever Bea had a relapse and he felt frustrated. He'd lift weights or pound the treadmill until sweat dripped off him and he would only stop when he felt exhausted. It probably wasn't good to work out that way, but it had been working for him so far.

'Maybe now that he's got some food in front of him, he'll stop interrogating you,' he said in a quiet aside.

Isla flushed. 'It's fine.'

'No. It's not.' He met her gaze. Conspiratorially. Sideways. Quick. A glimpse. But it was enough to cause a strange sensation inside him. As if he'd been hit. By a wave of something. Warmth. Affection.

No. Something stronger than affection.

Gabe frowned and speared a piece of bread and dipped it in cheese as he tried to analyse what was happening. He didn't like it. Didn't welcome it. He'd not felt this since he'd met his wife. Before she was his wife.

No. No. That's not it. It can't be the same.

Gabe dabbed at his lips with a napkin and took another fortifying drink of the champagne. His glass was nearly empty and now he felt like the one trapped in a corner.

Was Justin staring at him? Was Isla? Anyone else?

Isla thankfully now took control of the conversation and directed a question to Phillip, asking him about how he started the Garland Clinic.

As his senior partner and friend began pontificating about his great start in life, Gabe found himself retreating and glancing at his mobile phone, in case there were any urgent messages he needed to respond to. He wouldn't be the first consultant to walk out on the new-employee dinner because of some crisis at home.

But there wasn't a crisis, because no one was at home. Bea was at boarding school, as she always was Monday to Fridays, coming home only at the weekends. Suddenly he missed her. Missed his daughter like crazy and wished they were at home together, so he could sit in her bedroom and read her a story, the way he'd used to when she was little. Before she'd decided that she hated him.

When was the last time he read to her? He couldn't think. Couldn't remember. This feeling that he felt for Isla was confusing matters. Playing with his brain. 'Excuse me,' he said, getting up from the table and heading out to the veranda to get some fresh air and some perspective. Maybe it was the dress? Her eyes? Her scent? Her vulnerability?

Something...

Maybe it was all of those things and more.

Or maybe it's because I've not let anyone get close for far too long and, by my protecting her from Justin, she sneaked past my barricades?

Gabe leant against the stone and looked down into the gardens that were filled with flowers and blooms and fat bumble bees that were getting their last evening collection of pollen.

'Are you okay?'

He spun around at her voice, surprised. He'd not expected her to follow him out here.

Justin will have noticed. Damn it.

'Yeah. Yeah! I'm good. Just...needed a bit of fresh air, is all. It can get a little stuffy in there, sometimes...' He hoped he sounded convincing.

'Me too. I wasn't following you, though, so please don't think that. I wasn't even sure if you'd come out here. I just asked the waiter if there was somewhere *I* could go.'

He nodded, understanding. 'How are you enjoying your employee dinner?'

'Nerve-racking. I almost didn't come at all. This isn't my thing.'

'No. Nor me.' He sighed.

Isla frowned. 'Really? I always see you out and about.' Then she flushed. 'In the magazines. I know, I'm sorry. I shouldn't pay any attention to those, but my mother brings them round and... I know I shouldn't believe everything I see or read.'

'No, it's fine. Honestly, I get that a lot. A lot of my clients tell me the same thing. I'm kinda used to it.'

'Did you really go out for dinner once with Elizabeth Traynor?' she asked him, curiously.

Gabe laughed. 'Yes. But! It wasn't like it was shown. Celeb photographs and cosmetic surgery are very much the same. It's all about perception and what you can't see.'

She took a step towards him, looked over the veranda, then back at him. 'What didn't I see?'

'That we were at a party thrown by her agent. A woman called Cecelia Trent, who'd wanted us to meet to talk about Elizabeth getting some subtle nose work. And that there were a hundred or so *other* people there. That snapshot made it look like we were having some secret romantic rendezvous, but in reality we had loads of other people around us. They'd been cut out of shot.' Which was what Mack had intended. He'd seemed to make it his life's mission to paint Gabe as some sort of Lothario, when it blatantly wasn't true. To paint him as someone women shouldn't trust. But rich, handsome playboy doctor sold copies much better than doctor attends party.

Isla laughed. 'I see. Sorry.'

'It's okay. Just don't believe everything you see.'

'From now on, I will question everything. Maybe if I'd done that earlier, then my life wouldn't have gone to pot.'

He frowned. 'How so?'

Isla shook her head rapidly. 'It's nothing. Forget it. We all make mistakes, right?'

'We do. We're human. I think it's expected of us. Otherwise we'd be perfect and no one wants perfection, do they?'

She laughed, grateful to him for letting her off the hook. 'No. Though maybe don't tell your clients that.'

'No.' He watched as she leaned against the veranda. The way the white dress hugged her body, a small split in a side seam revealing a hint of thigh that made him feel all hot for some reason.

I cannot have some sort of crush on the new theatre nurse!

He had to end this. Stop it in its tracks. 'We should go back inside. Justin'll be wondering where we both are, or putting two and two together and coming up with five.'

'Right. Well, you go first. If we go back together that would definitely stir a pot.'

'Absolutely.' He pushed himself off the veranda and, without thinking, without realising what he was doing, he touched her fingers with his, in some sort of acknowledgement, as he passed her. A quick touch. A brief entwining of fingers.

Wait. What did I just do that for?

A gesture of support? Hopefully she saw it that way.

He entered the restaurant, feeling his face flaming with heat, and he stopped, out of sight of the veranda, out of sight of the table, and just took a moment to loosen his tie, to check his cuffs, to regain control over himself, before he put himself back out on display. Forcing a smile, he headed back to the table.

'Everything all right?' asked Phillip.

'Yes. Fine. Mmm-hmm,' he said, settling into his seat. 'Where's Isla?' he asked, to try and imply that they'd not just spent some time together alone on the veranda.

'Got a bit hot, or something,' Phillip replied. 'We figured you'd finished your starter, so we let the waiter take it away. Hope that was all right?'

'Yes, fine.' He'd forgotten about the food. Forgotten whereabouts they were in dinner. Two more courses to go. Two more courses and then he could plead work the next day and go home. Get some much-needed space from the new theatre nurse and some much-needed control over his responses.

'Actually, might I ask you a favour, Gabe?'

'Sure, what's up?'

'Well, I've had a long day and fancy a bit of an early night tonight—please the wife, you know how it is—and Mo needs to get back to his babysitter. I think Justin and the others want to go on to a godawful club or something, but Isla said she wants an early night… Would it be an awful imposition if I asked you to wait with her until her taxi arrived to take her home later on?'

'That's fine,' he said. Even though it wasn't fine.

It wasn't fine at all.

What would he say to her, standing out there, on the street, with her alone? He couldn't leave her there. It was the gentlemanly thing to do.

I just won't stand so close. Won't look her in the eye. Maybe I should apologise for the hand thing?

At that moment, Isla came back to the table and all the men, Gabe, Phillip, Mohammed, Justin, got up to stand, until she was seated.

'Everything all right, Isla?' Justin asked.

'Good, thank you.'

'Excellent.'

He sounded smug. Justin sounded as though he could see every little thought in Gabe's head and somehow knew about them meeting on the veranda.

Gabe couldn't look at him right now.

So he downed the rest of his champagne and poured himself some more.

CHAPTER THREE

THE LATE EVENING breeze was beginning to feel a little chilly. Isla was glad of her shawl as she pulled it close around her shoulders.

'Cold?'

'A little.'

'Here.' Gabe began to remove his dinner jacket.

'Oh, you don't need to do that!' she began to protest, even though she was grateful for the gesture and the warmth of his jacket instantly made her feel better. 'Thanks. It was nice of you to wait with me, but I'll be okay. You can go, if you'd like.' She was nervous. The two of them standing there, outside the restaurant. It had been a long time since she'd been outside with a man, alone, at night and the situation made her nervous. Even more nervous since that moment on the veranda when his fingers had caressed hers as he'd passed her by.

A jolt of electricity had shot up her arm, awareness spreading through her, making her feel something she'd not felt for a very long time.

Want. Need.

It was disturbing. Terrifying, almost. And with her boss! If there was one place you did not want to conduct a romance, it was at your job, because when it didn't work out, it could make life extremely difficult. And Isla felt as if she carried enough baggage already, without the bumpy road that a crush on her boss would entail. There was an imbalance of power in that relationship and that was fine when it was just work, because some people were meant to be in charge, but there shouldn't be an imbalance in an intimate relationship.

But his jacket felt so good around her shoulders and she appreciated the gentlemanly gesture. And she could inhale his scent. Damn, the man not only looked good, but smelled delicious, too! It was not helping with the inappropriate feelings! And he stood there, looking gorgeous in his white shirt and undone bow tie, hands in his pockets, as if he were about to walk a runway.

'This must seem a boring night for you,' she said.

Gabe turned to look at her, confused. He had been looking up and down the street as they waited for her taxi they'd ordered twenty minutes earlier, because he'd thought he'd seen something. 'Boring? Why?'

'Out with colleagues. Having to babysit me, when you could be out and about with some actors or models. Sipping champagne in penthouse suites and partying till the early hours.'

He smiled. 'Is that what you think happens?'

'Isn't it?'

He laughed. 'Well, yeah, but don't ever make the mistake of thinking that they're not boring. Those sorts of places are all the same. The *people* are all the same. They're networking, selling themselves and some of them are letting off steam in the worst ways possible.'

'If you don't enjoy it, why do you go to those places?'

'I get invited and it would be rude to say no, and sometimes I go because I haven't been out all week, or I had a difficult weekend and need to blow off steam myself.'

'Why would you have a difficult weekend?'

He shrugged. 'I don't. Not really. Perhaps difficult is the wrong word to use. I, er…have a young daughter. Beatrice. We, er—how shall I say this?—have a difference in communication style.'

'Oh. A pre-teen. Must be challenging sometimes? Is she at home?'

'No. She attends boarding school in the week. She comes home on Fridays, goes back Sunday evenings.' He looked up the road again as a car's lights illuminated the street as it turned the corner. 'This looks like you.'

He said he sometimes had difficult weekends. His daughter was at home weekends. Did they not get along? Some dads found it difficult to be with their daughters. Found they were having problems bonding, perhaps? She knew because that was what she'd experienced with her own father. He'd been in the army and had often been posted away for long periods of time and when he had come home, it was as if he hadn't known how to be a civilian. Hadn't known how to talk to her and so he hadn't bothered. She'd yearned so much for her dad to give her a hug, to tell her he loved her, that he was proud of her, to take an interest in her life, but he never had. Or had never been able to breach that chasm between them. He'd died never truly having had a proper, in-depth conversation with her about anything of note.

The taxi was pulling up in front of them. Isla shrugged off Gabe's jacket, to give it back to him. She stepped close, smiling, handing it back, her mouth forming a thank you, when suddenly there was a shout from behind them.

'Gabriel!'

They both turned and Gabe swore softly. 'Damn! Hide!'

Hide? There was nothing she could do but raise his

jacket to shadow her face as the whole street suddenly lit up with a flash of a photo being taken. Isla suddenly felt frightened, frozen to the spot, Gabe's jacket over the top of her head as Gabe himself swung open the taxi door and told her to get in quick.

Isla did so, clambering in, but she didn't want to leave him out there, all alone, without his jacket, with the paparazzi, and she called to him. 'Get in the car!'

Gabe looked at her, startled, then got in with her and he yelled at the taxi driver to just get going.

The car engine roared and they escaped, Gabe settling back into the seat with a sigh and an order for the taxi driver to go to Hammersmith. Then he turned to her. 'Sorry about that. Someone from the restaurant must have called someone, or texted someone, and then that happened.'

'How do you even live like that? Knowing someone could take your picture at any moment?'

She passed him his jacket back and he shrugged it on. 'I've got used to it. I don't like it, so I don't go out much. It got worse after I was snapped with Elizabeth Traynor. They thought they had a great fairy tale they could peddle. England's finest actress, single, beautiful, seen with eligible widower, out on the town.' He shook his head. 'It's what they chase. The fairy tale. Imagined relationships. Romances. It sells copies and ruins lives. But they don't care about that last part.'

'I'm sorry they do that to you. Do you think they got a good picture?' She hated the idea that she might now appear in some gossip mag: *Gabriel Newton's Mystery Woman!*

'I hope not, but I guess we'll find out.'

'Whereabouts in Hammersmith, love?' asked the taxi driver.

'Penny Road. Next to the Black Bridge pub.'

Gabe leant forward and passed a large note to the driver. 'Appreciate you keeping this quiet, all right?'

'Will do, mate.' The driver took the note and slipped it into his shirt pocket.

It was all very cloak and dagger. Isla wasn't sure how to feel and so she did what she always did. She giggled. Then laughed. Holding her belly, because it hurt so much as she guffawed at the whole situation, Gabe joining her. For a moment there, she'd thought she was in danger, but she hadn't been, and Gabe had rescued her and thrown her into a taxi and now he was paying that taxi driver to keep his silence! It was incredible! 'I never thought the evening would turn out like this,' she said, once she'd got her breath back. Breathing, trying to regain her composure.

Gabe was smiling. 'Nor me. Strangely. I'm sorry you got dragged into my mess.'

'It's okay. I had fun tonight, which was something I'd not expected.' And it was true. She'd not expected to enjoy a single moment of it. When had she last enjoyed herself like that? When had she last belly-laughed like that? Not for *years*. She looked at Gabe, because she wanted him to see that she wasn't offended. She wasn't upset.

He looked back at her. Those dark blue eyes of his twinkling in the shadows of the car. His hesitant half-smile. His gaze dropping to her mouth and then back to her eyes.

Isla swallowed as the mood shifted in the car. Felt herself grow hot.

'I've never been rescued by a maiden before,' he said softly.

She coloured, feeling heat bloom in her cheeks. Her

neck. Her chest. Feeling butterflies swirl in her stomach. 'It was my pleasure. To be honest with you, I've always felt like the one that needed rescuing.'

He was staring so intently at her that they didn't notice the car pull to a stop.

She was so busy staring into his eyes, allowing herself to drown in them, that she didn't even hear the taxi driver clear his throat and say, 'We're here, love.'

Gabe's hand reached up. Tentative. Slow. He caressed her cheek, his hand against her skin sending bolts of lightning through her body as she came alive, her breath catching in her throat.

'Ten quid. When you're ready.'

The driver's voice cut through the moment this time and Isla suddenly started and turned away, embarrassed, blushing. She pushed open the car door and reached into her clutch bag to pay the driver.

'I've got it. Don't worry,' said Gabe.

'No, I must pay. I—'

'It's fine. Honestly. Go inside.' Gabe had clambered from the car, too and stood behind her as she fumbled in her bag, this time for the keys to her friend's flat where she was currently staying until she could find a place of her own. She could feel the gazes of both men and it made her clumsy, the keys dropping to the floor.

Gabe reached them before she could and then, when they were both standing again, he passed them over.

She smiled at him, thankful, and inserted the key into her lock and opened the door.

Was she to ask him in for coffee?

No. She couldn't possibly do that.

'Thank you. For a…lovely evening,' she managed.

'Good night, Isla. I'll see you tomorrow,' he said, clearly waiting to make sure she got inside safely.

She gave him a nod and stepped inside, closing the door shut behind her and flicking the switch up on the lock to double-secure it. Isla let out a long breath and let her clutch drop to the floor. She kicked off her heels, then made her way up the stairs, feeling incredibly drained and unsure of what had just happened.

She and Gabe had had a moment.

A true, heart-stopping moment! And not just once, either! That moment at the restaurant, when he'd brushed past her on the veranda and his fingers had caressed hers. The way he'd protected her with the journalist and then the moment in the car.

He was going to kiss me!

What did that mean for them now? How were they going to work together?

Maybe I should go into his consulting room tomorrow? Ask for a private word? Tell him that nothing will come of it and that we'd both just been caught up in a moment?

Isla refused to get caught up in any fairy tale.

Because something bad always happened to the princess.

CHAPTER FOUR

'I THINK I just look tired. A bit droopy. I need you to give my eyes back their youthful appearance, because I used to be offered roles on television that were for daughters or young wives and the last role I got offered? Menopausal mother! I swear the next one that comes in will be for someone's granny.'

Gabriel smiled sympathetically. 'Have you had any eye surgery before?' he asked as he came around his desk to examine the face of a minor television celebrity who'd once had the recurring role in a soap opera of a wayward twenty-something.

'Not my eyes. Botox in my forehead. Lip fillers. Nothing more than that.'

He nodded. To him? Her eyes looked fine. Perfect for her age. Cleo Jones was in her late thirties, according to the press. In her medical file? Forty-three. But she did have ptosis, a little excess skin on her upper eyelid. The bags under her eyes, hidden by make-up, made her eyes look a little asymmetrical, so he could correct that. 'Have you ever been diagnosed with dry eyes? Or any type of eye condition?'

'No. I wear glasses to read.'

'That's fine. And do you smoke?'

'Socially.'

'It would be best if you could stop before the surgery as smoking can really have an effect on the speed of the recovery process.'

'Consider it done,' she replied. 'Anything to get better roles.'

Gabe sat back down and went through Cleo's medical history, past issues, if she was on any current medications. He performed a detailed examination of her eyes, her eyelids, her facial skin and assessed the underlying tissues. He took photographs from all angles and fed the images into the computer to show her what her eyes might look like post-surgery.

'That looks great!' she said.

'You understand that these are the optimum outcomes for surgery, but every surgery carries a risk. Blepharoplasty is a safe operation, relatively, and offers many aesthetic benefits, but it still carries a risk of infection, swelling, eye problems, bruising or even secondary surgery.'

'I do. I know you have to tell me the risks. But look at what happens to me and my career if I don't have this surgery. I lose work. I lose the best roles and you have no idea what that will do to my current state of mental health. I can't keep losing out to Petra.' He had no idea who Petra was, but assumed it was another actress.

'Well, let's schedule another appointment in two weeks. This will give you time to think about the procedure, read up on the risks and have some time to speak to our on-site counsellor.'

'I don't need a shrink.'

'Maybe not, but they are there to discuss any concerns you may have.'

'Two weeks? And then I'll have the surgery?'

'If you're still keen to go ahead, we'll get you booked in.'

'Good.' Cleo stood and reached across the table to shake his hand. 'I was told you're the best.'

'And the awards show last year told me that you were the best supporting actress.'

Cleo groaned. 'Supporting actress! I gave that role my all. I should have got lead actress.'

'Well, maybe this year? Or the next? Once you've recovered.'

She smiled. 'I shall hold you to that, Gabriel. We should meet for drinks one time. I'm having a birthday party in August. You should come.'

'Thank you.'

'I'll get Martin to send you an invite. Save the date!'

'I certainly will.' He said goodbye to Cleo and had gone to write up his notes when there was a knock at his door. 'Come in!' He didn't look up to see who it was. He figured it was probably Jane with a tray. She normally came at this time with tea or coffee and some biscuits.

'Can I have a word?'

Not Jane.

He glanced up. Swallowed hard.

It was Isla. Looking all nervous and anxious. Unable to meet his gaze. She looked...traumatised. It was the only word for it.

'Sure. Take a seat.' He indicated the recently vacated chair left by Cleo.

'No, thanks. I'll stand. This won't take a minute.'

Isla had lain awake all night, thinking. Listening to police sirens go past, patrons from the pub stumbling out of the door and making their way down the street. All the time, just staring up at the shadows on the ceiling, but not really seeing it. Instead, her brain had given her snatches of images. Thoughts. Feelings. The way Gabe had looked when she'd entered the restaurant. The way he'd leaned in to kiss her cheek. Phillip and Mohammed had done the same thing, too, but her brain wasn't rerunning *those* moments. The way Gabe had looked at her on the veranda right before he'd left, the brush of his fingers against hers, the way he'd leaned in towards her at the table in the restaurant to help her translate the French menu.

The way he'd looked at her in the taxi. Stroked her cheek. Gazed at her mouth.

That was day one. Day one of employment and already it was getting complicated and she *did not need* complicated in her life. She'd had that. Been paralysed by that. Had pressed pause on her life to deal with everything. She did not need Gabe to be another complication.

And so she'd got up that morning, determined to start this day afresh. She would eat, get dressed, go into work and be the best surgical nurse the Garland Clinic had ever seen! The thought had propelled her, rejuvenated her, had even made her feel that everything would be all right.

Until she'd opened her front door.

'I won't take up too much of your time,' she said, feeling a million emotions broiling away.

'It's fine.'

She nodded. Managed a smile that disappeared as fast as it came. All night she'd been rehearsing what she'd say. All morning, whilst she'd struggled to force down some breakfast.

Until she'd opened her front door.

But now that she was here, now that she was standing before him, it was as though all of those words, all of those fine sentences she'd constructed, had got clogged up in her throat at once. 'I'm just a theatre nurse. I'm just here to do my job and for you to be my boss.' She paused, needing to swallow down her nerves. 'Last night…last night a few things happened and those roles, those boundaries somehow…' She couldn't think of how to end that sentence.

'They got blurred,' he said, rescuing her.

Isla nodded. 'Yes. Yes, they did, and I don't think I can cope with…blurred.' She frowned, not sure if that sentence made any sense, but feeling it *somehow* did. 'Blurred is not for me. I need my life to be simple. Plain. Boring. To go to work, to do a good job and then to go home again. I don't need any more than that. I don't need to open my front door and have a bunch of journalists waiting to fire questions at me and take my picture!'

He stared back at her. Appalled. 'They found you.'

'Yes, they bloody well did! And they were waiting for me to come out! Waiting for me, like vultures, desperate to snatch at some scrap of meat left on the bones. Who was I? What was I to you? Whether we were serious!'

'I guess the taxi driver didn't keep his mouth shut, after all.'

She looked at him, blinking, surprised. She'd expected something more. She'd expected protests. She'd expected…what? Not this. Not this acceptance of everything she'd said. 'The taxi driver? That's what you're worried about? I had to run back inside my flat and hide. I had to clamber down the fire escape at the back, with an overnight bag, because I'm afraid they'll be waiting for me when I go back home! I've spent the morning calling friends I haven't spoken to in ages, looking for another place to stay, but no one's got anywhere and now I don't know what to do!'

He paused for a moment. Looked a little awkward, as

if to imply that his next sentence would only cause her more problems. 'I take it you've not seen what's online either, then?'

She blinked some more. Online? What did that have to do with…? *Oh, God! The paparazzi!* 'No.'

Isla watched, mute, as Gabe tapped at the screen and brought up the site of celebrity journalist, Mack Desveaux, and showed it to her. She stared and felt all of the air in her lungs leave her body as if in one breath. There she was, in picture form, behind Gabe, her face obscured by her shawl as she clambered into the taxi, Gabe obstructing most of the picture with his palm out to block the camera. The headline was *Who is Gabe's Mystery Woman?*

'Oh, my God…' She leaned against his desk and began to read the story beneath it.

Last night Gabriel Newton, thirty-eight, eligible bachelor, widower and millionaire, was seen outside exclusive restaurant Jean Luc's with a mystery blonde woman, who managed to escape into a taxi before her identity could be captured.

Questions mount as to who she might be. Gabriel is often photographed with some of the country's most beautiful women and he has never, to our knowledge, protected the identity of his female partners, so what makes this one so special? Ideas speculate whether London's most famously single cosmetic surgeon has finally found someone to settle down with, since the terrible passing of his beautiful wife, Ellis, with whom he had a daughter, now twelve.

If you can help us identify this woman, then please get in touch.

Isla read the article twice, three times, before she lifted her gaze and stared at Gabe. 'I don't believe this!'

'You're in shock, I know. I can only apologise that you have been dragged into this.' He sighed. 'Let me get you some tea. Tea is good for shock.' He pressed the intercom on his desk. 'Jane? It's Gabe. Could you bring in a tray of tea for two people, please? Thank you.' He came around his desk, unbuttoning his suit jacket, and settled into the chair next to her. 'I thought if they didn't know who you were, they'd leave you alone. I never expected him to use that protection as some sort of fuel for the fire that surrounds my public life.'

'I guess it's good that they don't know who I am yet, but...what happens if they do find out?' She didn't need that. Didn't need them putting two and two together and looking into her past and dragging up all that history she had. She'd tried to move on from that. This job, coming here, was meant to be a fresh start. She couldn't have it tainted and she most definitely didn't want the papers or gossip mags digging up her past as some sort of entertaining story. Because she'd been hurt. Badly. It wasn't fodder for the masses to dine on.

'I'll protect you. I have lawyers.'

'And have them believing it's something more than it is? It was a work dinner! Can't we just say that? They'll back down, then, won't they?'

'If only it was that easy.'

A knock on his door signalled Jane's arrival. The receptionist came in, placing the tea tray down on Gabe's desk. 'Isla? You all right?'

She pointed at the screen.

'Oh. Yes, I saw that this morning.'

'Could you give us a minute, Jane?'

'Of course.' Jane disappeared from the room, gently closing the door behind her.

'I'm so sorry, Isla.'

'It's not your fault.'

'But it is. They were following me. Looking for a story about me and I gave them one. Making a statement of denial will just continue to fuel the story, I'm afraid. It's usually best in these instances to just say nothing. Do nothing and then they'll move on to someone else, if we don't react.'

'And if they don't?'

'I'd have to speak to my advisors.'

Isla laughed bitterly. 'You have advisors? How the other half lives.'

'What do you mean?'

'That you're used to this. This intrusion into your life. Being seen about town with gorgeous women. That you have PR people, or whatever they're called! I'm just a nurse. Just a person who wants her private life to remain private.'

'So do I.'

'Then why do you court notoriety? Why court all of those women and tease the press? It must work for you, or you wouldn't have continued to do it after the first story.' She didn't mean to say all of this, but she was angry. Angry and scared and afraid to go home.

'I have never pursued notoriety!' Gabe retorted, sounding irritated. 'But this Mack guy is just pursuing some old grudge because my wife, Ellis, chose me, rather than him. And so when I went to a party, after my friends begged me to, I got talking to some young woman, who, yes, was beautiful and, yes, showed interest in me and I had no idea who she was! I didn't know she was famous!

But she made me feel a little less lonely, if only just for one night, and after that? Mack never stopped. Once he found out my wife had died, that I was somehow this eligible guy, he went crazy! I never asked for it!'

She looked at him, feeling hurt, feeling bad for them both. They were both victims of a gutter press that looked for anything they considered salacious to sell copies. Even something innocent could be twisted and presented as something else. Something more titillating. Like a new-employee dinner somehow actually being a secret tryst with some new love. 'I can't go home. They'll be waiting for me.'

'You could stay with me, if you need to. I have a big place. There's a set of rooms where the nanny usually stays when Beatrice is home for the six-week break.'

'Live with you? Won't that just feed the fire?'

'They won't find out. The building has private, secure, underground parking, my car has tinted windows. They'd never see you arrive or leave with me.'

'I don't know you. It would be awkward. Strange. We only met yesterday!'

'I know, but if you can't find a place… I'm just trying to protect you.'

'Hasn't worked so far,' she answered, without thinking, then realised how horrible and ungrateful it sounded. 'Sorry.'

'No, it's fine. If you want to make a statement, then I'll agree to it.'

She did not want to make a statement. She did not want to give them any more information about her than they already had. They still didn't know her name, because the ones outside her flat had asked her for it. The flat she was staying at was a friend's. She was renting it until she found herself something more permanent. A place of her own. But if she gave them a statement, she'd have to say who she was and as soon as they got that information… She'd gone back to her maiden name, but someone would surely see through that eventually… 'It would be easier if there wasn't something I didn't want dredging up again. I've tried to move on with my life, Gabriel. This is meant to be my fresh start.'

He frowned. 'Well, how bad is it?'

'It's bad.'

'Your CV was outstanding. I take it it was something private, then?'

She nodded. 'I want to be able to tell you about it, but…if I do, I don't want you making a big deal over it. Not any more.'

Gabriel seemed deep in thought. 'You should only tell me if you feel comfortable doing so. But I can assure you that I have never betrayed anyone's confidence before and I would not betray yours with anyone else here. Or out there.' He waved vaguely at the window, indicating the outside world.

'I don't want to talk about it here. I just want to get on with my job. Later, maybe.'

'Then *do you* want to stay at mine? The offer is there, until the press presence dies down.'

Isla knew she did not want to have to fight her way through a small skirmish each time she entered or left her home. And Gabe seemed really sincere. He was completely different from how she'd imagined him being. From reading about him in the gossip columns. And he was her employer! Well, one of them. How much time would she have to be alone with him, really? His daughter would be there on weekends, and workdays, she could maybe stay in her room? Lock the door, if she felt she needed to? 'Thank you. I might take you up on that offer. But what about your daughter? Won't she be confused if you have some strange woman stay at yours? Or is she used to it?'

Gabe smiled and shook his head. 'I've never had a strange woman stay at mine. Just nannies, or family members. No celebs. No one-night stands. I'm not that kind of guy.'

'Okay. Thank you. But just for a few days. No more than that.'

'A few days. Till the heat dies down.'

Isla gave a small, nervous laugh. 'I wasn't sure how this conversation was going to go. I'd practised it, but you never can tell how the other person might respond. I wasn't sure I'd still have a job after it, to be honest with you.'

'And lose a brilliant nurse? Never.'

She smiled at him, thankful for his understanding. 'Will everyone who works here say nothing to the press?'

'They never have before. I see no reason why they would now. I trust them. Wholeheartedly. Even Justin.' He smiled.

She nodded, knowing that trust, from her, might take a little longer. But if she was going to live with Gabe for a bit, then she would need to trust him. She hadn't been alone with a guy, for a long time. And now she was going to move into his house, even if it was only temporary. Two days? Three? Surely it would all be over by then?

But, more than anything, she knew she would have to tell him what scared her so much. What she was so afraid the press might find out that would make the story of herself and Gabe sell even more copies. Because Gabe wasn't the only one with a sad and tragic past. She had one, too.

And she'd never ever seen any version of her story in any kind of fairy tale.

CHAPTER FIVE

'THIS WAY.' Gabe opened the door from the parking garage that led to a small foyer that had two options. 'Lift or stairs?' he asked.

Isla eyed the lift and seemed to look wary. 'Stairs, please.'

He nodded and led them up.

There'd been no problem leaving work. There was a private parking area there, too, and at the end of their working day, he'd waited for Isla to be free, catching up on some paperwork, whilst she finished tidying the theatre from the last surgery. Cleaners would come in later this evening, to do the consulting rooms and waiting area. Then, when she was free, he'd walked her to his car and she'd got in, nervously, after placing her holdall in his boot, and he'd driven her home to his place near Hampstead Heath.

He'd already acknowledged to himself that day that what had happened had just been crazy. He'd only met Isla yesterday and yet here he was, inviting her to stay in his home for a day or two, until the press furore died down, but this was the type of life he lived now. He'd not been out to a party or socialising for a while and he'd hoped that maybe Mack had lost interest in him, but clearly not. His fifteen minutes of fame had long surpassed fifteen minutes and he was uniquely sorry that Isla had been drawn into it. He'd thought he was helping, trying to protect her. Trying to shield her. Instead, it had just made everyone think that he cared more for her than he had any other woman that he'd been out with.

Maybe he did?

The other women, they'd been temporary. Women whom he'd known he would only see for that evening. They were dinner companions, dancing partners, but they'd never been anything more than that. They'd been distractions, a way for him to forget how lonely he was and to pretend, even if it was just for an evening, that he wasn't alone. He never brought them home. Nor had he ever gone back to theirs. He wasn't that stupid. Not with the press around. In fact, the press had been an effective excuse for him to not have to date any more. His parents kept telling him that he'd be ready to move on from Ellis one day and maybe marry again, but he'd never believed that. And though the press were a pain, they were also helpful.

Isla, though, wasn't temporary. She was a member of staff. A member of his team and he would have to see her and work with her every day. She did not deserve the intrusion of journalists and their cameras, desperate for some image. And so he'd tried to protect her, believing that he was doing the right, chivalrous thing, and it had only become a nightmare for Isla and he'd felt guilty.

Offering her a safe haven had seemed only the right thing to do.

Unlocking the door to his house, he led her inside. 'Welcome home. Make yourself comfortable.'

'Thank you for this. I won't get in your way. You

won't know that I'm here,' she said as she followed him in through the hallway and into the main living space.

He saw her looking around and wondered how she viewed the place. Did she think it homely? Too masculine? He'd picked everything out himself. 'You can make yourself known. It'll be nice to have some company.'

She smiled nervously and he couldn't help but notice the way she clutched her holdall.

'Let me show you your room. You can unpack, take a moment to get settled in and look around. I'll make us both some supper.'

'You don't have to do that.'

'I know, but I want to, even though, I have to warn you, I'm not a great cook. I once set fire alarms blaring trying to boil an egg.'

Isla smiled. 'Well, maybe I can contribute there. I love to cook. I could cook for us, actually. A way to say thank you for letting me come here.'

He nodded. 'Let's show you your room.'

He led her up the stairs. There were two flights to get to her room, which was up in the attic spaces that had been converted two years ago, so were pretty modern. This was where Janice, the nanny that he usually hired to look after Bea during the six-week break, stayed. It was decorated in a soft grey colour, with white frames, sills and skirting boards. The dresser was a duck-egg-blue to match the bedside units of a double bed, adorned with many pillows and cushions of all textures. A door to the left led to an en suite bathroom with a shower.

'Is this okay?'

Isla nodded, a little dumbfounded. 'Okay? This is bigger than my friend's flat! It's perfect. Thank you.'

'Little bathroom through there, so it's entirely private,

and from the window over here…' he wandered over to it and opened the blinds to let in the late evening light '…you can see the heath. It's quite the view.'

'Wow.' She came to stand beside him. Looking out.

He couldn't help but turn to look at her as she gazed outside, her face filled with delight and wonder. He liked seeing that look upon her face. It changed her completely. As if whatever stress and baggage she carried every single day was lightened, even if just for a short time. Her eyes lit up, her cheeks glowed and he saw real happiness there. Real pleasure. All from a view that he took for granted every single day. 'I'll be downstairs. Want a tea or anything? Coffee? Something stronger, now that we're both not at work?'

She turned from the window, the sun creating a soft halo of gold around her head. 'Just tea, thanks. I'll unpack and freshen up, then I'll be down.'

'Take your time. There's no rush.' He didn't want to examine the feelings he was experiencing with her there. They were strange. Unexpected.

He'd not had someone to live with him at the house since Ellis died, apart from his daughter, or their occasional nanny, Janice. But that felt different from this. He knew Isla. Had a work relationship with her. Admittedly it was brand new, but still. It felt incredibly different.

It felt…nice.

Which was odd, because he'd got so used to living alone. Considered himself almost set in his ways. This was only going to be for a few days, but he thought… well, he thought it might be nice, even pleasurable to have her here. Someone to talk to in the evening. Someone to cook with. Someone to share a meal with. Adult company.

His thoughts whorled as he made tea in the kitchen.

Part of him telling himself he was being ridiculous, that there was no point reading anything into this. Isla was here because she had to be. Not because she wanted to be. She had been afraid to go home, because she'd been spotted with him. She was probably angry with him on some level, but wouldn't show it, because he was her boss, effectively. She seemed a lovely person, so she wouldn't say it, but he could bet that she felt that way.

Gabe did feel responsible for her being unearthed, but he was determined to make her stay here as comfortable as possible, so that the disruption to her life was as pleasurable as he could make it. And besides, there was something she wanted to share with him. She'd alluded to it at work. Something she didn't want the press to bring back up into her life and though, for the life of him, he couldn't guess at what it was, he hoped it wouldn't cause her any extra distress to bring it up with him.

After about fifteen minutes, he heard her footsteps on the stairs and she came into the kitchen.

'I…er…wasn't expecting guests, obviously, but we need to eat and so I've done a recce of the contents of my fridge and, embarrassingly, it's not much.'

She smiled. 'What do you have?'

'Eggs, milk, a tomato, potatoes and a jar of chillies,' he said. Then, embarrassed at such a short list, added, 'But I do have a full selection of herbs and spices.' He opened a cupboard door. 'A moving-in gift. I've not opened any of them, so they should be good. Or so far out of date that they ought to be labelled a hazardous waste.'

Isla smiled. 'I see. May I?'

He took a step back so she could acquaint herself with the items in his kitchen. Once she'd checked everything, she turned to him. 'Frittata?'

Gabe raised his eyebrows, 'You can make that?'

'Better than that. *We* can make that.' She smiled.

'What do you need me to do?'

She got him to peel potatoes. They didn't need many and, whilst he did that, Isla beat some eggs in a bowl with the chillis, some garlic and lots of black pepper from a pot that had not gone out of date. Not yet. When the potatoes were done, they put them on to par-boil.

'How did you learn to cook?' he asked.

'I used to help my mum when I was little. My dad worked away a lot—he was in the army—so I spent a lot of time with her. You pick some things up that way.'

'You cooked frittata when you were little?'

'No, not frittata. Mum was very much a meat-and-two-veg kind of woman. The most exotic recipe she ever cooked was a spaghetti bolognese and garlic bread. No, I had a lot of time at home a couple of years back and you wouldn't know it, because you work every day, but there are a lot of food and cooking shows on the telly these days. Whole channels devoted to it and I watched a lot.'

'Oh. Okay.'

'The thing that happened, the thing I don't want the press to find out about and bring back up, is the reason I was stuck at home.'

'You don't have to tell me if you don't want to. Not if it's upsetting. I completely respect your right to privacy.'

'I know. But you've offered me your home so that I can have some privacy and in turn I think I should tell you why. You've put yourself out for me and you didn't need to.'

'You don't owe me anything, Isla. It was my fault this happened to you in the first place.'

She smiled. 'Maybe. But I want to tell you. It feels right to tell you. I do want you to know. It will help you understand.'

'Okay. Shall we sit?' He indicated the small dining table that sat in the kitchen.

She felt nervous. Sick almost to tell him. To bring up something she'd sworn she'd never spend time thinking about again. But that had never been a promise she could keep, because the thing that had happened to her had had such knock-on effects on her life that it was with her every day. Every second. She never forgot about it and that was the problem.

'You know I used to work in a hospital as a surgical nurse.'

'Yes.'

'I loved my job there. I had great friends. Great colleagues. We were a family. I worked in A & E for a while, then moved into surgical. I worked in gynaecological surgery. We saw a great deal of cases there. The work was varied. I enjoyed it. One day, we had this patient come onto our ward. A lovely young woman, newly married. She and her husband were very much in love. She came in for a standard hysterectomy. She'd suffered for years with heavy periods and because she'd had two kids and wasn't planning on any more, the doctors agreed to remove her uterus. There were fibroids, all sorts of problems. We said we'd be able to make her life better.'

'Did it?'

'No. The surgery itself seemed to go well. It was afterwards when there were problems. When she came around from the anaesthetic, she seemed woozy, like most people, said a lot of funny things, but seemed fine. It was only when she was properly awake did we realise something had happened. Possibly a stroke. We did a scan and there was a clot in Broca's area.'

'Where we form speech.'

Isla nodded. 'She could talk, but her words were wrong. She mixed up nouns, she forgot names for people and we could see she was in distress. It was too late to use the clot-busting drug, so she had to have another surgery to remove the clot. I sat with her husband whilst it went on. He was terrified. Angry. They'd been told the risks of surgery, but no one ever thinks it will happen to them. He was angry at us and I had to get someone else to sit with him, as I began to feel uncomfortable. Unsafe.'

'Did he threaten you?'

'Not specifically. But I could see something in his eyes and I trusted my gut. We'd advised that the surgery was her best option—removing her uterus—her husband hadn't been so keen. He'd been wary of his wife having surgery. Had wanted her to try other ways to cope with the bleeding and the pain, but she wanted quick results. Permanent results.'

'What happened in her second surgery?'

'The clot was removed and she seemed to cope well with the surgery. But then her bad luck continued and she developed an infection. Her body, overwhelmed, went into sepsis. The doctors tried to get ahead of it, gave her antibiotics, but…she died.'

Gabe sighed. 'I'm so sorry.'

'I'd got to know her and her husband so well. He was devastated. Broken. I've never seen a man so…raw…with grief.'

Gabe swallowed.

Of course, he knew all about grief. She knew that he would understand that part, at least. Just maybe not the part that came next. 'You move on, don't you? As medical staff, you have to. You may have just lost a patient, but there's another patient in the next room and in the one after that and they're still here and they need comforting and support and your professionalism. I had to look after them and I did. It didn't mean I wasn't upset, I wasn't hurting, but it's part of the job. You switch off that part of you so that you can help someone else, and you blow off steam in the staffroom and tell stupid jokes and laugh in the face of such overwhelming upset.'

He nodded. 'It's part of the job.'

'Her husband didn't get that part.'

Gabe frowned now. 'How do you mean?'

'I didn't know, but he saw me. Heard me. Laughing in the staffroom at something and it created in him a rage that…' She swallowed. 'A rage that consumed him. He was waiting for me, in the staff car park, at the end of my shift.'

Gabe stood up straight, looking alarmed.

But she knew she had to go on. Knew she had to tell him the whole thing. She'd come this far, he needed to know. 'He came out of the shadows as I was looking for the keys to my car in my handbag. All I wanted to do was go home and raise a glass to his wife's memory. To shed my tears there. Only he stopped me. Grabbed me.'

Gabe stared. 'What did he do?' he asked quietly.

'He said I hadn't cared. That to me, his wife had just been a piece of meat and that he would treat me the same way. He hit me, with his fist, in my face. I remember falling to the ground, I remember, strangely, the smell of the parking garage—petrol, exhaust fumes, cigarettes—but, thankfully, not much of the attack that followed.'

Gabe rubbed at his face. 'Dear God…'

'He hit me. Kicked me. A lot. Broke four ribs, shattered my jaw. I believe he was going to do more to me. He ripped my uniform open, but I must have begun to scream or something, because people came running. He ran away, but I was able to tell the police who it was and he was arrested, whilst I had surgery to fix my face.'

Isla gave herself a moment to breathe slowly. 'He was put in prison for GBH, but he's out now. Good behaviour.' She smiled wryly. 'He thinks we ruined his life, so he ruined mine. He didn't go after the surgeon because he was a big, tall six-footer of a man, so he came after me because he heard me laughing at a joke. Because I was small. Weaker than him. An easier target for his anger. So, he ruined me. Ruined my marriage. Somehow it came between us. Karl was frustrated that he couldn't protect me, I was angry that he wasn't there when he'd meant to be meeting me after work and we ended up splitting up. It should never have happened, but our relationship had been tense before that anyway, so...it was just the final push it needed to go over the edge.'

'I'm sorry. That's why you don't want the press finding out who you are.' A realisation swept over his face. 'You were *Isla Green*, weren't you? I remember the case in the paper now. Because of your case we ensured our staff had a secure car park. That's why I thought I recognised you.'

'I went back to my maiden name.'

He nodded. 'What happened should never have been allowed to happen. I'm so sorry you had to go through that.'

'Not as sorry as me. It's made me wary of men. Wary of laughing at jokes. Of having fun. It always makes me feel guilty. Like I should never be happy again.'

'You can't let that man's bad choices rule your life.'

'I know, but it's easier said than done.'

The potatoes had begun boiling away at some point, and Isla turned them off and grabbed a strainer to drain off the water. She placed the potatoes on the side and turned to look at him. 'Your security means a lot to me. It's one of the reasons I wanted the job. To get back my career. To start afresh. To begin again. I don't need my past being dredged up. I've already fought so hard to put it behind me.'

He nodded. 'I won't let them bring it up.'

'You can't decide that,' she said softly. But she was grateful for his answer. His determination.

'Maybe not. But I can keep you safe. You need to trust me on that.'

He stood right in front of her now. Close. Too close? Isla smiled gratefully, but backed away. His proximity was too much. Her brain felt too full of thoughts. Ideas. Imaginings with him this close. He was handsome. More handsome than any man had any right to be and this close? That perfection was overwhelming. His blue eyes so bright. His lips so welcoming. His jaw, solid and square. But it was the way he was looking at her, that promise of protection, that he would keep her safe.

It was dizzying.

'Gemma Hargreaves?' His patient sat in the waiting room, looking nervous, her nose clearly bent out of shape, but, surprisingly, sitting next to her was Isla, in her scrubs, and she was holding Gemma's hand. Clearly some connection had already been made. 'Isla can come in too, if you'd like?'

'If that's okay?'

'Of course it is.' He stood back, smiling as they both

entered the room and sat down. 'You're here for a rhino-plasty consult, is that correct?'

Gemma nodded. 'Yes, as you can see it's a little out of shape thanks to an ex-boyfriend.'

Isla was holding her hand and now he understood why they had bonded. He examined Gemma, with her permission, talked her through her options, letting her know he would have to rebreak the cartilage in her nose to straighten it. She seemed to flinch at that, but unfortunately it was a necessary part of the process. 'But obviously you will be completely anaesthetised.'

'Will it hurt?'

'It will be uncomfortable, but we can prescribe you some painkillers and give you advice on self-care afterwards, so that we try to make it as painless as possible.'

'Sign me up,' Gemma said simply. 'I'm not going to let what that man did sit on my face for all to see for the rest of my life. It feels like he branded me and I want all traces of him gone.'

Gabe knew that he could fix the physical for Gemma. But the emotional hurt? The mental hurt? That might take longer. When she was gone, he turned to Isla. 'You okay?'

'I felt her pain. I'd brought a discharge form out to Jane on Reception and we were chatting when Gemma came in. She looked so nervous! So I sat next to her and she began to tell me her story and I just knew exactly how she felt. I guess we connected.'

'I'm not surprised.'

'When she spoke about trying to erase the brand he'd left on her...my heart almost broke for her. Do you know that most women are attacked by someone they know? By someone who supposedly loves them? It's a shocking statistic.'

'It must make it hard to trust anyone.'

'I'm always looking over my shoulder, you know? Wondering if he's there. If he still holds a grudge. The victim's justice worker assigned to me said that he'd changed in prison. Accepted his role in what happened and had sought forgiveness from God, but that he'd like to receive forgiveness from me, write me a letter, but I didn't want it. Now I'm terrified he'll find out where I'm living now and visit me, just to say sorry.'

'It's wrong that you should have that hanging over you.' He'd got closer to her, passed her a tissue when he'd seen that she was near tears from it. The man's sentence was over, but it was never going to be over for Isla. He'd wanted to comfort her. Make her see that not all men were like that. That some men were tender. Kind. Considerate. He hoped he'd made Gemma feel the same way. That he could be trusted.

She'd taken the tissue. Dabbed at her eyes with it, then laughed. Gulped. 'Look at me,' she said. 'I should be over this, right? It happened years ago.'

'Two years ago. Not that long.'

She leaned in, rested her head against his arm and the temptation to put his arm around her and pull her close was overpowering in its intensity.

But Isla was vulnerable. Fragile. He didn't want to take advantage. But she'd leaned into him, right? She'd sought comfort from him? So he lifted his arm, draped it around her shoulder, gave her a supportive squeeze to let her know that he cared and that she was safe here with him.

Gabe had never been a victim of crime. He'd never been assaulted. But he'd dealt with patients who had been and he knew trauma like this very often never went away. Victims carried it with them always. Like a shadow. Sometimes unseen.

She sniffed. Dabbed at her eyes and then looked up at him, gratitude in her eyes, thankfulness in her gaze, but something happened in that moment with him standing there, holding her close. Her looking up at him, her eyes glassy with tears of pain and fear.

He wanted to kiss her. Pull her close and take her in his arms and show her that a real man wasn't about violence, or strength or power. That a real man could respect her. Touch her tenderly. Value her. Admire her. Be wowed by her. And give her exactly what she needed in that moment.

She must have seen the intention in his eyes to kiss her.

Maybe his gaze had dropped to her full, very beautiful lips?

Maybe she'd sensed something in the way that he held her?

That realisation in her eyes, the realisation of his own how afraid she was of him in that moment, cooled his jets and he backed away.

He didn't want her to be afraid of him! He never wanted that from any woman!

'I…er…ought to get back to work,' she said, her cheeks ablaze with red.

'Of course. Yes. Thank you for your…assistance with Gemma. I'm sure she appreciated that very much.'

Isla nodded.

'It's good for people to know they have someone in their corner. I see it all the time when I go to India.' He thought of all the women he treated there. Women who'd had acid thrown in their faces from spurned men. Angry men. The women that turned up alone to his clinic frequently took longer to heal and get over their trauma than those that had support.

'I—I'll see you later.' And Isla slipped from his room.

Gabe sank into his chair when she'd gone, head in his hands. How had he let that happen?

When they got back home that evening, they settled into an awkward routine. Her watching him carefully, assessing him from across the room. He would chatter inanely about anything, keeping their conversations brief, light, uncomplicated. He expected at any moment that she would say that she would leave, go back to her place, but she didn't, because the press still weren't letting it go. They'd released an article guessing at who his mystery woman was and had suggested five women whom it might be.

All wrong, thankfully.

But tonight? Beatrice came home from boarding school. He'd already called her at school. Told her of their guest and why she was there and Bea had seemed fine with it. Happy almost that they would have a buffer.

He had to admit, he struggled when Bea was home. Always feeling as if he couldn't do anything right. That he was somehow letting her down. That he wasn't enough for her. She was twelve years old, but already he felt as if he were dealing with a teenager. She was so much more mature than her years and yet still a child. It was a confusing mix. For her, as well as for him.

Gabe always tried to make their weekends special. They had a week to catch up on, he wanted to spend time with her, yet she often just sat in her room.

Maybe with Isla there, it might somehow be different? Now he'd have two women who would be awkward around him.

He needed to go and pick her up. The boarding school was just outside London and, though he could pay for the school bus to bring her home, he liked to fetch her himself.

'I'll be back in a couple of hours,' he said to Isla as she began bustling in the kitchen. Part of him wanted to stay and be with her. To sit and talk to her and watch her as she cooked as he had this week. It was nice. It was easy. Being with Isla was surprisingly easy if they talked about inconsequential things. He'd not realised how much he missed having someone around the place. But was it Isla he liked, or just having another person? Ellis had cooked for him, too—knowing his inability to even boil an egg correctly without setting the place on fire. He'd loved his wife's cooking. Had loved walking through the door of an evening and having the delicious aromas of whatever she was cooking drift into his nostrils and dazzle his senses. 'What's on the menu tonight?'

'Just a casserole. Some roast potatoes. They'll keep in the oven until you're both back.'

'Well, hopefully, we won't be too bad, but it is London traffic and Friday evening, so...' He shrugged. Sometimes he and Beatrice got stuck in traffic jams for hours. It was never a problem for her. She'd just stick in her EarPods and listen to some music or an audiobook, whereas he'd have to sit there, hands on the wheel, cursing about delays and trying to start conversations only for Bea to not hear him at all.

'I'm looking forward to meeting her. You're sure she won't mind me being here?'

'Are you kidding me? She's going to love having you here. Means she won't have to talk to me!' he joked, even though, technically, he was being serious. He couldn't pinpoint exactly when it was that his relationship with

Bea had begun to falter. Her early years, up to the age of four, she'd been wholeheartedly reliant on him and not noticed that she was lacking in the mum department—even if there had been nights where her crying as a baby had been difficult and he'd dreamed of being able to hand her off to someone else, if just for a minute...

Had it been when he'd hired the first nanny?

When he'd sent her to boarding school?

When he'd bought her that bike for Christmas because he'd thought she was ready for one, even though she'd been asking for a keyboard all year? He could have bought both. Money wasn't a factor, but he'd not wanted to spoil her. Not wanted to throw money at her as a substitute for the lack of a maternal figure. He'd tried to raise her right and yet was failing her enormously. He'd even thought of pulling her out of boarding school, sending her to a normal one, just so that she could be at home all the time, but when he'd suggested it to her, she'd looked at him as if he were out of his mind.

'All my friends are there! Why would you do that?' she'd asked.

Well...yelled. She'd even slammed a door or two, as a teenager might have. And the thing was, he'd known that wasn't a solution, even when he'd suggested it. Because he would never have been home in time to look after her when she got back from a school day. He would have had to hire more staff to take care of her. Nurses to make sure she stayed well and did her clearance exercises. She'd probably end up with a better relationship with people he'd hired than she had with him.

So he'd kept her in Hardwicke Boarding School, kept bringing her home each weekend and kept hoping beyond hope that, one weekend, they would have a breakthrough.

They would understand one another. That he would somehow get back the daughter he missed so much. The daughter that he and Ellis had dreamed of.

'Do you…want me to come with you? Keep you company on the journey? We can turn the food down really low, or off, if you'd prefer, and reheat when we get back.'

Gabe was grateful for her offer. The gesture that offered to show everything was fine between them. That she was trying to put the near kiss to one side. But he wasn't sure how Bea would react to that. He'd told his daughter that Isla was just a colleague, hiding from the press, because of course Bea had seen the article herself. Her friends always showed her anything that had him in it. So, if he turned up with Isla, she might see something more in it? The way he had, briefly? 'That's very kind of you to offer, but—'

'Of course. It's okay,' Isla interrupted, blushing. 'I understand you'll want some alone time.' She walked away then, into the living room, to make it easy for him to go without her.

It was probably best, anyway. There'd be an awkward tension in the car on the way home, did he really want one going there, too? He and Isla stuck in that small space together? With no escape for either of them if one of them accidentally brought up something they shouldn't?

He had thought about kissing Isla and Isla had been afraid and he'd hated that. He wasn't someone to be afraid of. And though he knew it was nothing to do with him, but with her past, it still didn't make it any better.

One day, it might be. But not right now.

Gabe picked up the car keys from the hook on the side. 'Back soon!' and he took the stairs down to the car park.

CHAPTER SIX

ISLA LET OUT a huge breath of relief when she heard the door open and close, Gabe's footsteps retreating down the stairs to the car-park entrance.

Things had been awkward between them ever since he'd looked at her again as though he was going to kiss her. Honestly? She'd thought about kissing him, too, and that was what had terrified her the most. Not *him*. Not him because he was a man. But her own feelings! But she couldn't tell him that. That would make things even more awkward and she needed to hide out here—there was no place else she could go!

Hopefully, when his daughter arrived, it would make things simpler. Beatrice would be a buffer. They could talk to her, if not each other, and it would be nice to spend time with a young kid. She'd not spent any time around young kids for ages. Except her cousin's, but since moving to Hammersmith, she'd hardly seen them and she missed them. Kids were innocent. Kids were honest. They had no ulterior motives. They were funny. They enriched your life.

Isla dreamed of one day having children of her own. It was a dream that she'd always harboured, and when she'd married Karl, she'd thought that that dream was one step closer. They'd wanted to be married a few years and go travelling, though, before they had their babies, and so they'd not started trying, when Isla got attacked. To be fair, she'd not wanted to start trying back then, because she'd known things weren't right between them. They'd argued about simple things and she'd not wanted to start trying for a baby if they couldn't even agree about whose turn it was to do the laundry.

After the attack? Their marriage was even more difficult. The attack became the final blow that broke them apart. And her dreams of family, of babies, drifted away with the winds. Since then, she'd put the idea of having her own children to one side, believing that it could never happen now, because she wasn't sure if she could ever trust a man again to get close.

If you'd asked her months ago if she could envision a situation in a few weeks' time in which she would move into a man's house and live with him, as a guest, knowing that that man was some sort of celebrity surgeon, known for dating lots of beautiful women, she would have said no. Would have said it was crazy, and yet here she was. Cooking for him. Sitting with him in the evening and watching movies together.

That part? Was lovely, actually. Gabe didn't mind what they watched. He wasn't like Karl, who wanted to watch only action movies, superhero movies or war movies. Gabe was happy to watch romantic movies with her. Chick-flick movies. Ghost and haunted-house movies, which were her favourites. He'd sit on one couch. She'd be on the other. Each with a bowl of popcorn. And afterwards, they would sit and discuss what they liked, what their best bits were. If they thought certain scenes could have been different or better.

Isla liked that. She'd also liked discussing books with

him. Music. But food most of all, showing him recipes she'd found online and trying them out. Getting him to try her sauces as they were cooking, thrilling at his approval when he made all the right noises. She'd only been here a short while, but already she was beginning to feel incredibly at home. Gabe was letting her feel that way. Going out of his way to make her feel welcomed and comfortable, as if he knew what she needed.

Why couldn't it stay as simple as that?

Why couldn't they remain the friends and colleagues they'd been at the start?

Why had she felt attracted to him?

Why had she gazed at his mouth, milliseconds after his gaze had dropped to hers?

She'd thought about it. Thought about it a lot. Gabe might have a reputation as one of London's most eligible bachelors who had wined and dined many beauties in his time, but she also knew him as someone else.

He was kind. Protective. Loyal. A good friend. An excellent doctor and colleague. Intelligent. Easy to talk to. Friendly.

He'd made her feel protected. Secure. Safe. And that took a lot for anyone to do and he had done so in a matter of hours, and now?

It had changed.

Their relationship had changed. In that one moment that he'd held her in his arms.

She had changed.

And that was the most terrifying thing of all.

'Well, here we are. Do go and say hello to our guest before you vanish to your room,' Gabe said, carrying Bea's bags and books into the house.

Bea pulled her EarPods out of her ears. 'What?'

'I said—'

She grinned. 'Joking!' She shrugged off her coat and draped it over the stair banister. It fell to the floor, but she didn't notice as she headed into the kitchen, where he heard light voices and conversation as he grudgingly picked up her coat and put it on the coat rack where it belonged. Then he carried her bags upstairs and put them in her room.

The drive back had been as expected. Awkward. After her initial burst of conversation, where she'd moaned about having to wait *for ever* for him to show up, she'd got into the car and put in her EarPods. He'd ended up putting on the radio in the car, so he at least had something to listen to, as Bea hadn't spoken, except to ask what was for dinner.

'Casserole, I think, and roast potatoes. Isla's cooked.'

'Should taste nice, then.'

That had been it.

He'd yearned to ask her so much more. How her week had been. If she had any homework. What she'd been up to. How her health had been. If she'd done her clearance exercises daily, morning *and* night. But each attempt had not been heard and so he'd given up. He knew that he ought to have motioned to her to take out her EarPods and listen to him. Demand it, as her father, to get her to show him some respect. But they had such a short time with one another and it was already difficult. He didn't want to add any further resentment and so he let it slide, even though he knew it was probably the wrong thing to do.

He stared at the things in her bedroom. He didn't come in here often, but when he did he always noticed one particular thing. Bea had a photo next to her bed of her mother. The only one that they'd managed to take of Ellis holding Bea, who was only seconds old, before tragedy had struck.

Bea did not have a photo of her dad on her bedside table. He'd often thought of having one framed and putting it in here, to see if she'd notice, to see if she'd keep it out, but he wasn't sure he'd be able to take the rejection if she moved it, placed it in a drawer.

Heading downstairs, he was slightly taken aback to hear laughter coming from the kitchen.

'...and then she laughed so much soup spurted out all over and hit Mrs Midler in the face!' Bea laughed so hard she began to cough. A thick, heavy cough he was used to hearing.

He'd not told Isla about it yet. Maybe he ought to have? Because he could see the look of concern on her face at hearing the cough. But he was so used to keeping Bea's condition out of the public eye—he didn't need Mack making that into a sob story, too, to fit alongside his 'grieving widower' backstory—that was why he'd not brought it up.

Isla looked to him, as if to say, *Do you hear that cough?*

'Bea has cystic fibrosis. That's what you can hear,' he said in a soft voice, hoping that Bea wouldn't be offended by just telling their house guest.

'Oh. Okay.' Isla smiled at Bea. Accepted it and simply moved on, as if she knew not to make a big deal out of it. *Nurses!* 'And what did Mrs Midler do then?' she asked.

Bea beamed. 'She made this weird squeaky noise and ran from the room!' More laughter between them. Clearly they'd hit it off, already. He felt envy hit him square in the solar plexus. Isla and Bea hadn't been together for more than a minute or so and already his daughter had shared more with his house guest than she ever had with him.

'Oh, my!' Isla put on some oven gloves to open the oven and check on the food.

He had to admit, the house had smelt delicious when they'd walked back in. 'Sorry we were late. There was lots of traffic—I hope the food isn't ruined.'

'No, it's fine! I kept it on low. Bea, why don't you go freshen up and I'll start serving, if you're both hungry?'

'Starving!' Bea said, rushing off to use the downstairs bathroom.

Gabe watched her go. When she'd closed the bathroom door and he heard the taps running, he turned back to Isla. 'She likes you.'

Isla smiled. 'I like her. You have a smart and beautiful daughter. You should be proud.'

'I am. Not that she ever lets me show it.' He grimaced and washed his own hands in the kitchen sink.

'You okay?' She came to stand beside him, looking at him curiously.

'Yeah, just...' He searched for the words to explain how he felt about his relationship with his daughter, but Bea came back into the kitchen before he could say anything. He muttered that everything was fine and then began to lay the table. 'Juice, Bea?'

'Apple, please.'

'Coming right up. Isla? What drink would you like with your meal?'

'Juice is good for me, too, thanks.'

The roast potatoes were perfect. Crispy on the outside, fluffy on the inside. The casserole was thick with gravy and overflowing with chunks of beef, carrot, celery, mushroom and onion. It was a hearty meal. Delicious. 'This is amazing,' he said. 'I don't think I've had a casserole since I was little.'

'I've been trying to expand your dad's cooking repertoire the last few days, Bea. Hopefully, I've taught him some things, so that the two of you can eat at home more.'

'Good. Someone ought to have done it. I learn cooking at school, but so far we've only done basic things—scrambled eggs and jacket potatoes. Though I think next week we're poaching pears!'

'Lovely! Do you ever get to bring home what you cook? I'd love to try your pears, if you do. Maybe your dad could bring them into work, if I'm gone by then.'

'I don't think so. Cooking is on Wednesdays, so... I don't come home till Fridays.' Bea's eyes darkened.

'Oh, that's a shame. Well, maybe if you print the recipe, you could come home and do it?'

'Maybe!' Bea perked up and shovelled in another mouthful of casserole. 'How long do you think you'll be here for? All weekend?'

Isla shrugged and looked at Gabe. 'Whenever it's all died down, I guess. As long as I don't outstay my welcome!' She laughed.

'You'll never do that,' Gabe said, quickly. He wanted her to feel that she could stay as long as she needed. He, for one, was happy to have her stay and it sounded as though Bea wanted her here all weekend, too. And whatever made his daughter happy was fine by him.

More than fine. Honestly? It was so nice to see her smiling.

Isla got up early and decided to go full out on breakfast. Gabe had arranged a food order and allowed her to choose whatever she wanted and, knowing Bea would be back, she'd wanted to put on a nice spread for his daughter. A thank you. To both of them. It had to be difficult to suddenly have a stranger in your home and she appreciated their gesture.

By the time Bea and Gabe came downstairs, she'd cooked bacon, sausages, two types of eggs—scrambled and boiled—toast, warmed up some croissants and *pains au chocolat*, poured juice, brewed coffee and set out two boxes of cereal. 'Ta-dah!' she said as they both arrived in the kitchen.

Bea tried to smile, but then began to cough.

Isla had heard her coughing upstairs. A deep hacking cough that had alerted her to the young girl being awake.

'Bea, you need to do your clearance exercises,' Gabe said.

'I know.' Bea opened up a small cupboard off to the side of the kitchen and removed an oscillation vest. Cystic fibrosis patients used them to help shift the mucus that they needed to clear from their systems every day.

Isla bit her lip. Should she stay out of this? Or help? 'You okay, Bea? Want someone to help you?'

'She doesn't need help. She knows what to do,' Gabe said, picking up a glass of juice and taking a swallow.

Bea stared at him briefly as she coughed some more, then turned to Isla. 'That would be nice, thanks.'

Ah. Isla was being pulled into a battle between father and daughter. She didn't want to cause any more problems than were necessary, but she had offered to help. 'Okay.' She came to sit beside Bea. 'What do you do first?'

'Huff coughing.' Huff coughing, Isla knew, was to help shift this mucus from her lungs. It required a person to take in a breath, hold it and then actively exhale it with a huff, as if you were trying to fog up a pane of glass.

Bea sat up straight and tilted her chin slightly up, mouth open. Then she took a slow and deep breath, her eyes fixed on Isla, who was supporting and encouraging her. Coaching her. Bea held her breath for a couple of seconds, then exhaled it, forcefully in a huff, which caused her to cough more and bring up the mucus.

It was important to shift it from the lungs as the mucus contained bacteria and could make a CF patient extremely ill.

'And again, that's it. You're doing well.'

Isla was aware of Gabe prowling in the kitchen, watching, listening, but saying nothing. She wanted to look at him, check in with him, make sure he wasn't annoyed that she was helping, but watching Bea struggle through her coughing and helping her with tissues to wipe her mouth and nose was more important. She wanted to be present for her. 'That's it. One more.'

After the huffing, Bea said she had to do her clapping. It involved getting into certain positions and having someone slapping along her back to help release any sticky residue. 'Who helps you with that when you're at school?' Isla asked.

'Matron does it.'

'And is she nice?'

'Yeah. Not bad.'

'And your dad does it here?'

'Yeah.'

Gabe stepped forward to assume his role.

'I want you to do it, though,' Bea said.

Isla glanced at Gabe, saw the hurt upon his face. 'Your dad should do it. He knows what he's doing. I don't.'

'He can coach you. Can't you, Dad?'

Gabe paused and Isla saw his jaw muscles clench.

'Sure. No problem.' He began to talk her through the exercises. Stood back, whilst Isla drummed along Bea's back. She tried her best to involve him. 'Like this? Or should I do this?'

He seemed grateful for her questions. Clearly he cared so much about his daughter, but couldn't connect with her. Now all those comments he'd made at work about his weekends being tense made sense. Were Gabe and Bea always like this with one another? What had gone wrong between them?

Bea put on her oscillation vest and sat reading a book, whilst she not so quietly vibrated in a corner, coughing and disposing of her tissues in a special container she had at her side.

'How long does she have to wear that for?' Isla asked Gabe in the kitchen.

'About twenty minutes.'

'And she does this twice a day?'

'Yeah.'

'It must be very difficult, as a father, to watch your daughter go through that?'

Gabe looked at her in surprise, then nodded. 'It is. But it's harder for her. She saw a consultant a few months ago. He told her that she may need a lung transplant in a few years and that hit her hard. It's one thing to do this twice a day, but another to know that, despite it, you still might have to undergo a scary operation to save your life.'

Isla reached out and stroked his arm, without thinking. He'd looked so hurt. So terrified himself. He'd already lost his wife—was he worried about losing his daughter, too? 'You'll get through it. You both will.'

'Will we? You've seen how she is with me. She hates me.'

'She doesn't hate you.'

'No?' He didn't believe her, clearly.

But what could she say right now? She didn't know either of them well enough to know exactly what was going on here. 'It's difficult right now, but it's not too late. This is fixable. You've just got to be willing to try.'

'I'm always trying! But she won't let me in.'

Isla could see unshed tears forming in his eyes and wondered how long this had been going on. She knew herself what it was like to have a father she couldn't reach. She would miss him desperately when he was away, but then when he'd come home, he'd seemed to be a person she just couldn't reach. So she'd stopped trying and had begun to resent his strange presence in the house. It had been like living with a ghost. It had resulted in her, as an adult, going out with a variety of men that were unavailable. It had been a difficult thing to resolve and work on and she didn't want that for Bea, or for Gabe. Their lives were difficult and scary enough.

'What do you normally do each weekend when she's here?'

'Not much. She plays in her room. Listens to music. I work in my office.'

'Then change that. Don't stop trying to reach her, Gabe. She may not act like it, but she *wants* you to reach her. She's floating on a raft, out to sea in stormy waters. She needs the safe harbour of her father.'

'Well, then, what do you suggest I do?'

Whilst Bea was in the bathroom getting ready after breakfast, Isla and Gabe were standing in his daughter's bedroom doorway, looking in.

'There.'

'What?' Gabe tried to follow Isla's finger. Was she pointing at the wall, or the collection of teddies?

'The K-pop poster on the wall. Does she still like them? Listen to them?'

'Are you kidding me? She listens to them all the time.'

'Excellent!'

'Excellent? Why?'

'Because...' Isla had seen a promotional poster for them last week on the Underground and if she wasn't mistaken... 'Here. Look.' She passed him her phone. 'They're on tour and have a concert in Brixton tonight and tomorrow night.'

'Tomorrow night she'll be on her way back to Hardwicke.'

'So tonight, then.'

'You want me to get tickets? It'll probably be sold out.'

'You don't know unless you try.'

Gabe thought for a moment and led Isla back downstairs to his office. Tapping a few keys on his computer brought up some information. 'Sometimes it's not what you know, but who you know. I met this music promoter a year or so ago and he...yes!' Gabe pointed at the screen. 'He might be able to get us in, if there aren't any tickets left.'

He dialled the number of the box office and, as expected, the concert was sold out. But his music-promoter friend was able to use his clout to let them use his VIP box. 'And that way, no one will see us out together.'

'You want me to come too?' Isla asked in surprise.

'Of course! You think I'm going to suffer through this alone? It was your idea!' He laughed.

Isla smiled. 'You're not meant to be suffering. You're meant to be bonding with your daughter.'

'Isn't that the same thing these days?' He winked and then went to the bottom of the stairs and called up. 'Bea? When you're free can you come here a minute?' Gabe turned back to look at her. 'You think she'll like this?'

'I hope so. I guess we're about to find out,' she replied as they heard footsteps trotting on the stairs. Isla had to admit, she felt a small frisson of excitement herself. She'd never actually been to a music concert ever. And even though she wasn't familiar with the band, or their music, she knew they were hugely popular, so it had to be good, right?

Beatrice appeared in the doorway to her father's study. 'What's up?'

'We're taking you out tonight.'

Bea raised an eyebrow, suspicious. 'Where?' She sounded bored, already. Probably thinking her dad meant to take her to a supermarket or something.

'To see a show,' Gabe answered, smiling.

'I don't want to.'

'Not even when it's these guys?' Gabe turned his computer screen, so that Bea could see who he was talking about.

Her eyes widened in surprise, then she looked up at him. 'You're kidding?'

'Nope. I've got us a private box and, if we have time and it's not too late, we might be able to meet the band privately afterwards.'

'Really?' Bea's voice rose in surprise and awe. 'What time?'

Gabe checked the screen. 'Er…seven p.m. it starts.'

Bea squealed. 'Oh, my God, I've got to tell Jenny!' and she ran upstairs as fast as she could, a mixture of coughs and squeals, feet thundering, into her room to no doubt grab her phone and tell her best friend what she was doing that night.

Isla smiled. 'Well done. The first step in Operation Dad.'

Gabe was beaming. 'I think that's the first time I've made her smile like that in ages. It's a good feeling. I couldn't have done it without you, though,' he said, gazing at her with soft eyes. Eyes that were glassy with unshed tears.

Isla felt embarrassed under such close scrutiny. 'Of course you could.'

'No. I would never have thought of it. We'd have been two separate souls, in two separate worlds until she became a teenager and ran away or something, because she hates me.'

'Not true. She doesn't hate you.'

Gabe smiled. 'So...it's been a long time since I went to a concert. Think us oldies will need earplugs?'

She laughed. 'If cinemas are anything to go by, then... yes. I think we will!'

CHAPTER SEVEN

THEY WERE LATE leaving the house. Beatrice had tried on so many outfits that she couldn't make up her mind and then, when Gabe thought they could go, she began saying she needed to do something with her hair and put on some make-up.

'Bea, you're twelve, you don't need make-up.'

'But what if we meet Han Lee?'

Han Lee was the lead vocalist of Stride, the K-pop band that had taken the world by storm and the guy that Bea had as wallpaper on her phone.

'I'm sure he'll think you're great. Just as I do,' he'd said.

'But, Da-a-ad!'

He'd negotiated that she could do all of that in the car ride over, but that they must leave right now, or they'd be late and she'd never get to see them at all.

Isla had helped. Promising to sit in the back of the car with Bea and help her get ready.

Gabe was most grateful for Isla's help. It was crazy how his relationship with his daughter had changed so quickly in just *one day* with her around. Since hearing that they would be going to a concert, Bea had been different. Excited. Bouncy. Hadn't sneered at him, or rolled her eyes or any of the hundred usual things she might do if they had a conversation when she came home on a weekend. She'd texted her friends a lot. He'd heard her phone pinging with messages all day and when they'd sat down for lunch midday, she'd been so excited she almost hadn't been able to eat. But she'd sat with them. Chatted with them. Had actually smiled at him and given him a peck on the cheek before she'd gone back up to her room for the afternoon.

'What a difference a day makes,' he'd said to Isla as he'd helped her clear up the dishes.

'Imagine what she'll be like tomorrow,' Isla had replied, grinning.

'I think this might be our best weekend we've ever had.'

'Good. I'm glad.'

'And it's all thanks to you. Pointing me in the right direction. I think I'm so used to being the authoritarian, the teacher, the doctor, the physio, the nagger, that I forget to just be her dad.'

'I get it,' Isla had said. 'She doesn't have a mum and you want her to be brought up to take her illness seriously. You just have to remember that she's more than her diagnosis. The CF is a tiny part of her, as far as she's concerned.'

'Is that what she said to you, when you were both talking quietly, earlier?'

Isla had nodded. 'She thinks you don't see anything else. And I think, if you don't mind me saying, she hates the fact that you hide it from everyone. She thinks you're ashamed of having a sick daughter.'

'I'm not ashamed! I've just been trying to protect her. After losing my wife, I'm so terrified of losing Bea, too, that I crack down on her. Making sure she does everything right. Does her physiotherapy. Does her vest. Eats right. Exercises well. Thinks carefully of how she treats her body. I forget she's twelve. I forget that she just wants to have fun, like her friends, to live her life, but I've got her so tightly wrapped in a bubble that I never take her anywhere in case she gets sick.'

'I get it. I do. But you can't let her live her life like that. Because it isn't a life when you're so controlled by rules and regulations.'

Isla had spoken to him then about her father. His life in the army. Everything had had to be just so. Everything had had to be exact. Folded a certain way. Done at a certain time. So that he'd found it impossible to live his life normally when he'd come home and no one had been able to reach him. Gabe had felt her hurt. Empathised with her bewilderment at not being able to be enough to reach her father and chisel her way through to him. He'd wondered if he'd been doing the same to Bea.

He knew he had to let go of the restrictions he'd put her under. He'd thought he was keeping her safe. Keeping her healthy. But with him, she didn't get to live her life! No wonder she wanted to stay at her school, with her friends. It was where she was most free! At home, she felt trapped with him. A man she didn't understand, couldn't get close to. She must have been very sad indeed and he felt terrible for the way he'd approached his parenting.

So, driving to the concert, hearing Bea and Isla giggling in the back of the car as they listened to Stride through the car speakers was heavenly. It felt incredibly good to know that he was making his daughter smile. To make her happy. And though he worried about all the germs she might be exposed to by going to a music concert that would be closely packed with hundreds of people, he knew he had to let her live and experience the joy of life. Otherwise, what was the point? What was the point of any of it? Isla had been right, but why had he not seen it before?

When they parked up at the concert venue and his daughter emerged from the back of the vehicle, he openly gasped at what Isla had achieved with make-up for his daughter.

When Bea had said she wanted make-up, he'd imagined eyeliner, mascara, lipstick. His daughter trying to look older than her years. But again he'd got her wrong. Misread what she'd actually been trying to tell him. Because what she'd had done instead was that Isla had highlighted Bea's cheekbones, temples and just above her eyebrows with an icy blue colour and, in silver, had drawn on stars and sparkles, which were a motif the band used a lot in their promo. Bea looked amazing. Happy. Joyous.

'What do you think?' Isla asked him.

'I think you look stunning,' he said to his daughter, meaning it.

And Bea spontaneously hugged him, thrilled with his reaction and, shocked, unable to believe it, he took a moment, before lifting his own hands to hug her back, but by then it was too late. She'd let go again and was running off, hurrying them towards the entrance.

Gabe was stunned into silence.

Isla laughed, pulling down her own hat. He didn't think anyone had followed them here, but she was wary of being out and about with him again. Wary of being seen again. He'd noticed her grow more nervous as the day had passed and the time of the concert had got closer.

They showed their passes and were escorted to the VIP box, from which they had an excellent view of the stage. The venue was filled to bursting with people, mostly young girls, pre-teens and teenagers, though Gabe saw one or two adults, no doubt parents who had brought their kids. He felt an affinity with them. Wondered if they felt the same way he did.

On their way in, Bea had convinced him to buy some merch including a light up wand and, now they were in the box, he could see that almost every other person here had bought one, too. The concert had probably paid for itself already with merchandise purchases.

But he had to admit, the place looked great and, though he had to shout to be heard, he was having a good time. When the band came on stage, lights flashing, music thumping, everyone screamed with happiness. Stride looked to be a boy group and, not only were they good singers, but they performed dance routines, too, that he couldn't help but notice that Beatrice was copying as she sang and danced along. She coughed a few times and he was very much aware that normally, at this time of day, they'd be working on her breathing, her PT. Her oscillation vest. Getting her ready for bed.

It wouldn't hurt just this once to be late, would it?

A catchy tune began and he and Isla also began to dance. Just stepping from side to side, clapping their hands to the beat, smiling, having fun. He couldn't help but smile at Isla. She had given him this. This gift of this most precious time with his daughter. This chance to bond. And it was working out just fine! The VIP box meant Bea could enjoy something like this without him worrying that she might get sick from everyone else. They had a form of privacy. They weren't down in the pit with everyone else. He couldn't help but notice how some of the audience were pressed up tight against the security barriers, dancing, singing, waving banners, or their lit-up wands. In front of them were speakers and a line of burly protection detail for the band, who had their backs to the stage, watching the crowds.

'This is so great!' squealed Bea as they launched into another number. 'This is my favourite!'

She began coughing again and he tried not to freeze in fear, as he usually did when she had a bad coughing session, wondering if this would be the moment something went wrong. If this would be the time she couldn't catch her breath. If this would be the thing that would send her into hospital. It was a fear he lived with constantly and it was exhausting. But it was a burden he would carry, as her father.

'What's happening down there?' Isla grabbed his arm and pointed.

He turned back to look at the girls by the barriers. There seemed to be some sort of commotion. The bodyguards carrying someone over. A young girl. She didn't look conscious as they lowered her to the floor. 'Stay here with Bea,' he said, leaving their VIP box and making his way down the stairs to the main arena. He flashed his ID, told them he was a doctor and that he could help, and they let him through.

The young girl was being carried into a private area, away from the crowds, but he could still hear the throng, still singing, still celebrating. Could still hear the band singing.

'What happened?'

'We think she got crushed a little. Said she couldn't breathe and then she passed out,' said one of the burly guys in a neon-yellow jacket.

'She may have fainted.' He quickly examined her. She was breathing still, but was unconscious and he thought he could see little specks of blood in bubbles around her mouth, so he moved her into the recovery position and checked her pulse as someone arrived with a medical bag and oxygen. 'Thanks.' He attached a mask and tube to the oxygen, then placed the mask carefully over the girl's face. 'Do we know her name?'

Everyone shook their heads.

'Who is she here with?'

'Me! She's here with me. Her name's Lola.'

Gabe turned and saw a man he knew very well. A man whom he had had the displeasure of meeting once or twice before. A gossip columnist. A man who had helped make, not only his, but now Isla's life a misery.

Mack Desveaux.

But he tried to not let that put him off. Mack wasn't the important one here. It was Lola. So he pushed aside the years of irritation he'd felt with this man and focused on his daughter. 'I think she may have fainted. I've put her on oxygen. Any medical history I need to know about at all?'

Mack had rushed to his daughter's side and gripped her hand. 'No. She's perfectly healthy.'

Gabe nodded. Lola's pulse was fine and she was beginning to stir, colour coming back to her cheeks. 'That's it. Just breathe, Lola. You fainted a little.'

The young girl slowly blinked her eyes open, then groaned and winced, looking a little dazed to begin with, then frightened as she realised she'd lost consciousness for a bit. 'I feel sick. I hurt.'

'It's all right, pumpkin. I'm here. Dad's here.' Mack leaned in and kissed her on the forehead.

'Dad!'

'I know, honey. I know. It's okay. This man's a doctor. You're all right now.'

'You feel sick because you fainted, but don't worry, that'll pass.'

Gabe couldn't help but notice how close they were, and even though he disliked Mack immensely for having run a number of stories on Gabe he was hit with a wave of envy for how easy some people's lives were and wondered why his was anything but.

But the blood around her mouth bothered him.

'Is everything okay? Can I help?' Gabe whipped his head around at Isla's voice in the doorway behind him. What were they doing here? He'd told them to stay in the box. But there she stood, hands on Bea's shoulders, in front of her. 'Sorry. But Bea was worried.'

'We need to do a primary survey. There's blood around her mouth,' he said.

Isla stepped forward. 'She was crushed. She may have cracked ribs.' She glanced at Mack. 'Or something else.'

Punctured lungs. That was what she meant, but hadn't wanted to say in front of Mack.

Mack stood up. 'And you are?'

Gabe tried to motion quietly that she shouldn't say anything, but Mack was in the way and Isla couldn't see.

'Isla French. I'm a nurse. Let me help.' She pushed him aside to get to Lola. 'We need to check her chest. Has anyone called for an ambulance?'

'One's on its way,' Mack said.

Gabe asked Lola if it was okay to lift her top and examine her.

The young girl nodded, but began to cry.

Isla knelt beside him. Laid her hand on his. 'Let me.'

Gabe nodded and sat back.

There were marks on Lola's chest, consistent with intense pressure from the barrier. A bruise already forming, just beneath her breasts in a narrow straight line, red and purpling. Isla gently palpated Lola and when the young girl winced, she slowly lowered the girl's top to maintain her dignity. 'Definitely two cracked ribs that I could feel,' she murmured to Gabe. 'Could be more, but she needs an X-ray to confirm. Whether her lungs are damaged from the break is hard to say, but judging by the blood? I don't know. She may have bit her tongue or lips.'

'Lola, can Isla check your mouth?'

The young girl nodded again and reached for her dad's hand. He squeezed it.

They removed the oxygen to check her mouth, but could see no signs of oral damage. Lola might very well have punctured lungs. Maybe even a collapsed lung? She did seem hungry for air. 'I'm going to update the ambulance.' He pulled his phone from his pocket and began to dial.

They drove home in near silence, thinking about how the evening had ended.

Isla sat in the back with Gabe's daughter. Occasionally smiling at Bea, she tried to get her attention, but it was difficult, because after the paramedics had helped that young girl into an ambulance Gabe had pulled her to one side and told her exactly who Lola's father was—Gabe's personal nemesis, Mack.

It would all come out now. She'd be in a gossip column again! Her past. The attack. Everyone would know. Everyone at her new workplace. They would all look at her with sympathy. They would all want to ask questions, when she'd thought she'd put this thing behind her. But most of all? It would reveal her location to the man who had originally attacked her. He would be able to find her and, though she didn't think he was a threat any more, she didn't want him just turning up one day to make an apology.

But the other thing, the thing that had made Gabe mad, was that she'd brought Bea into the room with Mack. He'd done his utmost to keep his daughter out of the spotlight that had focused on him, and she could see from the back seat of the car how stressed he was about all of it. His frown. The furrow in his brow. The way the muscle in his jaw clenched and unclenched. The way his fists tightened on the steering wheel. How white his knuckles were. How forcefully he changed gears.

In the house, he threw his car keys onto the counter instead of hanging them up on their little hook as he strode into the kitchen, grabbed a glass, filled it with water and then glugged it back, before letting out a massive sigh and leaning against the counters, head bowed.

Isla took Bea upstairs to help her with her coughing and PT, feeling it was probably best to give Gabe some space. She wanted space herself. She wanted to pack her things and run again. But she was sick of running! Sick of hiding who she used to be. Her days here with Gabe and, lately, Bea, had been wonderful and she didn't want to lose that. And though Gabe had felt guilty for pulling her into the spotlight, now she felt guilt for putting that spotlight on herself and Gabe's daughter. She wanted to apologise to him. To tell him she would move out again. Find someplace else.

But first, Bea needed taking care of. She'd been late doing her clearance exercises and it had showed, immediately. As the paramedics had begun to place Lola on a backboard to carry her out to the ambulance, Bea had begun to cough.

Her coughing fit in front of Mack and his daughter had been spectacular.

'*Hey, is she okay?*' Mack had asked.

'*She's fine. Come on, Bea.*'

Gabe had tried to usher her from the room.

'*She sounds sick.*'

'*She's not infectious,*' Gabe had answered.

'*How do you know?*'

'*It's not Covid, it's CF,*' Isla had said, thinking she was being helpful. Putting Mack's mind at rest that *his* daughter, who had just fainted, who had fractured ribs, who might have a punctured lung, would not catch anything from Gabe's daughter.

And in that moment, she had seen Gabe close his eyes in dismay. How could she have not thought? How could she have just blurted it out? It had not been her information to tell.

It took a while to get through Bea's clearance exercises. She was so excited about the concert still, had so enjoyed her special night out, no matter how it had ended. She'd even told Isla how proud she had been to have seen her dad in action. And Isla, too. Seeing how they helped people. She'd never really seen it before.

But Isla had taken a huge misstep and she felt so bad. Especially because Gabe had offered her his home. Had offered her a haven, even though they had barely known one another.

Eventually, Bea fell asleep and Isla slipped from her room and stood at the top of the stairs, anxious about going down them and seeing Gabe and apologising. She knew she ought to be more focused on the fact that she had just told a paparazzi who she was, that she was the mystery woman seen with Gabe the other night and that they would bring up her past and make her live that night-mare all over again, but all she could think of was Gabe. Of how she'd told Mack that his daughter had cystic fibrosis. Of how she'd let *him* down, after the sacrifices he had made for her.

She found him in his office, staring at a blank document, the cursor waiting, blinking silently. 'Hey. How are you doing?' she asked, feeling nervous about his response. Would he answer her? Ignore her?

'I'm all right. You?'

Isla nodded and came further into his room, leaving the door open behind her. 'Despite the ending, Bea had a good time tonight. You made her incredibly happy.'

He seemed to ignore her attempt to begin this positively. 'Is she asleep?'

'Yes. It took a while. She was so excited and then her clearance exercises took some time.'

He nodded, steepling his hands in front of him as he considered his screen.

She wondered what he was working on. 'What are you up to?'

He seemed to think for a while. 'I'm trying to write.'

'Write what?'

'A book. I'm trying to write a book. I've been planning it for some time, got it all laid out. Characters. Setting. Plot. I thought now would be as good a time as any to actually make a start, but now that I've opened up a document, I can't seem to find the words…'

She was surprised. 'Oh. Well, I've heard that some people can get writer's block. Maybe that's what you have?'

'Maybe. Or maybe I'm so wound up right now that it would be impossible for me to write anything!' He let out a heavy sigh. Rubbed his face with his hands.

Isla felt her cheeks colour. Knowing she was the source of his irritation. And she felt fear too. The last man she'd apparently wound up had attacked her. Put her in hospital. Caused her to have surgery and counselling. 'Gabe, I'm sorry! I didn't know who he was! I thought I was helping! I thought…'

The fire in his eyes was incredible and she couldn't look at him. Couldn't bear to see the disappointment, the betrayal, the hurt that she had caused him. She stood up. Knowing she couldn't stay here any more.

'I'll go. I'll leave first thing in the morning.'

'What? No! Why would you leave?' He sounded confused now.

'Because I told Mack about Bea. I betrayed your trust, your daughter's privacy.' She began to head out of his office, but Gabe was fast. Very fast. And before she knew it, he was standing in front of her, blocking the doorway.

Her heart began to pound and she felt herself backing away in fear. 'Please…stop.'

Her bottom lip felt trembly. She looked up at him with such apology.

Gabe looked horrified to see the fear on her face. He backed away. 'I don't want you to leave,' he said softly.

'But I told that guy everything—'

'Isla! Listen to me. I don't want you to leave.'

She braved a proper look at him and saw tenderness in his gaze now. Where had the anger gone? She *had* seen it, hadn't she? Now she was beginning to doubt herself. Recognised herself settling into an old pattern of behaviour, of not being sure if she could read an intention or an emotion in a man's face. 'But, but…you're angry with me and you have every right to be.'

'I'm not angry with *you*,' he insisted.

Confused, she looked up at him. How could he be angry with himself? He'd not done anything wrong. He'd not blurted out private information to a gossip columnist.

'I'm angry because… I'm angry because it's all *changed*. I was protecting you, I was keeping you safe, and now I can't even do that! It's going to be in Mack's rag tomorrow. Who you are. Your past. And I thought I could stop that and now I can't. Your life is going to be ruined by that man, who, because he has an interest in me, will now want to chase you.'

'That's not your fault.'

'It is. I just feel like…' He groaned. 'Damn it! I just feel like I fail every woman that I care about. I couldn't protect my mum when she went through cancer. I couldn't protect my wife or my daughter from getting sick and now I'm failing you, too.'

'Gabe, you couldn't control any of those things. Your wife passing isn't on you. Bea's cystic fibrosis isn't on you and nor is the situation that I find myself in.'

'But I wanted to protect you. I thought I could keep you safe. You have no idea how much I longed to do just that. Just once, I wanted to win against the battle of life.' Gabe walked away from her and slumped into his chair, head in his hands. 'Bea was an accidental pregnancy. Ellis wasn't ready yet. She wanted to work a bit more. See more of the world. But she fell pregnant and suffered horrendous morning sickness. Every time I heard her in the bathroom, I felt guilty. She spent three days in labour and I felt guilty for every painful contraction she went through that did nothing to progress the birth. She was terrified when they rushed her into surgery for a C-section. Bea's heartbeat was decelerating and not recovering. I thought I might lose them both.'

Isla knelt in front of him, listening to him speak. This was the first time she'd heard him share his pain and she knew it was important to listen. He'd listened to her and though she knew he'd lost his wife, she'd not known the details. Nor had she looked them up on the Internet, figuring that he would tell her when the time was right.

'Bea was small and weak, her lungs weren't great and she needed to be on oxygen, but Ellis got to hold her briefly. We thought, naively, that everything was going to be all right, but then Ellis suddenly lost consciousness and all these alarms went off. I took Bea from her and passed her to the NICU nurse.' Gabe rubbed his hands through his thick dark hair. 'She had an amniotic embolism. It had travelled to her brain, caused a massive stroke. She never woke up. I felt it was my fault. I'd got her pregnant. I'd convinced her to carry on with the pregnancy and then she was dead and my daughter could barely breathe and I felt so incredibly powerless and guilty for it all.'

'It wasn't your fault, Gabe.'

'I knew there was cystic fibrosis in my family,' he replied, looking glum. 'My sister, Sarah, had it. She needed a lung and liver transplant when she was twenty-three. She died from surgical complications.'

Isla's heart broke for him! He had been through so much! 'I'm so sorry.'

'I knew I might be a carrier. We found out, much later, that Ellis had been a carrier, too. We should never have had a child and every time Bea coughs, every time she struggles to breathe, I feel guilt.'

'You can't say that! People that have cystic fibrosis can lead incredibly happy and joyous lives!'

'I'd never seen that. I just remember seeing and hearing suffering all the way through my childhood. And now

I see it in Bea. And she won't let me comfort her. She's never let me get close. And now there's you. I got you into this mess, put upheaval into your life as you were looking for stability and I couldn't even keep you safe.'

'Listen to me, Gabe. It's. Not. Your. Fault. None of it, all right? You've got to stop shouldering the blame for everything that goes wrong.'

'I've always felt this way. Even as a child. I try to escape it. When life feels dark, when life feels lonely and terrifying, I go out. Find someone to spend time with, put a smile on my face, no matter how short a time.'

'You're talking about all those female celebrities?'

He nodded, looking embarrassed. 'It's shallow and pathetic, I know. You don't have to tell me. But sometimes they make me feel better. Make me feel less alone. Until I come home, anyway, and the house is empty and the silence screams at me.'

'It's not shallow. You did what you did because it was all you knew how to do. But you're different now. And stop bringing yourself down! Think about all the good things that you are! You care so much about the people around you! You're intelligent, you're kind, empathetic. You go out of your way to accommodate people and even offer them a place to stay. You protect them. You're loyal. A true friend,' she said, placing her hand on his knee to get him to look at her. Because she needed him to know just how much good he'd put into her life. How much she had enjoyed being with him.

'This last week that I've spent with you has actually been some of the happiest days I've had in a very long time. So if you're going to perform an account of your life and you're going to measure your success with people, then you damn well make sure you take that into account, too!'

Gabe looked at her. Smiled. 'You're an amazing person, you know that?'

She blushed. 'I try. Despite everything, I try.'

'This past week has been some of my happiest days, too.'

Isla looked into his very blue eyes and lost herself in them. It was as if they were the only two people in the whole world as they sat together in the dim light of his office, the only light source the screen on his computer. He really was an amazing person and she hoped that he could see that. Wanted him to know just how he'd made her feel. And when he reached out with one hand to stroke her cheek, she felt her breath catch in her throat.

His touch was so soft, so delicate, and in that moment, she wanted more. They were both two lonely souls, who had both been through so much, and surely it was only right that they find comfort in one another? It had been so long since a man had touched her like that. Since a man had touched her at all.

After the attack, she and Karl had allowed a vast chasm to open up between them and after they'd split up, it had been like wandering in the wilderness. Isla had allowed herself to be lost, had preferred to wander alone. After all, it was safer to be that way. To not let any man close, and why would she? She'd doubted her ability to understand just exactly what they were feeling. To wonder if they were seeking comfort, or whether they hid a mean streak of violence that was about to be unleashed on her. Men were physically so much stronger than her. She wasn't a big person. Isla was average. About five feet seven. Light build. Thin, rather than shapely. She'd allowed herself to hide behind her uniform. Behind her baggy scrubs. She'd done nothing in the intervening time since her attack to advertise herself as an attractive woman to men, because she didn't want them to notice her.

But with Gabe? That barrier had come down. Because she knew that he saw her. That he understood her.

And now, as his hand cupped her face and he slid off his chair to kneel opposite her on the floor, his face only inches away from her own, her heart thudded in her chest with sweet anticipation.

Was she ready? She felt ready. She felt safe with him. This moment in time. It felt right. She'd come down those stairs expecting an argument, expecting to have to move out, and instead here they were, staring into each other's eyes, blood pounding so loudly in her ears it was like being back at the concert.

She couldn't help but glance at his lips. His mouth. Anticipating what it might be like to kiss Gabe. Would he kiss her sweetly? Gently? Would the shadow of stubble make her skin burn when he pressed his lips to hers? What would he taste like?

When had she last been kissed? With tenderness? With love? She couldn't remember and her body yearned for it. Her last touch from a man had been extremely violent and it was taking huge amounts of courage here to just sit and wait and see what would develop.

Gabe moved closer. Slowly. Imperceptibly.

She could feel herself grow hot, her breathing catching in her throat, and she closed her eyes, ultimately in an act of trust and submission, and waited for the press of his lips against her own. And when they did, she let out an involuntary noise. A small noise. Not a groan, not a cry, but a sigh. A sigh because she knew she could trust him to treat her right, to be aware of her past and to know that he must take baby steps with her.

His hand went to the back of her head, his fingertips slipping through her hair and gently holding her to him as their tongues met and she felt her insides melt with desire.

All the pain, all the hurt, all the suffering that she'd kept inside from the attack seemed to release in that moment. It was one thing to be brave and to start again and to put on a mask, but that kind of living was hard. It was exhausting! And lonely, too. But in this moment with Gabe, kissing him, one hand on his chest so she could feel the heat of him, the strength of him, his pounding heart, she let that mask slide and she was just Isla again.

The Isla that she'd kept hidden. The Isla that she'd tried to protect. The Isla that wanted to be normal and to be loved. The Isla that had just tried her best in life. The one who dreamed of a fairy-tale ending. Who'd imagined marriage and children and growing old with someone. For too long, she'd kept that version of herself hidden away, afraid to allow it to bloom, because when she had been that person before? It had all been stripped from her in a single act of violence that had had far too many ripples of consequence.

And yet here she was. Finding tenderness. Finding affection and gentility.

And, my God, he's a good kisser!

At some point, they came up for air. She wasn't sure how long they'd been kissing. Time had seemingly slowed. But when they did, she slowly opened her eyes and gazed into his. She was shocked. Surprised. Moved almost to tears.

He looked deeply into her eyes and she saw a question there.

What do we do now?

Their relationship had changed now, because of that kiss. Before, he'd been her employer, her boss, her friend and salvation. A co-conspirator. Her haven.

But now? He was something more. That kiss had been a torchlight, a beacon, to announce that they both were attracted to the other. That they both had feelings for the other. So what happened now?

Isla didn't want to rush things. She didn't want to make another mistake. She was so terribly afraid of doing that, and what if they'd ruined things now? What if it was awkward? She needed this sanctuary and what if he expected more?

'Gabe... I think that...'

She didn't know how to say she wanted to apply the brakes. Not without upsetting him. Men, in her experience, always wanted more from her, right?

'We should take it slow,' he said for her. Softly. Understanding.

Reassuring.

He smiled to let her know he knew what she was thinking. Feeling. Afraid of.

'We go at your pace. We have all the time in the world, Isla, to get this right. And I will take every second of it, to make sure that you feel comfortable.'

And she was so relieved. So grateful to him in that moment. That he understood her. That he'd listened to what she'd been through and would have known her hesitation. Isla felt seen. As if she needed to cry, so grateful was she for his reassurance. 'If that's okay?'

Gabe smiled, staring deeply into her eyes. 'Of course it is. There's a lot at stake here.'

And he was right. Because this wasn't all about her,

was it? Gabe had his own history. His own reasons to hesitate. This wasn't just about him. He came as a package. He had a daughter, who had needs. Who probably needed a mother, but Gabe, protective over his daughter, would not choose anyone. Nor introduce them to Bea, unless he was sure of them. The man had lost a wife under tragic circumstances and he blamed himself for it all. He would feel hesitant about a relationship, too.

So this was a good thing, that they were both being careful. Both being happy to slow things down.

The kiss was a landmark moment. How they moved forward from that was very important. Part of Isla wanted to run away very fast! A kiss was one thing, but something more? Because when she closed her eyes, she could still feel how it felt to have that man fumble at her clothes, to humiliate her even more. He would have assaulted her in a much more terrifying way if those people had not come into the car park and disturbed him. Trying to imagine Gabe unbuttoning her blouse, or removing her clothes, made her shiver and she wasn't sure if it was in a good way.

But she did know she didn't *want* to be scared any more. She wanted to be brave. She wanted to live life unapologetically. Live loud. Live free. But the fear of getting hurt again ran like an undercurrent beneath everything.

'I'd better say goodnight,' she breathed, staring back into his eyes, wondering whether to kiss him again. Instead, she lifted the hand that had been on his chest and gently stroked his face. Her fingertips feeling every bit of stubble. The solidity of his jaw. The way he leaned into her hand and closed his eyes.

'Goodnight, Isla. Sleep well,' he whispered back, opening those intense blue eyes of his and smiling back at her.

Oh, I'm in deep trouble here.

Would she be able to sleep? Probably not for a very long time.

And if she did?

Her dreams would be full of him.

CHAPTER EIGHT

GABE DID NOT sleep well. He'd lain in bed, his mind full of the events of last night, dreading just what would have been printed about himself and Isla in the gossip rags.

He wasn't one for ordering newspapers or magazines, but he did look at them online to keep up with the headlines and as he sat up in bed and picked up his tablet, about to search for Mack's blog, he noticed he had an email flagged as urgent. He went into his email app and saw the email was from Mack himself and it had an attachment. Frowning, curious, he opened the email.

Gabe,

Just wanted to thank you for last night in looking after my Lola. It was nice to meet your daughter and Isla too. Thought I'd give you an update—Lola did have two fractured ribs but thankfully her lungs were just fine! I don't know what I would have done without you there. So…rest assured, I've called off the crew from watching Isla's place and any exposé of her identity or Bea's condition will never come from me.

You have my respect, my guy.

Mack

He clicked on the attachment. An old stock photograph of him from some awards do, dressed in a tuxedo, but instead of a glaring exposé, which he'd been expecting, there was something else instead.

Gabe Newton—Superhero Doc!

Eligible bachelor and surgeon to the stars, Gabe Newton, went from surgeon to superhero last night at a concert for K-Pop group Stride.

Gabe was attending the concert with his daughter, Beatrice, twelve, when an incident near the stage saw the superhero surgeon leap into action.

Stride had been performing a medley of their latest hits, including such greats as 'Why Don't You See Me?', 'Dark Desires' and their best-selling number-one single 'Clouds', when the audience, mostly filled with young teenage girls and their parents, experienced a surge against the barriers due to one member of the band, Han Lee, deciding to tease the audience by stretching out his hand. This surge resulted in a young girl, nine years of age, getting pushed against the barrier and she fainted.

Security guards pulled the unnamed girl free and removed her to a room for treatment, where they were met by Gabe, who treated her until paramedics arrived. The young girl was taken afterwards to the hospital, as a precaution.

Gabe and his daughter then left the concert venue.

It is understood that the band sent their best wishes to the young girl and gave her a private audience in hospital.

Stride go on to their next concert in Brighton, before beginning their tour of the US. Stride have been touring since last year, performing to sell-out crowds all around the world.

The Brixton venue has assured this columnist that safety procedures will be updated in light of this incident.

Gabe stared at the article. There was no mention of Isla! Mack hadn't used the information he had about him at all!

Wow, the guy has a heart.

All Gabe could think of was that he'd wake up to an exposé article and, with her cover blown, Isla would move out again, and he didn't want that. She was such a breath of fresh air to his life. She was helping him get closer to Bea, but, more than any of that, he wanted her to stay. Even though he knew that was selfish. Isla probably wanted her life to just be normal again. To live in her own place. Not be hiding out somewhere. And Mack had called off the attack dogs outside Isla's place.

That means she can go home.

His feelings in response to that shocked him. The idea that he might be home alone again, without her, without her bubbliness, without her smile, her presence...

I don't want her to go.

How quickly someone could unexpectedly change your life.

Because he believed Mack. The man would not send a message like that, after what Gabe had done for Mack's daughter, and then go back on his word. The man might be a gutter snipe, but he'd always kept his word.

But to tell Isla she could go home? After things had changed so much?

Because there'd also been that kiss...

He felt desire flood him at the thought of it and he

had to push it away. At this moment, Isla was still fragile and he didn't want to be responsible for breaking her.
He would move slowly. Be guided by her. Be aware of
how he spoke to her at the clinic—he didn't want anyone
knowing about them. And thanks to Mack they wouldn't
have anything to explain. They already knew that first
picture was the new employee's dinner. They knew that
he'd offered her a place until the furore died down, and
last night? She'd simply gone with him to a concert for
his daughter. They'd accept that version of events, surely?

Downstairs, he heard movement in the kitchen. Isla
was up. She always got up early. He often found her busily
beavering away making breakfast for them. How quickly
his home life had changed in the past week or so! Dressing, after showering, he made his way downstairs, hoping
that things would not be awkward between them after last
night's kiss. They would have to act normally for Bea and,
besides, he had to drive her back to school this evening.
Maybe that car journey would be better than the others?

Isla was putting a tray of something in the oven.

'Morning,' he said softly, glad that he could face her
happily and not have to show her an article exposing her.

She turned and smiled at him, blushing slightly. 'Good
morning.'

'What are those?' He pointed at the oven.

'Oh, dinner rolls, for later. I thought before Bea goes
back to school we could take a picnic somewhere.'

'A picnic? Out in public?'

She nodded, folding a tea towel. 'We could find someplace quiet. Where no one would notice us. I wasn't going
to suggest anything, but then I saw Mack's article online
and...' she smiled, her face softening in a rosy, happy glow
'...he didn't *say* anything about me. Did you see it yet?'

He nodded. 'I did. He emailed it to me. I was just as surprised as you. Perhaps the man isn't the stone-hearted monster I always thought he was.' He knew he needed to tell her that she could go home. That her friend's flat was safe again, even if, selfishly, he wanted her to stay. 'And he said something else, too.'

Isla looked curious. 'What did he say?'

Gabe pulled up the email on his phone and showed it to her, even though he knew she would leave. He watched the expression on her face change from curiosity, to shock, to joy.

'He isn't going to say anything?'

Gabe shook his head. 'No.'

'I don't have to hide out?'

'No.'

'I could go back home?'

'Yes.'

But then he saw something on her face. Something that made him think that she didn't want to leave here, either.

'But I don't mind if you stay. I'd like you to stay.'

'You would?'

He nodded. 'Yes. I mean it doesn't have to be for ever, or anything!' He laughed, nervously. 'But you don't have to leave right away. You could...stay until your birthday, or something. I know Bea would like to celebrate it with you here.'

Now she was nodding, as if she was considering his suggestion, mulling it over in her mind. 'Well, if it's okay with you...then I'd very much like that.'

'It is.' He wanted to reach for her. Pull her into his arms and squeeze her tight, but he didn't want to scare her, either. This had to go at her pace, not his.

'Then that means I don't have to be captive here. We

could do something outside London today. Away from
any journalists. Where people are less likely to notice us.
Make the most of Bea's last day. It'd be nice to make it
memorable before she goes back to Hardwicke.'

He smiled at her. So glad she'd agreed to stay. She was
so thoughtful. 'Bea's always wanted to go on a picnic.'

'Then it's settled.'

'Great. We can ask her when she comes down.' He
poured himself a coffee from the machine. 'Are you sure
you're happy to be seen out and about with us? People
might think if they saw us picnicking together that we
were some sort of family.' He wasn't sure if even he was
ready for that and the idea of it made him feel strange.
He'd only ever imagined a family with Ellis. Picnicking
with his daughter and Isla might be seen as their relationship being somewhat more serious than he'd hoped
to convey to everyone at work. He didn't want work to be
awkward or rife with gossip.

'I could wear a hat, or large sunglasses. You could wear
a baseball cap. Go where no one expects us to be.'

'Sounds like a plan. Sounds like you've done this before.'

'Hidden from everyone?' She managed a wry smile.
'I had to, after the attack. People wanted interviews. Ex-
clusives. My phone rang off the hook constantly and I
couldn't bear to stay in the house feeling like a prisoner.
So I found ways to hide in plain sight.'

'Such as?'

'I'd walk my parents' dog. People don't notice dog
walkers, you sort of blend in. They notice the dog more
than you. Or walk around holding a takeout coffee. You
look like you belong with one of those.'

'You sound like a spy.'

She laughed. 'Sometimes it felt that way.'

'Well, we don't have a dog we can borrow, so where do you suggest?'

'We'll find a park, or open space. What about Richmond Park? Or there's lots of open space around Hampton Court Palace. We could find a little nook there. Have a picnic, or ice cream.'

Gabe nodded. Sounded good. As he gazed at her, he wondered about her beauty. She seemed totally unaware of it. She never seemed to bother with make-up. She always put her blonde hair up in a bun or ponytail. She had that easy, relaxed beauty. Natural. English rose. Did she not know how beautiful she was?

He'd felt something last night with his lips pressed to hers and his fingers in her hair. He'd felt moved. He'd felt...well, guilty to begin with. Isla was the first woman he had properly kissed like that since Ellis. Yes, he'd been on dates with women. Lots of first dates. But he'd always escorted them safely to their front door, like a proper gentleman, and pecked them on the cheek as a goodbye. Once, maybe twice, he'd kissed them on the lips, but it had always been short, sweet, perfunctory and he'd not felt a thing except sadness.

With Isla last night? It had been different. He'd felt himself awakening, as if he'd been in hibernation for a long, long time and her kiss had begun to warm him. To pull him from the winter he'd been in and back towards spring. Where everything was new and blossoming and full of hope.

He'd become used to being shut down. To working, socialising to order, but he'd never been present in the way he had been last night. It had been a dazzling feeling, to realise that he was still there, beneath the layers of mourning that he'd been smothered in for a long, long time.

It had been many years since Ellis died and he'd been like a monk for all of it. And now that part of him had been awakened, he couldn't help but feel pulled towards Isla.

Maybe when Bea was back at school and they were on their own again, they could explore what they'd begun last night?

Upstairs, he heard coughing. Lots of it. So he got Bea's oscillation vest out of the cupboard and her tissues and waited for her to come downstairs to start her clearance exercises.

'Morning,' she said, as she stumbled blearily into the kitchen, still in her pyjamas, wiping at her eyes with a sleeve.

'Juice or water?' Isla lifted up a bottle of juice and wiggled it at his daughter.

'Juice, please.'

'Sleep well?' Gabe asked, coming in to sit beside Bea at the kitchen table.

'Yeah. I had some really weird dreams, though.'

'Yeah?'

He sat listening to Bea as she told him some weird, convoluted dream about a grizzly bear hunting her at Hardwicke, wondering if Bea realised that this was the first time they'd ever done this. Had a natural conversation where she talked to him as if he was a loving father and not someone that she had to battle with. It was a marvel and he would have talked to her about anything. He got distracted from talking to Isla, wanting to revel in his daughter's attention. When she'd finished and she'd started her huff coughing, he decided to tell her their plans for the day. 'We thought we'd go take a picnic in Richmond Park. What do you think?'

Bea was coughing, wiping her mouth with a tissue. 'A picnic? Really?'

Gabe nodded, smiling, loving the look on his daughter's face.

'Yay!' A huge bout of coughing took hold of her then and Gabe got up to help pat her on the back to clear it, as she seemed to be having difficulty.

'But if you need to rest, maybe we should stay in.'

'No! I wanna...go!' she said, coughing some more.

Gabe looked up at Isla, hoping that she would back him up. Bea's coughing seemed a little worse this morning than the last few days and now he was wondering if he should have taken her to the concert, after all. Nothing was worth ruining his daughter's health. 'Maybe you should rest. You're back at school later. Perhaps it's a bad idea to push you again after last night's excitement.'

'Dad! No. I'm fine. Listen.' And she smiled at him, only doing a little cough, now and then.

'Isla, what do you think?' Gabe asked.

Isla was buttering toast, but she stopped to look up at them both. 'I think that you and Bea need to spend time together, but I also think your chest sounds a little clogged this morning. Why not have the picnic in the back garden instead? We can still make it special. It's a lovely day and you get the best of both worlds. We'll have games and everything, but if your chest is bad, we've got everything here to respond to it. What do you say?'

Bea seemed to consider it, but another bout of heavy coughing, where she struggled to breathe, seemed to decide it for her. 'Okay. Picnic in the back garden. But I get to choose the music.'

'Deal,' Gabe said, reaching out to shake his daughter's hand.

Mack's article had surprised her. She'd thought she would wake this morning and see her name and history splashed across his gossip column, but he had omitted her *completely*, instead focusing on the fact that Gabe had taken care of Mack's daughter. She'd thought that this morning, with her cover blown, she'd have no more reason to stay here at Gabe's and she'd have to return to her friend's flat and face it out all over again.

But that hadn't happened and the realisation that she could stay at Gabe's a bit longer? Had pleased her. Especially after last night's kiss. It was as if their little bubble remained intact. Their little secret. This attraction that had been building was still theirs alone. It was nice to have a secret. It was nice to feel this way. When last had she felt this frisson of excitement for a man?

When she'd first met Karl? No. Not even then. She and Karl had been friends first. Colleagues first. What had built between them had been comfortable. Easy. They'd shared a drunken kiss at a work's do and had somehow begun a relationship that way. And though she'd liked him a lot, there'd not been the excitement that she felt with Gabe.

She'd often wondered, as she did now, if she'd fallen for Karl because he was the exact opposite of her absent father. Karl was ever present. He was steady. Sure. Never let her down and encouraged her at work to go for promotion. When she came home, he was always there. They ate meals together. Went out together. He listened to her.

But had it ever been enough? She'd often felt as if something was missing, but could never pinpoint what, but now, with Gabe, she wondered if it was down to attraction. Desire. Karl had been comfortable. Sex with him had been nice, but had it ever blown her world? Looking at Gabe, she somehow imagined that intimacy with him would be...

I can't think about that.

The idea of her exposing herself to him like that. Submitting to him like that. Being vulnerable. It almost seemed too much. When she was attacked, that man who went from beating on her to ripping at her clothes made her feel vulnerable and she couldn't imagine ever being so passionate with Gabe that he'd be able to ravish her with passion, without her freaking out.

I'm not fixed yet. Maybe I'll never be?

When Bea disappeared upstairs to get dressed for the day and washed, Gabe cleared up the table and as he passed her in the kitchen, he brushed his hand against hers.

Heat raced up her arm and caused goosebumps to break out over her skin and she smiled to herself. A picnic here in the privacy of their own garden would be nice. Making food for it would be nice. Playing games and laughing with Bea and Gabe would be nice. Like pretending she had a family of her own, only without all the responsibilities and realities of one. She never did anything like this when she was a child. She couldn't remember any family activities, to be honest.

When the water began to run in the bathroom above as Bea washed, Gabe came to stand behind her and she could feel his presence, close in proximity. What was he doing? Isla turned slightly and he was inhaling the scent of her hair.

'What are you doing?' she asked, smiling, knowing exactly what he was doing.

'Just…being present. Enjoying that you're here.'

She laughed, nervously. But, despite her nervousness, was enjoying it, too. Was she brave enough to turn around and face him? See what happened? In a moment of crazy courage, Isla turned to face him, smiling, one eyebrow raised.

Gabe stepped closer, smiling back. One hand went either side of her at the kitchen units and, though he had penned her in, she was not afraid. Because it was Gabe. And he was safe. He excited her. He was not a threat. Not yet, anyway.

He leaned in. Came closer. His mouth so close to hers, their noses brushing, teasing her with the idea of a kiss, but not actually kissing her.

It was almost more than she could bear. Her insides were a tumult, her stomach was flipping, her blood was pulsing and her breathing had become erratic, but, despite all of that, she smiled. Laughed.

And the Eskimo kiss became a soft, gentle, real one.

CHAPTER NINE

'OKAY, LADIES AND GENTLEMEN, let's just go through our pre-operative checks. Patient is confirmed as Laurence Haworth and he is here for a deep plane facelift. Date of birth is July twelfth, 1984, so forty years of age.'

Isla checked the paperwork and then the label on the patient's wrist to confirm. 'All present and correct.'

He nodded and checked with the anaesthetist that they were happy to proceed.

'Patient is fully sedated,' he agreed. 'BP riding steady at one twenty-two over eighty-one. Pulse at seventy-one beats per minute and oxygen saturations at normal levels.'

'Then let's get started.'

Gabe was feeling optimistic. Bright. For the first time in years, he'd had a good weekend with his daughter. They'd got closer. He'd felt as though she was finally allowing him to love her and show that love, without considering everything he said as an attack.

It was all down to Isla. She was who he had to thank for this. Yesterday, they'd had a lovely picnic in the back garden together and then they'd all driven together to take Bea back to Hardwicke Boarding School.

It had been nice. And surprisingly frightening how easy it was to imagine them as a family.

'I spy with my little eye, something beginning with B.'

They'd played I Spy in the back garden as they ate their picnic and Bea had been winning.

'You can't keep picking things beginning with B,' Gabe had said, joking.

'It's my turn. I can pick whatever letter I like. Come on! B!'

'Bumblebee?' Isla had guessed.

'Nope.'

'Brickwork?' Gabe had guessed.

'Nope.'

'Beautiful young lady?'

'No!' Bea had chuckled.

Gabe had grabbed at a daisy from the lawn and passed it to his daughter, who had laughed, taken the flower and tucked it behind her ear.

Then she had plucked it back out. *'But this is close!'*

'So, it's a flower?'

'I'm not telling!' Bea had laughed.

'Bluebell?'

'No.'

'Begonia?'

'I don't even know what that is, Dad!'

Bea had collapsed laughing, which had become another coughing bout, and he'd had to pat her on the back to help clear it.

'Butterfly bush?'

'Ooh! So close!'

'Buttercup?' he'd guessed.

'Yes!'

Bea had raised her hand for a high-five, which he'd met with his own, and then she'd instantaneously reached for him to give him a congratulatory hug.

He'd been so startled, so surprised. Bea had never initiated physical contact with him before. Their arguments with one another, their frequent misunderstandings, had kept them apart for a long time. So to be holding her, hugging her, at her desire, had meant so much and almost brought a tear to his eye.

Isla had noticed, of course.

He'd caught her looking at him afterwards, as he'd pretended to think of a letter for his turn in the I Spy game, and she'd smiled happily for him.

He'd been happy, too.

And then, driving Bea back to Hardwicke, they'd arrived at the private school, parked up, got out her things and walked Bea up to her dorm. Normally when he did this, he would awkwardly say goodbye and then leave, as Bea had made it quite clear she didn't want him embarrassing her in front of her friends. But this time, she'd given them both a huge hug and a squeeze and had happily waved them goodbye from her window.

Gabe had left her behind for the first time looking forward to when he could collect her again. Now he couldn't wait for Friday evening, so he could pick her up again and they could continue growing their bond.

'So, I'm working below the superficial muscular aponeurotic system because this allows me to create tension at the level of the fascia, which in turn allows for a tension-free skin closure for better results,' he explained to Isla.

'I see.' She sounded fascinated and he loved that she was so interested in his work.

'Suture, please.'

She passed it over and he tied his knot.

'Cut.'

Isla snipped it with scissors.

'The patient does have some jowling, and he's asked

me to address this too, so could I ask you to apply pressure here on the buccal fat pad?'

Isla let him guide her to place her fingers.

'Perfect. I'm going to make a small incision here.' He made a small incision in the overlying fascia and then began to tease out some of the buccal fat. 'Bipolar cautery, please.' He made sure to avoid injury to the facial nerve. 'That's it. Four zero nylon, please.'

They worked well together. They were efficient and the operation was running smoothly. Isla was an excellent theatre nurse. Gabe couldn't help but look up and smile at her as they worked, and he was about to thank everyone for their assistance when suddenly the machines monitoring Mr Haworth suddenly started blaring alert noises as his pressure dropped and his heart rate went into ventricular tachycardia.

'Oxygen saturations are dropping!' said the anaesthetist.

'Increase the oxygen,' he ordered. 'We may have to cardiovert if this keeps up. Isla? Get the pads ready, please.'

Isla grabbed the defibrillator and opened Mr Haworth's gown to place the chest pads in case they needed to shock the patient.

'One sixty-two BPM,' advised the anaesthetist. 'One-seventy.'

Alarms were blaring.

'Do you think he's having malignant hyperthermia?' Isla asked.

'Possibly. Let's take him off anaesthesia, please.'

'He's in ventricular fibrillation!'

Ventricular fibrillation was dangerous. Life-threatening and needed immediate treatment to stop the patient from going into cardiac arrest. 'We need to shock him back into regular rhythm. Clear!'

Isla punched the button and Mr Haworth's body jerked in response to the shock. 'Still in arrhythmia.'

'Beginning CPR.' Gabe began to do chest compressions. It had been a long time since he'd had to do anything like this, but he was glad to observe, as if from a distance, that he and his team, including Isla, remained calm. They knew what to do. Isla used to work in A & E. She was a good nurse. 'And clear!' He shocked the patient again.

Mr Haworth's heart returned to a regular rhythm again.

They all breathed a sigh of relief. 'Thank the stars. Okay, let's get him bandaged up and taken to the high-dependency ward. I want fifteen-minute obs on him. If you could apply the antibiotic ointment and apply the pressure dressing before he goes up?'

Isla nodded. 'Of course. Well done.'

'I think Mr Haworth will be very pleased with his results. Once he gets over the shock.'

'So do I.'

Her eyes gleamed with happiness over her surgical mask and he felt the urge to go over to her, pull that mask down and kiss her now that the adrenaline was not coursing through his body.

But they were at work and he couldn't do that, so he tried to keep his tone brisk as he thanked everyone in the room for their assistance and then left Theatre to scrub out.

As he washed his hands, he wondered how long he and Isla would be able to hide their feelings for one another at work. At home, it was easier. Especially now that Bea was back at school, too. Since their kiss, it was all he could do to not think about her. He wanted more, but he knew he had to move slowly. Kissing her was amazing. So amazing, he'd begun to wonder what it might feel like to do other things to her, but he didn't want to scare her off. She'd been through a trauma. He would have to be guided by her, when she was ready for more.

But by God, he wanted more! Moments like this showed him that life was short and could be taken from you unexpectedly.

'We've placed you in a compression bandage, Mr Haworth. You'll need to wear it for at least the first twenty-four hours continuously. This is to minimise swelling and ec-chymosis.'

'What the hell is ecchy...eccthee...?'

'Ecchymosis?' She smiled at her patient. 'It simply means bruising.'

'Then why don't you say bruising?'

She smiled. 'Sorry. We medics have our own terms for things and we get used to them, forgetting that not every-one knows what they are. You'll need to keep your head elevated for about the first week, so sleep on lots of pil-lows. And, as explained before, no rigorous or physical activity for two weeks.'

'Okay. Should be doable. But the big doc here is looking at me as if something bad happened. Should I be worried?'

Gabe smiled. 'As far as your cosmetic surgery is con-cerned everything went very well, Mr Haworth, but the surgery did present with a complication. You went into an arrhythmia and we needed to shock you and do CPR. Now this could simply be because your body was too tired from the anaesthesia, but it could also imply that there may be a weakness with your cardiac system and I would like to refer you for further testing, just to make sure that you're okay and that there's nothing wrong with your heart.'

'There might be something wrong with my ticker?'

'We won't know for sure. Your pre-surgical tests did not show anything at all worrying, so I'm hoping it was nothing more than your body growing tired from the procedure, but let's get you referred and checked out just to be sure, okay?'

Mr Haworth nodded.

'I'll refer you to Mr West. He's the best in the business and he'll be able to see you soon.'

'Thanks, Doc.'

Gabe smiled. 'And now I'll leave you in Nurse French's very capable hands.'

When Gabe had gone, Isla turned back to her patient. 'Tomorrow we'll check your drain and do the dressing removal.'

'Yes, miss.'

She smiled at him. 'We'll make appointments to see you again in four days and seven days to assess the wound. But you have our details—any problems or questions, don't hesitate to ring us.'

'Will do.'

'You have someone to look after you when we let you home?'

Laurence nodded. 'My wife.'

'Is she coming later?'

'She should be here any minute. She wasn't a fan of me getting the surgery. She said I looked just fine as I was. But I didn't feel fine. I don't think I've aged well. Lots of stress at work and all that, which might explain the old ticker, too, but my wife still looks like she did when she was twenty. Everywhere we go other guys would be eyeing her up and assuming I was her dad or something.'

'Surely not?'

'I'm telling you the truth. I just wanted to feel youthful again. Recapture that spirit of confidence of looking in the mirror again. To stand by my wife's side with pride. Now I've got to worry about something else.'

'I'm sure she's very proud to stand by you. And try to look at this as being fortunate. You've been given a warning. A chance to do something about it and take action.'

Laurence tried to grin. 'I do like your spin. You ought to have gone into politics, miss!' He laid his head back against the pillows and closed his eyes.

Isla left him to rest. Though patients often went home within a few hours of the surgery, they liked to monitor them first, check their observations and make sure there were no complications after their surgery and anaesthetic. And patients like Mr Haworth needed extra stays. Extra monitoring.

As always, she'd been thrilled to watch Gabe work, and seeing him cope with the emergency? She'd been very proud of the way he smoothly went from calm and controlled to reacting fast and thinking on his feet and keeping control of the situation. She enjoyed assisting all of the partners in the Garland Clinic, but Gabe especially. When she saw his name on the board, she'd look forward to it all day, getting to spend that extra time with him, even though she shared his home, too. He was an exquisite surgeon. Polite. He didn't have a God complex. He wasn't arrogant, as she'd thought he might be, before she began working here. He was an educator. Kind. Funny.

Surgeries were done for the day and they were getting

ready to go home. She knocked on his office door, before going in. 'Hi. You ready?'

'Just a sec. I need to send an email.'

She stepped over to his bookcase and perused the titles whilst she waited. Behind her, she heard the sounds of his keyboard as he typed and she realised she was so looking forward to getting home and cooking for him and...what? This was their first night alone in the house since Bea went back to Hardwicke. Would they kiss again? Snuggle on the couch? Or would he want more?

Isla glanced at him.

His brow was furrowed, his lips moved slightly as he spoke the words to himself as he typed. He was such a handsome man and when she looked at him, she felt for him, for all the pain that he'd been through. They'd both experienced trauma. His wife had died, unexpectedly and tragically. He'd been left to look after a daughter that had struggled to breathe. He'd been alone all this time.

Was he lonely? Was he looking for someone who could give him a commitment? Not just him, but his daughter, also? Or was he afraid of getting hurt again?

What did Gabe see when he looked at her? Someone he could have fun with? Or something else?

It was the something else that worried her. Though she craved a family of her own, to one day hold a baby of her own, she feared the steps she would have to go through first.

It was so strange to desire intimacy and yet be so terrified of yielding to it at the same time. When people were hurt, you helped heal them by hugging them. By showing them that you loved them. It was never just words. It was acts of love, too. But what was a person to do when that very act scared the living daylights out of you?

She had no doubt that Gabe would be tender and kind. But that didn't help any when she still suffered the occasional flashback. When she saw the face of her attacker lunge close as he decided he wanted more than to just beat her... His eyes...his face...the spittle. The things he'd said, the names he'd called her, as he'd torn at her uniform.

Isla swallowed and closed her eyes, dismissing the images, banning them once again and forcing them to the back of her mind.

She couldn't ever imagine Gabe being rough, or scaring her. But she needed to be brave enough to let him try.

Could she do that?

Was there a way?

Maybe I need hypnotherapy or something.

Because if she were to ever be intimate with Gabe, she'd want to enjoy it. All of it. Every moment. Not be fighting flashbacks. Gabe was such a special person, he deserved someone who would enjoy his every touch. Who would shiver with delight, not fear, at his fingers caressing their skin. Who would close their eyes and sigh with pleasure and revel in the moment.

I deserve to be able to feel that way when he touches me.

She'd not heard him switch off his computer, or get up from his desk, so when he was suddenly behind her, his hand on her arm, she jumped.

'Sorry.'

'No. It's okay. I was just lost in my own daydreams there.' She smiled at him, not wanting him to feel guilty for something that was not his fault.

'Ready to go home?' he asked softly, smiling at her with such tenderness.

'Yes. Absolutely.'

CHAPTER TEN

SHE'D SAT IN the car with him on the way home and they'd enjoyed a pleasant journey, her stomach grumbling with hunger because she was starving. She was determined to cook something nice when they got back.

'What are you doing?' Isla looked at Gabe with a smile upon her face.

They'd got home quite quickly and she'd told him she was going to cook a mango curry and asked could he get the red curry paste from the fridge. Talking about whatever it was might be easier whilst they were cooking.

'It doesn't seem to be here.'

She laughed. 'In the door, second shelf down, right next to the sweet onion chutney.'

'Aha! Got it. Thanks. I could have sworn it wasn't there a moment ago.'

'How are you a world-class surgeon, who can see two nerve endings that need to be spliced together, but you can't see a red jar that's right in front of you?' She laughed again as she stood at the counter chopping courgette and yellow peppers.

'Because I'm a man. Genetically programmed to not see what's right in front of me when I'm looking for it.'

'Right. Okay. Do you think you could go in the pantry and see if you're able to find me some shallots?'

'I don't know, let me try.' He passed her the jar of curry paste, then went to the pantry, opened it up and rummaged in the onion bag. 'How many?'

'Three or four should do it.'

'Coming right up.'

She loved cooking with him. It was the shared activity of it, the camaraderie, the fact that though Gabe could do all manner of expert things in a surgical theatre, his skills in a kitchen were less so. He'd burned sausages the other day. He'd said it was because he'd got distracted, found things to do whilst food was cooking and then forgot he was cooking, until the smoke alarm had reminded him rather loudly. But he did like cooking with her and she liked the fact that, in the kitchen, the boot was on the other foot. At work, Gabe taught her, educated her, tested her knowledge and skills, and yet in the culinary arts, she was the teacher and he the pupil.

It was nice. Karl had never been interested in cooking. He liked the end result, but he never wanted to cook. He'd always let her do it and so she'd spent many hours in the kitchen alone. Having Gabe with her, helping, telling her stories about his day, or his life, or sharing jokes with her? It was so special. So delightful. She knew she'd miss it incredibly when she finally returned home.

Because that would happen at some point, right? She'd have to go home at some point. She couldn't stay here for ever—he'd invited her as a temporary thing. But she loved that they could cook and share car journeys and in-jokes with one another and, at the end of the day, Gabe would kiss her goodnight.

It was going to be her birthday soon. It would fall on a weekend, when Bea would be back, and she was so looking forward to it. Having a birthday as part of something special.

Isla hummed to the music playing on the radio as she placed the chopped shallots in a pan, with a little oil, and began to fry them, adding a spoonful of garlic paste as the onions began to cook. Was there any better smell in the world than that? 'Can you pass me the courgette and peppers, please, before you eat them all?' She smiled at him as he passed her over the dish with the chopped vegetables.

'You know you're bossy in the kitchen?'

'Am I?'

'Yes. But I like it. It's assured. It's confident. And I like to dine on food that's been cooked by a confident chef, who knows food and has a refined palate.'

'I'm not sure I have a refined palate, but I'll take the compliment.'

'You didn't ever think about becoming a chef?' he asked.

'Not really. I think I always wanted to be a nurse. Didn't you always want to be a doctor?'

'Actually, no. I always thought that I'd be a K9 police officer growing up.'

'Really?' She looked at him in surprise. 'What stopped you?'

'Dog allergy.'

'You're kidding?'

'Nope. I break out in hives. So I looked to become something else. I'd always been interested in medicine, too, and decided to become a GP. But then, during placements in training, I discovered a love for surgery and here we are.'

'Oh.'

'What?'

'Nothing. It's just that…when I think of my future… of what it might look like when I settle down and hopefully have a family of my own, I've always imagined I'd have a dog. I don't know what I'd do if I ever found out I was allergic.'

'You could take antihistamines.'

'Or get a dog that's allergy friendly. There must be some, right?'

'Well, let's see.' Gabe got out his phone and began scrolling for information as Isla added ginger and the red curry paste to the softening vegetables. This was most definitely procrastination and it worried her. 'Here we go! You can have a Yorkshire terrier. Apparently they have hair, rather than fur, so they're hypoallergenic.'

'Great. You could get yourself a terrier, too.'

'I've always pictured myself with a German shepherd. I'm not sure a Yorkie is my jam.'

'I'm sure you'd find them adorable if you got to know them.'

'I guess. I could train it to be a guard dog, too, right?'

She laughed. 'Absolutely! Why not? People need ankles.'

The DJ on the radio suddenly began to play a song that Isla hadn't heard in ages. It took her back to her teenage years. To hearing it and dancing to it at her first ever party.

'Oh, I love this song!' She began to sway.

'Then dance with me.' Gabe turned down the hob and then took Isla's hand and led her out into the centre of the kitchen and pulled her into his arms.

She couldn't help but laugh. Blush a little. Dancing in the kitchen. Pressed up close. She thought that maybe they'd sway together for a little bit, he'd twirl her around a few times and then they'd go back to cooking.

Only that didn't happen.

He held one of her hands close against his chest. With the other he led and she was pressed up close to him. Very close. They'd kissed before, their lips might have met, but she'd never felt the length of him pressed up against her like this.

Isla felt herself grow hot. A heat of awareness, of desire, of apprehension washed over her. She did not know what was going to happen and that was not a feeling that she was comfortable with.

Since the attack, Isla had controlled every aspect of her life. Who she allowed to get close. Who she allowed herself to get attached to. Friends. Colleagues. Family. Romantic attachments had never been allowed as she'd always been afraid of letting anyone close, because as soon as someone invaded her close personal space, she often felt herself freaking out and so it had just been easier, the last year or so, to keep everyone at arm's length.

And now she found herself in Gabe's arms, marvelling at the way his thumb was stroking her hand against his chest, the way his beautiful blue eyes were gazing at her.

I want this. I want this all the time.

Her heart thudded in her chest. Her mouth went dry and she had to fight the urge to break away. Her brain screamed at her to break it off, to go back to cooking, to where the situation was friendly and warm and safe, but her heart, her body, which had been starved of love and comfort and gentle touch, wanted her to stay exactly where she was.

It was dizzying. Confusing.

Which voice to listen to?

He wasn't doing anything threatening. He wasn't being rough. He was being kind. Gentle. And now he'd laid his head against hers and they moved to the music and she closed her eyes and told herself to just focus on that. The movement. The rhythm. The normality. It was just a dance. He wasn't trying to feel her up. He wasn't trying to remove her clothes. They were just dancing. And this song wouldn't last for ever, so...

Just enjoy it.

And so she tried. Maybe ninety per cent of her tried. The rest? Was on full alert. Waiting for something bad to happen. Because something always did.

Panic washed over her in a wave.

'I haven't danced like this in ages,' Gabe said, softly.

'No?'

'I never danced any slow songs with anyone. Not like this.'

'Oh.' She wondered if he was struggling with the moment, too? If he'd not danced with anyone at parties like this, was his last slow dance with his wife? 'You must miss Ellis, so much.'

He stopped dancing. Pulled back to look at her. 'Of course. I will always miss her. She was taken from me before her time.'

It was as if a wall came down between them, and they separated. 'I didn't mean to imply that you were dancing with me like that because you missed her. I was just thinking who you must have last slow-danced with.'

His eyes had darkened. 'It was with Ellis. We danced the night before she went into labour with Beatrice. I stood behind her and danced because her baby bump was so big.' He swallowed.

'I'm sorry you lost her like that. Truly.'

He nodded. 'I've been trying to move on. Sometimes I forget her. I can go a whole day and not think about her and then, when I remember, I feel so guilty. Holding you in my arms and hearing her name at the same time made me feel...' He didn't say guilty.

But she knew that was what he meant.

She had made him feel bad and she hadn't meant to. They'd been having a moment and she'd spoiled it. But had she done so deliberately? The song had been coming to an end and she'd been worrying about what would come next. If they'd carried on dancing, holding each other close, would it have progressed to something more? Because she'd been scared of that. Had she self-sabotaged the moment? And if so, what did that mean?

That she wasn't ready for intimacy?

And clearly, Gabe still had a hang-up about his wife.

'I'll carry on with dinner. Why don't you get a glass of wine?' She realised she'd said something a wife might.

You relax, honey... I'll cook dinner.

Maybe she ought to rethink this living arrangement? Maybe she ought to go back home? Clearly this thing between her and Gabe was reaching a turning point that she wasn't sure either of them were ready for.

She couldn't handle intimacy. He was still missing his wife.

But the truth was, she'd begun to like it here. She'd begun to feel settled. Going to bed at night, knowing that Gabe was near, like a security blanket. Living in her perfect, comfortable home. Driving into work with him, driving home with him. It was all very domesticated. And Bea? She loved Bea. She was a wonderful young woman and they got along great.

What would her life return to if she gave all of that up?

Would it be as empty as it was before?

Would she feel as alone as she had?

And how would Gabe take her leaving? Because he seemed to like having her here.

She would be leaving because of herself. Because she was afraid of what it would mean for them if she stayed. Because the truth was—she could feel her feelings for Gabe were growing. Exponentially. It was why she had allowed him to get so close. It was why they had kissed. It was why she had allowed him to pull her close for that dance.

But fear was an insidious thing.

It crept into the cracks of a person's armour and took hold.

Isla just had to decide whether she wanted to live in fear of the past, or step boldly and bravely into a new future.

CHAPTER ELEVEN

GABE CONTEMPLATED ISLA'S comment about Ellis. She was right. He *did* miss Ellis, but he'd not been thinking of his wife when he'd been dancing with Isla.

Well, not much. He'd briefly thought of her when he'd taken Isla in his arms. A wash of guilt that he'd been holding another woman in his arms. Another woman that he'd wanted to pull close. Wanted to hold. And as they'd danced, as they'd swayed, bodies close, the scent of her dizzying his senses, the feel of her wakening his body so that base, primal desires had been threatening to drown out everything else his brain was capable of thinking about, he had forgotten Ellis. No longer stuck in the past. He had been very much in the present. His breathing ragged. The softness of her fingers in his. The way she'd felt against him. And he'd very much begun to think of the future.

What it would look like for him. For them.

And as thoughts of *them* had filled his brain, of how she might fit into his life, Bea's life, as he'd imagined them together, crazy to believe that he had been doing, Isla's statement had cut through it all.

You must miss Ellis.

Of course he did. But it wasn't as raw as it once had been. The pain of losing Ellis, of realising that he'd been abandoned by her to raise their daughter alone. He'd not told anyone, because he'd felt bad about it, but he'd been angry with Ellis for leaving them, even though he'd known it wasn't her fault. She would not have chosen to die like that. Ellis would have wanted to raise Bea. To be there for her daughter through every step of her life. School. Prom. University. Relationships. Career. Ellis would have wanted to be there for it all. But she wasn't, was she? She never would be. And he'd grown to accept that.

You must miss Ellis.

Why had she said that? Because she meant it? Because she thought that their dancing together was moving too fast? Was it her way of pushing him away? Had she felt his body stirring in response to her? His need, his desire for her, his base thoughts scaring her away because she wasn't ready for anything physical like that? They had kissed. Deep, passionate kisses. Kisses goodnight. Kisses good morning.

He liked kissing her then. He wanted to kiss her more. But the most confusing thing for Gabe was that he was starting to make plans. He could imagine them together so easily. Isla being a part of their life. Isla cooking in the kitchen with him every day. Sharing meals. Cooking with Bea. Going out on trips together. He wanted to take Isla places. Restaurants. Cafes. Theatre. Abroad to different countries and cultures that they could explore together. To India, to share his work with her there. He could imagine them doing that so clearly. So easily.

Bea liked her. No. Scratch that. Bea *loved* Isla. And they'd only spent one weekend together. It was as if they'd been best friends straight away.

He'd not been looking for a mother figure for Bea. He'd

not been looking for a relationship at all. But here she was, in their lives, and it was getting complicated.

Isla's statement had simply reminded Gabe that he'd actually *forgotten* his wife. For just a short time. But the cruelty of it was that when he'd been reminded, he'd been holding another woman close, which had somehow made the guilt worse. And he'd felt bad, because it meant, clearly, that he was moving on. Stepping into the next period of his life.

Ellis would have wanted him to be happy, he knew that. She would never have wanted him to be single for the rest of his life, living in solitude to raise his daughter and watch her go out into the world.

'Anything I can do?'

She was putting out two plates. 'You could drain the rice.'

He was glad to be given a job to do. He liked feeling useful. 'Sure.' He placed the colander in the sink and poured the rice into it, draining the water.

Their next patient had come in for a breast reduction. And she'd been very nervous, yet also excited, when Isla had fetched her from the ward for the walk into Theatre. 'I can't believe today is the day. You have no idea how long I've waited for this.'

Isla had smiled. This was what she loved. Knowing that a surgery was about to make a patient's life much better. Laura was petite. Only five feet two. But her breasts were overly large for her frame. 'I bet.'

'Years of backaches. Years of sore indentations in my shoulders from bras that look like they were constructed by the military. Years of wolf whistles and attention I never wanted from men. Being felt up without giving permission. That ends today.'

Now Gabe stood over her, explaining what they were hoping to achieve today.

'Patient would like us to go down to a more comfortable and less painful thirty-four C.'

'She'll have to get used to having a new centre of balance. And she told me that she's really looking forward to buying pretty bras for a change. Little lacy things and attracting guys who like her for who she is rather than the size of her breasts. Do you know she told me that she'd had three guys go out with her who *only* stayed until they'd seen her naked? And then they dropped her.'

'Really? Some guys...' Gabe seemed disgusted as he asked her to pass the scalpel.

Isla had endured wolf whistles from afar before. Stood at a crowded bar and felt someone grab her bottom for a cheap feel. She'd felt the male gaze before, as if they were undressing her with their eyes. And of course there'd been the attack. Where she'd felt that, because she was a woman, she'd been attacked because she was physically weaker than him. That she'd not been seen as a person, as an individual with worth, but just something to be used. How cheap it had made her feel. Her attacker had not been able to force his rage against the loss of his wife, against death, against strokes or infections, and so he'd gone for the easier, more accessible target. As if she were disposable. That was the thought and feeling that had sat in her mind in the first few weeks after the attack. That she was worthless. It had taken a lot of time for her to find her pride and her power again. To feel confident.

Gabe didn't make her feel weak. He made her feel special. As if she was worth something. And he'd been taking the time to get to know her properly. She loved the way he gazed at her at night, when they were watching a movie or the television and he thought she hadn't noticed. The way he'd smile at her. Be considerate of her. Fetch her drinks. Snacks. Last night? He'd rubbed her feet for her. That had been...interesting.

They'd been watching some action flick. One of her favourite actors. Isla had been at one end of the couch, Gabe the other. Her legs had been aching that day. She'd done a lot of steps at work and so she'd lifted her feet up onto the couch and Gabe had just lifted them onto his lap and begun massaging them!

It had been heavenly! His fingers expertly massaging out the knots and aches in her arches, her soles, her toes. His warm hands smoothing over her skin, over tired muscles in her lower legs, manipulating her ankles, his thumbs applying soft pressure, his fingers stroking her.

It had taken every ounce of willpower for her to not moan with pleasure. And when the film was over? She'd closed her eyes and sunk further into the cushions and allowed him to continue. To feel him touching her, in a non-sexual way, but giving her pleasure, was almost orgasmic. To realise that she could be touched by a man and not feel threatened. To realise that she could trust Gabe to respect her boundaries. He hadn't tried to run his hand further up her legs. He hadn't tried to pull her closer to touch her elsewhere. He hadn't tried to make it sexual.

Yet somehow, it had been. To her, anyway.

And the most wonderful thing about it? She had, briefly, wanted him to. She'd thought, *What would it feel like to have him trail his fingers up my calf, past my knee and up my thigh?* The thought had made her heart pound, had made her groin ache and her breathing increase, but at the same time, she'd been terrified. So much so, she'd opened her eyes, smiled at him and reluctantly pulled her feet free of his manipulations.

'Thank you,' she'd said.

'You're welcome.'

He'd smiled back at her and his eyes had been so dark and mysterious, she'd wondered what he'd been thinking, too. Had he been holding back? Had he wanted to do the same thing to her? Allow his hands to go exploring? Wandering? When she'd gone to bed that night, she'd lain there, clutching at her duvet, thinking about Gabe lying in his own bed just a few doors away.

Had he been thinking of her, the way she'd been thinking of him?

Gabe carefully made an incision around the nipple, the areola and down each midline of the breast. 'Tell me, what are the risks of breast reduction?'

She liked it when he quizzed her.

'Bruising. Numbness. Sometimes there can be a difficulty with breastfeeding afterwards. Sometimes the nipples don't take and they can be lost. But that's rare.'

He nodded. 'And why am I using liposuction?'

'To remove excess fatty tissue in each breast. It helps to reduce the volume.'

'Good.'

Liposuction always looked quite violent, but the results from it could be very good indeed. It did create a soreness and tenderness after the surgery, but that could be managed with pain medication and maintaining movement in those areas, so that the patient didn't stiffen up.

'I'm now going to reshape the breasts to try and maintain what?'

'Similarity in size and shape, but the breasts may be different after surgery once swelling has gone down.'

'Good. You know your stuff.'

'I've watched you do this twice before and your results have been terrific. Seeing the ladies come in for check-ups afterwards? They seem so happy with their surgery.'

'That's what it's all about. I'm going to place the drains now.' He sewed the drains into position. One under each breast so that any extra blood or fluid might drain away into two holding pots at the end of each drain. The Garland Clinic offered patients special bags that the drains could be held in, so the patient didn't have to carry them around.

'It's looking good,' she said. 'She's going to be happy, I think.'

'Okay. Are you happy to do the bandages and the support bra?'

'Absolutely!'

'All right. I'm done! Let's get her to Recovery and monitor her, but she should be able to go home by the end of the day.'

'Perfect.'

At the rear of the Garland Clinic, there was a small walled, private garden with a bench, beneath a pergola. If the weather was nice, sometimes the staff would sit out there and eat their lunch, or, if they were on a morning or afternoon break, sit out there with a coffee or tea.

Today was one of those days. The weather was surprisingly warm. There was almost no breeze and the sun was shining brightly. They'd just finished Laura's surgery and it had gone well. Isla had escorted Laura up to Recovery and she was under observation for a few hours, before she'd be allowed home.

Isla had been thinking about what Gabe had said. About changing people's lives and how easily they could manage that with a few cuts and a few well-placed sutures. Of course, there was more to it than that, but, at the end of the day, that was what it was.

Isla wished she could remove the memory of her attack. Her life would be so much easier if that particular scar on her soul could be excised. Was it possible? Would she ever be able to forget?

'You look lost in thought.' Gabe's voice came from behind her and she turned on the bench to see him coming towards her, with two mugs. 'Brought you a tea.'

'Thanks.' She took the tea from him.

'Penny for them?'

'Just thinking about the past, that's all.'

'Oh. Past good, or past bad?'

'Past bad. Wondering how to excise the stuff you don't want. Make the new you happier with yourself. More confident.'

She knew he'd understand. He dealt with people who tried to do that every day. 'Well, you have three options. Option one, you accept who you are, warts and all. Accept that you are unique and that it's not the cards that you're dealt, but how you play them.'

She smiled. 'I'm not sure I want to play these cards.'

'Okay, option two is...you find a way to move forward. Get rid of what you don't need. Refuse to let baggage hold you back. Go forth no matter what and let the past be damned.'

'And option three?'

'You find someone to help you. Someone who makes

you feel better about option one.' He smiled at her. 'That's what I did.'

Isla raised an eyebrow. 'Who? Ellis?'

'No. It was you.'

'Me?'

'My life was just fine before you came along. At least I thought so. But then you arrived and something changed. My life is brighter. Happier. I feel more content. I'm looking forward to my daughter coming home tonight.' He joked, winking at her, before taking a sip of his tea.

Isla laughed. 'So what you're saying is that my life could be heaps better with the right person by my side.'

'Yes.' He raised his mug as if toasting the suggestion.

She clinked it with hers. 'And how do I know who that person is?'

'I think you'll know instantly. Deep down in your heart. It may be hidden to begin with. Covered over by thick blankets of fear, or shame or denial. But you'll know, because that person will be the one you think of all the time. The person that is never out of your thoughts. The person who you imagine doing things with, even if that scares you.'

'You're all of those things,' she said quickly, not having realised that she wanted to say it, but it had just come out anyway. As if she'd wanted to say it, before she got too scared to if she thought about it first. She felt her cheeks colour at having showed her cards. Her thoughts. Her feelings.

He smiled and looked her directly in the eye. 'You're all of those things for me, too.' He looked back at the clinic, made sure that they couldn't be seen from the door, or windows, and then he leaned over and planted a kiss on her lips.

She felt a thrill run through her at his words. He felt the same way? She'd hoped, but he'd not actually said anything and so she hadn't wanted to assume.

But his words made her happy.

'You've changed my life,' he said softly when the kiss ended, looking deeply into her eyes.

Isla stared back at him. Shocked. Surprised. Happy. Afraid. They'd known each other mere weeks and yet they'd become so close, so quickly, from having spent so much time together. If they meant this much to each other already, what did that mean? Where was this thing going? Because if it was going to get serious, Gabe might expect more from her. Physically.

And what if she couldn't?

What if the past stopped her?

Because she didn't want to lose someone as incredible as him.

'You've changed mine too,' she said, reaching up to stroke his face, wishing she could tell him so much more. Admit to so much more. But she was afraid her words might entrap her further. Maybe it would be best to hold back until she was sure of whether she could be physical? Maybe they should put on the brakes? She'd thought about going home. About getting some space from him. But then she'd promised to stay until after her birthday on Sunday. To still be there for when Bea came home, so they could spend her birthday weekend together.

And that was another thing. If she got involved with Gabe seriously, then she would become a stepmother of sorts to Beatrice. Was she ready for that? Prepared for all that that would mean?

'I should go back in,' she whispered and kissed him quickly one more time, before getting up and leaving him alone on the bench. She hated walking away. She hated leaving him. She'd wanted him to say more. To tell her all the things she wanted to hear.

But she'd been scared. Because if he'd said all those lovely things, the three words she longed to hear, she would have been terrified of saying them too.

CHAPTER TWELVE

THIS TIME WHEN she volunteered to go with him to collect Bea from school, he agreed. There was nothing more he wanted than to spend as much time as possible with Isla. Because he had no idea if she would even be with him after her birthday weekend and so he wanted to enjoy every second. She had become incredibly important to him and, this weekend, he planned to sit with Bea and ask her how she truly felt about their house guest. Because it was one thing to get along with someone if you thought of them as just a guest, or a friend, but quite another to consider having that person in your life more permanently, as a mother figure.

So, the more time he gave them to bond, the better.

As usual, the traffic was heavy. Maybe even heavier than it had been last week. They were stuck in bumper-to-bumper traffic at a point that didn't usually get congested and he was having a difficult time trying to see past the cars in front of him, to find out why. But as they inched forward, they both became aware of flashing lights. Car hazard lights and, beyond that, debris on the road. Long scaffolding poles and broken glass. An accident? There were no emergency service vehicles there yet, so it must have just happened.

'We ought to stop. See if we need to provide assistance,' Isla said, taking the words right out of his mouth.

As he parked up, off to one side, he put on his own hazards and Isla rushed off to give assistance as he removed the orange cones he kept in the back of his vehicle in case of breakdown. It was one thing to offer help, but you needed to be safe to do so. They were out and vulnerable on a busy roadside. Then he ran to catch up. He had a basic first-aid kit in his car, but it was only gauze pads, bandages, plasters, gloves. He grabbed the gloves and passed them to Isla as they assessed the driver and passenger in the car.

A scaffolding pole must have fallen from the lorry far up ahead, bounced onto the road and then up and through the windscreen. The driver must have swerved and hit the metal barrier on the side of the road. Luckily, the pole had gone through the centre point, missing both driver and passenger, but they had multiple cuts from broken glass, were both in shock and the passenger's legs were crushed into a tiny space where the side of their car had crumpled in. Unfortunately, they'd been driving a classic car and so it didn't have the safety reinforced cage that modern cars had.

Gabe glanced ahead. The driver of the truck with the scaffolding poles was getting out of his cab and beginning to run back to offer assistance. He was fine. There were no pedestrians or other vehicles involved, so they could focus on these two people. He pulled his mobile from his pocket and dialled 999, informing them of the situation.

'Emergency services are en route to your position, sir.'

'Inform them that there is a doctor and nurse on scene.'

The female passenger was crying, hiccupping breaths. The male driver was calmer.

'Sir, tell me your name.'

'Paul. And this is my wife, Janelle.'

They were an older couple. Maybe mid-seventies? 'Any medical history I should know about, Paul?'

'I'm on blood thinners.'

That would explain the profuse bleeding he was having from his head.

'My wife has high blood pressure and is being treated for lung cancer. We've just come back from the hospital. She's had chemo today.'

Gabe's heart sank. That wasn't good. 'Okay, Paul, Janelle. I'm Gabe and I'm a doctor and the fine young lady next to your wife is Isla and she's a nurse. We're going to help you until the paramedics get here. What I'm going to do is ask you both to sit very still, whilst I perform a primary survey on you both, okay?'

It had been a long time since Gabe had worked in Accident and Emergency. He'd done a few months' worth of shifts there as a junior doctor and, though he'd enjoyed it, he'd not enjoyed the tragedies. The upsetting stories where he felt as though, no matter what they did, they could not save a life. Or change a life. Or make someone better. He'd lost count of how many times he'd taken a patient's family members into a family room to break bad news and it had almost broken him. He'd got out of A & E as quickly as he could. Not entirely sure where he wanted to specialise in those early, exhausting years.

Behind him, cars crept by. He was aware of stares, of being watched. Even of people with their phones out, recording as he assessed Paul and Janelle. Paul was in pretty decent shape considering what had happened. Shock, cuts and abrasions, and undoubtedly whiplash, but without scans and X-rays he couldn't be sure of anything. He would need to maintain Paul's cervical spine, so he told Paul to sit still and not move, whilst he assessed Paul's wife. She was in much worse shape, losing consciousness, and her entrapped legs looked as though they might be broken beneath the knee. Isla maintained Janell's C-spine as Gabe clambered into the back to hold Paul's head steady.

He could hear sirens now. Could feel relief flooding through him at their approach. Even Paul reached out to grab his wife's hand and squeeze it reassuringly. 'They're nearly here, Paul. Janelle will get the help she needs and pain relief to make her more comfortable.' Thankfully, Janelle was still breathing evenly as she drifted in and out of consciousness.

Gabe glanced at Isla, who knelt beside him in the back seat of Paul and Janelle's car. Her eyes were full of fear. 'It'll be okay,' he whispered as paramedics arrived in view and asked Gabe for an update on the situation.

He told them what he could. They placed cervical collars on Paul and then Janelle. Paul was taken out of his vehicle relatively easily and placed into an ambulance and taken away, though it took longer for Janelle. Police took their statements and they were told that they could go. They needed to. Gabe was very much aware that Beatrice would be wondering where they were.

'Honey? It's Dad. Sorry we're running late, but there was an accident. We weren't involved, we're fine, but we had to stop to render assistance,' he said, calling her on his mobile before he started driving again.

'Oh, okay. I guess I'll see you soon, then?'

'Half an hour. Tops.' He couldn't wait to hold his daughter safely in his arms. It was at moments like this, when life came close to death, that people felt the need to hug their loved ones close. When Gabe had lost Ellis and he'd been all alone in the hospital, except for his poorly newborn baby daughter, he had held her in his arms and gazed into her little face and wondered what her life would be like without a mother. He'd not been sure he'd be up to the task of parenting alone. He'd been scared and then her oxygen alarms had gone off and nurses had rushed in and taken Beatrice from him and put tubes down her and he'd stood there, shocked, listening to the alarms on her machines, and backed away, not sure if he had the strength to lose her too.

But something had kept him there. Hope. Fear. Those two opposing forces had bound him to stay. He had been the one left. The one responsible for her. She'd no longer had a mother, she'd needed a father to fight for her and he'd vowed to do that every day of her life. Determined to bring her up right, and maybe he'd gone about that the wrong way, which was why they'd begun to feel a separation between them, but Isla was the glue putting them back together. He reached across for Isla's hand, as Paul had done to Janelle, and squeezed her fingers.

'You okay?' she asked.

'Yeah. You?'

'I think so. That was scary, huh?'

'Yeah. But I'm no stranger to scary.'

She nodded. 'Nor me.'

'Doesn't mean we're experts, though, does it? We still stumble blindly through the difficult parts of life.'

Isla laughed. 'Ain't that the truth? Do you think we'll ever be experts? Do you think we'll ever be confronted with something scary and just brush it off and calmly wade through it, anyway?'

'I'd like to think so. But maybe scary is there for a reason? Maybe being scared is what propels us to be better? To have faith in ourselves. Or more confidence. Maybe we should view scary as an opportunity for personal growth?'

'Gabriel Newton, plastic surgeon extraordinaire *and* philosopher.'

He smiled. 'You know what I mean.'

'I do. In fact I've been thinking about fear a lot just lately.'

'You have?'

'Of course. This situation we're in...that's scary. My feelings for you...*us*...that's scary.'

He made the turning into Hardwicke then. He wanted to answer her, to say something wise and important and considered, but he couldn't think of what to say, so he said nothing as he drove up the long driveway to the front door, where Beatrice was waiting with her tutor, Mr Sansom.

Bea gave him a lovely hug when he got out of the car and then she hugged Isla, too.

He couldn't help but smile.

'Mr Newton? Might I have a word?' asked Mr Sansom.

Gabe looked at Isla.

'Bea? Let's get your bags in the car, whilst your dad talks.'

He was grateful for Isla to distract his daughter. 'What's up?' he asked.

'I just wanted to make you aware that Beatrice has had to make one or two visits to the school nurse this week, due to her coughing. She seems fine, but I can't help but worry that maybe her cystic fibrosis is taking a turn and I thought it best to keep you updated. I did email you during the week about it. I assume you saw that?'

Gabe frowned. There had been an email from school, but he'd not read it. Normally when he got emails from the school, it was about events or fundraising, or concerts, never anything important like this. He felt bad for not reading it. 'You should have tried to call me.'

'I did, but you were unavailable at the time. In surgery, I do believe, so I left a message with your secretary.'

Damn. It must be somewhere in my inbox and I never saw it!

'Right. Well, thank you for letting me know. I'll do an assessment at home and keep an eye on her.'

'Of course. You have a good weekend, Mr Newton.'

'You too.'

Gabe clambered into the car, feeling a niggly worry at the back of his mind. Was Bea's CF getting worse, or had she just had a rough week? Her coughing had been worse after the concert. Had she picked up an infection? Or was this nothing? Was this Bea's tutor being overly cautious? 'Ready to get home?' he asked, looking into the back seat.

As if on cue, Bea coughed heavily, then nodded, her eyes watering.

He felt something strange and dangerous settle in his stomach and, with a feeling of foreboding, he drove home.

CHAPTER THIRTEEN

'I WANT TO take you into work. Show you around,' Gabe said to Bea when she'd finished her morning clearance exercises.

'Really?'

'Yes. I'd like to show you where I work. What I do.' He looked a bit twitchy.

'And...?' Bea asked, raising an eyebrow.

'And we have machines and equipment there so I can check you out a bit.'

'There we go.' Bea looked smug. 'That's what Mr Sansom was talking to you about, huh? That my cough had been bad last week?'

Gabe smiled. Caught out. 'He may have mentioned it briefly. Don't you want to see where I work?'

'I do. I'm kind of interested in medicine, actually. But you don't need to worry about me, Dad. I'm fine. We'd been trampolining and I may have just done more of it than I should.'

'Trampolining?' Gabe sounded concerned. 'Bea, you know you have to be careful.'

'I know, Dad, but you've got to trust me.'

Gabe had been so worried last night, he'd sat on the stairs, listening to Bea cough in her bedroom. Her tutor's comment had really unnerved him and he'd even considered getting her old baby monitor out of storage and putting it in her room.

'I'm not sure Bea would like the idea of you monitoring her with video and audio now that she's nearly a teenager in her own room,' Isla had said.

'I can hear you guys! If you're gonna chat out there, can you do it quieter? Some of us are trying to sleep!'

They'd both smiled and headed downstairs, but they'd stayed up later than normal, enjoying a glass of wine, and right before they'd gone to bed, Isla had even massaged Gabe's shoulders. He'd felt so tense! But she'd soon soothed out his knots and to hear him sigh with pleasure had made her feel good, too.

When they arrived at the Garland Clinic, that Saturday morning, it felt strange to be there. Of course, it was empty of patients, but Phillip Garland was there, in his office, catching up on some paperwork, and the cleaners were in, working hard.

Gabe introduced Bea to his boss and then showed her his own consulting room.

Bea looked around it, smiling. 'This is all yours?'

'Yes.'

'You have a picture of Mum and me on your desk.' Bea picked up the framed photo and smiled at it.

'Yes.'

Isla wanted to slip her hand into his. To comfort him. This was a big thing for the two of them. They were reconnecting in ways that Gabe could never have imagined just a few short weeks ago.

Bea put the picture down. 'Where do you operate?'

'Theatre. I'll take you, but you mustn't touch anything.'

'Really? You don't want me touching sharp scalpels and

things? Shocking.' She laughed and followed him down the corridor towards the theatres.

Isla followed them, watching them walk side by side as Gabe gave his daughter the tour. They entered Theatre and Bea marvelled at the bright lights, the equipment and the 'cutting table', as she called it.

'Does this ever drip with blood? Like, do you have to mop it up off the floor?' she asked with marvellous glee.

'Thankfully, no.' Gabe smiled.

At that moment, Isla's phone rang. 'Excuse me for a minute.' And she went to take her call.

When Isla was gone, he took a chest X-ray of Bea to make sure her lungs looked okay, before he asked her the question that had been on his mind for a while. 'Can I ask... what do you think of Isla?'

Bea turned to look him right in the eye. 'She's great. I really like her. She's made you a happier person.'

He smiled. 'You think so?'

'Think so? I know so! I've never seen you smile so much. Weekends are a little less stressful now.'

'You noticed that?'

'I notice a lot of things, Dad. You like her, huh?'

He sucked in a breath. 'I do. I like her a lot. She's been hurt before and I don't want to make any mistakes in causing her any more pain.'

'Sure.'

'And so I wanted to check in with you, now that we can talk to one another, about how you'd feel about Isla becoming...' He didn't know how to finish off the sentence.

'Becoming your girlfriend?' Bea smiled, finishing it for him.

He guessed girlfriend was as good a term as any for now. 'Yeah.'

And he would absolutely go by Bea's decision. It was important. He wanted to show Bea that he respected her too. She was growing up now, as Isla had said. He had to respect her as a growing woman. She was becoming her own person. Independent. Which was what he'd wanted when he'd sent her to Hardwicke. She was strong. Wilful. In many ways she was just like her mother. And he would not enter any serious relationship without his daughter's approval of any woman that would become a serious component of her life.

'I think she's great. You should go for it.'

'Really?'

Bea nodded. 'Really.'

He gave Bea a hug then. Really squeezed her tight, laid his head on top of hers. They were still hugging when Isla came back into the room, her face grim.

'What's wrong?' he asked, feeling a deep concern rise up at the look on her face.

'There's an article about us. It's everywhere.'

Back home, Gabe turned his monitor so that she could see and there, emblazoned across the screen, were pictures of her and Gabe at the road traffic accident, obviously taken by a passer-by in a car, and her whole identity revealed.

Gabe's mystery blonde turns heroine at roadside!

It was all there in black and white. The accident yesterday, her and Gabe helping out, but it seemed that someone had managed to talk to Paul and Janelle, who'd wanted to thank the couple that had helped them roadside and named them. From that, it had taken whichever gutter journalist this was to discover her past and share it in the article.

She felt herself grow cold.

It was out. Everyone would know now.

'I don't believe it. How did they find out?'

'How do they find anything out? They dig and dig until they strike gold. I'm so sorry, Isla. I tried to protect you as much as I could.'

She nodded, but already her mind was racing with thoughts. Feelings. But overall, she felt kind of resigned to it. 'Maybe it's a good thing that it's out now.'

Gabe looked up at her, confused. 'How do you mean?'

'Well…hiding a part of my past, pretending that everything is fine, trying to be someone new, wearing a mask…it's *exhausting*, Gabe! Maybe now I can just be me and if people want to talk about it, let them. Because look at what it's done to me so far. I changed my name, I lost my marriage, my job that I loved. I moved away, got a new job and had to move into your house, uprooting *your* personal life, just to protect mine!'

'I didn't mind. I've loved having you here. So has Bea.'

'I know.' She smiled at him. 'But there's no point in hiding any more. They all know. The world and his wife. I should just go back to my friend's flat and start again.'

'After your birthday? As promised?'

Another smile. He was being so sweet. So nice. To show that he wasn't eager to get rid of her, and she appreciated that. 'After my birthday.'

'I think I'm getting a cold.' Bea stood in the doorway to the kitchen and she did indeed look a little poorly. Her nose was red, she was sniffing and wiping her nose with a tissue and as soon as she finished, she sneezed, which set off a coughing fit.

Gabe walked her over to the table and sat her down. 'Your chest X-ray was good though. I'll get you some decongestants. Isla, could you do her a hot water with honey and lemon?'

'Sure.'

He sat down with his daughter at the table and reached for her hand. 'Anything I can do?'

'Let me eat ice cream?'

'No.'

She smiled. 'Worth a shot.'

Gabe grinned. He liked this easy nature they had between them now. Now that they could talk to one another without it always being a battle of wills. Why couldn't he have seen what his daughter needed before now? He'd believed that, being Bea's only parent, he had to be really hard on discipline to make sure that she grew up with the right head on her shoulders, but he'd forgotten all the rest that she'd needed. A soft place to fall. Someone who would listen. Someone who would let the occasional thing slide and who would take an interest in her likes and needs. He'd been so focused on staying on top of her CF, not exposing her to risk, that he'd never thought about music concerts or taking a step back from the role of disciplinarian.

Isla had taught him differently. In one short weekend, she'd shown him what was possible and he knew now to not have a knee-jerk reaction where his daughter was concerned.

'Here. Sip this. But be careful. It's hot,' Isla said, setting down a mug and pressing the backs of her fingers to Bea's head. 'No temperature, so that's good.'

'We need you to be better for tomorrow.'

'Isla's birthday? What are we doing?'

'I thought a show at the West End and then dinner for all three of us, but if you're ill, then maybe we should postpone?'

'It's just a cold! I'll be fine. Which show are we seeing?' she asked.

'You can help me decide.' Isla smiled.

Isla woke to the sound of two people badly singing 'Happy Birthday' as her bedroom door was opened and in walked Gabe and Bea, with a birthday cake with a fizzing sparkler candle on it. Laughing, she sat up in bed and waited for Gabe to deposit the cake on her lap. As the candle fizzled out, she clapped her hands. 'Thanks, guys! Is this why you wanted me to have a lie-in?'

'Yes. We get to spoil *you* today.'

'Aww, you don't have to do that. How are you feeling, Bea?' Yesterday, Bea had coughed and sneezed her way through the day, and they'd ended up vegging on the couch and watching movies and, eventually, Bea had got her ice cream.

'I'm fine. Just the sniffles and sneezes.'

'How were your clearance exercises this morning?' She'd heard her going through her routine downstairs.

'Same as always. No better, no worse. Dad can stop panicking.'

Isla looked to Gabe for confirmation and he gave a nod as he passed her two birthday cards. 'Happy birthday, from both of us.'

Isla thanked them and began to open their cards. The one from Bea had a dazed, scruffy-looking dog on the front, with hair sticking in all directions. It said, *You don't look that old!* and inside was a message that read, *Happy Birthday, Isla! Hope you have a lovely day! Love Bea.* With three kisses.

'Thanks, Bea.'

Gabe's card had a teddy bear on the front, and the teddy was holding a big bunch of beautiful flowers. Inside, the message read, *Happy Birthday, Isla. You're the gift in my life. Love Gabe.* With a single kiss.

'Thank you.' She wanted to kiss him, but Bea was there and they'd not really spoken to Bea about the two of them having feelings for one another. Or so she'd thought.

Because in that moment, Gabe stooped to drop a kiss on her cheek.

She blushed and glanced at Bea, but Bea was smiling.

'It's cool. I know. By the way, I made you this.' Bea passed over a small wrapped present, tied with a pink bow.

She knew? When had Gabe talked to her? 'You made me something? Bea!' She reached forward to give Bea a hug, then tore into the wrapping and discovered a small purse that had a hand-embroidered flower on it.

'I made it in textile class.'

Her heart was overflowing. 'Bea, it's beautiful. I'll treasure it always.'

Bea beamed. 'What do you want for breakfast?'

'You're making it?'

'I am.'

Isla glanced at Gabe, who gave her a small nod to let her know that Bea would not be left unsupervised in the kitchen and that he'd be helping. Gabe had been getting better in the kitchen, but what would be the easiest thing for them to prepare? 'Poached egg on toast?'

'Coming right up.' Gabe leaned in and this time

dropped a kiss upon her lips, before he stood and removed the cake.

Isla flushed, glancing at Bea to see her reaction, but Bea was just smiling at the two of them and when her dad had begun going downstairs, Bea turned in the doorway and said, 'He likes you a lot, you know. He said you'd been hurt before, but…please don't hurt him. He's been through enough.'

Isla stared at Bea. 'I like him a lot. He's a very kind, generous man.'

Bea smiled and headed downstairs to help cook breakfast.

He felt an element of nervousness as he got dressed for going out with Bea and Isla. Gabe might have been seen out with some of the most known female celebrities out there, but he had never been seen out and about with another woman *and* his daughter at the same time. He knew what the press would make of it and he'd warned Isla, too, but she'd simply sucked in a deep breath and said, *'Fine.'*

He was proud of her for not being scared of them any more. She was most definitely stronger than him. To him, the press had become something he had acquired. A thorn in his side. Something that had become a nuisance. Honestly, sometimes he'd been photographed just going out to get milk. But Isla? She wasn't going to let them see that she was bothered any more. They'd found out her biggest secret, they'd written about her past and splurged it across their pages and, quite frankly? Isla was of the opinion of what else could they do to her? Nothing, was the answer. They might speculate, they might ask her for a quote, they might chase her with their cameras, but she was refusing to run any more and for that he admired her.

It took strength to do that. And he'd discovered, since getting to know Isla, just how strong that she was.

He couldn't believe that she would leave after today! He didn't want that. He really wanted her to stay. He loved having her here. Loved waking up in the morning to the sounds of her in his kitchen. Sometimes she'd hum to music, or be singing in that cute, off-key way that she had.

He loved sitting across from her at the breakfast table and discussing their upcoming patients for that day. He loved the drive in to work with her. They'd listen to the radio and there'd be a music quiz on that one station they listened to and they'd both try to outdo the other. On the drive home, they'd let off steam, and at home, they'd cook together and then eat together and watch a movie or series that was streaming.

He loved the way she smelt when she came downstairs after a bath or shower, her hair wrapped up in a towel on top of her head. He loved the way she felt snuggled next to him on the couch. He loved the way they'd kiss each other goodnight. He loved knowing that she was sleeping, safe and secure, just a few rooms away from his at night. And he loved that Bea loved her too.

After today? All of that would be gone.

He'd be living alone again all week. Seeing her only at work, and he knew it would not be enough.

Somehow, he would like to convince her to stay. But how? What if she thought it was moving too fast?

I'll start by giving her a birthday to remember.

Once he was in his tux, he went to check that Bea was ready, only to discover Bea was being helped to choose her outfit by Isla, who looking stunning in an emerald wraparound dress and heels.

He'd seen her once in heels before. At the new employee

dinner. They emphasised her shapely calves and the swish of her skirt as she moved. Her waist was neat and gently rounded, perfecting her hourglass figure. And she'd done something remarkable with her hair, curling her normally straight blonde hair so that it fell in gentle waves around her neck and shoulders. Her eyes smouldered and her lips, highlighted by a lipstick, looked edible.

'Wow! You look amazing!' he managed to say.

Isla smiled at him, her eyes looking him up and down. 'So do you. Now all we have to do is find a dress for Bea. We can't decide between the red or the blue.' She held up two dresses on their hangers. 'She likes the red one, but feels the blue might be more appropriate for a restaurant. What do you think?'

Gabe glanced at his daughter, feeling as though this question was some sort of test for him to pass and he wanted to get it right. So he thought for a moment. 'The blue might be more appropriate for the restaurant, but, if I remember correctly, the last time you wore it, you said the elastic at the waist irritated your skin, so I'm going to say the red one, because I know you have the perfect shoes to match.' He waited with bated breath to see if she would approve.

Bea grinned and nodded at Isla.

He'd passed!

'Red, it is. We'll leave you to get dressed. Call me if you need me to do the zip at the back.' Isla left the room with him, closing the door softly behind her. 'Well done.'

'Thank you,' he said, feeling kind of smug.

'You know there was a secret third option?' Isla asked him with a tilted head and a smile.

'Ah, you mean the white dress with the butterflies on it?'

'I do!'

'But she won't wear that at night, because bright lights shine through it, so I discarded it as an option.'

'You have been taking notes!'

'All thanks to you.' He leaned forward and dropped a soft kiss upon her lips. He'd been wanting to do that all day. The desire to touch her and hold her had been getting stronger of late. He wanted to do so many things to her. To explore her. Taste her. But he'd been holding back. Holding back even more with Bea here. 'You know I had the chance to speak to Bea briefly when I gave her the work tour.'

'I do.'

'About you. Us. What her thoughts were on there possibly being an us.'

Isla stopped smiling and looked serious. 'And what did she say?'

'She said she didn't mind. That she liked you a lot and could see that you made me happy.'

She seemed to relax again. 'Oh. Good! I'm glad.'

'Me too.' He reached for her fingers with his. Felt them entwine. Imagined their bodies entwining and brushed his lips over her neck, inhaling her scent, only to break away guiltily when Bea's door suddenly opened and his daughter came out and asked Isla to do her zip.

He glanced at his watch as a distraction exercise. 'We ought to start making a move or we'll miss curtain up.'

'Okay. Let's go!'

CHAPTER FOURTEEN

ISLA HAD NEVER been to the theatre before to see a show. She'd been to the cinema, but never a show, or even a music concert, except for the one with Bea. And they had to go to a matinee showing and then eat around six, to get Bea back to Hardwicke by late evening. So the show was a treat. A special experience in which she loved everything about it. She'd not been sure how engrossed she would be in the story, but there were music, songs, laughter and even a moment where she found herself leaning forward, so caught up in the moment that she actually found tears in her eyes at the end, when the lead female character might lose everything she had fought for. When the cast came on stage to take their bows and applause, she stood and clapped the loudest. If she knew how to wolf-whistle? She'd have done that, too.

'That was amazing!' she said to Gabe as they came out of the theatre and headed to the car so that they could drive to their dinner reservation.

'Wasn't it?'

'I really liked the prince,' said Bea. 'He was funny.'

Isla turned to look at her and smiled. 'He was so funny!' She laughed, thinking of his antics. 'How's your cold?'

'I'm all right. Just a blocked nose, mostly.'

'And how does your chest feel? No tightness?'

'No.' And, as if prompted, she coughed to show that she could without it overwhelming her. 'Where are we going to eat?'

'De Luca's. It's Italian,' said Gabe.

'Yes! I see a pizza in my future!' said Bea, rubbing her hands together.

Isla smiled and turned back to Gabe. He looked happy. Content. She wanted to reach out and lay her hand on his, but she was nervous with Bea there, watching, even though she now knew that Bea wasn't opposed to them being together. Dared she?

'Have we been there before?'

'No. But I picked it because it has good reviews and there's a kids' area there, where you can play video games if you get bored of being with grown-ups.'

'Cool!'

Isla smiled. If Bea did go off to play on the video games, perhaps she and Gabe could share a nice moment together? That would be wonderful, as the time before she had to return home was ticking by so quickly. Now she'd made the decision to leave, she was beginning to regret it.

What was waiting for her back at her friend's flat? Damp. That window that, even when closed, still produced a draft. Empty rooms. Stuff that didn't even belong to her, but to her friend. All that was hers were her suitcase and some food in the fridge that had probably gone off by now, anyway, so…

But there was no reason to stay here any more. Her secret was out and the whole reason for her staying with Gabe had been to protect that secret. There was nothing to protect any more and so she had to go. She couldn't expect Gabe and Bea to keep putting up with her. Those two needed their space to grow and it would be good for

Isla and Gabe to get some space. Living in each other's pockets was fine at the start of a relationship when they were still in a honeymoon period and everything was fresh and new and exciting, but if this relationship was to move at a steady pace, then they'd each need their own space to breathe. Because sometimes, being with Gabe, she felt that she couldn't think clearly. Especially when his lips were at her neck and her hands were in his, or when kisses grew more passionate and her senses assailed her.

Isla smiled as they entered De Luca's. It was deceptively intimate. Lots of round tables. Candlelight. Soft piano music. White table linens and a single rose in a bud vase on each table. Wooden panelling adorned with awards for cooking and pictures of various celebrities with the chef blocked off the view of an area filled with computers and consoles, but a small screen in the corner allowed them to keep an eye on Bea as she went to explore it.

The waiter came and took their order. Gabe ordered a plain cheese pizza for Bea as she'd requested, with doughballs and a salad, and Isla and Gabe ordered arancini for starters and *branzino* for main—oven-baked sea bass, with lemon, garlic, herbs and a white-wine fennel sauce.

As the pianist tickled the ivories, Isla sat forward to look Gabe in the eyes. 'Thank you for this. I'm loving every moment of my birthday with you and Bea.'

He sat forward too. Reached for her hand. 'I'm glad. I wanted to spoil you and I am, though if we'd had to spend your birthday, at home, in jammies, watching a movie on the couch, I would have tried to make that special, too.'

'Any time with you is special,' she said, smiling. Meaning it. Meeting Gabe had changed her life. He'd gone from being her boss to someone close. Someone she truly adored. She knew she could trust him and that meant a huge deal, because she'd not thought she'd ever learn to trust a man again.

It gave her hope. That, one day, she might attain all those things she'd ever dreamed of. A marriage. A family. She'd once thought—feared—that she would always be alone, but maybe now that wouldn't be the case?

When the food arrived, they called Bea back to the table and they sat and ate together as a family. It felt nice. Isla was happy. Bea and Gabe were great company. Funny, warm, companionable. They all laughed at the same things and she could feel herself get excited for things that Bea had coming up at school. She was going to audition for the school's end-of-year production and they talked about what her audition piece could be and Isla really hoped that Bea would do well.

Gabe chatted a little about his next trip to India, telling her all about the work he did out there. 'And I'd love it if you'd come with me, Isla.'

India! 'I've never been. I've never been out of Europe. In fact, the farthest I've ever been is France. Are you *sure*, Gabe?'

'Absolutely. I think you'd make a vital contribution to the work over there. We always need good surgical nurses and I think it would be a brilliant experience for you.' He paused. 'And I'd like you there with me.' He reached for her hand. Squeezed it.

It was a big decision. One that excited her. 'Well, yes. I'd love to! Thank you!' she gushed.

He leaned in, pecked her on the cheek and she coloured.

As expected, when they came out of the restaurant, she found herself looking for photographers, but there weren't any, thankfully.

On the drive home to get changed and collect Bea's things for school, Bea was yawning heavily and coughing a lot. She needed to do her evening clearance exercises before returning to Hardwicke and so they were doing their level best to keep her entertained. But once they were home, they had an hour or two before they needed to get going and Isla popped upstairs to get changed out of her dress and into something more comfortable for taking Bea back to Hardwicke.

It was going to be hard to say goodbye to Bea, because, after today, she wasn't sure when she'd next get to see her. Hopefully next weekend, if she and Gabe arranged something.

She removed the dress and placed it on a hanger and wrapped herself in a bathrobe whilst she decided what to wear, and was standing in front of her wardrobe, lost in her thoughts, when she heard a gentle knock on her bedroom door.

'Come in,' she said, expecting Bea.

But it was Gabe.

She smiled at him and self-consciously pulled her bathrobe more tightly closed. 'Hey. Thank you for today. I had a great time.'

'Me too.'

He closed her bedroom door behind him and came to stand beside her. 'I can't believe you won't be here tomorrow. My life won't be the same.'

She smiled. 'Nor mine.' She leant into the wardrobe, grabbed a pair of jeans and a light blue sweater, only for Gabe to turn her towards him. Pull her close and look deeply into her eyes.

'Would it be wrong of me to say I don't want you to go?' He looked truly conflicted.

'Of course not. It shows you care about me.'

'I do. I truly do. And I never thought I'd feel this way about someone else. I'm beginning to believe that everything just might turn out great. That I won't lose everyone I love.'

Love. Was he saying he loved her?

Isla leant in. Kissed him. 'I feel the same way, too.'

He seemed to think for a moment. 'Then don't. Don't go. Stay with me.'

She hesitated. Actually thought about it. 'But what would that mean?'

'Whatever you want it to mean.'

'Like a real relationship? Something we'd admit to everyone? All the people we work with? Our families? Friends? The world?'

He nodded. 'Yes.'

Isla didn't know what to say! She had dreaded leaving. But she worried that they'd started this relationship weirdly. They'd moved in with one another, without dating, without getting to know one another. Would it cause ructions later on? That they'd missed steps?

'Isla… I never thought I could love another woman after Ellis… You've proved me wrong.'

Her own heart filled with a rush of happiness then. For him to say this, after all he'd been through with his wife. Her feelings for him were just as strong, but they'd not tested one another yet. Not fully. She had not been physical with him at all. They'd only kissed.

But he'd told her he loved her and she loved him and that required a celebration.

She leaned in for a kiss. A slow kiss. A passionate kiss. With the kiss she wanted to tell him everything. Wanted to show him how much he meant to her. To let him know that her feelings for him ran just as strong. Just as deep.

And as the kiss deepened he pushed her back against the wardrobe and she gasped with delicious heat that washed over her.

His hands, which before now had never strayed far from her hair, or neck, or waist, began to move up her body, and for the first time she felt his hands at her breasts, his thumbs brushing over her nipples, through her bathrobe, and the pressure of his desire against her.

Sex. He wanted sex.

And though she wanted more than anything in the world to be able to lie with him, already she could feel her panic building. She felt trapped. Claustrophobic. In a situation of her own making that she needed to escape from. She was just in her robe! She was vulnerable. He could have her naked in seconds! She got flashbacks of her attack, remembered the feel of that man's fumbling hands at her clothes, the way he'd tried to grab her, tried to get more and, suddenly, Isla was panicking and pushing Gabe away. 'Stop!'

He stepped back, eyes glazed with desire and guilt. 'I'm sorry. I didn't mean to—'

Isla suddenly felt cold. Afraid. What had she done? She wasn't ready for this! How had she ever thought she would be ready for this? 'No, I—'

There was a knock at her door and then Bea was coming in. 'Should I take this with me, do you think? I want to lend it to Harriet.' She was holding a book she'd bought and seemed totally oblivious to the tension in the room.

'Er...sure. Why not? Let's let Isla get dressed, so we can go,' Gabe said, ushering his daughter from the room.

Clearly he felt embarrassed, but so did she! How could

she have feelings for him and practically tell him that she loved him, but would not be able to be with him *physically*? She couldn't play with his emotions like that—hadn't *he* been through enough? Hadn't they *both* been through enough?

This will never work. I can't believe I could ever be ready!

And how could she face him now? Clearly he couldn't face her. Her rejection, pushing him away, had upset him—he couldn't wait to escape!

Isla rubbed at her face as tears welled in her eyes. Would she ever get over this? Maybe those dreams of family were all pipe dreams. Maybe she'd been a fool to think that having feelings for someone would be enough to overcome the past.

She glanced at her jeans and sweater, then back at the wardrobe, and she knew she couldn't stay.

The drive to Hardwicke was difficult. Isla had not answered him when he'd knocked at her door to say they were ready to go and it had hurt him that she couldn't speak to him. Figuring it might be easier to talk when Bea wasn't around, he'd made a decision. 'I'll take Bea into school, then when I get back, we should talk,' he'd said quietly to her closed door.

She hadn't answered, but he'd known she was in there, listening.

He'd laid his forehead against the door. He hadn't wanted to leave to take Bea to Hardwicke. He'd wanted to stay there. He'd wanted to sort this out. He'd felt awful! He'd asked for too much before she was ready. But he hadn't been able to help himself. She'd told him she felt the same way about him, they'd had a lovely day together and he'd missed being able to touch her and had wanted more and when they'd begun kissing…it had become so passionate, he'd craved more of her. Simple as that. He'd lost his senses as his need for her had grown. Forgetting he'd needed to go slowly. And now he was taking his daughter away, losing her, as well as walking away from Isla. He didn't want to lose her.

'Everything all right?' Bea asked in the car. Their journey had been completed in silence, because his mind was awash with regret and things he should have said. Should have done.

'Fine.'

'You don't look fine. You look sad.'

He glanced at Bea. Saw the concern on her face. 'I think I might have ruined Isla's birthday.'

'What did you do?'

How could he explain that to his daughter? She was twelve years old! 'I made a silly mistake, that's all, and it upset Isla.'

'Was it when I came into her room with my book?'

'You noticed that?'

'Anybody would have noticed that.'

'It's okay. Don't you worry about it. I'll sort it out when I get home. Apologise.'

'Make sure you do it properly. Mr Sansom says an apology should have three parts.'

'Really?' He couldn't believe he was taking romantic advice from his young daughter.

'Yes. We had this big class debate after Shawna fell out with Roland and everyone took sides.'

'Whose side did you take?'

'Shawna's.'

He pulled into the driveway of Hardwicke. 'And what

are the three parts of an apology?' He figured right now that any advice would help, because he sure felt stuck about it all on his own.

'Hmm, let me remember... Oh, okay, I've got it. First of all you have to admit that the other person is upset about something and say you are sorry, but Mr Sansom says you really have to sound like you mean it.'

Gabe nodded. He could do that.

'Then, I think you have to admit that you did something wrong and work out how to put it right.'

'Okay, and the third part?'

'Make it better. Take the steps to actually make it right.'

'What did Shawna and Roland decide on?'

'She promised that she wouldn't put glue on his chair any more if he stopped calling her names.'

Gabe nodded, but he really wasn't worrying about Shawna or Roland. He figured those two were fine. What he needed to do was apologise to Isla for asking for more than she was ready to give. No. For trying to take more than what she was ready to give. He needed to accept his part. Show her that he knew what he had done wrong and the steps he would take to fix it. 'How did you get so wise?' he asked, leaning over to peck Bea on the cheek.

'I stayed here at Hardwicke.' She smiled at him, then the smile faltered. 'Will Isla still be your girlfriend when I get back next week?'

Gabe paused for a moment. 'I hope so. I hope so with all my heart.'

Isla felt an utter coward. She hadn't wanted to be there when Gabe got back from driving Bea to Hardwicke and so the second they'd gone down to the car park, she'd called a taxi and returned to her friend's flat. There'd been no photographers, so that was something. Maybe someone else was more interesting than she was, and she was glad. Because her life had enough misery in it—she hadn't wanted to have to fight her way to her front door.

The flat felt cold. She rubbed at her arms but wasn't convinced the cold was from the flat. It was inside her. The flat was stale and so she opened up the windows to let in some fresh air. A thin layer of dust was on the shelves and, normally, she would have taken care of it, but right now? She didn't care. She slumped on the couch, seeing, but not hearing the drone of the television, lost in her turmoil of thoughts.

This place did not feel like home. Home had been where she was earlier today. A place where she had felt safe and cherished and loved. This place? Was a stopgap, nothing more, and honestly? She didn't want to be here. Maybe she could have taken a walk someplace? But you needed your wits about you in London and she knew right now that if she went out and about she wouldn't be concentrating. Just lost. She wiped her eyes and sniffed, feeling an utter failure. Gabe would never get to see the Isla she was before her life had changed for ever and that made her feel sad. That she couldn't be who she wanted to be.

A man like him deserved a woman who could love him back the way he needed. He was a red-blooded male, strong and passionate. He was *not* going to want to live the life of a monk!

A knock at her door startled her from her reverie.

Who was it? Who even knew she was back?

Could it be Gabe?

Her heart pounded at the possibility and she glanced at the clock on the wall. Had there been enough time for him to, not only go to Hardwicke and back, but also find her gone and make the only logical conclusion as to her whereabouts?

The answer was yes.

She got up and went to the door. Curious as to who was waiting outside. She peered through the eyehole and saw Gabe on the other side. Because of the distortion, she couldn't see if he was mad or sad or anything at all. 'What do you want?' she asked through the door, her heart breaking.

'Only to speak with you. Preferably face to face, but I can do this through a door, if you want the rest of the people in this block to hear me,' he said, sounding calm and friendly.

And he was right. They'd already had enough of their relationship put into the public eye. Maybe some of it, especially this most important part, should remain private? Isla pulled back the chain and opened the door, stepping back.

'Come in.' She was not afraid of him. She had no misconceptions about whether he'd be angry or mad with her, because she knew him well. He'd just want to talk. That was all.

He followed her into the small living room.

'It's not your place, but it's home,' she said, attempting a joke.

'Is it, though?'

She looked up at him.

Gabe shook his head. 'May I sit down?'

She indicated a chair and sat opposite.

'I'm here to apologise. I'd like you to hear me out and if, at the end, we can't agree on a way forward, then by all means I shall leave you in peace and see you at work tomorrow, but I really hope that you'll want to hear me out.'

Isla nodded. She wanted to hear what he had to say. Just to be near him again was wonderful and she'd hated the short time they'd been apart, thinking that it might all be over.

'I'm sorry for what happened before. I'm sorry if I upset you, or made you feel scared. Frightened by my unthinking actions. I was wrong to push for more before you were ready. I should have gone more slowly. Waited for you to guide me as to when you were ready for more physical contact and awaited your consent on that. I was wrong and I hate that I've upset you, or scared you, or made you think of what happened to you from before. That was not and will never be my intention and, if you'll permit me, I'd like to make amends. Show you that I can move at your pace and will be guided by you in the future.'

'You think we have a future?' she asked, terrified.

'I do.' He smiled. 'An incredible one! We're good together, Isla! At least, I think so! I never thought I could love someone again and yet here I am. I love you and I want to be with you in any way that you can manage to be. I can go slow. I can wait for you to be ready, and if it's the case that you'll never be ready? Well, then, that's perfectly fine, too. But I would like you to be a significant part in my life. In Bea's life, too. And I would love for you to come home, so we can begin that life.'

Isla almost couldn't believe it! He was saying all these wonderful things! 'I want to be ready. I want to work towards being ready. Maybe I need some more therapy.' She laughed nervously. 'But I would like to be with you very much. Are you sure you can wait for me? I don't want to punish you by holding you at arm's length. Not when I love you with all of my heart, too.'

Gabe smiled. 'You do?'

'Of course I do!'

He got up. Came over to sit beside her. Gently took her hands in his. 'We can do this, you know.'

She nodded. 'I'm sorry I ran.'

'I'm sorry I pushed.'

'You think we'll ever get to be where we'd both like to be?'

He smiled. 'I'm *already* there.'

She wanted to kiss him. 'Then let's go home.'

EPILOGUE

One year and one day later

SHE SLIPPED FROM his arms and crept across the bedroom floor, trying not to make a noise. She didn't want to wake Gabe. Neither of them had got much sleep and now that he was sleeping, she wanted him to get some rest.

Yesterday had been her birthday and, unlike her birthday from the previous year, where Gabe had treated her, she'd decided to give him a present.

They'd been intimate before, of course. It had taken about eight months before she'd felt ready to go all the way with him, and it had been everything she'd ever dreamed it would be. She'd been a little nervous! Like, what if, after all of this, they weren't sexually compatible? But that idea had been blown away in an instant. Gabe's very touch had been enough to make every sensory nerve ending in her body sing. He'd been gentle. Delicate. Moving slowly. Taking his time. Savouring every inch of her, the way she'd felt she could savour him. She'd not wanted to be passive. She'd wanted to take what she wanted, too, and his groans of pleasure as she'd teased and tempted him had filled her with a sense of her own feminine power and control.

The realisation that making love with Gabe no longer had to be something that she feared had been inexplicably powerful. That it was something that she'd be able to enjoy had been a wonderful surprise.

They'd taken small steps in the lead-up to it. Isla had employed a therapist, who'd suggested they take the notion of sex away completely and instead just do small things. Little, intimate things. A touch here. A stroke there. A kiss. A lick. And if she didn't want to go any further, then she didn't have to. In fact, the therapist had forbidden it.

Which had made her want it all the more.

Her sexual homework had become something that Isla had begun to look forward to as each week passed and holding back had become something with which they'd both struggled. One week, the therapist had suggested that Gabe do nothing but just lie there and let Isla do what she wanted to do. He wasn't to hold her, or guide her, and, basically, just lie back and think of England! Isla had wanted to throw caution to the wind and go further, but Gabe had been the one to remind her that they shouldn't.

She'd been a little upset at that. Feared that he didn't want her. But he'd shown her differently by going over and over the last step they'd been allowed. It had involved him using his tongue in a very particular way and she'd welcomed it. Over and over again as she'd revelled in her power and her femininity and realised that she could guide this, too. She wasn't weaker than him. She wasn't submissive. Gabe's physical touch, their lovemaking, could be something that gave her power and control and it was all that they had needed.

And the week when the therapist had told them that they could engage in full lovemaking if she felt that she was ready? Isla had come home, grabbed Gabe's hand and pulled *him* up the stairs!

She smiled at the thought of it. At all the nights they'd

had together since then. She and Gabe had built something beautiful, something wondrous, and she was so thrilled with her life. With her love for Gabe and Bea.

She closed the door to the en suite quietly and crept to the cupboard where she'd hidden the box. Isla had always wanted to create her own family and they'd had genetic counselling, too, due to Bea's cystic fibrosis. And so they'd spent many nights enjoying each other. Almost as if they were trying to play catch up with all the nights they'd spent at each other's side without being allowed to go all the way.

Her period was a couple of days late. Not much and it was probably nothing, but she'd wanted this so much and for so long, she simply had to know the truth.

If the test was negative, then that would be disappointing, but it would also be fine. They'd not been doing this all that long and they still had all the time in the world to get pregnant. She would be sad, but it would pass, because she still had the love of her life. And she had a wonderful stepdaughter in Bea. Not officially her stepdaughter, not yet. They weren't married. But that was how she felt about Bea. She loved her too.

To be able to give Bea and Gabe this gift of a sibling? Another child? After all their struggles? After all that they'd both been through? It would be amazing.

And secretly, selfishly, just for herself, she yearned to have a baby. Gabe had already experienced that with Ellis, but Isla never had. She'd never ever had a scare, or anything. She'd never come close. But now she was and she wanted this more than anything.

She took the test and placed the stick on the side beside the sink and waited. There was a full-length mirror in the en suite and she looked at herself. Front view. Side view, running a hand over her belly, imagining it swelling and filling with child. She thought she felt a little different, but maybe that was just her imagination? Maybe that was just being overly hopeful? But she'd been tired lately.

And yesterday? On her birthday? It had been a long day of celebration and she'd wanted to be in bed early. They'd gone to bed at eight p.m. Lain in each other's arms and laughed about the day. She'd turned to face him. Had entwined her naked body with his and looked deeply into his eyes as her hands had begun to explore. She'd not been tired enough for that. Now that she could, she wanted to enjoy intimacy as much as she could with Gabe.

He was perfect. He was her everything. And if this test was negative? He still would be. If it was positive? Then he'd still be her everything, but somehow so much more. She wanted his child in her belly. She wanted to grow their family. Her ultimate power as a woman.

Was it time? How many minutes had elapsed? Enough? What if she looked and it was still too early? But she couldn't wait any longer. She'd waited enough.

Isla crept over to the stick, closed her eyes and sucked in a steadying breath, before opening them again and looking down.

Pregnant

She gasped, her heart pounding and expanding with joy as she studied it closer just to make sure.

She heard Gabe stir in the next room and knew she'd have no way to keep this from him, to plan a surprise way of telling him, because she wanted him to share in her joy, to share in this precious moment that she would remember for the rest of her life. 'Gabe? You awake?'

'Yes.'

'Can you come in here a minute?'

There was a pause and she imagined him creeping across the bedroom floor, naked, grabbing his robe maybe?

'Everything okay?' he asked, opening the door.

She turned to him. 'I hope so.' And she lifted the test and watched as his smile broke across his face.

'We're having a baby?'

She nodded and laughed as he picked her up and spun her round in his arms.

'My God, how I love you! You've made my life, my heart, so happy.'

'Well, I hope there's room for more love in that heart,' she said, smiling.

'Are you kidding me? Of course there is. You make it possible.' He dropped to his knees, rested his hands on her belly, cradling it, and kissed it. 'Welcome to the world, little one.'

* * * * *

If you enjoyed this story,
check out these other great reads from
Louisa Heaton

A Mistletoe Marriage Reunion
Finding Forever with the Firefighter
Single Mum's Alaskan Adventure
Bound by Their Pregnancy Surprise

All available now!

MILLS & BOON®

Coming next month

NURSE'S TWIN BABY SURPRISE
Colette Cooper

'I can see you're dressed in scrubs but I can't just let you crack open this man's chest without confirming your identity.'

Glittering sapphire eyes met hers and her breath locked in her throat. He was even more stunning in the flesh than he was on screen...almost impossibly so. She was aware the team around them were continuing with the CPR – compressions were being quickly but steadily counted aloud; monitor alarms still rang out reminding them the patient's vital signs were critically outside of parameters. She knew what was going on around her but for a moment, the centre of her focus were the two deep blue eyes looking back at her, laser like, penetrating, silently assessing. Her determined resolve not to find him attractive wavered. Straightening the front of her uniform, her instinct telling her to look away, she held his gaze.

'Max Templeton,' he replied, one dark eyebrow raised and clearly having completed his appraisal of her, 'cardiothoracic consultant.' Was he trying to supress a grin?

Continue reading

NURSE'S TWIN BABY SURPRISE
Colette Cooper

Available next month
millsandboon.co.uk

Copyright © 2024 Colette Cooper

COMING SOON!

We really hope you enjoyed reading this book.
If you're looking for more romance
be sure to head to the shops when
new books are available on

Thursday 19th December

To see which titles are coming soon, please visit
millsandboon.co.uk/nextmonth

MILLS & BOON

FOUR BRAND NEW BOOKS FROM
MILLS & BOON MODERN

The same great stories you love, a stylish new look!

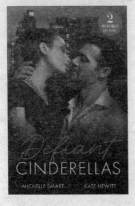

OUT NOW

Eight Modern stories published every month, find them all at:

millsandboon.co.uk

afterglow BOOKS

Afterglow Books is a trend-led, trope-filled list of books with diverse, authentic and relatable characters, a wide array of voices and representations, plus real world trials and tribulations. Featuring all the tropes you could possibly want (think small-town settings, fake relationships, grumpy vs sunshine, enemies to lovers) and all with a generous dose of spice in every story.

♪ @millsandboonuk
⊙ @millsandboonuk
afterglowbooks.co.uk
#AfterglowBooks

For all the latest book news, exclusive content and giveaways scan the QR code below to sign up to the Afterglow newsletter:

SCAN ME

afterglow BOOKS

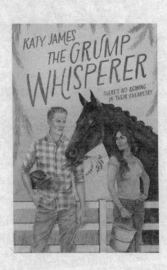

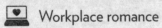 Workplace romance

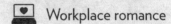 Workplace romance

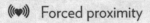 Forced proximity

 Small-town romance

 Spicy

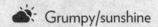 Grumpy/sunshine

OUT NOW

Two stories published every month. Discover more at:
Afterglowbooks.co.uk

LET'S TALK
Romance

For exclusive extracts, competitions and special offers, find us online:

- **f** MillsandBoon
- **X** @MillsandBoon
- **◎** @MillsandBoonUK
- **♪** @MillsandBoonUK

Get in touch on 01413 063 232

For all the latest titles coming soon, visit
millsandboon.co.uk/nextmonth

OUT NOW!

3
BOOKS
IN ONE

Tammy
WEBER

Tina
BECKETT

Sharon
KENDRICK

Workplace
ROMANCE

A CHRISTMAS DATE

Available at
millsandboon.co.uk

MILLS & BOON

OUT NOW!

Available at
millsandboon.co.uk

MILLS & BOON

OUT NOW!

3
BOOKS
IN ONE

SECOND CHANCE
FOR
Christmas

A.C.
ARTHUR

MARION
LENNOX

SUSAN
MEIER

Available at
millsandboon.co.uk

MILLS & BOON

OUT NOW!

3 BOOKS IN ONE

A *Christmas* HOLIDAY ROMANCE

KIANNA ALEXANDER   MEG MAGUIRE   ELIZABETH BEVARLY

Available at
millsandboon.co.uk

MILLS & BOON

MILLS & BOON
A ROMANCE FOR EVERY READER

- **FREE** delivery direct to your door
- **EXCLUSIVE** offers every month
- **SAVE** up to 30% on pre-paid subscriptions

SUBSCRIBE AND SAVE

millsandboon.co.uk/Subscribe